Praise for the InCryptid novels:

"The only thing more fun than an October Daye book is an InCryptid book. Swift narrative, charm, great world-building . . . all the McGuire trademarks."
—Charlaine Harris, #1 *New York Times*-bestselling author

"A remarkably enjoyable series, and rapidly becoming one of my favorites. Keen characterization, a rich and weird world full of nifty critters, plenty of action, even an underlying sense of humor that serves to defuse the darker twists."
—Tor.com

"Seanan McGuire's *Discount Armageddon* is an urban fantasy triple threat—smart and sexy and funny. The Aeslin mice alone are worth the price of the book, so consider a cast of truly original characters, a plot where weird never overwhelms logic, and some serious kickass world-building as a bonus." —Tanya Huff, bestselling author of *The Wild Ways*

"McGuire's InCryptid series is one of the most reliably imaginative and well-told sci-fi series to be found, and she brings all her considerable talents to bear on *[Tricks for Free]*. . . . McGuire's heroine is a brave, resourceful and sarcastic delight, and her intrepid comrades are just the kind of supportive and snarky sidekicks she needs."
—*RT Book Reviews* (top pick)

"A joyous romp that juggles action, magic, and romance to great effect." —*Publishers Weekly*

"McGuire has created a rich, tongue-in-cheek, and wholly unique urban fantasy world."
—Barnes & Noble SFF Booksellers' Picks

"*Discount Armageddon* is a quick-witted, sharp-edged look at what makes a monster monstrous, and at how closely our urban fantasy protagonists walk—or dance—that line. The pacing never lets up, and when the end comes, you're left wanting more. I can't wait for the next book!" —C. E. Murphy, author of *Raven Calls*

**DAW Books presents the finest in urban fantasy
from Seanan McGuire:**

InCryptid Novels

DISCOUNT ARMAGEDDON
MIDNIGHT BLUE-LIGHT SPECIAL
HALF-OFF RAGNAROK
POCKET APOCALYPSE
CHAOS CHOREOGRAPHY
MAGIC FOR NOTHING
TRICKS FOR FREE
THAT AIN'T WITCHCRAFT
IMAGINARY NUMBERS*

SPARROW HILL ROAD
THE GIRL IN THE GREEN SILK GOWN

October Daye Novels

ROSEMARY AND RUE
A LOCAL HABITATION
AN ARTIFICIAL NIGHT
LATE ECLIPSES
ONE SALT SEA
ASHES OF HONOR
CHIMES AT MIDNIGHT
THE WINTER LONG
A RED ROSE CHAIN
ONCE BROKEN FAITH
THE BRIGHTEST FELL
NIGHT AND SILENCE
THE UNKINDEST TIDE*

Coming soon from DAW Books

THAT AIN'T WITCHCRAFT

An *InCryptid* Novel

SEANAN MCGUIRE

DAW BOOKS, INC.

DONALD A. WOLLHEIM, FOUNDER

1745 Broadway, New York, NY 10019

ELIZABETH R. WOLLHEIM

SHEILA E. GILBERT

PUBLISHERS

www.dawbooks.com

First Printing, March 2019
1 2 3 4 5 6 7 8 9

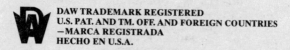

For Whitney.

Make a wish and count to ten;
I swear you'll make it home again.

Price Family Tree

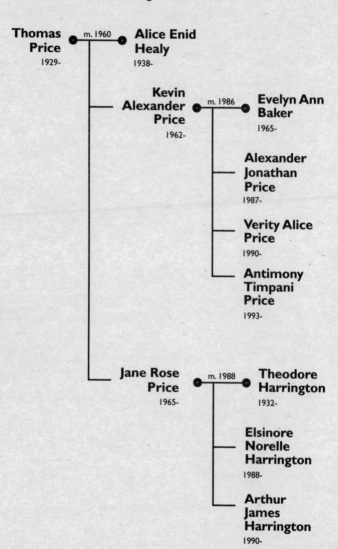

Thomas Price
1929-

m. 1960

Alice Enid Healy
1938-

Kevin Alexander Price
1962-

m. 1986

Evelyn Ann Baker
1965-

Alexander Jonathan Price
1987-

Verity Alice Price
1990-

Antimony Timpani Price
1993-

Jane Rose Price
1965-

m. 1988

Theodore Harrington
1932-

Elsinore Norelle Harrington
1988-

Arthur James Harrington
1990-

Baker Family Tree

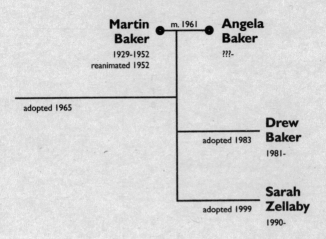

Martin Baker
1929-1952
reanimated 1952

m. 1961

Angela Baker
???-

adopted 1965

Drew Baker
1981-
adopted 1983

Sarah Zellaby
1990-
adopted 1999

Clarity, noun:

1. Ease of perception or understanding; lucidity.

Crossroads, noun:

1. A place where two roads cross.

2. A place where bargains can be made.

3. See also "places to avoid."

Prologue

"Children are a blessing. Like all blessings, occasionally they're also a curse."

–Evelyn Baker

The woods near Portland, Oregon, about to do something really stupid

Three years ago

THE STACCATO RHYTHM OF a woodpecker slamming its beak against a pine tree echoed through the woods, filtered and distorted by densely-packed branches. There were no other sounds, not from the birds and animals that lived there, and not from the human girl who hung by her knees on a bough in one of the larger trees, a knife in either hand.

Antimony sometimes thought that if she were to total up the amount of time she spent upside down—between her work with the family and taking the occasional header during roller derby—she'd probably be able to qualify as an honorary bat. As it was, she'd come to find inversion strangely soothing. It definitely helped to straighten out the kinks derby practice left in her spine.

Somehow, she didn't think the rest of the team was going to take "spend a lot of time hanging out upside down in trees" as a therapeutic tip.

Also unlikely to catch on with the rest of the team: floating. Fern seemed happy about it, but Fern wasn't human and, for her, being in a situation where she could dial her personal density down to something roughly akin to a blowup doll was probably really, really relaxing. She drifted gently up from the ground and grabbed the nearest available branch, stopping her ascent before she could reach the top of the trees.

"I have good news and bad news," said Fern. "Which one do you want first?"

"The bad news, please." Antimony didn't bother keeping her voice down. They weren't hunting anything arboreal: attracting unwanted attention wasn't a concern. More importantly, her siblings were only about two hundred yards away, working their way toward her. If she wound up in a bad situation, one phone call would bring her backup running.

She wasn't the biggest fan of her older brother or sister, but that didn't mean they didn't know how to do their jobs. If there was one thing she could count on, it was them following their parents' instructions to the tediously detailed letter.

"Well, it's definitely a unicorn," said Fern. "It has all the unicorn-y bits. Like the horn. Also the blood. I did *not* expect a unicorn to have that much blood on it. Are unicorns usually covered in blood?"

"Every unicorn I've ever seen has been."

"Oh."

"Is the good news that it's already super dead and I can come down from the tree and we can go out for pizza?" Antimony's hands tightened on her knives, clearly telegraphing how annoyed she'd be if the unicorn had been handled without her.

Fern glanced at Antimony's hands, but wisely didn't comment. She had known her friend and teammate long enough to know when she was facing a fight she couldn't win. "No, it's alive and bloody and armed—um, horned—and heading this way, so it's probably going to get here soon. The *good* news is that Karen is single again."

"Karen—what?"

"You know, Karen. The blocker from the Concussion Stand. Um, she skates as Can't Believe It's Not Beater?"

"I know who Karen *is*, I'm just not sure why that's good enough news to bring it up when we're in the middle of a unicorn hunt."

Fern looked at her with wide blue eyes, increasing her density just enough to let her gaze slightly up at Antimony, like a particularly trusting child. Sometimes Antimony envied that trick. No one knew exactly how sylphs were able to change their personal density—not even the sylphs, who usually shrugged and went about their business when asked—but they were good at it. Good enough to fly, or at least float, when the need arose. Also good enough to turn themselves into the proverbial immovable object.

Antimony wasn't good at anything like that. In a family of Lilu, ghosts, dimensional travelers, and telepaths, she was just Ordinary Annie, the unnecessary third child. And nothing was ever going to change that.

"Karen likes you," Fern said patiently. "I mean, I don't understand why, since you're sort of mean sometimes—not to me, but to the other girls during practice, when you think they're not focusing enough—and it's not like you ever hang out and talk to anybody, and the last time you came to a party you just leaned against the wall drinking Diet Coke and glaring at anyone who tried to get you to dance, but she does, and she's single. So I bet if you asked her out, she'd say yes at least once."

Antimony raised an eyebrow. "Why would I be doing this, exactly?"

"Because dating is fun and smoochies are fun and you're lucky enough to have members of your own species around to do smoochies with, so you should at least try once in a while. You said you thought you might like girls. This is your chance to find out."

"Okay, one, I doubt Karen wants to be my bisexual experiment, and two, I told you, I'm not looking for anyone right now. Not on the team, not off the team, not at the grocery store, not on the weird cryptozoologist dating site my cousin Artie keeps threatening to set up—"

"He's not really going to, is he?"

"Uh, no. Half the signups would be Covenant assholes trying to infiltrate us, and the rest would either be overcommitted LARPers or some bored Bigfoot looking for someone to catfish. He's smarter than that. He may not always *act* smarter than that, but he is."

"Oh." Fern bobbed in place, clearly relieved. "Good."

"Yeah, good. But really and truly, I'm not interested in dating right now. If there's someone out there for me, I'll find them eventually. I mean, they'd have to be pretty weird to be interested in," Antimony waved a knife, indicating her entire inverted self, "all this. So maybe it's not going to happen."

"It will. I know it will. Someday your weirdo will come."

Antimony snorted. "Whoever it is, they must have been very, very naughty to wind up stuck with me."

Fern opened her mouth to object—she didn't like anybody saying bad things about her friends, not even her friends—but stopped as a bloody, vaguely equine shape trotted into the clearing below. Wisely, Fern shut her mouth and pointed.

Antimony turned to follow Fern's finger. Her smile in that moment would probably have been enough to hurt her dating prospects, such as they were, for the foreseeable future. It was the smile of someone finally being allowed to start breaking things.

"All *right*," she breathed, sheathing one of her knives and reaching under her vest to produce a Ziploc baggie filled with raw steak. It had been pressed against her side long enough that it was virtually at body temperature, and the smell, when she broke the seal, was strong.

Fern wrinkled her nose and didn't say anything. She kept not saying anything as Antimony dropped the baggie like a plummeting meat bomb. It burst when it hit the ground, strewing chunks of steak everywhere. The unicorn's head snapped up, nostrils twitching.

It really was a horrifying creature, bearing less resemblance to a My Little Pony than to a horse that had been sent to the glue factory, murdered everyone it found there, and come looking for revenge. The only part of it that could be considered beautiful or majestic was the long, spiraling horn that emerged from its forehead. The horn shone like mother-of-pearl, despite its thin coating of gore.

Fern whimpered. It was a reasonable response.

"Shhh," said Antimony, and pulled another bag of steak—this one laced liberally with rat poison, because there's no kill like overkill—out of her vest. She was grinning as she dropped it. In a very soft voice, she continued, "See why I don't date? You try explaining this to your significant other, and see how single you are in the morning."

The unicorn was under the tree, nosing at the spilled steak. As it began to eat, Antimony unsheathed her second knife, winked at Fern, and unhooked her legs from the branch where she'd been hanging.

The unicorn never saw what hit it.

One

"Don't look back. You'll never see anything
but what you're doing your best to leave behind, and you're a lot more likely to trip and
fall down, which gives it another chance to
eat you."

–Frances Brown

A large corn maze somewhere in the middle of Ohio

Six days ago

THE WIND BLEW ACROSS the corn with a sound unnervingly like a million bones rattling in the distance, a
skeleton army marching on our position. I've never seen
a skeleton army, but if they exist, I'm absolutely positive
they'd be marching on Ohio. There's nothing else to do
in Ohio. It's just corn, corn, skeleton army, possibly evil
corn maze, football, corn.

When they show farms in the movies, the ground is
always soft and loamy, inviting. It's ground that says
"hey, have a picnic on me." This ground wasn't like that.
This ground was hard and dry and seemed to consist of
equal parts petrified dirt and rocks, which dug into
my butt in a way that managed to be simultaneously
uncomfortable and invasive. I tried to squirm unobtru-
sively. All I did was work a few particularly pointy
chunks deeper.

Sam grimaced. "Is it ants? Please tell me it's not ants.

You can lie if you want. In this one situation, I give you full and enthusiastic permission to lie."

"It's not ants," I said. "I think I'm sitting on a rock."

"I know you're sitting on a rock. I'm sitting on at least six rocks." Sam leaned back on his hands. "I feel like this farm is missing its true calling. Get rid of the corn, harvest rocks."

"I doubt a rock maze would attract nearly as much in the way of tourism."

"Okay, first, this is Ohio, there is no tourism. There's just bored teenagers looking for someplace to go on a Friday night. Second, how much tourism do you think they're getting, with all the mysterious disappearances? Ballpark figure?"

"They got a lot of bonus tourism after the first couple disappeared." If there's one thing humans and sapient cryptids have in common, it's the burning desire to gawk at the site of an accident—and that goes double when you substitute "mysterious disappearance" for "accident." One mysterious death or missing teenager is a short-term gold mine for the heartless entrepreneur. As long as you don't mind building your success on a foundation of bones, you can make a lot of money.

The trouble begins when the deaths and disappearances keep happening. The "lightning never strikes twice" school of morbid curiosity can turn into "maybe I should have a vague sense of self-preservation" with reassuring speed, and the crowds stop coming.

The corn maze where we were enjoying the wonders of nature had been the site of not one, not two, but *eleven* disappearances since the start of the Halloween season. Always couples, always in their late teens or early twenties, and always fitting the "would totally sneak away to make out in the corn maze" demographic.

(Not as narrow or specialized a demographic as you might think. I know for a fact that my older sister went all the way in a corn maze with one of her high school boyfriends. She came home with husks in her hair, a smug expression on her face, and the phone number of the guy who'd been driving the hay wagon. My brother never got lucky in the corn as far as I know—although it's also possible that Alex has more of a sense of discretion than Verity, which hello, not hard—but he definitely took a few girlfriends to walk the supposedly haunted trails and hold hands in an atmosphere of delightfully artificial fear. Sex and terror go hand in hand.)

Sam frowned, tilting his head back until he was gazing at the sky. The nearest city was far enough away that it was a gorgeous deep black, splashed generously with stars. The moon was a perfect bone-pale circle, looking down on us like a single unblinking eye.

"Didn't you say you had family near here?"

"My maternal grandparents," I confirmed. "They live in Columbus. My cousin Sarah was staying with them the last time I checked. She hasn't been well." That's putting things mildly. Sarah is a cuckoo, a kind of pseudo-mammalian cryptid telepath. She's a nerd fantasy on the outside, all long black hair and big blue eyes and books on complicated mathematics. On the inside, she has more in common with a tarantula wasp than she does with your average mathlete. She's not human. She's only technically a mammal. Evolution made her, threw up its hands, and went home.

Cuckoos are psychic, and that's what got her into trouble. Most cuckoos use their telepathy passively, letting it make the world easier for them without actually exerting any effort. A few years ago, Sarah used her telepathy actively, in an attempt to save my sister's life. She succeeded. Verity lived.

She also failed—or at least, she also paid. Her telepathy hasn't been working right since she used it to manipulate the memory of some Covenant goons, and when a telepath's powers go on the fritz in the real world, it's not the cute two-issues-and-resolved dramatic twist like you get in the comic books. It's scary and it's grueling and sometimes I'm scared that Sarah is never going to be back to what passes for "normal" with her.

We'll love her no matter what. She's family. But I miss spending hours online chatting with her about her latest math obsession, and what's happening in the comics, and whether she's ever going to tell Artie—one of my other cousins, not actually related to Sarah; the family tree is complicated—that she's hopelessly in love with him. I miss *Sarah*. I wish I could be sure she was coming home.

I wish I could be sure I was.

Sam glanced down, a hopeful look in his eyes. "We could go visit. Let them see that you're okay."

I threw a handful of corn husks at him. "What part of 'in hiding from my family for their own protection' don't you understand?"

"The part where I'm tired of sharing rooms in shitty motels with Cylia and Fern, and I'm sort of hoping your grandparents have a guest room."

"Uh." I raised an eyebrow. "Am I wrong to interpret that as 'I miss getting laid, and I think my chances are better in your grandparents' house'? Because if so, wow, do I suddenly have some questions about your pre-me dating life."

Sam snorted. "Please. You met my grandmother. Between her overprotective 'I will end you' routine and the whole monkey thing, you know I wasn't getting any before you came along."

I threw another handful of husks at him, just on general principles. Sam laughed. I grinned. Despite the rocks digging into my butt and the whole part where we were sitting in a field known to be the site of multiple disappearances, this wasn't the worst way to spend an evening. Maybe my standards are lower than they should be. Honestly, I don't care.

We were closer to my grandparents than I liked—no more than a hundred miles from Columbus, and that was being generous—but it hadn't been a choice, not once we'd heard how many people had gone missing from this one sleepy little town. Their only real tourist attraction was the corn maze, more than a mile across and capable of holding hundreds of people at the same time without any of them being in eyeshot of anyone else. It was the perfect combination of domesticated fear and light exercise, and it had been running for years without problems. As we got closer to Halloween, the maze would—in an ordinary season—be overrun with hired teenagers in spooky costumes, paid to make the night more interesting.

This wasn't an ordinary season. This hadn't been an ordinary season since the week after the maze had opened, when the first pair of teenage lovebirds had gone into the corn and failed to come back out.

A lot of things hunt in cornfields. Some of them are human: all those movies about serial killers and farm-hands who figured out that scythes can reap knees as easily as they reap wheat didn't come from nowhere. Others are born of desperation, families of ghouls or harpies or other occasional man-eaters getting stranded in the middle of nowhere and going for an easy meal. I'm not excusing it. For one thing, I'm a human, and I enjoy not being eaten. For another, no one deserves to die that way. But it happens, and it's always going to happen, and all we can do is try to minimize it as best we can.

Thing is, most human serial killers are sloppier than whatever had been hunting in the corn. And most non-human killers are all too aware that this world doesn't belong to them anymore, if it ever did, and are smart enough to move on after a meal or two. Becoming an urban legend is the first step toward becoming a corpse.

Whatever was hunting here, it was something that liked the corn, but wasn't smart enough to pack up and go somewhere else to avoid attracting attention. That meant it was likely to keep killing, and killing, until the season ended and the farmers came to raze the field— and depending on what we were talking about here, that might be when the real trouble started.

My name is Antimony Price, although I've been known to call myself quite a few other things when the situation demands it. I'm a voluntary exile from my family. I'm a fugitive from a monster-hunting organization called the Covenant of St. George that would be delighted to use me to get to the people I love. I'm a roller derby player. I'm a cheerleader. Most of all, above everything else, I'm a cryptozoologist.

Cryptozoology is possibly the only scientific discipline that still thinks we're living in the Pulp Era. Our goals are twofold: conservation and concealment. When we can, we help supposedly fictional creatures stay under the radar and flourish, waiting for the day when they can come out of the shadows and book their appearances on *Ellen*. Unicorns and dragons, chupacabra and bogeymen, we find them and help them as best we can. We also study and properly document them. Their habits, their biology, and—where applicable—their society. This world has lost too many things already. If we're going to lose more, the cryptozoological community is damn well going to make sure their stories have been written down before that happens.

And that's all well and good, but when your job involves things that could give Godzilla nightmares, it can sometimes get more action-adventure than anyone's life really ought to be. Cryptids can't be allowed to go around eating humans, for a lot of reasons. Sure, we have plenty of humans compared to the number of available wadjet, but when people get eaten, other people notice, and then things get messy. So when something like "multiple mysterious disappearances in Ohio corn maze" crops up—no pun intended—it's on someone like me to go in and figure out what the hell is going on.

To be honest, it was sort of a relief. We'd been in the car for weeks, following whatever meandering backroads Cylia thought looked interesting, and I was going out of my mind with boredom. A little cornfield creature feature was just what the doctor ordered.

(Not to downplay the virtues of boredom, mind you. Cylia's seemingly random road choices were being guided by her preternaturally honed luck, courtesy of her jink heritage. We'd had more flat tires, near-accidents, and unplanned rest stops than any six ordinary voyages . . . but we'd also missed the speed traps, avoided the possible bottlenecks, and made our way from Florida to Ohio without the Covenant of St. George making an appearance. She was sucking down minor bad luck to balance a fairly major piece of good luck, and she was doing it without complaint or visible strain. I might never be able to prove it, but at this point, I was more than reasonably sure I owed Cylia my life.)

Sam sat up straight and leaned forward to tap my knee with one long-fingered hand. "Hey. Penny for your thoughts."

I favored him with a smile, allowing it to become sappier than I would have dared in more direct light. I hate being sappy. I hate knowing people can look at me and understand how much I care about the asshole I'm smiling at. The asshole who was, in that moment, sitting in the dirt alongside me, willingly going along with a plan that most people would have dismissed as a slower, less entertaining form of starting a barfight for the sake of letting off some steam.

In a just world, Sam Taylor would have found a nice carnie girl, someone who planned to spend her whole life on the flying trapeze, someone who didn't come with a complicated family history and an even more complicated personal present. He deserves better than me. He deserves the world. Too bad I'm going to kick the world in the teeth if it ever tries to come between us again. I already did the "running away for his own good" routine, and it wasn't enough to save either of us from the inevitable. So screw nobility. Annie Price loves Sam Taylor, and that's how it's going to be.

It doesn't hurt that he's ridiculously good looking, regardless of what shape he's in—although I'm probably biased. He's tall, broad-shouldered, and built like the acrobat he is, with naturally tan skin and features that nicely blend the Chinese and European aspects of his heritage. He's usually scowling, or at least frowning, when he has to walk around pretending to be human, but that just makes it better when he relaxes. When he *smiles*.

Sam is a fūri, a kind of therianthrope cryptid whose natural form is the sort of anthropomorphized monkey that wouldn't look out of place in a *Teenage Mutant Ninja Turtles* toy line. I've never been much of a furry, but like so many good geek girls, I had an early crush on Nightcrawler from the X-Men, and Sam's the next best thing. If we ever go to San Diego Comic-Con together, I'm going to talk him into dyeing himself blue and laugh myself sick as he suddenly sprouts a legion of admirers.

At the moment, he was wearing his human shape, his dark hair hanging over half his forehead and his feet covered by battered sneakers he could kick off in less than three seconds flat if he needed to. It was part of the lure. All eleven disappearances had been couples, and in the cases where they'd come to the corn maze with someone else, their friends had tearfully confessed that they'd split the party because the missing had wanted some "alone time" in the corn. They'd all been human, too, at least as far as a crawl through the archives of the local paper had been able to confirm.

There was no way to prove for sure that all those people had disappeared from the corn maze itself. They could have wandered off, and there had been no signs of an abduction. Better, from the perspective of the local police, there had been no blood. As all the missing were above the age of eighteen, the farm wasn't an active crime scene . . . yet. To make sure no one got the bright idea of making it one, Cylia and Fern were parked on a frontage road behind the maze, with Cylia twisting local probability to make sure no one human wandered by while we were working.

"Hey." Sam tapped me again. "Did you hear me? I said penny for your thoughts."

"Sorry. I was thinking."

"Thinking what?"

"That it's awesome how my job involves making out with my boyfriend in the middle of a potentially haunted cornfield."

Sam rolled his eyes. "You're so weird sometimes, Annie. You get that, right? You understand that you're not a normal girl?"

"That's why you love me, right?"

His smile was bright enough to make up for the lack of light, and even sappier than mine had been. "Damn straight," he said, and leaned forward to kiss me.

Kissing Sam while he was in human form was unusual enough to demand my full attention. Structurally, his face doesn't change much when he transforms, but he's always a clean-shaven human, and has full, remarkably fluffy sideburns when he's relaxed enough to go fūri. Two boyfriends for the price of one.

Boyfriend. There's a word I never expected to become relevant to me, Antimony "pit traps are more interesting than dating and boys don't like girls who can hit harder than they can" Price. I mean, boys other than my brother, who is a) weird, and b) my *brother*, ew. I'd been figuring on a life of happy solitude, broken when I needed to punch someone or set something on fire. And then snide, snarky, unavoidable Sam Taylor had come along, and now I was stuck in a relationship I had absolutely no interest in getting out of.

One of his hands slid up my side, presumably to distract me from his other hand, which was creeping under the hem of my shirt. I slapped it lightly away and kept kissing him. The corn rustled louder around us, despite the lack of any obvious wind. Sam pulled me closer, and this time when he slipped his hand under my shirt, I let him. The clots of dirt digging into my ass and thighs seemed suddenly a lot less important than seeing how tightly we could press our bodies together, his hands roving across my body, my hands pressed flat against his back, fingers digging in for purchase.

The corn rustled louder still. Sam bent his head to kiss my neck, lips brushing against the curve of my ear as he straightened.

"Now?" he murmured.

"Not yet," I replied, and kissed him again.

This is something slasher movies, inaccurate and frequently sexist as they are, get right

Lots of things don't like it when humans have sex—or even indulge in excessive heavy petting—in their vicinity. There's nothing puritan about it. Sex is loud and messy and distracting, which means it simultaneously frightens away the local prey animals and transforms the humans in question into easy pickings. For everyone who'll break off from their paramour to ask what that noise was, there are ten who'll make the jump to "maybe it was the wind, boobs are great, whee" all on their own. Which means sneaking up on someone who's having sex is measurably safer than most of the alternatives.

Sex is also the mechanism via which humans make more humans, and after centuries of people following "kill it with fire" as if it were a sacred commandment, most of the intelligent creatures we share this planet with have good reasons to genuinely *hate* humans. We're tiny, virtually defenseless persistence hunters who can't stop killing each other. We don't have claws, or fangs, or poison, or telepathy. We can't transform into something bigger and stronger, we can't hibernate for centuries, we can't do anything. And somehow we still managed to take over the world. Humans are terrifying. The last thing anything with a brain wants is to leave humans alone to make more humans.

(It doesn't help that a remarkably large number of

intelligent cryptids have adopted "look as much like a human as possible" as a survival strategy. From therianthropes like Sam to jinks like Cylia, there are dozens of nonhuman species hiding among the human population. Which means that human couple getting busy in your local monster's hunting grounds could actually be a couple of bigger, meaner monsters playing defenseless in order to lure in an easy meal. It's a hard world for a giant impossible carnivore.)

If you're in the middle of nowhere and worried about something attacking you, have sex, or at least indulge in some therapeutic making out. The odds are good that whatever you're scared of will choose that moment to attack. And if you happen to be heavily armed, well, it'll be a good way to work out the frustration of being interrupted.

A cryptozoologist is always prepared for mayhem, whatever form it takes.

Sam's hand cupped my breast, familiar and strange at the same time. Looking back, I realized I couldn't remember the last time we'd made out while he was bothering to stay human. Unlike most therianthropes, fūri default to their more simian form: it's the human that's a transformation, and hence the human that takes work to maintain. I'm not sure he *could* have sex without losing control of the specific tension that lets him look like just another hot guy on the street, and I'm not cruel enough to ask him to find out.

Besides, without going into unnecessary detail, let's just say that having a significant other with a prehensile tail is occasionally its own reward.

I groaned despite myself and bit down on his shoulder, leaning forward until my hair fell over my face. The corn rustled louder behind me. This time, I knew there was no wind. The corn was moving on its own—or, more likely, something a lot more material than the wind was moving it.

What felt like a hand made of spidery roots caressed the back of my neck. I reacted instantly, whirling away from Sam and pulling the small scythe out of my waistband in the same motion. The "hand" withdrew, but not fast enough: the edge of my blade caught it across the palm, slicing it neatly in half. The severed portion of the hand fell, twitching and writhing as it separated into its component parts—a handful of twigs, roots, and twisted corn husks.

"Corn Blight," I snapped, scrambling to my feet. "Sam, get the can."

"Everywhere has corn blight!" he replied. "Corn blight doesn't try to kill you."

"That's 'Blight' with a capital 'B'!" The corn was still moving, shaking and rustling like an entire platoon of creepy kids was hiding on the other side. That would have been nice. A little Stephen King action would have been a delight compared to what we were actually standing in the middle of-slash-up against and potentially about to be eaten by.

When you say "monster," people think of bears and alligators, or manticores and dragons. Big things, terrible things, things that can chase and catch and hunt. They forget, for the most part, that there's more to the world than the animal kingdom.

Fungus, for example. Fungus is everywhere, in everything. However much we can see—a mushroom, a toadstool, a patch of mold—there's so much more beneath the surface, wrapping its roots through whatever it finds, using the world to nurture itself. Fungus outmasses and outbreeds everything else on the planet. Most of it is fairly calm, content to spend its life consuming and reproducing and not bothering anyone. The rest . . .

Well, the rest can be a problem.

"Sam, go," I hissed.

"I don't want to—"

"You *go* or we both *die*. Not a hard call. I'll be here when you get back."

"You're a real jerk sometimes, you know that?"

"I do." I took my eyes off the corn long enough to throw a grin over my shoulder at him. It wasn't a surprise to see that he'd relaxed into his natural form. If anything, it was a relief. When he's not focusing on looking human, Sam is faster, stronger, and sturdier—all good things in a fight. "Now go, so I can stay a breathing jerk."

He rolled his eyes and was gone, leaping into the air with an ease that I could only envy and vanishing into the rustling rows of corn.

Speaking of rustling. I returned my attention to the corn in front of me, and the half-glimpsed shape that had retreated there after I sliced off a chunk of it. I pulled the other scythe from my waistband, holding them in front of me. Not my preferred weapons, but knives aren't as effective against an entire killer cornfield as I might like, and flexibility is sometimes the key to survival.

"All right," I said. "Come on if you're coming, or stop wasting my time."

The corn rustled and was silent. I tensed, bracing myself.

The corn attacked.

Blights-with-a-capital-B are thankfully rare. Their spores can only sprout under very specific conditions, and those conditions aren't met as often as they used to be. Something big had wandered into this field at the start of everything—a deer, maybe, or someone's sick cow. It had made it into a part of the maze where people didn't go, and it had died, and it had had the bad luck to do it atop a Blight spore. The fungus had woken up in response to the feast, sending its hyphae deep into the flesh of the unfortunate animal, and it had grown, and it had eaten well.

The smell of the Blight would have been horrific

during those early growth stages, when it was nothing
but decay and hunger. That must have attracted its first
victim, some farmhand or local civic employee who had
managed not to be included in the list of official disappearances by virtue of being gone long before the first
kissing couple dropped off the radar.

Well, I'd found them. All of them.

The Blight rushed at me in the fungus-wrapped, corn-
swaddled form of that unidentified first victim, an unspeakable scarecrow creation of meat and rot and fury.
Its hands, one missing half the fingers, were outstretched
to grasp and tear at my flesh. It would have my throat out
if it could, feeding itself in the warm spray of my blood
while its hyphae worked their way into the meat of me,
beginning the process of conversion.

Blights are awful things. They're about half as smart
as the smartest thing they've eaten, and since this one
had been eating humans for a while now, it was clever
enough to lurk, plan, and pounce. It had been going after
the distracted couples because it knew they were easy
prey. Its only mistake—so far—had been assuming that
Sam and I were equally distracted.

I grinned, gave my scythes a spin, and met it halfway.

My parents started my self-defense training when I
was four years old. It would have been sooner, but I'd
been the youngest and quietest of three, and I guess
they'd thought they had a little time. The only reason
they'd figured out how wrong they were was because I'd
started setting tripwires around the living room, which
was pretty impressive for someone who was still figuring
out how to tie her own shoes. What can I say: I've always
been an overachiever.

The Blight moved fast but jerkily, like it wasn't fully
connected to its own body, probably because it wasn't.
It was a vast, slow fungal intelligence, operating its
terrible meat puppets for its own benefit. The one it
had chosen to take us out lunged for me. I spun my
scythes as I danced to the side, cleaving its arms off at

the elbows. It howled, the sound more animal than anything else about it, and lunged again.

This time my strike took its arms off at the shoulders. They snapped like the hollow, rotten things they were, spilling out the smell of rot and a cascade of writhing maggots and dried-out corn cobs. The Blight would eat anything it could get its substance on, spreading and growing, stripping the land. The corn was already infected, every bit of it, and I spared a moment's thanks for the fact that this corn had never been intended for eating: the commercial crops were in a different field. What we were about to do wasn't going to leave the family who owned the farm destitute and starving.

Bored, maybe. The maze was *officially* closed for the remainder of the season.

There are traditions all over the world—or at least everywhere corn is grown—of burning the cornfields at the end of the harvest. It's supposed to help the soil. Whether it does, I couldn't tell you, but I know a good burning is the only reliable way to kill a Blight once it takes root, and a few preemptive burnings will pretty much guarantee your farm stays clean. Assuming you catch it before your brain is a swampy mess of fungus and you no longer remember what it is to burn.

Another Blight-body lunged from the corn, strands of fungus and clots of corn silk tangled in the rotted remains of its long brown hair. It didn't have eyes, just pulsing pits of Blight, but it tracked me all the same, and as I staggered backward to avoid its grasping hands, something else grabbed hold of my ankle.

Eleven disappearances, at two people per disappearance, plus the person who'd originally fallen into the corn to incubate the Blight spore equaled way more bodies than I was equipped to handle alone. I spun and hacked at the hand holding my ankle, hoping Cylia's field of improbable luck was holding and the thing hadn't managed to break the skin. Blight aren't zombies, they're fruiting bodies controlled by a greater, if subhuman, mind, but every cut and scratch increased my chances of infection, even with the best fungicide on the market. I'd rather skip the risk, thanks.

I swung the scythe in my left hand for the nearest Blight, only to have it twist at the last moment, so the blade embedded itself in the broadest point of the Blight's chest. I realized what was about to happen an instant too late to do anything about it. The Blight fell, and in the process, wrenched the scythe out of my hand.

It was smart enough to know I needed my weapons if I was going to win, and it had sufficient bodies that it could afford to sacrifice a few in the name of victory. I, on the other hand, only had *one* body, and if I lost it, I was fucked.

A Blight grabbed my right wrist. I slapped it on the shoulder as hard as I could, expecting it to burst into flames. It did not oblige. I froze.

You know the only thing worse than developing semi-controllable pyrokinesis? Losing it and being suddenly faced with the reality of a world that refuses to burn just because you asked it to. The Blight yanked me closer. I switched the scythe to my left hand and started hacking, trying to get the thing to let me go before it could reach me with its terrible teeth. Belatedly, the thought that maybe going up against an entire cornfield full of man-eating fungus on my own wasn't the *best* idea I'd ever had—and I've had some really terrible ideas.

"Annie! Duck!"

I stopped hacking and hit the ground the second I heard Sam shout. The Blight's arm was weakened enough from my repeated blows that it couldn't hold me when gravity was on my side; it let go and howled. It was still trying to decide whether it should charge the newcomer or drop and rip my throat out when the jet from the flamethrower hit it squarely in the face.

Yes, flamethrower. When you can't generate your own flames, artificial flames will do. I rolled away from the thrashing pyre the Blight had become, and kept rolling as

Sam directed the flames in a wide arc, igniting multiple Blights and a substantial amount of the corn.

"Remind me again why we didn't do this in the first place?" he shouted.

"Because we had to be sure it was Corn Blight, and not something really nasty!" I scrambled to my feet, grabbing the second flamethrower from its place against his leg.

God, I love my job sometimes.

Two

"Keep on falling in love, no matter how
much it hurts you. Eventually, it'll end up
giving you a safe place to land."

–Enid Healy

*About two hundred miles outside the city limits
of New Gravesend, Maine*

Now

"IF YOU'D STOP SCRATCHING it, it would heal faster."

"But it itches *now*."

Cylia glanced up, her eyes meeting mine in the rearview mirror. "And whose fault is that, exactly?" she
asked, voice cool. "I told you not to fight a field. A field
is bigger than you. No question, no contest, no way you
were going to win."

"But we *did* win," I objected. "We burned the Blight
to the ground. The field is clean, the farmer isn't going to
be eaten by evil fungus, everybody wins." Not everybody.
The Blight's victims had been consumed enough that the
fungus had weakened and worn away their bones. When
the fire came and cleansed the fungus away, there had
been nothing left to hold the skeletons together. Maybe a
forensic anthropologist could have sifted through the
dust and ashes to find conclusive proof that at least
twenty-three people had died there. Maybe not.

For the families of the victims, there would be no

closure, no confirmation that their loved ones were gone. There would just be the aching question, forever, of what had happened to them. It was difficult to think about that and not draw parallels to my own family's situation. They didn't know where I was or what I was doing or whether I was even still alive.

Well. They probably knew I was alive. I was pretty sure my dead Aunt Mary was allowed to tell them if I died, and the mere fact of that sentence making sense is proof that my life is damn weird.

"You need to be more careful," said Cylia. "You can't count on luck to save you every time. Believe me, I should know."

I wanted to bristle and object that I hadn't been counting on luck to save me, that I'd been counting on tactical planning and years of training for situations even stranger than "and then I convinced a cornfield to attack me by making out with my boyfriend." Good sense caught up with me at the last second, reminding me that counting on luck was exactly what I'd been doing.

Dammit. I hate it when other people are right. I slumped in my seat, careful not to pinch Sam's tail. He had it wrapped around my waist, and had since he'd fallen asleep about a hundred miles back. The poor guy was exhausted.

We all were. Travel is fun when there's an end in sight, but when you're on a seemingly endless road trip through the middle of America, there comes a point where the weariness settles into your bones and latches on like a novel new kind of parasite. I don't know how the routewitches do it. They have to travel to preserve their power. Maybe that dependence comes with an increased tolerance for diner hamburgers and gas station bathrooms. Me? I don't have any of that, and I was ready to commit violence for the sake of a shower with decent water pressure.

"Are we there yet?" I asked waspishly.

"Almost," said Cylia.

I blinked, sitting up straight. "What?"

"I said, almost." This time when she looked at me in the rearview mirror, she was smiling. "We're almost there."

I stared at her.

Of the four people in the car, Sam was the only one who was visibly not human. As always, he'd slipped into his fūri form as soon as he fell asleep, which was why he was wearing a hoodie, with the hood pulled securely over his head. If we got pulled over, he'd be able to shift back to his less simian guise before anyone got a good look at him. And of the four people in the car, I was the only one who was *actually* human according to any standard definition.

Fern and Cylia look superficially alike. Both are skinny, pale, and blonde. But where Fern is a fairy-tale princess turned live-action derby girl, with skin like cream, enormous blue eyes, and a dancer's build, Cylia is tall and freckled, with eyes the color of pondwater and bones that seem to be constantly on the verge of breaking through her skin and running off on their own adventures. She's remarkably strong, for all that she doesn't have much in the way of leverage, and favors shirts without sleeves that show off her biceps and tattoos at the same time.

Both of them used to play roller derby and, presumably, will again when we eventually finish our road trip from hell and turn toward home. That was where we'd met: on the track, where Fern and I had been skating for the Slasher Chicks, and Cylia had been skating in one of the competing local leagues. We'd always gotten along, and after this little road trip of the damned, I strongly suspected any return to Portland would be accompanied by Cylia switching leagues. You can't help someone take a sponge bath in a truck stop bathroom without forming the kind of bond that simply won't go away.

They have something else in common, apart from the roller derby and the general "make me feel like I'm at a family reunion" blondness: neither of them are even partially human, unlike Sam, whose mother was as human as they come. Fern is a sylph, a walking fuck you to the laws of physics. Her density is sort of optional, and she can make herself heavier or lighter with a thought. It shouldn't work. Biology and physics both say it shouldn't work. But she does it anyway, because what's the point in having scientific laws if you can't break them once in a while?

And I'm glad we've already accepted that idea, because Cylia is worse. She's a jink, one of two known species of human-mimicking, luck-manipulating cryptids. (The other species, the mara, mostly just eat the stuff. We are not big fans of mara. And by "we," I mean "anyone with any sense.") Things tend to go her way, although her lucky breaks are always accompanied by little misfortunes, like getting to the one motel in twenty miles that has any vacancies and discovering we'll have to share a bed. Things that will inconvenience but not endanger.

It says something about her skill at working the luck that she can keep it that consistent. Most jinks who survive to reach adulthood are like that. They learn what they can bend and how far they can push it, and they hone their craft on the sharp, unforgiving knife of knowing that the first time they screw up, the Covenant of St. George will be knocking on their doors, having miraculously tracked them down. Luck goes both ways. If yours is bad enough, it'll serve the ones who hate you.

Cylia's husband, Tav, died as a consequence of his own bad luck, having spent their years together manipulating the world to keep her safe. It had been an act of love, and I was pretty sure that if it had been possible to ask him—if one of the family ghosts had been able to find him lingering in whatever afterlife waits for the jinks and mara—he would have said he had no regrets. Cylia had been safe while she was with him, and now that she was without him, she had a firm enough grasp of her own capabilities that she was doing just fine.

For the moment, anyway. Technically, the smart thing for her to do would have been to put me out of the car, since at last count, I had the Covenant of St. George, the sorcerers who ran Lowryland, and the crossroads themselves all wanting a piece of my ass. Getting far, far away from me would be safer and more sensible than taking me on a cross-country road trip.

Thankfully, no one has ever accused my friends of having sense.

"Where are we going, exactly?" I asked. "Did you throw darts at a map again?"

"Better," said Cylia. She sounded serene, but I could hear the cracks behind her calm demeanor. Being in the car for weeks was wearing on her as much as it was wearing on the rest of us. Maybe more, since I don't drive, Sam preferred not to—he had to stay human to do it, and that made him uncomfortable—and Fern's driving could be described as either "enthusiastic" or "hazardous." Cylia had been behind the wheel almost constantly since we'd left Florida. She deserved a break.

That didn't mean I was willing to trust her definition of "better" quite yet. "Meaning . . . ?" I said carefully.

"Meaning I dialed a number at random and told the person who picked up that I was calling about the house," she said. "That's why I spilled my coffee yesterday."

"You spilled *everybody's* coffee yesterday," said Fern.

She wasn't wrong. Cylia had knocked over so many cups that I was pretty sure the tank top she'd been wearing was now permanently brown. It had been a small streak of bad luck, but it had gone on for the better part of a day, culminating in a gas station coffee machine somehow coming detached from the wall and shattering at her feet. We'd barely escaped that one without being scalded.

"What about the house?" I asked.

"Well, we're renting it for the next three months," said Cylia. She sounded smug. Maybe she was just thinking about taking a real shower. "Three bedrooms, lakeside access, barn that probably doesn't actually contain livestock, and plenty of privacy. Best of all, the owner is doing it all under the table while he's off backpacking around Europe—he was cagey enough about where he's going and why that the dude is either a routewitch powering up for the dry season or smuggling something, and—honestly—I don't care. The place is furnished, utilities are included, and it's within our budget."

"Um," I said. "None of us have jobs, and I don't really have much money. Neither does Sam."

"I do," said Fern brightly. "I saved all my paychecks, and I didn't have to buy uniforms while we were at Lowryland."

"You were a princess," I said.

"I still am in my heart," she said.

Cylia laughed. "It's fine. I've got it covered. Tav had a *lot* of life insurance, and he died a natural death. He's still looking out for me. And when he stops, I'll start buying lottery tickets."

"Fair enough," I allowed. As long as she never went for the big score—no miracle escapes, no multimillion dollar jackpots—her luck would last. She knew what she was doing. "Did you at least get to see the house?"

"Nope," she said, laughed again, and kept on driving.

The trouble with people is that we're all stories already in progress. Even before we're born, we have history, who loved who, who left who, who betrayed a global organization of monster-hunting assholes for who—the usual. I'm no different. I used to think maybe I could be, that I'd somehow be the one who broke the family mold and found something new to be, before I realized that family molds are never as close or confining as we think they are. I'm my own person, unique in the annals of my

family tree, but that doesn't mean I'm not a part of the
lineage that made me.

Either four or five generations ago, depending on how
you start counting, my great-great-great- grandparents
decided they didn't want to be genocidal jerks anymore
and quit the Covenant of St. George with as much fuss
and bother as they could manage. They died a long time
before I was born, but I've read their diaries, and they
were capable of a *lot* of fuss and even more bother. They
moved to America after that, figuring an ocean between
them and their old bosses might be enough to keep the
vengeance to a minimum.

They were mostly right: it took a long, long time for
the Covenant to send someone to check up on their way-
ward lambs. The story might have bent in a very different direction after that, except that the Covenant decided
to use "checking up on the heretics" as a punishment for
one of their less obedient soldiers, and shipped the man
who'd go on to become my grandfather off to the middle
of nowhere to make sure their former members weren't
making any trouble.

No one in my family has *ever* been able to resist trouble. Not only had my great-great-grandparents been
making trouble, they'd been making more family members. Two generations of them, to be exact. By the time
the dust settled, Grandma Alice was married to Grandpa
Thomas, who was missing—as in "yanked into another
dimension"—and the Covenant believed we were all
dead, a happy situation that managed to endure for two
more generations before my older sister, Verity, outed us
all as alive on national television.

If that's confusing, don't worry about it. Sometimes it
confuses even me, and I lived through it, day by agoniz-
ing, irritating day.

After Verity spilled the beans on our survival, we
needed to find out what the Covenant knew, which is
where one of their creepier habits came in handy. See,
the Covenant of St. George is a secret society with a

limited number of members and an even more limited capacity for recruitment, since it's not like the continued existence of the cryptid world is exactly public knowledge. In an effort to keep this from becoming a serious problem, they've been running a breeding program for centuries. As in a "we tell you who to marry, we tell your kids who to marry, we craft the future of your family one carefully curated pairing at a time" program. Because *that's* not fucked up and wrong.

The Covenant breeding program has resulted in a bunch of families with consistent "looks" created by genes capable of beating up every recessive in the neighborhood and taking their lunch money away. All the other women in my family have what the Covenant calls the "Carew look," thanks to my great-great-grandmother, Enid Carew, and my great-grandmother Fran, who looked enough like Enid to make it kind of creepy when my great-grandfather married her. Every Price woman in my generation is short, petite, and very, very blonde.

And then there's me. Tall and busty and brown haired and perfectly Price in every way, as in Grandpa Thomas, as in "I look like the representative of a bloodline the Covenant no longer recognizes, since Grandpa was the last of them, and he hasn't been seen in decades." So when Verity decided to turn us all into targets, it made sense that I'd be the one sent to infiltrate the Covenant, since there was no way they'd recognize me. What could possibly go wrong, right?

Right.

To be fair, my infiltration of the Covenant seemed to go well—so well, in fact, that the Covenant sent me to infiltrate a carnival suspected of harboring at least one killer cryptid. The Spenser and Smith Family Carnival, to be precise, where I'd found the suspected killer cryptid, and stopped her before she could kill anyone else . . . and where I'd met Sam Taylor, grandson of the carnival's current owner.

Sam Taylor, the boy—the man—who'd put an end to

my longstanding "dating is a waste of time" policy, through sheer dint of being such an asshole that my options boiled down to kissing or killing, and you know what? Kissing was *way* more fun.

Only the Covenant disagreed since Sam wasn't human. The Covenant disagreed with a lot of things, including my belief that the rest of the carnival should be spared. None of *them* had been killing people. That didn't matter to the Covenant. That especially didn't matter to my handlers, one of whom had died in the effort to extract me . . . or to Leonard Cunningham, the current heir apparent to the entire mess. He'd twigged to me as a Price almost as soon as he'd met me, and he'd allowed the whole charade to play out as a sort of a test of my character.

I'd passed. He'd allowed me to live. He'd even allowed me to escape and go into hiding, secure in his fanatic belief that I'd eventually come crawling back. He was wrong—God, he had to be wrong—but getting out of the Covenant's surveillance band had also meant getting out of my family's reach. I hadn't spoken to any of them since I'd left to go undercover. If not for my dead Aunt Mary, they would probably have believed that I'd been captured, or killed, or—worst of all—converted to the cause.

(I've mentioned my dead Aunt Mary a couple of times now. I'll get to her soon, I swear.)

Where does a girl go when she's running from her family, her not-quite-boyfriend, and the largest monster-hunting organization on the planet? Lowryland, Florida, of course. One of the biggest and most successful amusement parks on the planet, which means it's also one of the most crowded, which means tracking spells couldn't follow me there. It was a great idea, up until I ran into the secret cabal of magic-users who were secretly running the place. In what felt like no time at all, I wound up semi-apprenticed to their leader, who siphoned off most of my magic in order to fuel a massive conspiracy of luck-theft that had caused an unknown number of injuries, deaths, and disasters in and around the Park.

Nothing in my life is ever simple, I swear. To make matters worse, in the course of getting away from the fuckers running Lowryland, I was nearly killed by a runaway roller coaster, and found myself in a position no one in my family had been in since my grandfather's day: I found myself making a bargain with the crossroads. Which is where my dead Aunt Mary comes in.

See, Aunt Mary is a crossroads ghost, which means she was a human when she was alive, and went to work for whatever the hell the crossroads actually *are* when she died. She's like a public defender for the people who feel the need to make bargains with something too big and too powerful for the human mind to fully understand. The crossroads speak. They offer things. Mary explains why taking those things would be a bad idea. She offers alternatives. The alternatives are usually "don't do this, death would be better, you will be sorry forever if you do this."

I did it. I did it to save myself, and to save Sam, who had been swept away by the same roller coaster. I did it for the sake of my family, and because I'd been scared out of my mind by the thought that I would never go home. Maybe my intentions weren't entirely pure, but I was pretty sure the crossroads didn't care. They appreciate a little honest selfishness.

They saved my life, and they saved Sam's life, and they took the fire out of my fingers as collateral against a favor to be performed later. One day soon, they were going to call on me to do something for them, and when they did, I wasn't going to be in a position to refuse.

I glanced at Sam sleeping in the seat next to me, and felt a deep, fierce possessiveness clamp around my heart, holding so tight that for a moment, I struggled to breathe. It had been worth it. It had all been worth it.

I put my hand on his knee and closed my eyes. Maine. We'd be in Maine soon, and there would be time to rest and regroup and decide what we were going to do next. Cylia's luck had led us to this house. It would be safe. It would be fine. For a little while, at least, we could stop running.

That idea had never sounded so good.

🐾

The car door slammed hard enough to wake me up. Not just me: Sam's tail tightened around my waist before letting go, disappearing back to wherever it went when he returned to his human form. Therianthropes are walking violations of about a dozen scientific principles at any given time, including conservation of mass.

"Where are we?" he asked groggily.

"Hang on and stay human; I'll find out." Growing up with a family like mine means learning how to wake up very, very quickly under pretty much any circumstances, since the alternative could involve getting eaten. I unbuckled my seat belt, opened the door, and stepped out into the pine-scented air of someplace that was definitely *not* the rolling fields of farm country.

I was standing on a gravel driveway. Trees pressed in on all sides, packed together until they were basically a horror movie waiting to happen. The sky overhead was a dark so deep and clear that it contradicted itself, becoming a virtual sea of stars that glittered, silver-bright, against the blackness. They weren't the only source of light: the moon was huge, gilding the land in silver and glinting off a distant slice of what I assumed was a lake, since it didn't look active enough to be an ocean.

At the end of the driveway, a house that could easily have nabbed itself a starring role in *Attack of the Return of the Blair Witch: Part III* loomed against its background of trees, windows glowing dimly behind gauzy curtains.

Cylia stood in front of the car, harshly lit by the headlights as she exchanged a stack of cash for a set of keys.

The man next to her glanced uneasily at me, attention snagged by the motion. Cylia snapped her fingers.

"Eyes here," she said, not unpleasantly. "Focus on the nice lady with the nicer money. Lovely, lovely money. Three months of wandering-around-Europe money. Is there anything we need to know about the house?"

"The upstairs shower is finicky," he said. "You have to turn the hot water up twice as high as you think you do. There are snakes in the boathouse, but they're not venomous, and they're useful at keeping down the mice. There's an account that pays the utilities automatically, so there's no chance of the power being shut off, but it goes out sometimes anyway, when there's a storm up. Best to keep your flashlights ready to use."

"Not haunted?" she asked.

He laughed, more nervously than I was comfortable with. "Not so's anyone would notice."

In my experience, that usually meant "not haunted, but there's something unpleasant in these woods that eats people, and I'd rather you didn't ask me about it." That was fine. Once we got settled, I had every intention of spending a little time as something unpleasant in the woods. If I found the original unpleasant thing, we could have a contest to determine who was worse. I'd win. I always won.

"Great." Cylia made the keys vanish into her pocket as she smiled at our new landlord. "Have a wonderful time in Europe. We'll see you in December."

"About that . . . if you don't mind me asking, what brings you out here? Fall's not the most hospitable season for visiting Maine."

"Maine has a hospitable season?" I blurted. They turned to look at me. I shrugged. "Sorry. Just . . . between the mosquitoes and the snow, I didn't realize there was a tourist-intensive time of year."

"We're here for the leaves," said Cylia. "We just love a pretty tree, isn't that right?"

"Sure is," I said, and bared my teeth in an approximation of a smile.

Cylia lifted both eyebrows in what I recognized as the universal gesture for "get back in the car before you ruin everything." I got back in the car. Sam, still apparently human, gave me a mistrustful look.

"Is she buying drugs? Please tell me she's buying drugs, and not selling one or more of us to the local zoo."

"She's paying the rent on the house where we're going to be living for the next few months." I glanced at the front seat. Fern, who could probably sleep through the fall of the Roman Empire, was still out cold. "Apparently, the upstairs shower is finicky. I'm cool with that, since it implies the existence of a downstairs shower, meaning we have access to multiple showers."

"Is that—" Sam began, and caught himself. "What am I saying? Of course, it's safe. Cylia wouldn't be paying the man if it wasn't safe."

Cylia was done paying the man. He waved at her before he walked down the driveway, passing the car without a single look as he receded into the night. Cylia followed him as far as the driver's-side door, which she opened and slipped through, plopping herself behind the wheel.

"We'll figure out permanent sleeping arrangements in the morning," she said. "For tonight, find a flat surface and enjoy getting some rest in a bed that isn't moving or rented by the hour. Home, sweet home."

She started the car, and we drove on toward the future, which looked like it might at least have better plumbing than the past.

Three

"If cleanliness is next to godliness, bleach
is proof of the existence of the divine."
                                    —Jane Harrington-Price

Waking up in an unfamiliar house in New Gravesend, Maine

WAKING UP TO DISCOVER Sam had functionally tied
himself to me in the night was no longer unusual,
or particularly surprising. He'd grown up with his family's carnival, never more than a few feet from people who
knew what he was and didn't have a problem with it. By
choosing to run off and follow me, he'd given up the kind
of safety and security most cryptids will never know, and
he'd done it without being asked. If wrapping his tail
around my ankle or waist while we slept meant he didn't
feel quite so unmoored, I was cool with it.

What I hadn't realized was how much I'd come to
take that contact as a security blanket, a sign that the
world was sticking with its new, somewhat idiosyncratic
normal. But when I opened my eyes to find myself alone
in the middle of a wide, bare mattress—no sheets or
blankets in evidence, nothing but a single caseless pillow shoved under my head—my first response was fear.
Piercing, unfettered fear, the kind I normally associated
with free fall and near misses.

I sat up. Sam didn't appear. It wasn't so much that I
didn't like being alone—I don't have a problem with

being alone—but that for the past several months, getting Sam away from my side had basically required a crowbar. We were both a little insecure after everything we'd been through, and while I might have eventually started seeing his presence as clingy, we weren't there yet. So why was I alone?

The room was good-sized. It had to be, to accommodate the king-sized bed I was sitting in. The curtains were insufficient to block out the sunlight, but judging by its brightness, I'd slept until almost noon. Gingerly, I rolled out of bed, retrieved my jeans from where I'd clearly abandoned them the night before, and started for the door.

Everything after the conversation in the driveway was a blur, and not a very detailed one. I dimly remembered being shaken awake again, which implied that I'd gone back to sleep before we'd reached the house. I didn't remember getting my things out of the car. Maybe I'd left them where they were for the night, trusting our isolation to keep them from getting stolen.

Outside the door was a long, cool hall, dust motes dancing in the air. The runner down the middle of the floor was the kind of faded wine-red flower pattern that seems to spring spontaneously into being in old houses the world over. It didn't provide any cushioning as I walked, although it could probably become a tripping hazard in a pinch.

Photos of people I didn't recognize and would probably never meet lined the walls, hung with care above locked barrister bookshelves full of leather-bound old volumes that didn't look like they'd been touched in twenty years. I kept walking until I heard people talking quietly up ahead—and, more importantly, until I smelled bacon. That was enough to make my shoulders unclench. I took my hand away from the knife strapped to my wrist—more proof that I'd fallen into bed without taking the time to get properly undressed. I'm happy to sleep with weapons under my pillow. I'm less happy about sleeping with weapons actually on my person. When a bad dream can lead to a punctured kidney, nobody wins.

(This is just one of the many reasons that I feel developing sorcery as an adult is unfair and unreasonable, even if it's not uncommon among sorcerers—although sorcerers are pretty uncommon to begin with, making this a problem for one percent of one percent of people, if that. Before the fire was taken from my fingers, I wasn't waking up stabbed. I was waking up *on fire*. Not the kind of party I enjoy.)

The stairs were narrow, but not rickety, and carpeted in a rug that matched the one in the hall. At least our temporary home wasn't a hovel. The third stair from the bottom creaked when I stepped on it. That would be an easy enough fix. Give me a hammer and some nails and I could take care of it in under an hour. The idea was pleasant. It had been way too long since I'd been able to spend an afternoon just improving my living conditions.

The living room at the bottom of the stairs was complete with couch, comfy-looking chairs, and one of those big televisions that look expensive until you realize they're more than a year old. We could probably buy a more recent model at the local Goodwill or equivalent for under a hundred bucks, which explained why the owner had left it here while he filled his house with strangers. It was still nice to see. I could watch bad horror movies and eat popcorn and not be running for my life for fifteen minutes.

I'd never watched a horror movie with a boyfriend. I liked the idea. It's more fun when there's an excuse to get cozy, and when the monsters aren't, y'know, real.

I followed the smell of bacon across the living room to the dining room, which was dim due to lack of external windows. Someone laughed, the sound coming from behind a closed door, and I hesitated.

The last time I woke up to surprise breakfast, it had been my Aunt Mary doing the cooking, and while that had been a delight—no one makes pancakes like

someone who's been doing it for more than fifty years—
it wasn't like she and I were currently exactly on what I'd
consider speaking terms. She was furious with me for
making my crossroads bargain, even though I'd done it
to save my life. I couldn't really blame her for that, although I could resent her a little for being willing to let
me die if it meant the crossroads wouldn't have a claim
on me. I like being alive. It's how I get things done.

Mary can find me anywhere I go. It's one of the advantages of being her specific kind of ghost. If this was
her trying to make a peace offering, maybe it was time
to let her. I took a deep breath and opened the kitchen
door.

I was almost disappointed when I stepped into the
kitchen and found Fern standing at the stove, flipping
bacon strips with a fork. She looked up at the sound of
my footsteps, already smiling even before she saw me.
"It's eleven," she informed me brightly. "You slept until
eleven. I didn't know you knew how to do that."

"Is there coffee?" I asked.

"Coffee, toast, and bacon. No eggs. There weren't
any eggs in the fridge. No milk, either. Cylia has a list
going over on the table. Check the fridge and cupboards
and write down anything you want her to get from the
store."

"Right," I said, casting around until I found the coffee maker. It was old-fashioned, twenty years old if it
was a day, but the coffee was black and hot, and the
sugar was sweet, and when I put them together, it started
to feel like maybe I was going to finish waking up after
all. "Where's Cylia?"

"She's cleaning out the car. Sam went for a walk in
the woods. He wants to know how many neighbors we
have."

"Mmm," I said, spooning more sugar into my coffee.
Knowing the location and number of the neighbors mattered more to him than it did to the rest of us. If there
were too many of them, he'd need to spend most of his

time either indoors or making the effort to seem human. But if we were isolated, he could finally relax.

For his sake, I hoped he could relax.

The coffee was good. The bacon was better. I sat and ate and added things to the shopping list, some essential— bread and canned soup and mac and cheese—and others frivolous—marshmallow fluff and sugared cereal and microwave pizzas. There was a microwave. I could once again live on my natural diet of salt, fat, and artificial cheese.

Fern finished cooking and sat down across from me to eat her own breakfast. After we'd both swallowed more fried pig than was strictly good for us, she asked, "Do you like it here?"

"I don't know yet," I said. "I'll get some shoes on and go for a walk, assuming Cylia doesn't want me to come to the store with her."

"I think she's excited to have some time to herself," admitted Fern.

"That's what I figured," I said. "Do *you* like it here?"

Her smile was immediate and bright. "It's wonderful. There's a little room up in the attic with bars on the window, so I can have it open all night and not worry about floating away." Her smile dimmed. "I mean. Unless you want it. We're supposed to pick our rooms today, now that we're all awake."

"Okay, first, us picking rooms doesn't mean you automatically lose the one you want, so no, and second, I'm looking forward to sharing a room with Sam for more than a couple of days. We need to figure out all the ways we get on each other's nerves. So a 'little' room isn't going to work for us. I'm happy staying where we slept last night, unless Cylia has another suggestion."

"Oh." Fern relaxed. "Good."

I took the last bite of bacon and chewed thoughtfully, watching her. We'd been trying to look out for each other during this unwanted adventure, taking care not to push anyone too far. Despite that, Fern had been actively fraying. She needed privacy as much as the rest of us, if not more. I had no idea what "normal" social activity looked like for a sylph. Did they enjoy and crave company as much as humans did, or did they prefer solitude?

One more question that may never have a real answer, courtesy of the Covenant of St. George. The large, harmless cryptids, like Fern and Cylia, were among the hardest hit by the purges. They're not teetering on the edge of extinction like the manticores are, but they don't have anything resembling the kind of community they would have once, before the humans decided this planet was ours and ours alone.

Sometimes I sort of hate my ancestors.

We finished our breakfast in comfortable silence, and I washed the dishes while Fern wrapped the leftover bacon in foil and tucked it into the fridge. With that done, we looked at each other awkwardly for a moment before, in unison, we started to laugh.

"Okay, this was weird and all, but I'm going to get my shoes and see if I can't find Sam out in the woods," I said. "I'll try not to go out of earshot. If you need me, just whistle."

"Sure, Annie," said Fern. She stepped around the table and hugged me, hard, before I could move away. "It's going to be good here. You'll see. We're going to get to rest."

"I hope so," I said, hugging her back. Then I turned and left the room. Time for a walk in the woods.

It was a beautiful day. Early fall in Maine is neither too cold nor too hot, but is instead as close as the state comes to putting on its best dress and inviting people to the party. The house was surrounded by a large grassy patch, less "lawn" and more "private meadow." I stopped at the edge of it, looking back and trying to assess our temporary home by daylight.

It was a pretty standard piece of New England construction, built to keep heat in and cold out, covered in double-paned windows that stared judgmentally out on the world. The porch wrapped most of the way around the ground floor. I looked at it and thought about the last lazy days of fall, about spending them counting fireflies and eating hamburgers and laughing, finally safe, finally able to breathe.

Three months was a lot of time to regroup and recover. It was also a lot of time to let the guilt catch up with me. My family had to be going out of their minds with worry. But again, time. Now that we weren't focusing on running, maybe I could figure out a way to set up a line of communication with my cousin Artie. If anyone in the family knew how to use the Internet to talk in complete privacy, it was him.

Cylia hadn't just found us a temporary home. She'd found us a way to start hoping again. I appreciated that more than I could put into words. Turning away from the house, I made my way into the trees, leaves crunching under my feet, and I was alone in the world, and it was glorious.

I watched carefully as I walked for signs that Sam had passed through, or that something else had. I didn't know these woods. I'd never been to Maine before, and I didn't have any of the family bestiaries to prepare me for what I might find. There are cryptids everywhere in the world, which only makes sense, when you consider "cryptid" means "science doesn't know about it yet." New species are discovered every year, brought into the scientific fold and lifted out of cryptozoological obscurity. These days the word mostly gets used to mean the big stuff some people say is real and other people say is a big hoax, like Bigfeet, unicorns, and the occasional giant snake.

(Always assume the giant snakes are real. The alternative is finding yourself being slowly digested in the belly of something you didn't want to admit existed, and while I'm as fond of healthy skepticism as the next girl, I'm a lot *more* fond of continuing to have my original skin. As in, the one I was born with, not the one the snake has left me with after a little recreational swallowing me whole.)

Woods like these—dark, and dense, and clearly mostly ignored by the locals, either because they were full of ticks or because the people who lived around here had better things to do with their time—are a paradise for the smaller, shyer, less dangerous cryptids of North America. There were probably angler tortoises and tailypo living in the underbrush, and if I found a creek, I'd also find bloodworms nestled fat and comfortable in the mud, getting ready for their long winter hibernation.

I made a mental note to do exactly that. A surprising number of things can be lured in with bloodworm ichor, and my field kit was less "running low" than it was "nonexistent." If I was going to take a long field trip-slash-exile from my family, I might as well try to gather some useful data while I did it.

Poison oak looks the same no matter where it's growing. That's a good thing. Ticks are harder to watch for. That's a bad thing, and I stepped carefully, trying to avoid kicking any bushes that looked specifically likely to harbor a large and hungry arachnid population. Lyme disease would not exactly improve my year.

I was so busy watching the ground that when I finally stopped and looked up, I had no idea where I was.

Whoops.

Trees stood sentinel around me, tall and silent and unmoving. Their branches blocked enough of the sun to have created a series of clear patches through the wood, places where the underbrush was thin, and I'd been automatically following them as I walked. That would make it easier for me to find my way back . . . maybe. Paths like that, in woods like these, have a tendency to branch.

The light was golden, filtered through the changing leaves, and everything had the vaguely unreal air of a

Normal Rockwell painting. I breathed in the scent of loam and growing things, feeling the tension leave my back inch by struggling inch. This wasn't like the woods back home, which smelled of pine and pitch and petrichor, but it was close, so close, and there was a hint of winter in the air, warning me that the days of wandering peacefully through the trees weren't going to last forever. Better get my time in while I could.

I started walking again, paying more attention this time. A few branches had been broken recently; something had been through here. I shifted my path to follow the damage, and when I stepped around a particularly thick-barreled tree, I saw him. Sam. He was standing in a clearing, back to me, attention focused on something in his hands. He'd acquired a heavy wool coat somewhere, probably in one of the closets at the house, and had the collar turned up to cover most of the back of his head. It made sense. He was a carnival boy, born and raised, and he'd always spent the winter tucked safely away either indoors or in a place where snow was a rumor, rather than a reality. The idea of a fall and early winter in Maine was probably simultaneously fascinating and terrifying.

Learning how to move through the woods without making noise is Price Family Survival 101. I've been sneaking up on rangers and forestry workers since I was seven. It was easy to start stepping lightly and moving with deceptive speed, like I was channeling my inner Jason Voorhees. Minus the machete and the murderous rage, natch. In only a few seconds, I was standing behind my runaway boyfriend.

Never cover a jumpy person's eyes when they're standing in the middle of the woods unless you want an elbow to the sternum. I didn't, so I put my hands on his shoulders instead, leaning in close at the same time.

"Guess who?" I murmured, only inches from his ear. His very human ear. His very human, very alone in the middle of nowhere—

Oh, crap. I realized what I'd done half a beat before the man in front of me shouted and whirled, his hands already raised defensively. He was holding a book, and used it to partially block his face, like he thought I was going to start throwing punches.

I wasn't there, of course. I was three feet back from my starting position, my own knees slightly bent, ready for flight or a fight, whichever came first. The man stared at me. I stared back.

He did not, seen from the front and without the veil of my road-weary assumptions, look a damn thing like Sam. He was white, for one thing, with blue eyes and an angular face that seemed designed to have made him seem worried even when he wasn't. I mean, he sort of had good reason to be worried, since a strange girl had just grabbed his shoulders in the forest, but that was beside the point. His hair was dark and shaggy enough to have created the right silhouette when combined with the bulk of his coat. Hindsight, as they say, is always twenty-twenty, and never more so than when you've accosted a total stranger.

"Um," I said. "Sorry. I thought you were somebody else."

The man stared at me, lowering his book in order to stare with more of his face at the same time. That was another place where his angular bone structure and rather remarkably thick eyebrows served him well. He could stare disbelievingly like nobody's business.

"Who did you expect to *find* in the middle of the woods on a Thursday morning?" he demanded. He had a faint New England accent, the sort of thing that would no doubt be used as a quaint character trait on a CW drama, but which really just made him sound even more judgmental than the average man on the street. "The Jersey Devil doesn't come this far north."

"To be fair, if you were the Jersey Devil, I think the wings would have sort of given you away before I went and grabbed you," I said. "For which I am sincerely sorry, and which I will never do again."

He kept staring.

"Come on. I didn't stab you or set you on fire or throw things at you, I think you can stop looking at me like I'm some sort of serial killer."

"You're not from around here, and you're in the middle of the woods, which isn't exactly what I'd call *normal*," he said, voice taking on a strident note. I'd spent enough time around my cousin Artie to recognize the sound of someone working themselves into a tizzy. "There's nothing around here except—"

The man stopped mid-sentence and went back to staring at me.

"Oh, no," he said.

"If you were about to say 'there's nothing around here except that house that was for rent, which is a reasonable walk that way,'" I pointed vaguely, "then you're in the neighborhood of reaching a logical conclusion. Hi. I'm assuming you're my new neighbor."

"Oh, *no*," he repeated, with more heat. "He wouldn't. He wouldn't dare."

"If by 'he' you mean 'the man who rented us the house,' then yes, he would dare. Has dared. We have a contract for the next three months and everything." I crossed my arms. My willingness to play nicely— engendered, for the most part, by my own mistake—was fading fast. "He's off to Europe, and we're looking forward to an exciting adventure with the upstairs shower, which is apparently finicky. Hi. I'm Annie. You are?"

Using my real name, even in its shortened form, was risky. Using my "Melody West" identify, which had been well and truly blown by my time in Lowryland, would have been even riskier. "Annie" is a common name, where "Antimony" is not. It would be fine.

And if it wasn't fine, these woods looked like they'd offer plenty of places to hide a body.

"James," the man said stiffly, pulling himself into a locked, upright position. He was tall, taller than me, taller than Sam. If he hadn't been slumped, there's no way I could have gotten them confused.

Honestly, if I hadn't been exhausted, there's no way I could have gotten them confused. All this time on the run had done more damage to my situational awareness than I'd realized. "Nice to meet you, James, and again, sorry for startling you. I didn't mean to. You live around here?"

James hesitated. I could see the debate on whether or not to lie raging in his eyes. I sighed.

"You're the one who told me there was nothing anywhere near here, thus implying you'd have to be from somewhere nearby. I'm *trying* to make conversation. Do you think you could meet me halfway? Maybe? This will be a lot easier for both of us if you do your share of the heavy lifting."

"Excuse me if I'm not proficient in the art of having conversations with strange women who accost me in the middle of the forest," he said.

"You're excused," I replied. "Now can we start this over, or do we need to spend some more time riding the roller coaster of shame around the recrimination mountains? Because you seem nice and all, and I really am sorry I upset you, but I have shit to do today, and this is getting old."

James blinked. Then, to my surprise and relief, he laughed. He was a lot less intimidating when he laughed.

I mean. The man didn't look like he knew what strength training *was*, and there was absolutely no question of whether I could take him in a fight, but there's something about scowling strangers in unfamiliar woods that triggers a mild "maybe I fucked up" response in most thinking creatures.

"I'm sorry," he said. "I guess I take myself too seriously sometimes. Can we start over?"

"Without me mistaking you for my boyfriend and

scaring the crap out of you? Absolutely." I extended my hand. "Annie Brown."

"James Smith," he said. His grip was firm without being painful; his palms were dry. "So you're renting my cousin Norbert's house?"

"I guess," I said. "A friend of mine made most of the arrangements. I slept during the drive over. Tall guy, sort of nervous-looking, said he was on his way to Europe to spend a couple of months backpacking?"

"You'd be nervous, too, if you had a name like 'Norbert,'" said James. "But yeah, that's the one."

My real name is a lot closer to "Norbert" than it is to something as ordinary as "James." I didn't comment, just smiled and said, "I guess that means we're neighbors, assuming you don't lurk around isolated woods for no specific reason."

"I live that way," he said, and pointed at the densest part of the wood, in the opposite direction from the house. That was a relief. I didn't mind sharing the woods—look at me, getting all possessive already—but it was good to know we'd at least have *some* privacy. Sam was going to need it. "Just me and my dad."

"Oh," I said.

He grimaced. "Is this where you call me weird for living at home?"

"Not at all," I said. "I lived with my parents until very recently. I liked it. I don't see any reason to move out if you're comfortable."

"I don't know if I'd go that far . . ." James trailed off mid-sentence as he realized what he was saying. Cheeks flaring red, he stepped away, moving his book behind his back. "Welcome to the neighborhood. I'm sure I'll see you around."

"I'm sure you will," I agreed. I knew a dismissal when I heard one. Offering a genial nod, I turned to go back the way I'd come.

"Wait!"

I stopped, looking over my shoulder. "Yes?"

"You should be careful out here. These woods aren't necessarily safe."

I smiled, showing him all my teeth. "No," I said. "I guess they're not."

This time when I started walking, he didn't call me back. I walked into the trees until I was what I considered a safe distance away, and when I looked back over my shoulder, I couldn't see him at all. That was a start. Much as I wanted to be nice to the neighbors, I hadn't been expecting to meet them in the middle of the woods.

Not that I knew where I was. Between the unfamiliarity of the trees and the time spent talking to James, I had no idea whether I was moving toward the house or whether I was just getting myself more lost.

"And me without a compass," I muttered, turning to consider the trees. They seemed to consider me right back. "Okay, well. Won't be the first time."

I started walking again, following the paths shade and the local animals had cut through the underbrush, chasing the last of the tension brought on by my unexpected encounter from my shoulders. I don't know how long I wandered, sunk into the pleasant, near-hypnotic act of walking through the woods, before I heard something rustle overhead. Whatever it was, it sounded way too big to be a raccoon or a tailypo, which didn't leave many options. I stopped walking. I smiled.

"Took you long enough," I said.

Sam dropped down in front of me, landing with the ease of long training. All fūri are graceful when compared to humans. A fūri like Sam, who's spent most of his life on the flying trapeze . . .

When he moves, it's poetry. There's no other way to describe it.

As usual, he was barefoot, letting his simian toes grip the ground for purchase. His tail curled high behind him, a visible barometer of his mood. He was relaxed, comfortable even, and why shouldn't he be? We had the better part of a forest all to ourselves. For the first time since leaving the carnival, he didn't need to worry about getting caught because he'd decided to let his hair down. So to speak.

"I didn't even know you were out here until I went back to the house and Fern told me you'd gone for a walk," he said. "Did you know Cylia was going to the store?"

"I'm hoping that's past tense by now, since I'm going to want lunch when we get back." I stepped forward and slung my arms around his neck, leaning in to plant a kiss on his lips. "Hi."

"Hi," he replied, and wrapped his own arms around my waist before pulling me close and kissing me much more firmly.

I've never been a girl who did much kissing, and I feel genuinely fortunate to have found myself a boy who didn't have much more experience. I mean, I think we're getting pretty good at it—neither of us has any complaints—but that, plus the thing where he's a monkey more than half the time, has done a lot to keep me from getting self-conscious. Kissing somebody who looks like they're about to anchor their own sci-fi movie franchise is distracting enough that we've been able to just get on with things, like figuring out where to put our hands.

When we finally broke apart, I was breathing fast and his cheeks were red, which made me want to start kissing him again. I tamped the impulse down as hard as I could. Fun as it would be to spend the day making out in the woods, we had things to do.

"I ran into a guy somewhere that way," I said, waving a hand vaguely. "Human. Be careful out here."

"I've been watching for humans since before you knew how to work a crossbow," Sam said.

I lifted an eyebrow. "What kind of dismissive comment is that, exactly?"

"The kind that realized halfway through that it didn't know where it was going," he said, smiling lopsidedly. "So, yeah. Thanks for the warning."

"No problem," I said. "He seemed nice. Apparently, we're renting from his cousin. If something breaks, he's probably who we'll call."

"Should I be jealous?"

"Only if you think my taste runs toward tall, dark-haired assholes."

Sam blinked. "Uh, that is *exactly* what I think your taste runs toward. I now present exhibit A, myself." He waved a hand, indicating the entire length of his body. "But since I also know there's something I can do that some random human in the woods can't, I'm going to skip jealous in favor of smugness."

"Oh?" I asked. "What's that?"

Sam grinned before grabbing me by the waist and leaping into the air, landing on a branch easily fifteen feet above the ground. I squeaked at the impact. His grin got wider and yes, there was more than a small element of smugness in his expression.

"See?" he said. "I'm way more fun than some random asshole. I'm your *favorite* asshole." He kissed me quick and leapt off the branch, carrying me along with him as he began making his way through the forest.

When I was a kid reading comic books with Sarah and Artie, I never imagined myself as Gwen Stacy. I was much more into the idea of being Peter Parker, or better yet, Jessica Drew, someone who was badass and awesome in my own right. Not that Gwen wasn't cool, it's just that Gwen had a nasty tendency to wind up dead, regardless of the timeline, and that isn't my scene. Since hooking up with Sam, though, I was starting to understand the appeal.

As a human, the trapeze is as close as I can reasonably come to flying. My sister is into free running, which is mostly about falling with style, and she does what she can within the limits of her human anatomy, flinging herself off the side of buildings and using a combination of momentum and acrobatic training to translate meaning into motion. I may not like her much, but I'll be among the first to admit that what she does is impressive as hell.

Sam takes all that and throws it out the window. Take a monkey's strength, speed, and grace, and scale it up for a human frame. Then combine it with a lifetime of intensive training, and what you'll get is the closest thing I'm ever likely to meet to the real-world Spider-Man. He kept one arm wrapped around my waist, tight enough that I didn't worry about falling, and hurled himself through the trees with the casual fluidity of a man who had absolutely no concerns about falling. I put a hand over my mouth to keep my laughter inside. People don't usually look up. It's one of the weirder facts about people. Even if they did, we were moving quickly enough that it was incredibly unlikely we'd be seen. Someone laughing overhead would be a lot harder to explain.

Sam shot me a concerned look when I moved my hand. I lowered it just enough for him to see me smiling. He flashed a quick, understanding smile of his own and kept going, the woods whipping past all around us, the world turned green and magical.

Then we were dropping out of the trees at the edge of the artificial clearing containing our new home. Sam let me go as soon as I had my footing. He stepped into the shadow of the woods for a beat, and then swore softly as he moved to stand next to me, human and barefoot in the autumn chill.

"You need to carry a pair of flip-flops if you're going to do stuff like this," I said.

"Normally I do. I was just so excited by the idea of actually stretching out some of the kinks in my back that I forgot." He shrugged, expression wry. "Next time."

"Every rock you step on will be a reminder of that promise."

"Gee, you're sweet. How did I ever find a girlfriend as sweet as you?"

"Just lucky, I guess." I leaned up to kiss his cheek. "Come on. Let's go see if Cylia is back from the store."

We walked together across the open field, him hopping and swearing every time he stepped on a rock, me trying not to laugh at him, and it had been a long time since I'd felt that hopeful or that genuinely at peace. It was a nice change.

It was really a pity that I already knew it was never going to last.

Four

"Sometimes it's important to stop and breathe. It'll improve your mood. It'll also improve your aim. Nothing fixes most problems like shooting them in the head."

—Alice Healy

Entering a slightly less unfamiliar house in New Gravesend, Maine

CYLIA'S CAR WAS BACK in the driveway. Everyone was safe: everyone was home. I took Sam's hand as we walked around the corner of the house, heading for the kitchen door, which was propped open to let the afternoon air inside. As we got closer, we could hear Cylia telling Fern where to put the groceries. I grinned and sped up, pulling Sam with me, until I was finally able to stick my head inside. Then I stopped, blinking.

Fern was balancing on a chair, loading staples—sugar and salt and rice and dried beans—into the cupboard above the pantry. Cylia stood a safe distance away. If Fern fell, she could bleed off enough of her density that she'd bounce off the floor like a big, really weird balloon. If Cylia fell, we'd wind up at the local emergency room.

The amount of care Cylia was taking to stay clear, though . . . "How much bad luck does the universe owe you?" I blurted.

Cylia turned to offer me a twisted smile. "Hello to you, too," she said. "Enough that it's going to hurt when it hits me—and it should *only* hit me. I told the luck to find this place for my use. I'm expecting a twisted ankle, or for the car to blow all four wheels at the same time, or for my wallet to get lifted. That doesn't mean I need to give things a chance to swing in the other direction. I'd rather be neutral than lucky."

"Raise your hand if you like your personal weirdness better than the idea of constantly doing bookkeeping for reality," said Sam dryly.

"I can't raise my hand, or I'll hit myself in the face with the pancake mix," said Fern.

"Did you buy the *whole* grocery store, or only the parts that looked interesting?" I asked.

"One of the possible expressions of my current luck deficit could involve my credit cards getting turned off for a week," said Cylia. "Fern has her cards, and I know you have cash, Annie, but Sam's broke—"

"Sorry our carnival caught fire," he said.

"—and it's not like any of us are working. I wanted to make sure we could eat without resorting to petty larceny."

"Or hunting," I said. "This looks like the kind of place where I could find deer." The thought of a nice piece of venison made my mouth water. Hunting with Dad—and occasionally Grandma Alice, when she was in the right dimension during deer season—had been one of my favorite parts of childhood. It had been recreation, a way to contribute to the household, and training for a future that would almost inevitably involve needing to shoot people, all at the same time.

Most people go their whole lives without needing to point a gun at another intelligent being and pull the trigger, and sometimes I envy them. That also means most people, confronted with a situation where they *need* to point a gun at somebody and pull the trigger, will freeze up. It's not a failing. It's a trait I've sometimes wished I could share. But there was no way my siblings or I were getting out of this fight. Even if we'd wanted to go off and be "normal," to become accountants or dentists or whatever, we would always have known too much, and we would always have needed to be able to defend ourselves.

"Is it the kind of place where you can find a shotgun and a hunting license?" asked Cylia. "I really don't want us messing with the local law until the bad luck hits."

"Give me a few days, I'll figure it out." I moved to investigate the contents of a brown paper bag. "Who's making dinner?"

"Not you." Cylia moved the bag out of my grip. "You'd make spaghetti with maple syrup and canned tuna, or something equally horrifying. You may be the only human in the house, but you're also the only person who doesn't eat like one."

"Youngest child." I shrugged. "If I wanted my food to survive in the fridge, I needed it to be as unappetizing as possible. Have you and Fern talked about rooms yet?"

"I want to keep the one we slept in last night, if that's okay," said Sam. "That's a great bed, and the rafters are perfect for me to do my stretches without putting anyone else out."

Cylia shot him a startled look. "Okay, not the reasoning I was expecting, but sure. Fern's happy in the attic, and I found a bedroom off the living room that will work perfectly for me. That way, we have someone sleeping on every floor. Helps us keep watch for robbers."

"What reasoning *did* you expect?" I asked.

"You've got the bathroom to one side and the library to the other, which means even if the walls are thin, nobody's going to hear you having sex," said Cylia. "I honestly figured I'd be getting the privacy argument."

I perked up. "There's a library?"

Sam groaned. "Oh, great. Now we've lost her."

He wasn't wrong; I was already heading for the door.

What people sometimes forget about my family, when we're being all badass with our knives and our bullets and our ability to keep fighting even when we're long past the point where anyone with any sense would have given up is, well . . .

We're *enormous* nerds. Seriously. I am the inevitable result of a lineage which includes researchers, librarians, and the kind of animal lovers who think everything, no matter how potentially deadly, deserves the chance to flourish. While they observe and take notes, naturally. It's not science until somebody writes it down.

I pounded up the stairs. The door to the room where Sam and I had spent the night was open, propped by my suitcase, which Cylia must have carried in from the car while I was wandering in the woods. The doors to either side were closed. I tried the one on the left: bathroom. I tried the one on the right. It opened easily, and all my wishes came true.

"Jackpot," I whispered, taking a moment to stand there and just breathe, glorying in the anticipation of stepping through.

The library had clearly started its existence as two rooms of reasonably average size, before they were joined into one mega-room, like an architectural Voltron. Floor-to-ceiling shelves lined the walls, blocking everything except for the fireplace and the single, relatively small window. As if that weren't enough, the shelves were packed—absolutely *packed*—with books. Old books. Cloth-bound and leather-bound and—I'm not a book snob, I love my paperbacks as much as the next girl, but there's a certain degree of weird literary bullshit that will never, ever come out in paperback.

I exhaled and stepped into the room as if in a daze, slowly walking along the shelves, letting my fingers trail along the spines of all those lovely books. Most were dusty. The few that weren't seemed to be mostly local history and folklore. That was good enough for me. Snagging the first one off the shelf, I sank into the confines of a nearby armchair and allowed the text—dry as dust, but filled with so many things I didn't know, and hence hungered to learn—to carry me away.

The book, *A History of New Gravesend, Maine*, by one Nathanial Smith, was about as interesting as the title implied, in both possible directions. He spent an entire chapter on the architecture of the local sewer system and barely spared a page and a half for a dramatic fire that had consumed half of downtown, but which had, in its aftermath, provided what he referred to as "multiple opportunities for redevelopment." That seemed like a pretty shitty way of saying "all the poor people burned to death."

I wasn't the only one who thought so. I turned the page to find that someone had written, in tidy ink letters, "Bastard never saw a tax loophole he wouldn't exploit. Check ownership records for area, ref. Dunning. Possible someone tracked land profit?"

Normally, I would have been annoyed to find that someone had been writing in a book, especially a book as old as this one. In this case, I was delighted. When trying to learn local history, the real story is usually in the footnotes and the indices, hidden in the places where people don't want you to look.

Dunning. The name was familiar. I unfolded myself from the chair and, sure enough, found Dunning's *Families of New Gravesend* on the shelf two volumes over from where I'd found the first volume. I pulled it down, along with three others that seemed likely to show up in further footnotes, before returning to my chair.

This town could be as boring as bathwater, a place where nothing interesting enough to make a Wikipedia page out of had ever happened, but I was going to find out. I was going to learn it *all*, every story, every secret. I had three months to do it in.

I was so engrossed in my unplanned research project that I didn't notice how dark it was getting outside the window until someone knocked on the doorframe and cleared their throat. I looked up. Sam was standing there, ringed in light from the hall behind him.

"Dinner's ready," he said. "Find something good?"

"How long have I been up here?" My stomach grumbled. However long it had been, it had definitely involved missing lunch. That was almost . . . well, nice. I hadn't had the opportunity to spend a day sunk in a book since leaving Portland. It felt like I was getting back to normal, at least for me.

I liked the idea of getting back to normal.

"Long enough that if you hadn't left the door open, we would probably have been afraid you'd died," he said. "I unpacked all our stuff. And made the bed. And offered to make you a sandwich. You didn't notice."

"Oh." I offered him a sheepish smile. "Sometimes I get really into my reading."

"Uh, yeah, I'd say. If you were any more into your reading, you would actually be *inside* the book."

"Never go into a book. Either it's a dimensional portal, which is bad, or it's some sort of Dungeons and Dragons-style mimic-thing, which is also bad, although in a less 'we'll never find your body' sort of a way."

Sam blinked at me slowly. "You know," he said finally. "I like you exactly the way you are, because I am not stupid and do not want you to hit me with a shoe for implying that there's something wrong with you, but you were a lot easier to understand when you were just the annoying chick who wanted to throw knives at my head."

"Don't worry." I got out of my seat, setting the books I'd been reading carefully aside for later. "I'm still the annoying chick who wants to throw knives at your head. I've just diversified my interests."

"See, you say that like it's reasonable, but all I hear is 'blah blah blah, I'm probably going to stab you in my sleep.'" He wrapped his tail around my waist, pulling me closer while he placed his hands to either side of my face. Then he grinned and kissed me.

When he pulled back, he said, "On the plus side, the make-outs are amazing."

"That's what I'm here for," I said, leaning in to kiss him again. There was something so refreshing about being goofy and sappy and not worrying that somebody would see us. This was the first time we'd really been able to stand still since the start of our relationship, the first time I'd been able to kiss him without either forcing him to stay human or checking to see whether the motel curtains were closed. It was nice. It was special.

It was never going to last. Good things never do.

"What's for dinner?" I asked.

"Cylia made a sort of goulash with pasta shells and hamburger and stuff," he said. "It smells amazing. There's parmesan cheese for the rest of you, and no dairy at all for me."

"She remembered."

His smile was almost shy. "She did."

Cylia had been my friend long before she met Sam. Sam, on the other hand, had grown up sheltered by an entire carnival of people who loved and looked out for him—and who had warned him, over and over again, that if he was ever exposed to the rest of the world, he'd wind up in a zoo, or worse. Humans are not historically kind to things we don't understand. Even without the ever-present threat of the Covenant of St. George, a cryptid in today's world has a lot to worry about.

Meeting Cylia and Fern, who weren't human and weren't from the carnival and didn't give a damn what he was, just that he was good to me, had been a revelation. It had been nothing short of miraculous to him that they could care about him enough to keep track of little things like the fact that he was lactose intolerant, or that he didn't like riding in the front seat because then he couldn't risk falling asleep. People are a lot more likely to notice when the guy in the passenger seat is a monkey than when it's just another dark shape in the back.

"Goulash is better when it's hot," I said. He unwound his tail from my waist and took my hand, and together we made our way down to dinner.

Cylia had set the table, putting the pot on a trivet in the middle. "You're doing the dishes," she said, pointing her spoon at me.

I nodded. "Seems fair."

Fern was buttering bread. She looked up and smiled. "Did you find something to read?"

"Is that an actual question, or are you just being polite?"

Fern thought about it while the rest of us were taking our seats. Then, nodding solemnly, she said, "Actual question. I mean, we're all exhausted. You could have decided to take a nap. I've had three showers so far today, because I can. I'll probably have another one before bed."

"I admire your dedication to exhausting the local water table," I said. Cylia handed me a bowl of goulash. I sprinkled cheese on the top as I thought about how to phrase things. Finally, I said, "I've been reading books on local history. They're about as interesting as you'd expect for a small town in the middle of nowhere. Lots of 'and then there was a feud over who owned the chickens, which went on for fifteen years, long after both the chickens and the original participants were dead, because it was something to do.' This may be Maine, but that doesn't make it Stephen King territory."

To my surprise, Cylia relaxed visibly. "Oh, thank the Fates," she said.

I blinked at her. "Did I miss something?"

"Luck brought us here; luck found us this house," she said. "And it's perfect for what we need, have you noticed that? It's *perfect*."

A warm current of unease worked its way through my stomach. "Perfect things exist. Besides, this house isn't perfect. The water pressure in the upstairs shower's hinky."

"There's a master bedroom right next to a library," said Cylia. "There's an attic bedroom with bars on the windows. We're surrounded by the kind of forest where a six-foot monkey can run around and not worry about being seen by strangers. It's not perfect in the 'will win awards' sense. It's perfect in the 'does it suit our idiosyncratic little group of weirdoes' sense."

The unease grew stronger. From the look on Sam's face, he was experiencing something similar. "So why does this make us *not* being in Stephen King country a good thing?"

"That's one of the ways the luck could have equalized," said Cylia. "It could have decided, hey, we got the perfect house, in the perfect town, with the perfect unmarked graveyard filled with angry spirits out back. Or the perfect family of hungry ghouls looking for a group of tourists no one would miss. Or—"

"I get the horrifying picture," I said. "Boring town is better. Check. But doesn't that mean we're still waiting to see how the luck is going to equalize?"

"It does," admitted Cylia. "It also means we'll have a little time and can get our footing before we have to fight for our lives again. Sometimes boredom is its own punishment. Now, can someone pass the pepper?"

Dinner was exactly as advertised: filling, delicious, and hearty in that summer camp kind of way, like we were storing up calories against the possibility of never getting to eat again. Cylia was a pretty decent cook, as long as what you wanted was carbs, protein, and vegetables that came out of a can. Sam, after tucking away three helpings, paid her the highest compliment in his vocabulary.

"You cook like a carnie."

Cylia laughed, and Fern laughed, and even I laughed, as much out of relief as amusement, because this was really happening: this was real life. We had our own place, and the space to stop and breathe and just *be* for a little while. I'd never realized, back when I was spending my days on my cousin Artie's bed complaining about the X-Men and my nights on the track with the rest of my team, how much I needed to stop once in a while.

As promised, I did the dishes, and Sam, who had grown up in a carnival boneyard where everyone was expected to pull their weight, dried them and put them away, and by the time we were finished, both Fern and Cylia had gone to their respective rooms and shut their doors, leaving us alone in the kitchen. They might as well have left us alone in the house. It had been so long since I'd had privacy, *real* privacy, privacy that wasn't stolen in a motel restroom or the middle of a cornfield filled with killer Blight, that for a moment I didn't know what to do with it.

I stared at Sam. He stared back.

"Um," he said finally. "Am I being weird and creepy and so totally a dude if I say I really, *really* want to go upstairs to our bedroom with the door that shuts and locks and walls that don't connect to any place where someone else is trying to sleep?"

"No, because I was about to say the same thing."

The look of relief on his face was profound enough that it was almost comical. "Race ya," he said, and took off like a shot.

There is no planet where I can keep up with Sam, and so I didn't even try. I was tormenting myself as much as I was tormenting him, and still I took the stairs with the decorous grace of a Jane Austen heroine, one hand on the railing, one foot in front of the other, stretching out the journey until every nerve I had was screaming. There might not be fire in my fingers anymore, but there was still fire in my blood, and it wanted to burn—oh, God—it wanted so badly to burn.

The bedroom door was closed when I got there. I opened it, stepped inside, and was treated to the sight of a perfectly made bed, the covers turned down in obvious invitation, the pillows—which must have come from a hidden linen closet—plumped and ready. All that was missing was my boyfriend.

So I did what people don't do. I looked up.

Sam, holding himself perfectly still in the corner by bracing his hands and feet against opposite walls, grinned at me. His lips were drawn tight across his teeth, as always, keeping the expression from turning into a threat display.

"Found me," he said.

"I wasn't aware we were playing hide and go seek." I closed the door, clicking the lock into place as a precaution before bending to unlace my shoes. I tried to look unconcerned, like I didn't care how long he hung out on the ceiling rather than getting his ass to floor level and ravishing me.

"And I wasn't aware that we were playing keep away." There was a soft thump.

I continued untying my shoes. "Haven't you ever heard of delayed gratification?"

"Oh, let's see." The springs on the bed creaked. "First, I had to wait for you to tell me you weren't just some weirdo who happened to come with a pair of talking mice. Then, I had to wait until I got up the courage to ask you out. *Then*, just when I'm thinking hey, maybe I'll actually get to touch a girl, I find out you've been lying to me since the minute we met."

I glanced up sharply, suddenly tense. Sam was sitting on the edge of the mattress. He offered me a small, almost twisted smile before pulling his shirt off over his head. That helped with some of the tension, even as it made other elements of it worse. Say what you like about the risks of the flying trapeze, but you won't find a better workout this side of the circus.

"That's over, that's settled and done," he said, tossing his shirt to the foot of the bed. "I lied to you, you lied to me, we canceled each other out. Still put a crimp in our sex life."

"Theoretical sex life, at that point." I stepped out of my shoes and unbuttoned my jeans. "We weren't sleeping together yet."

"We were in my dreams," he said wistfully and paused to watch as I gracelessly rolled my jeans down my hips and kicked them off. "The reality is better. But, you know. Stuff kept getting in the way. Like the asshole assassins, and you burning down the carnival and running away, leaving me behind."

"It was for your own good."

"Uh-huh. Try pulling that trick again and see how far that excuse gets you. Small hint: not far." Sam folded his arms. "Then I had to *find* you, and then I had to deal with wacko assholes who wanted to suck the luck out of the world like little kids with an orange, and then we were on a road trip for weeks with people I didn't really know, and anyway, I think my gratification is *plenty* delayed at this point. My gratification is going to summer school and watching all the other gratifications running around playing baseball."

I paused in the act of unfastening my bra. "You were homeschooled at the carnival. Do you even know what summer school *is*?"

"Shut up."

"I'm just saying, that metaphor sort of got away from you somewhere."

"And I'm just saying, shut *up*." Then he was kissing me, and one hand was busy finishing what I'd started with the bra, and conversation was no longer a necessary part of our evening.

Prior to Sam, I would have said my interest in dating—limited as it was—was doomed to stay pretty much hypothetical. I hadn't been a virgin, thanks to a few beer parties in high school combined with a burning desire not to wind up tied to the altar of the next cult that needed a specific kind of sacrifice, but that had been more about practicality and physicality than actually making a connection with anyone. Sex had been something that could happen, that wasn't so frightening it needed to be avoided, but that I didn't think about on a regular basis.

Turns out having a significant other who likes sex and likes *me* and really likes combining the two changes my priorities a bit. The extra hands don't hurt, either.

When we were finished, exhausted and sweaty and content with one another, we brushed our teeth, cleaned up as much of our strewn clothing as felt reasonable, and fell back into bed, this time for less aerobic activities. I was asleep almost as soon as my head hit the pillow.

I woke some unknown length of time later, spine rigid, hairs on the back of my neck standing on end. I held myself perfectly still, reviewing things that might have woken me. My dreams had been pleasantly abstract and were already fading, leaving none of the thin veil of unease that came with nightmares. Sam was sleeping solidly beside me, his breath a steady constant too soft to be the reason I was awake. His tail was wrapped loosely around my left wrist. I tugged. He let go, making a small sound of discontent, and didn't open his eyes.

Whatever the cause of my unwanted wakefulness was, it wasn't in this room. It was—

There. A sound, faint but distinct, from outside the bedroom. Not outside the window, where it could have been any number of woodland creatures, from bunny to bear: inside. Someone was moving around nearby. Someone who sounded too large to be Cylia. I'd already eliminated Fern. If she needed to be on this floor for some reason, she would have dropped her density until her steps were the next best thing to inaudible. No one robs a house like a sylph.

Moving as quietly as I could, I slid out of the bed and retrieved my jeans. It only took a few seconds after that to find my bra and tank top. It felt a little silly to be putting my tits away to go and investigate a creepy noise in my house, but that's one of the things the women in horror movies always get wrong. If there's something that might slow you down in a fight—like, say, leaving your boobs to flop around free-range and cumbersome—you deal with it *before* the fight gets started.

Guns are a bad idea in a rental house. I belted a set of throwing knives around my waist and eased the door open, stepping gently out into the hall.

The house was dark and close enough to silent as to make no difference. There are always sounds in an old house at midnight. The rumble of the heating system, the soft settling of old timbers as they sink deeper into their positions, the whistle of the wind outside the walls. At the moment, I was grateful for every familiar, predictable noise. As long as I was careful, they would cover for me.

A dim light was coming from under the library door, too dim to be anything but a flashlight. I looked at it, eyes narrowing. Any chance that it had been Cylia, unable to sleep and looking for a nice book on civic history to ease her into dreamland, died with that light. She would have flipped the switch. She would have used the overheads.

We had an intruder.

I drew a knife as I placed a hand on the library doorknob. The air felt electric with the confrontation to come. I took a slow, careful breath, centering myself, and shoved the door open.

There was a yelp as the person inside realized they were no longer alone. I didn't see them: they dropped their light, whatever it was, and the library was cast into darkness. That was fine. I closed my eyes to keep any shadows or outlines from distracting me, balled my free hand into a fist, and swung, missing by at least a foot.

Blind fighting—the art of punching people while you can't see them—is a useful skill to have, which is why my parents insisted my siblings and I all develop it, if only for the inevitable day when we'd be trying to punch a robber in a rented house in Maine. It's all about knowing the space and following the sounds inside it. The intruder backpedaled away from me, every step broadcasting their location.

I swung again. This time, I was rewarded with the pleasant crunch of knuckles mashing against cartilage.

"My nose!" exclaimed a male voice. I drew back to swing at him a third time. I was keeping my knife until and unless I really needed it. Punching burglars is much easier to explain to the local police than stabbing them. Stabbing them can cause . . . problems.

Our intruder had better reflexes than I expected— that, or it had been long enough since I'd had a good sparring partner that I was getting rusty. Either way, my fist smacked into a palm rather than hitting his face, and pain followed immediately after. Not searing pain. Not even the dull pain of hitting something too hard for my hand to take. No, this was the brutal, bitter pain of thrusting a hand into a pocket of subzero water that had miraculously remained unfrozen, dropping the temperature of my skin into frostbite territory almost instantly.

I shrieked, jerking my hand away, and kicked the intruder's feet out from under him. There was no point in trying to be quiet, not when all the available backup was mine. Sam was already going to be pissed that I'd gone looking for the intruder without him. He'd be *livid* if I got myself frozen to death because I didn't scream.

The intruder fell hard, with a grunting sound that confirmed the location of his head. Great. I dropped to one knee, feeling it strike home against the bottom of his crotch, and leaned forward to press the edge of my knife against his throat. It wasn't the sharpest blade, since it was designed for throwing rather than slashing, but I was pretty sure he'd get the idea.

"What the hell are you doing in my house?" I demanded.

The light clicked on before he could answer, and James Smith—the man from the woods—squinted in pain and surprise against the glare. I gaped at him. That gave him the chance he was looking for. Moving fast, he grabbed my wrist. Cold flowed from his fingers into my skin, and I dropped the knife as my hand forgot how to clamp down. I howled. He tried to roll away.

"*No*," I snarled, and punched him again with the hand he'd frozen first. My knuckles hit his nose with an audible crunch, followed by a bolt of pain that seemed to travel all the way to my shoulder. If I hadn't broken something, I'd at least bruised it, in both of us, and I was going to need medical attention.

His head snapped back, smacking against the floor so hard that his eyes rolled back and his body went limp. I staggered to my feet, one hand hanging functionally useless, the other hand aching so badly that I could feel my pulse in the traceries of pain, and stared at the unconscious form of literally the only person I'd met since getting to Maine.

Well, fuck.

Five

"Death is not the last great adventure. Death
is the natural consequence of getting the last
great adventure wrong."

–Mary Dunlavy

*The library of an increasingly familiar house in New
Gravesend, Maine*

IT HAD BEEN FIFTEEN minutes, and the feeling was returning to my right hand. The skin was red and
chapped, like I'd been outside in a bad snowstorm. My
joints ached, but I didn't think I was going to lose any
fingers. That was the good part. James Smith was tied
securely to a chair, his hands covered in oven mitts that
would keep him from grabbing hold of anyone else. That
was the better part.

Cylia leaned against the wall, dressed in a fluffy yellow bathrobe that made her resemble nothing so much as
a malevolent daffodil come to pass judgment on the
weak. She still looked friendlier and more understanding
than Sam, who was in human form, wearing only his
jeans, and glaring at James like he was trying to decide
how to dispose of the body. Which, let's be fair, was
probably pretty close to the truth. It turned out Sam
didn't like it when people froze his girlfriend.

Gosh, I loved that man.

Fern was outside, checking the house perimeter to
make sure James had been acting alone when he broke

in. We already knew how he'd entered: one of the panes in the library window was shattered in a snowflake pattern, like it had been exposed to sudden, shocking cold. He must have frozen it, smashed it, and then reached through to unlock the window and let himself inside. The sound of the glass breaking was what had woken me up.

James looked at me warily. A thick trail of dried blood connected his left nostril to his upper lip. There wasn't much visible swelling; I hadn't managed to break his nose. Pity. I couldn't justify punching him again, either, not until we'd managed to get some information out of him. If he stopped talking, maybe then I could punch him. That was a fun idea. My hand hurt, and everyone was grumpy as hell, and punching was just the thing to make me feel better.

"Let's try this again," I said. "Why did you break into our house?"

"It's not your house," he said sullenly. "It belongs to my cousin."

"What a lovely, subtle, pointless clarification," I said. "That makes my hand feel *so* much better. Which reminds me. What did you do to my hand?"

"I didn't do anything to your hand," said James. "You're the one who punched me in the face and tied me to a chair."

"Actually, I did that, on account of how you broke into our house and broke my girlfriend's hand." There was a low, dangerous note in Sam's voice, one that promised a remarkable amount of pain to anyone who got in his way. "The knots would be a lot tighter if she'd done it."

"I didn't break her hand," protested James, shooting an alarmed look in Sam's direction. The oven mitts we'd taped over his hands flexed with the movement of his fingers.

"No, you just froze them a little." I held up my left arm. A red, angry handprint was etched in the skin around my wrist. It didn't hurt as much as my hand, but that wasn't saying much. "I'm going to lose skin. Not too much, I don't think. Not sure I care how much. It was my skin, and I didn't say you could have any of it."

"And *I* didn't say you could go breaking windows on the house I just rented," interjected Cylia. Sam shot her a sour look. She shook her head. "I'm upset about her being hurt, too, but I'm also the one who promised to pay for any damages incurred during our stay. Windows are expensive. Give me one good reason I shouldn't call the police right now."

"My father's the chief," said James. "Please call the police. I'm begging you. I'm sure he'll be really interested in why I'm tied to a chair with a broken nose instead of safe at home where I belong."

"Your nose isn't broken," I said defensively.

Cylia put a hand over her face. "Of course, his father's the local police chief. Of *course*. Of all the luck." She muttered the last like it was the direst curse in her vocabulary, and for a jink, maybe it was.

I focused on James. "You broke into our house," I said. "We didn't kidnap you. We were defending ourselves against a home intrusion."

"This is Maine," said James, like that explained everything.

Maybe it did, in whatever weird little world he was inhabiting. I turned to Cylia. She lowered her hand and met my eyes, expression despairing.

"He's right," she said. "I forgot. For a few minutes, I forgot."

"Forgot what?" I asked.

"We're in New England. It's like . . ." She took a breath, clearly trying to organize her thoughts. Then she turned toward Sam. "When you were with the carnival, how did you feel if some townie wandered backstage, where they weren't supposed to be? Were you welcoming? Happy to see them? Or did you tell them to get the hell out?"

"We told them to get the hell out," he said, voice still rough and angry. "We didn't like strangers."

I could testify to that. Our first meetings had been a dance of snark and snipe, him trying to bait me into walking away and leaving the carnival forever, me trying to convince him I deserved a chance to prove myself. "What does that have to do with anything?" I demanded.

"New England is a lot like a carnival, or a secret society, or the insular group of your choosing," said Cylia. "I mean, they welcome tourists, they can't close their doors against the whole world, but in most of the small towns around here, they'll choose the familiar over the strange every single time. If we call the police and tell them we have the police chief's son tied to a chair, the fact that he's the one who broke into our house won't matter one damn bit. What's going to matter is why is his nose broken, why did you have a knife in your hand when you went to confront him, all the things that *shouldn't* matter. Because we're strangers. Because we're new. Because we don't belong here."

"A cat can have kittens in an oven, but that doesn't make them muffins," said Sam.

I eyed him. "What?"

"Something my grandmother used to say." Sam looked at the red marks on my wrist, then back to James. "So if we can't call the police, what do we do?"

"We get the shovel out of the car and we deal with things the old-fashioned way, I guess. Maybe I'll *actually* break his nose, since you all keep saying I did it." I sighed heavily as I turned my attention to James. "Someone else is going to have to do most of the digging. My hands aren't working properly for some reason."

His eyes widened. "You wouldn't."

"You broke into my house, you froze my hand, and you're lying about basically everything except, I assume, being the chief of police's son," I said. "I don't know how you deal with unsolvable problems here in New England, being a stranger to your town and all, but where I come from, if someone presents you with a situation you can't win, you don't say 'well, guess Starfleet wants me to fail this exam.' You say 'what would James Tiberius Kirk do,' and then you shoot the asshole who broke into your house in the head and go about your business."

James' eyes widened further, although not so much with fear. "Did you seriously just use the Kobayashi Maru as a threat?"

"The what?" asked Sam.

"It's a *Star Trek* thing, and yes, I did," I said. "There's no such thing as an unwinnable scenario."

"Oh, my God," said James. "But cool. Cool. I clearly didn't actually break into the house, and am having a very vivid and painful dream. Awesome. I can deal with that."

"Nope," I said, and leaned over to flick him in the nose. My fingers ached at even that small gesture. He rocked back in his chair, gasping from the pain. Worth it. "Not a dream. You're about to die at the hands of a house full of nerds, unless you want to change your song and tell me how you froze my hand and why you broke into the library."

Eyes full of tears, he sat up straighter and fixed me with a haughty look. "You wouldn't believe me if I told you."

"Let me guess: puberty hit, and you discovered you secretly had strange and inexplicable powers, powers that required you to stand apart from your fellow man, at least until you received a call from Professor Xavier's Institute for Higher Learning, and—"

The flicker of interested, wary curiosity that had been growing in his eyes flickered and died. I stopped talking and looked at him for a moment. Really *looked* at him, trying to see the man beneath the blood, bad decisions, and bravado.

And when I saw him, I recognized him.

"Hang on a second." I took a step back. "I was making a bad X-Men joke, since again, house of nerds, but until you realized that . . ." I stopped talking, mind racing wildly.

There *are* cryptids that thrive in cold places. There are even cryptids, like the yuki-onna, who can create cold when they need to, much as there are cryptids—like the dragons—who can create heat. It's not a completely un-heard-of trick. But James . . . I was willing to bet on James being human. Call it intuition or call it long training, but nothing about him screamed "cryptid" to me. My track record isn't one hundred percent—I thought Sam was human until he showed me otherwise—and yet. Punching someone in the face is usually a good way to get them to reveal anything they might not want you to see.

Just in case, I leaned forward, well into James' personal space, and squinted at his eyes. They were blue, but lacked the delicate snowflake scaffolding inside the iris that I would have expected from a yuki-onna. "Are you wearing contacts?" I asked. "Please be honest. I'll poke you in the eye if you lie."

"You're really aggressive," he said. "No, I'm not wearing contacts. Why?"

"Because you froze me with a touch, and you started getting nervous when I mentioned suddenly discovering abilities that people around you wouldn't understand, and fire is more common, but we can't all be Jean Grey, can we, Bobby?"

"Can you *please* start speaking English instead of geek?" demanded Cylia. "I'm not following you."

"That's okay," I said, eyes still on James. "He's following me, and that's what matters. He's a sorcerer, aren't you, James? You freeze things with a touch. How many times did you shatter your pillow before you got it under control?"

"Wait, really?" Sam stood up straighter. For a moment, I thought he was just interested. Then he took a step forward, advancing on James, and I realized the uncomfortable truth: he was *livid*.

James realized it, too, and leaned back as far as the ropes would allow. "I don't know where she's getting any of this, but I swear—"

"Because see, if you're a sorcerer, even a shitty one, you clearly have enough of a grasp of what you're doing that you're not freezing yourself all the time. You're not pissing icicles. Which means you can mostly keep it under control. Which means you froze her *on purpose*, and I am not cool with that. I am sort of the opposite of cool with that."

"I didn't mean to!" James yelped. Me punching him in the face didn't appear to have distressed him nearly as much as being loomed over by a shirtless man who looked like he could break way more than noses. "I thought I was being quiet, and she startled me, she *hurt* me, I was just defending myself! I wasn't trying to hurt anyone! I thought I had time!"

"Time for a home invasion?" I asked, pulling his attention back to me. "What sort of schedule is that?"

"My cousin had been looking for renters all month," said James. "I thought I could get him to agree to let me caretake the place. I was even willing to pay for utilities, since I knew he was heading for Europe. He wasn't supposed to find anyone who was willing to stay in here."

"Please don't tell me the house is haunted," said Cylia.

For the first time, James looked genuinely nonplussed. "What? No. Why would I be worried about that? Ghosts are harmless."

"Depends on the ghost," I said. "Eyes on me, Jimmy-boy. We're not done talking."

"Don't call me 'Jimmy,'" he said, suddenly scowling. His hands flexed. The oven mitts were my favorite thing. I loved the oven mitts. "That's not my name."

"Sorry," I said. "Still, eyes here. Why did you want this place? What's here that matters enough to break in when you know a bunch of strangers will be trying to sleep? We could have done a lot worse than breaking your nose, you know."

James took a deep breath, clearly steeling himself. Then, choosing his words with exquisite care, he said, "There's something horrible feeding on people who don't know what else to do, who think they don't have any other options. I need the books here so I can stop it."

"Oh," I said faintly. "Is that all?"

"I'd be a lot happier if the asshole was still wearing the oven mitts," grumbled Sam, casting a narrow-eyed glance at the dining room table where James sat with Cylia and Fern. They had promised to hold off on figuring out what sort of cosmic horror was getting ready to eat us all until I could make a pot of coffee. I needed something hot to wrap my hands around as much as I needed the caffeine.

Sam didn't need any caffeine. He'd been looking at James like he wanted to bounce the guy off the nearest bridge since the break-in, and he wasn't calming down. I couldn't blame him. If Sam had been the one hurt, I would probably already have been dragging James toward a shallow grave.

"He's playing nice, so we're going to do the same," I said, picking up the tray of coffee mugs.

Fern's check of the outside hadn't found any sign that James was working with a partner. He hadn't even driven to the house. There was a bicycle next to the mailbox, and a folding ladder propped against the wall outside the library window. So far, everything he'd told us had proven to be true, except for the whole "I didn't freeze you I don't know what you're talking about" routine, and I genuinely couldn't blame him for that. I would have done the same thing if I'd been the one tied to a chair with my hands covered.

It was funny. I'd never met an untrained sorcerer before, only people like the assholes at Lowryland; James Smith was possibly the closest thing I had to an actual peer, and I had no idea what to say to him, or even where to start. "I'm a sorcerer, too, but I sold my magic to the crossroads in exchange for not drowning, and maybe I'm never going to get it back, and maybe I'm okay with that" didn't feel like the sort of thing that was going to fly. Either he'd think I was lying to build rapport, or he'd think I was out of my mind for ever letting my magic go.

To be honest, I wasn't sure which side of that conflict I'd fall on. Sam following behind me like a particularly surly bodyguard, I walked back into the dining room and put the tray of coffee cups, sugar, and milk down in the middle of the table. My hands barely shook at all.

"Good news: I don't think you did any nerve damage," I said, with more cheer than I actually felt. "That means I probably don't have to kill you."

James looked abashed. "I really am sorry," he said. "I've never frozen a living person before. I didn't realize how much it would hurt you."

"Makes sense," I said. I took a seat and a cup of coffee at the same time. Sleep could wait. "Like I said, fire's more common, and fire-based sorcerers generally can't burn themselves. You probably can't give yourself frostbite, so how would you know what it would do to somebody else?"

"Don't do it again," snapped Sam. He sat next to me, somehow still managing to loom.

That was going to get old fast. "All right: introductions. Everyone, this is James Smith, who I met in the woods. James Smith, this is everyone."

James looked expectantly around the table. No one offered a name, not even Fern who was looking at him with uncharacteristic wariness. He seemed to deflate a bit.

"Sorry," he said. "I guess I don't deserve you trusting me just yet. But . . . how do you people even know what a sorcerer *is*? It took me months in my mother's library before I found a name for what was happening to me. Who are you? Where did you come from?"

"My grandfather was a sorcerer," I said. It was true, and enough of the story to be believable. "Fire, not ice.

He accidentally toasted a lot of stuff before he figured things out."

James' eyes lit up as he sat up straighter in his chair. "Really? Can I meet him? I've never met another sorcerer."

"You're not going to meet this one," I said. "He's been gone for a long time. I never got to meet him myself."

"Oh." James' shoulders slumped. "I'm sorry for your loss."

"Yeah, well. Every family has to suffer a few." It's difficult to say how much of a "loss" Grandpa Thomas really is. Grandma Alice insists he's alive somewhere out there, and that she's going to find him. Most of the family thinks she's deluding herself, but since she's regularly carrying more ordnance than a small gun store, no one wants to tell her that. I . . .

I thought she was deluding herself, too, until I made my own deal with the crossroads. Some of the things they said make me think she might be right. He might still be out there somewhere, trapped and scared and waiting for her to save him. I don't know what to hope for anymore. I don't have so many grandparents that I can afford to leave them trapped in eternal limbo. I also don't know how I'm going to tell Grandma Alice that she's not crazy without triggering a full-out assault on the crossroads, and I don't think even she could survive *that*.

James looked down at the table. "I know about families and losses. My mother was a sorcerer. Ice, like me. She was good, too, at least if I believe her books. I remember her making it snow in the kitchen when I was a kid, like it was no big deal, and she'd be laughing, and it was . . . it was magic. I always hoped I'd get magic just like her."

"What happened?" asked Cylia. Her voice was surprisingly gentle.

"She got sick," said James. He matched her gentleness with bitterness, until every word was dripping with it. "She had magic and she had knowledge and she had money and none of it mattered, because she got sick and she died and she left me alone with a man who wouldn't know magic if it flew up and bit him in the face."

"Your dad doesn't know?" I blurted.

"No, and I'd ask you not to tell him, except for the part where he wouldn't believe you if you did; he'd just think you were trying to screw with him. If you don't want to have the chief of police and uncle of your landlord watching you like a hawk, you won't say a word." There was a bone-deep stubbornness and no small amount of pride in the look he gave me. I recognized that expression. It was the face of a man who was accustomed to being the smartest person in the room.

Most of the time, that look was on my own face. I'd never realized how obnoxious it was. "We're not going to tell him," I said. "What good would it do? It's not like I can force you to make ice in front of him, and I'm pretty sure punching you in the face again to get you to freeze me wouldn't make your dad very happy with us, even if you don't get along. You're a sorcerer, you make things cold, you must be a delight in the middle of the summer. What books are you looking for?"

"Mom couldn't keep her library at home without making my father suspicious. He married her because she was pretty, and because she knew how to keep house, and because he was smart enough to recognize a good thing when it looked him in the eye, but she had to make a lot of concessions to make things work." James' smile was small and even bitterer than his words, if such a thing was possible. "She married him because she loved him, so I guess we all get to fuck up once. Anyway, she got my cousin Norbert's parents to let her have a couple of shelves in the library, since they liked her so much, and they knew my father wasn't as big on books as they were. They're still here. The books, I mean, not the parents. They died a long time ago."

"People do that." I'd been in a room with someone's private manuals of sorcery and spellcraft, and I had somehow managed to spend my time reading municipal land records. That basically summarized my life. "So you need her books to learn more about this horrible thing you mentioned, and you didn't get them out of here before we moved in, which meant breaking into the library in the middle of the night. Got it. What's the horrible thing?"

"You wouldn't believe me if I told you," said James.

"We believed you about the freezing-my-girlfriend thing," said Sam sourly. "We're at least trying to believe you about your weird family shit. Maybe try us with the next piece."

"I don't—" James began. Then he stopped, catching himself, and looked around the table. All of us were watching him expectantly. "Okay. You might believe me. You people are really weird. Are you some kind of cult?"

"We're carnies," I said, voice flat.

James blinked before apparently accepting this. He shrugged once, picked up his coffee, and asked, "Have you ever heard stories about people going to the crossroads to make a deal? Like, a *big* deal, something they couldn't get any other way?"

I stopped breathing. Literally stopped. My throat felt like it had closed, slamming shut and refusing to let anything through. Sam gave me a worried glance, putting his hand on my arm. I shook my head, motioning for him to stay quiet.

James didn't even notice. He sipped his coffee, shoulders drooping in what might have been resignation, or might have been relief. He was finally getting the chance to tell people what he was afraid of. And maybe we were serious or maybe we were weird stoners who wouldn't believe a word he said, but, either way, we were strangers, and there was nothing we could do to use what he told us against him. There was a power in that. A sincere, cleansing power.

"There are stories about the crossroads everywhere

in the world. If you go to a place where two paths cross, there's power there, and maybe you can make a deal with it, and maybe it can give you whatever it is you've always wanted. What's interesting, though, is if you go back far enough, the deals . . . they were always small, and maybe people regretted them and maybe they didn't, but there was *balance*. At the end of the bargain, no one walked away feeling like they'd been cheated."

"What changed?" asked Cylia.

"It's 'what,' and it's 'when,'" said James. "It takes work to find records that go back five hundred years, but I did it. I called in favors, I volunteered at local history days, I bribed people in other countries to go to *their* museums and copy manuscripts for me, and I did it."

"How long?" I asked.

James looked at me. "Five hundred years, give or take a few decades," he said. "The first records I've been able to find of a crossroads bargain turning *bad*, taking more than the person who made it intended to pay, are from the late fourteen hundreds. People seemed genuinely shocked, like prior to that, going to the crossroads had been extreme but understandable. Divination via the crossroads fell off sharply, and some places began to talk about them as places where witches congregated. What's interesting is that if you read carefully, it's pretty clear that this is when the witches *stopped* congregating at the crossroads. It was like they realized something had changed, turned dangerous, and they didn't want to have any part of it."

"Witches?" I asked carefully.

"They're not the same as sorcerers," said James, a faint lecturing note coming into his tone. He was clearly enjoying this: he had the opportunity to talk about things most people would never listen to without laughing. That probably didn't happen very often. "There are all kinds of witches in the world, and some of them draw power from the road. There are probably a few of them traveling around North America right now, maybe even with a carnival like the one . . . you all . . ." He stopped, looking around the table again.

Under other circumstances, the sudden blend of hope and fear in his eyes might have been amusing. He was looking for commonalities, or at least for people who could understand him. He was looking, in his own sideways manner, for witches.

"Sorry," I said. "None of us are witches, route or otherwise."

"Route?"

Inwardly, I winced. "If they draw power from the road, it makes sense, don't you think?"

"I suppose so," he said. "But yes: after the crossroads changed, the witches started avoiding them. There's some evidence that they tried to warn people away, and got killed or driven from their homes for their trouble."

"People don't like things that are different," said Sam bitterly.

I leaned over until my shoulder brushed his, eyes still on James. "What does all this have to do with anything?"

"I thought I said." James took a deep breath. "The crossroads prey on people when they're at their weakest. The crossroads *hurt* people. They can be any place where two roads or paths cross, but there are always places that have . . . weight, for lack of a better word. Places where the crossroads are more likely to hear you."

I knew what came next. God help me, I knew what came next. I didn't say anything.

"One of those places is here, in New Gravesend. It's easier to reach the crossroads than it ought to be. People do it by mistake, sometimes, and they get hurt. They get hurt *bad*. Some of them . . ." His voice caught in his throat. When he finished, it was quieter, more introspective. "It's not how things are supposed to be. I know it's not. The crossroads weren't always like this, and now that they are, someone has to stop them. *I* have to stop them."

"That's impossible," I said.

"No, it's not." James looked me squarely in the eye. "There's a way, and I know how."

I stood so abruptly that my chair scraped, hard, against the floor.

"Excuse me," I said, and left the room. The others could make excuses for me, if they wanted to. Sam was more likely to glare at James until one of them exploded. That was fine. I had to go. I had to get out.

The front door was locked. I fumbled it open and let myself outside, walking along the wrap-around porch until I reached the swing on the left side of the house. It looked out on the woods, and the moonlight glinting off the thinnest slice of the distant lake. I sat down, my heart pounding so hard it felt like I could taste it.

"All right," I said softly. "You can come out now."

The air changed around me.

"Hello, Annie," said Mary. "Long time no see."

Six

> "There's no honor in running away from a debt. There's no shame in running away from a bullet. Learn to tell the difference as early as you can."
>
> –Evelyn Baker

Outside on the porch, preparing for an awkward conversation

"NOT LONG ENOUGH, BASED on the conversation I just had," I said, keeping my eyes on the lake. The water sure was pretty. It must have been wonderful in the summer, when the sun was hot and the lake was cool and everything made a certain sort of seasonal sense. "How's the family?"

"Worried about you." The porch swing creaked as she settled next to me. Dead since before my grandmother was born, and she can still have mass and substance when she wants it, can still move through the world like she belongs there. It's a neat trick.

Her eyes always give her away, at least to people who know what to watch for. Mary Dunlavy—Aunt Mary to three generations of Price children, all of us growing up under her careful eye, with her wiping our spills and kissing our booboos, the eternal babysitter—has eyes like a hundred miles of empty highway, every color and no color at the same time. Look into them too long and you'll see the cornfields waving next to an Iowa offramp, the tangled forests of Oregon and the sunset splendor of Arizona. Everywhere the road is, she is, because she serves the crossroads, and they've marked her, permanently, to make sure she never forgets.

As if she ever could have. Being dead and bound to work forever for an eldritch horror masquerading as a piece of roadwork isn't exactly the sort of thing a person forgets.

"I'm sorry to worry them," I said.

"They know. Believe it or not, they trust you enough to believe that if you're not coming home, it's because you have a good reason."

I snorted. I'm the baby of the family, not the heir and not the spare, not the good kid or the exciting renegade. I'm just Antimony, the one without ambition or direction or any of the other things someone my age is supposed to have. The idea of them having faith in me was almost ridiculous. Oh, my cousins might—Artie and Elsie and even Sarah, if she was currently capable of remembering who I was—but my parents? My siblings? No way.

"I don't know how much longer I'll be able to keep track of you the way I have been."

I opened my mouth to ask her why not, and froze, the implications of her statement sinking in. Slowly, I turned to stare at her.

Mary was wearing her usual seventies hippie gear, several decades too modern for her actual date of death, but remarkably well-suited to her straight white hair and those impossible eyes. A climbing clematis vine was embroidered up the side of her peasant blouse and around the squared-out neckline, until it looked like it was trying to strangle her one carefully stitched tendril at a time. She looked exhausted. No small feat, for a ghost. But she smiled, ever so slightly, as she met my eyes, and she nodded, the tiniest inclination of her chin.

Mary is the family babysitter. Somehow, she's managed to turn that into a loophole in her contract with the crossroads, an excuse to keep following the family around the world—or, more specifically, to keep following the *youngest member* of the family. The one who most recently needed babysitting. As the last born in my generation, I'd enjoyed Mary's company and occasional protection longer than either of my siblings or any of my cousins. If she wasn't going to be following me anymore . . .

The loophole was closing. "I'm guessing asking you *who* is going to have the baby would be a little too close to something useful," I said.

Mary nodded again, more firmly this time. "I can't tell you. The crossroads would love to get a tighter hold on you right about now, and that means real information is off the table. But you already knew that."

"Yeah, I did," I said, pushing the idea of a baby—a *baby*, a Price baby—to the back of my mind. "Just like I knew you'd be showing up tonight. I didn't want you to pop in inside. You would have given our poor houseguest a heart attack."

"Might have solved a few problems if I had," said Mary regretfully.

That's the thing about Mary: she's a good person in a bad situation, and she has never, to the best of my knowledge, liked her job. The crossroads call. The crossroads cajole. The crossroads convince, and the whole time, Mary—or another ghost like her—is there, trying to explain why this is a bad idea, why the person making the deal should walk away. And almost always, she loses. By the time a person goes to the crossroads, they're not interested in being convinced to stop. They know what they want, and they're going to get it if it kills them. Which, sometimes, it does.

"Maybe," I said. "I'm guessing this isn't a friendly visit."

"No."

"I haven't seen you since Lowryland. I was starting to think you were avoiding me."

"I have been. The crossroads have always known your name, Annie. Now they know where you are, and they know what it tastes like when you're afraid. They *want* you."

"I already owe them."

Mary shook her head. "No. I mean, yes, you owe them, but they haven't beaten you. They haven't taken you. They hate your family."

"Wh—" I caught myself before it could become a question. "I guess why that's the case would count as one of those questions I'm not supposed to ask."

"I guess it would," Mary agreed. "I really wish you'd had the chance to meet your grandfather."

"Me, too."

"Thomas Price never met a strict letter of the law he didn't feel like subverting. It's like he thought life was a riddle that could be solved in a way where no one had to get hurt—or maybe where only the people who deserved it got hurt. Remember, he started out Covenant. Slippery as he was, he still had some pretty firm ideas about morality."

I held my tongue. If she was talking, it was because she wanted me to hear something. All I could do by interrupting was increase the chance she'd have to stop.

"Sometimes I thought he married your grandmother in part because the Covenant had been so fixated on him finding a way to subvert her and bring her back into the fold. Not that Alice hasn't always been stubborn in her own right—they were a pair. No matter what else I can say about them, I can say with conviction that neither of them would ever have found someone better suited to their specific brands of crazy. And I got you, and your siblings, and your father, out of the deal." Mary's smile was fleeting. "It would have broken my heart if the family tree had ended with Alice. I'm really not qualified for any jobs but babysitting, and people don't hire you if you don't have references these days."

"I'm not planning on having children any time soon," I said.

"I know, but your brother and sister both want to, and

that should be more than enough to keep me busy for a while." Mary looked down at her hands, resting between her knees, and said, "Your grandfather knew about the crossroads. He knew to avoid them, and he knew if he ever made a deal, they'd do their best to hurt him. He stayed away as long as he could."

"Lot of people stay away for their whole lives."

"You didn't."

Silence fell like a hammer, smothering all the natural night sounds of the forest around us. I tried to speak. Nothing happened. She had me dead to rights, and what's more, she had just, in her own sideways manner, answered one of the questions that had plagued me for my entire life. What could have driven a man like Thomas Price, a scholar, a sorcerer, a former member of the Covenant of St. George, who knew *exactly* what kind of danger the crossroads represented, to make a bargain with them?

What, if not the life of the woman he loved? Mary had said, when I made my own crossroads deal, that she'd been the one to broker the contract for Alice Healy's life—Healy, not Price. They hadn't been married yet, and so far as I knew, my grandmother had only gone to the crossroads after she had a ring on her finger and an empty place where her husband should have been. That visit had ended in fire and tears, but no bargain, which led me to believe the crossroads had asked for something she wasn't willing to give up, not even to save the man she'd go on to spend the next forty years searching for.

Sometimes I wonder whether families are less complicated when they don't insist on running around messing with the supernatural and getting themselves locked into unspeakable bargains with the other side of the veil. Then I realize I'd rather not know. Better or worse, this is what we've got, and this is what we're keeping.

"When your grandfather went to the crossroads—and remember, you didn't ask any of this, I'm talking because I want to, and you can't stop me—they'd been waiting for him for a long, long time. He had power. He moved through a world filled with chaos, and sometimes he made it worse and sometimes he made it better, but always, always, he made it more fair. That was what he cared about more than anything. The crossroads looked at him and saw someone who could help them if he belonged to them, but who could hurt them if he didn't. They wanted him for *years* before he came to them, and when he did, they offered a bargain that should have given them everything."

"But it didn't," I guessed flatly.

"Never could have. Tommy, he was . . ." Mary stopped, and smiled a small, sad smile. It was impossible to look at her and not be reminded that she'd known him when he was young, with his entire future ahead of him. When he'd been Thomas Price, Covenant man, and not my grandfather. Finally, she said, "He was stubborn. They laid a labyrinth at his feet, and he fought every step to keep from going around the next corner. When he finally ran out of room to run, when he finally paid what they'd been asking all along, well. The crossroads had never meant to sink that much power into him. They'd been expecting an easy kill. They hated him for what he did, and they've hated the rest of your family ever since."

"Which, I suppose, is all by way of saying I'd better watch my ass," I said.

"*No.*" Her tone was fierce enough to make me stop and straighten. She glared at me. "You've already failed to watch your ass. You didn't watch it, and you didn't let me watch it, and now you're in up to your neck. Screw watching your ass. Now is when you start listening. Now is when you *do as you're told*. Even if you don't want to, now is when you listen, because otherwise—"

Mary stopped mid-sentence, mouth opening and closing soundlessly. No: not quite soundlessly. She raised a hand to her throat, clutching at it and making a faint choking noise. Then she burst like a smoke-filled balloon, leaving a thick mist hanging in the air for a single terrible moment before the wind carried it away.

"She really needs to learn when to stop talking," said an unfamiliar voice.

I turned. A teenage girl was leaning against the porch rail, brown hair pulled high into a ponytail, eyes as cold and mercurial as midnight in the desert, as the road that runs past a deserted graveyard. She was wearing a red-and-gold letter jacket over a pleated red skirt and a gold sweater; matching ribbons were tied in her hair. Something about them looked wet and bloody in the porchlight.

I know a cheerleader when I see one; we recognize our own kind. And I know when we're not cheering for the same team. I balled my hands into fists against my knees, swallowing the urge to jump to my feet and demand answers. That would be a bad idea just now. I could already tell.

"Where's Mary?" I asked.

"Our mutual employers called her back to remind her who she works for, and who she works against," said the girl. She pushed away from the railing, walking languidly toward me. "My name's Bethany. I'm your new caseworker, for lack of a better term."

There was something old-fashioned in the way Mary shaped her vowels, easily dismissed as a regional accent if you hadn't spent time around people from her generation, all of whom seemed to have the same softness in their "a"s, the same roundness in their "o"s. Bethany didn't have that accent. Bethany sounded like she was my age, or close enough to it as to make no real difference.

Bethany was also very, very dead. Her eyes alone were enough to tell me that.

"Give her back." Now I did stand, and was gratified to find that I had a few inches on the dead girl. If all else failed, I could punch the ghost a few times to make myself feel better.

"Oh, she'll be fine, once she remembers her place," said Bethany. "Mary-Mary, quite contrary, has a longer leash than most of us are allowed. Loopholes. It's always loopholes with you people. I say 'you people,' but I don't mean you in specific, Antimony Timpani Price, sorcerer, debtor. The crossroads gave you everything you asked for, and all they asked in return was a favor to be performed later, when the time was right. I assume you remember?"

"I don't think I could forget if I wanted to."

"Good," said Bethany, and she smiled—the sweet, serene smile of someone who actually enjoyed her job. "The crossroads are ready to call in your debt. Once your task has been performed, they'll return the fire they borrowed from your fingers, and you'll owe them nothing more. You'll be free. You can make another bargain or never speak to them again, whatever you prefer. Won't that be nice?"

"That'll be swell, which means there's a catch for sure," I said warily. "What do the crossroads want me to do?"

"Nothing major. Just find out what the sorcerer James Smith knows—how much he's been able to learn, and from what sources, and how—and then kill him."

"What? I'm not going to *kill* someone! That wasn't the deal."

"That was precisely the deal. One favor. Whatever the crossroads need. And they need the boy dead. I don't understand why this is a problem. You're a Price. I know about you. Killing is basically why you exist." Bethany smiled, cold but not cruel, like a single human life held literally no value to her.

And maybe it didn't. Mary had always cautioned us against talking to other crossroads ghosts, although she'd never been willing to tell us exactly why it was a bad idea. I'd always sort of assumed she didn't want to risk someone else figuring out the right combination of terrible suggestions that would convince us to make a crossroads bargain. But what if it was simpler than that? What if the fact that she had a living family to care for and look after had been enough to keep her from losing track of her own humanity? She'd been dead for a long time. She still loved the living. That was more than could be said for a lot of ghosts.

"Well?" said Bethany. "Time's wasting. Make your choice."

If the crossroads wanted James Smith dead, that meant he was onto something. That meant he was probably at least a little bit right. And if he was at least a little bit right . . .

"I know what I have to do," I said.

"Good girl." Bethany smiled. "Remember, we need to know *how* he's learned these things. Be his friend. Make him trust you. We'll be watching."

Then she was gone. I waited, counting slowly to one hundred. Mary didn't come back. Dully, I realized she might not *be* coming back. Maybe that weird, rambling story about my grandfather had been the last warning I was ever going to get from her.

Until that moment, standing alone in the dark, I hadn't really felt like I was doing this without my family. They were distant, yes. I couldn't call them or ask them to support me. But if I'd died in Lowryland, or somewhere out there on the road, Mary would have made sure that they knew.

I could call for Rose. She'd come, if she could. It wouldn't be the same. I was suddenly aware of the tears rolling down my cheeks. I swiped them fiercely away. No. I was a Price. I was a derby girl. I wasn't going to cry over this.

I was going to kick its ass.

I turned and stalked back into the house, letting the door slam behind me. The others were still in the dining room. All of them turned at my arrival, James and Fern looking relieved, Sam and Cylia looking neutral. Well, that told me who the good cop-bad cop pairing had been.

"Sam." He sat up a little straighter. I pointed to the kitchen door. "Lock it down."

He blinked. "You mean—?"

I nodded, and he was gone, still human-form but moving at a speed that strained the bounds of credulity. I turned back to the table.

"Cylia, you got a piece of paper I can borrow?"

"In my purse," she said, sounding bewildered. "It's on the sideboard."

"Got it." Cylia's purse was a big black leather monstrosity that could probably have been used to smuggle things up to the size of a live chicken. I dug into it, rummaging until I found a crumpled piece of paper and a Sharpie. Then I returned to the table, sitting down next to James, who looked like he wanted nothing more than to move his chair away from me. That was reasonable. I had, after all, disappeared outside for an extended period of time, only to come back furious and ready to spread that fury around.

It was almost a good thing the crossroads was keeping my fire away from me, because I would have burned the whole house down without even raising my voice.

Pushing the paper to where James could see it, I uncapped the Sharpie and wrote CAN YOU WARD AGAINST GHOSTS? Then I handed it to him, nodding toward the paper.

Give the man this much: he was smart enough to catch on immediately. He took the Sharpie and wrote, in neater, more conservative letters, ONLY IN THEORY. NEVER TRIED MYSELF. NO GHOSTS AROUND HERE.

Oh, I doubted that. There are ghosts everywhere. It's just that most of them don't give a damn about people unless we're interfering with them in some way, and so they leave us alone. I took the Sharpie back. WHAT YOU NEED?

James hesitated before reaching for the pen. SALT, he wrote. ROSEMARY. CLEAN WATER. THREE

IRON NAILS. GRAVE DIRT WOULD BE NICE, BUT CEMETERY IS A MILE AWAY.

"Don't worry about it." I stood. "Cylia will help you get the things you need to make the cookies. I have the special spices upstairs."

When James realized I was saying I had grave dirt already on hand, his eyes widened, his general expression taking on the air of a man who had made very poor life choices. But all he did was nod and say, "I'm excited to find out why it's so important I start baking."

"Oh, believe me," I said. "It's a life changer."

Seven

"Life is a death sentence. Get as many stays
of execution as you possibly can."
— Frances Brown

In the kitchen, waiting for the wards to come slamming down

Sam's check of the perimeter had come up as empty as Fern's: we were alone. The windows were closed, the doors were locked, and other than the five of us, nothing bigger than a tailypo was currently engaged in going bump in the night. Except for the ghosts, of course, and they were the problem.

Sam leaned against the kitchen counter, a cup of coffee cupped between his long-fingered hands, his tail occasionally snaking over to wrap, ever so briefly, around the outside of my wrist. Then he would pull it back and look mistrustfully at the closed kitchen door, like he expected James to come bursting through at any moment.

"I wish you'd tell me what the hell is going on," he said.

"I wish I felt like I could," I replied. "Just give it another few minutes, and then we should be able to talk freely."

Sam scowled but didn't argue. He knew better than that, and he knew something was upsetting me. I was hoping he'd been able to make the logical jump from "James is studying the crossroads" to "Mary probably stopped by for a visit," although asking him to continue onward to "I think the crossroads have done something terrible to her, they've assigned a new ghost to make sure I keep my side of the bargain, and—oh, by the way—they want me to murder James" was a bit much.

The next time his tail wrapped around my wrist, I caught the tip of it between my fingers, tugging lightly. He responded by wrapping it around my thumb, holding me where I was. I offered him a somewhat strained smile.

"This is how it's always going to be, you know," I said. "This is what normal looks like when you're doing it with me. I hope that's not a deal breaker. I mean, I'll understand if it is. I'm not sure I'd want to be in a relationship with me, if I had a choice."

Sam blinked. Then, to my surprise, he laughed. "Are you kidding? I figured *that* out the night I found you fighting a giant spider-woman in the boneyard. If I wanted to spend time with you, normal was never going to be on the table. I just don't like that you can't tell me what's going on."

"Soon," I promised. "Really soon. I'm not keeping secrets because I want to, I swear."

"I believe you."

The smell of burning paper trickled under the kitchen door. Sam whisked his tail out of my fingers. I glanced at him. He was back in human form, still shirtless, and even crankier-looking.

"This is supposed to happen," I said.

"Great. All this *and* your new friend happens to be a pyromaniac."

"I asked him to set the fire, if that helps."

"Okay, weirdly enough, it doesn't. It doesn't help *at all*." Sam gave the door a venomous look. "I sort of like not being charcoal."

"I love you, too," I said.

A look of horrified realization washed over Sam's face. "I didn't mean—"

There was a light knock. "You two decent in there?"

Cylia called, before opening the door and sticking her head inside. "James says he can't be absolutely sure it worked without having a ghost to test the wards, but he's about ninety percent sure. Ninety-five, maybe. Now do you want to come out and explain why you asked him to do that, and why you couldn't help?"

"Sure." I set my coffee mug on the counter. The last thing I needed right now was more caffeine. I was already more than wired enough.

In the dining room, James was using a hand towel to meticulously remove each scrap of ash from his fingers. He glanced up when he heard my footsteps, frowning at the sight of Sam trailing along behind me.

"Fun night, huh?" I asked. "Bet you didn't think this would be the end result of your little adventure in breaking and entering."

"It's definitely put me off my life of crime," he said dryly.

"Where's Fern?"

"She took the casserole dish out back to hose the embers, so we don't start a *real* fire," said Cylia. "It was a stroke of luck that we found a cast iron casserole dish in the first place."

"Good luck, so there's that," I said. "Look, James, I haven't been exactly straight with you."

He rolled his eyes extravagantly. "Really? The woman who punches robbers after accosting them in the woods, knows about ghost wards, and has a sorcerer for a grandfather, not being entirely straight with me? Forgive me while I die of shock."

"Wait," said Sam. "Not just general wards, but *ghost* wards? Why would you—aw, fuck, Mary. Was she here?"

"Yeah," I said. "She came to talk to me when I went outside. That's why I was gone so long."

"Who's Mary?" asked James. He turned to Cylia. "I feel as if I'm missing something rather important here. Could you please remind them that I can only help if I understand what's going on?"

"Sorry, kiddo," said Cylia. "Half the time I feel like I'm waiting for the movie."

"Mary is my aunt," I said. "She's dead. She's also a crossroads ghost."

Slowly, James' head swung back around, until he was staring at me with wide, disbelieving eyes. "A crossroads ghost," he said, in a tone of exquisitely careful horror. "As in, a mortal spirit bound to serve the interests of the thing I'm planning to destroy."

"Yup," I said. "That would be her. Nice lady. You'd like her, except for the part where she came to try and warn me about what was going to happen now that we've met you, and the crossroads sort of punished her. I'm trying not to think about that too hard until I know our options. For right now, she's missing, and a ghost named Bethany is filling in for her. Mary has always had my best interests at heart, even when they've conflicted with the interests of her employer. Can't say the same about Bethany."

"I . . . what?" James kept staring at me. "No. Crossroads ghosts don't have mortal relationships. It's part of what gets them chosen. They have no family, or minimal family, and when they die, the chance to continue interacting with the material world is tempting enough to let the crossroads convince them to become a very specific sort of haunt. They can't be someone's aunt."

"I don't know how you know more about the way this works than I do, but Mary's an exception," I said. The sad part was, I knew *exactly* how he knew more about the way the crossroads worked than I did. He'd made them his field of study, whereas my family had spent the last two generations living in the shadow of what happens when you let them get too close. Mary had asked us—begged us, even—to stay away, not to ask questions that might attract the wrong kind of attention, and we'd loved her enough and accepted them as enough of a natural phenomenon that we'd done as we were told.

I felt a little sick, to be honest. If the crossroads were

something that could be fought—something that could even be destroyed—how many people had died while my family carried on treating them like they didn't matter? Like they were something that only lured the weak or unsuspecting when we, out of everyone in the world, should have known better?

James opened his mouth to answer. Then he stopped, shut it, and simply looked at me for a very long moment before he said, "If you don't explain right now why you have an 'exception' to every rule I know attached to your family, and why you knew enough to ask for wards when that 'exception' was replaced by someone you didn't trust, I'm leaving."

"Good luck with that," said Sam.

James raised a hand. The air crackled around it, becoming crystalline, like the air on a winter morning during a hard freeze. "I don't think luck will have much to do with it," he said.

"Luck *always* has something to do with it," said Cylia. "We're all dancing to Fortune's tune, whether we believe it or not. Now you boys back down and play nice, or I'll show you just how much luck can affect the outcome of a fight."

"She'll do it, too," I said. "She fights mean."

"No," said James. He shook his head. "I refuse. You're the only person here who's bothered to give me a name, and all of you talk in riddles and act like it's normal. Well, it's *not* normal. Yes, I broke into your house, and yes, I'm sorry I did that, but it doesn't give you the right to treat me like a fool. I want the books. Give them to me and I'll be on my way. You never have to see me again. I refuse to stand here and be made fun of."

"Everyone, chill," I said, and winced immediately after. "Everyone, forgive me for accidental ice puns and *calm down*. James, no one is making fun of you. This is difficult for us, too. We didn't . . . I mean, this isn't what we were expecting."

"It's sort of what I was expecting," said Fern, who had

been quiet up until this point. To be honest, I'd almost forgotten she was there. I turned to look at her. She shrugged. "Things always get weird before they get bad. We're in the weird phase. Bad is next. That's why we have to trust each other and start working together. Annie, did Mary come to tell you the crossroads knew about what James was trying to do?"

I nodded.

"Okay." Fern walked up to James and extended her hand. "My name is Fern. It's nice to meet you. I wish I could have met you when things were better, but I guess this will do."

"Um." The brittle glitter disappeared from the air around James' hand as he lowered it and clasped Fern's fingers. "Thank you for telling me your name."

"If Fern's in, I'm in," said Cylia. "I'm Cylia."

"Sam," said Sam. He didn't sound happy about it. I still couldn't blame him.

"You already know my name," I said. "I'm Annie. Annie Price."

There was no flicker of recognition in James' eyes at the sound of my surname. Normally, that would have been nice. Just my luck that the one time I *wanted* all the baggage that came with my name, I met someone who didn't care about the cryptid world except where it intersected with the crossroads.

"Names are a nice start," said James. "I still want to know why you have an 'exception' following you around."

"Aunt Mary died a long time ago," I said. "But she started off haunting her father. I guess he was old enough that the crossroads didn't think he'd be much of an anchor, and they were right, because he died pretty soon after she did, but by that point, she was already babysitting my grandmother. It might not have been enough, if my family hadn't known about ghosts. But they did, and when they found out Mary was dead, they didn't care." That was the simplified version. Oh, they'd cared, all right; they'd cried for the girl they'd come to love, whose death had somehow been so overlooked that she'd been able to slip right back into the life she'd left behind. And then they'd kept right on treating her like Mary, like who she was transcended everything else.

Maybe it had. Maybe that was why she was the only crossroads ghost who'd managed to maintain so much autonomy that she'd been able to continue being herself, being happy, even after everything else had changed.

"Your family is fine with dead people hanging around," said James disbelievingly. "No problems, sure, come and haunt my house."

"Not all of us," I said. "My great-aunt Laura used to ward her trailer against the dead because they didn't let her sleep. That's how I know about wards, even if I can't draw them." I'd never bothered to learn. The only ghosts who were likely to interfere with my daily life were Mary and Rose, and I wanted both of them there.

"Got it," said James. "Why are we warding the house now if your aunt is such an 'exception'?"

"Because like I said, my aunt is gone, and the ghost the crossroads have sent in her place doesn't seem nearly as friendly." There was something coolly familiar about Bethany, something I couldn't quite place. I was almost certain I had never met her before, alive or dead. I would have remembered her school colors, if nothing else, because cheerleaders never forget a spirit bow. "The crossroads . . . fuck. I don't even know where to start."

"Try the beginning," said James. "That generally works for me."

I took a deep breath. "All right. Did you see anything in the news about the accidents at Lowryland?"

James Smith was a decent audience: it took more than half an hour to explain the events that led up to my leaving Lowryland, and he only interrupted twice, both times to ask for clarification of something that needed more background to make sense. I was almost grateful for the pauses. They left me the space I needed to edit out cryptid involvement without actually lying. Sam, Cylia, and Fern might be willing to tell our new neighbor their names, but it was up to them when—and whether—they revealed the fact that none of them were as human as they looked.

When I reached the part about my bargain with the crossroads, and what I'd agreed to, his eyes became very wide and his cheeks became very pale. The air around him glittered as the temperature in the room dropped, not quite plunging to zero, but definitely trending away from the comfortable.

Finally, I said, "And that's all. That's why the crossroads are watching me."

"They want you to kill me, don't they?"

It was a simple question, almost casually asked: how's the weather, what are you doing for the holidays, do the crossroads want you to kill me? I still had to stop and brace myself against the table. Sam placed a hand against the small of my back, steadying and stabilizing me. I shot him a grateful look. He looked back, familiar even in his unusual humanity, before returning his attention to James. I did the same.

"Yes," I said. "They do. Although they want me to become your best friend first, so I can tell them everything you know. And supposedly in exchange, they'll put the fire back in my fingers and let me go on my merry way, no longer in debt to anyone for anything."

"They won't, you know," he said. "They'll have some reason you didn't quite follow their orders and need to do them one more favor before they let you go."

"I know," I said.

"You'll never be free of them."

"I know that, too."

"So why did you—?"

"Knowing doesn't change the fact that if I hadn't agreed to their bargain, I would have died, and Sam would have died, and a bunch of other people I care about would have died, and sometimes a bad deal is better than no deal at all." I shook my head, fighting the urge to glare. It would have been so easy to start blaming him for the destruction of our "take a break and recover for a while" plan. It would have been so *easy*. "I needed the chance to figure out how to get through this. I took what I could get."

"Are you going to kill me? Should I be getting ready to defend myself?"

I hesitated. Salvation came from an unexpected source.

"Of course she's not going to kill you," snapped Sam. "What the hell kind of people do you think we are? We didn't have to tell you any of this. And if she'd been planning to kill you, believe me, you'd be dead."

"That isn't as much of an endorsement as you think it is," said James.

"Except for the part where he's right," I said. "Seriously, James, if I'd been planning to kill you, why would I have told you about it? You were already primed to believe whatever I said, because you want someone who understands what's going on, who knows how to say 'sorcerer' without turning it into a Dungeons and Dragons joke. All I needed to do was tell you I was scared of the crossroads and ask for your help. I told you the truth. That means something."

"Maybe it means none of you are very good liars," snapped James.

"Oh, to hell with this," said Sam, and stood, shifting and blurring as he did, until there was an anthropomorphic monkey where the man had been. Still shirtless, which provided an excellent view of the lines of fur running along his spine and the sides of his shoulders. And a lot more relaxed all of a sudden—something James didn't seem to properly appreciate. He was staring at Sam, eyes even wider than before.

Sam leaned forward, resting his hands on the table,

tail curled high in what I recognized as a display of dominance, like a biker flexing in the parking lot. Everything about his posture was informing James in no uncertain terms of who the winner would be if things got physical.

Too bad any fight they had wouldn't restrict itself to the physical. Sam could hit harder and move faster than a human, which just meant James could freeze him more quickly than he could the average boxer. I put a hand on Sam's forearm, indicating that I wanted him to stay where he was.

Sam either didn't notice or didn't care. Eyes narrowed in frustration, he said, "Annie isn't lying. If you think she is, you know where the door is. And if she *were* lying to you, you'd never know. Believe me."

"You're a monkey." The statement was almost flat, divorced from all emotional response. That made sense, since James was clearly on the verge of freaking out.

"I'm a sylph," said Fern, not to be outdone.

"I'm not a *monkey*, I'm a *fūri*," said Sam grumpily. "You're a monkey, too, if you think I am. We're both primates. I'm just a primate who can swing from trees and then go sit on airplanes."

"Airplanes?" asked Cylia.

"Some seats were not designed for people with tails." Sam managed to make it sound like some dire pronouncement, heralding the fall of nations.

I swallowed my laughter. It would have hurt his feelings, which was really too bad. A little levity would not have been welcome right about then. "Sorry about the limitations of human ingenuity," I said.

"Forgiven." Sam wrapped his tail loosely around my waist, still staring at James. Again, I had to swallow laughter. "So are you going to call me a monkey again, or are you going to listen?"

"You're not human." James turned to Fern. "You're not human either. A . . . sylph? Aren't those air spirits?"

"Sort of," she said, with a broad shrug. "I can make myself lighter or heavier when I need to. It's easy."

"This is too much." James looked back to me. "All of this is too much."

"This is life," I said. "Why do you hate the crossroads so much? Unless you were leaving something out before, they didn't kill your mom. And you don't seem civic-minded enough to be this upset about them just existing."

"I don't make friends easily." James made the admission slowly, as if it pained him.

Sam snorted. I rewarded him with a light elbowing. He snorted again, this time at me, and rubbed the spot where my elbow had hit his side.

"You're not alone in that," I said.

"Hey, I make friends just fine," said Cylia.

"I don't," said Fern.

James looked down at his long-neglected coffee. "I was a smart kid, and I was a hurting kid, and I was a little bit of a know-it-all. It was the easiest way for me to cope with what I was going through. I studied hard. I got gold stars and my teachers admired me and my peers knocked me into mud puddles and called me names. All of them hated me . . . except Sally."

"Sally?" I prompted.

He glanced up and smiled, suddenly vulnerable, suddenly achingly sad. Or maybe not so suddenly. The roots of that sorrow were traced all through the lines of his face, growing in the fertile soil they found there.

"She was in my second grade class. We'd never really talked—like I said, I didn't make friends easily, and Sally was pretty and funny and everybody liked her, and I knew better than to get too close unless I wanted to get my ass kicked. And then one day I was sitting on a bench reading, and this kid, Billy Maxton, he ran up and pushed me to the ground and started kicking me." A note of wounded confusion slipped into James' voice, all the harder to hear because it was so familiar.

He wasn't the only one who'd been a smart, mouthy kid who got along better with the teachers than with the other students. Elementary school had been a special kind of hell for me. Ditto middle school. High school had brought cheerleading and its associated challenges, and probably saved my life. Without something to focus on and give me a place in the social pecking order, I would eventually have been eaten alive.

"She was on the other side of the playground, but she saw me go down. She ran over and jumped on him, and started punching him again and again, screaming about how he wasn't nice, he wasn't a nice boy, she was going to tell everyone he wasn't a nice boy." The confusion faded into admiration. "It took two teachers to pull her off him. She skinned her knees all to hell, but she didn't mess up her hair at all, and I pretty much fell in love with her right there. Sally was amazing. She could have been anybody's friend. *Anybody's.* There wasn't a kid in that school who wouldn't have been lucky to even touch her hand, and she chose me. I don't know why. She never told me."

Sam's tail tightened around my waist, and I knew what he was thinking. There are very few people in this world who will love and treasure us for who we are, rather than who they think we have the potential to someday become. For James to find one of those people was amazing. For him to lose her . . .

"When did she make her bargain at the crossroads?" I asked.

He glanced at me, then looked back down at the table. "We were seventeen," he said. "She was looking at getting out of here, finding some scholarship or something that would give her a free ride to college. Not because she needed it, necessarily—her family's pretty well-off. Because she wanted something that meant I'd get to go, too. I don't know how . . . I mean, most kids go to the financial aid office, you know? But we'd been pounding the pavement for months, applying for everything, applying every*where*, and my grades were great, but I didn't have any extracurriculars and my father said he didn't see why he should pay to send me to spend more time rotting my brain reading when there was plenty for me to do here at home. And she knew . . ."

James stopped. Just stopped. He stared off into space, saying nothing, doing nothing, barely breathing. The rest of us were silent, waiting for him to snap out of it.

Finally, he said, "She knew about my mother. Who else was I going to tell? Sally was my best friend. I told her everything. I told her how maybe someday I'd get magic, too, and then I'd make sure she had whatever she wanted, forever. I told her how it was going to be okay, if we could just figure out how to fix things. And she knew about the crossroads. Mom never went there, but she wrote down everything she knew. She gave *directions*. I swear, I didn't know Sally was going to follow them."

"Of course, you didn't," I said. He glanced at me, expression pleading for explanation, for absolution, for something to lift the veil of guilt he'd been looking through for years. It was almost painful, how much I wanted to give that to him. We weren't friends, although we might be eventually, but there are some burdens no one should be required to carry alone. "You *understood* the crossroads. Maybe not everything about them, or you'd have chained her to a tree before you'd take the risk, but you knew they were bad and you knew that smarter people than you had tried to make a bargain and been burned, and there wasn't any fire in your fingers or frost in your hands, you couldn't possibly have expected to win. So you knew you'd never go, and that meant Sally would never go. She was your best friend. She was the person who listened to you. You just forgot that sometimes the people who love us are willing to do things *for* us that they'd never dream of doing for themselves."

Sam's tail tightened around my waist. I wasn't just talking about James and Sally anymore. He knew it. He wasn't going to let me go.

James flinched. "So you think it's my fault that she went."

"No. It would be your fault if you had left books laying around open to the pages on the crossroads, if you'd mentioned them over and over again in an effort to get her interested, if you'd *asked* her to do it. We're not responsible for the things people do when we haven't asked them to save us. She was trying to save you." I took a breath. "What happened?"

"I don't know." His voice was soft, almost dull. "She left a note that said she'd worked it out, she'd figured out how to word her bargain so it couldn't be used against her, and she went while I was at the library. I was volunteering. Trying to punch up those extracurriculars enough to let me get the hell out of this town. I was—"

He stopped, catching himself, before he continued, "Anywhere two paths cross can be a focus for the crossroads, but there are some places they like better than others. Places where things have gone wrong in the past. There's an old tree on the other side of the wood. Kids call it the hanging tree, and they don't remember why, but they don't go there alone after dark, either, and when dogs go missing near it, they're never found. There's a crossing in sight of the tree. It's not a good place. As soon as I realized Sally had gone to find the crossroads, I knew that was where she would go."

He fell silent. I could see his frantic journey in the way his throat worked, the way his jaw clenched. Wherever he'd found her note, it had been far enough from the hanging tree that he'd been forced to run, maybe, or grab his bicycle and go, seventeen years old and racing against his best friend's love for him as he tried to snatch her from the jaws of a monster she didn't fully understand, nor ever could.

Finally, softly, he said, "The ice woke up when I was halfway there. I think . . . I think that's the moment when her bargain was sealed. I think she asked the crossroads to give me something that would mean I definitely got out of this town, and so they unlocked the magic I'd inherited from my mother and acted like it was some big gift, instead of something that would have come along in its own time if I'd just been patient, if I hadn't complained to Sally about how I was afraid it was never going to happen. It was so cold. I couldn't control it. I didn't understand what was happening. I froze my handlebars. They snapped off in my hands, and I crashed into a tree."

He reached up, touching a small scar on his forehead as he said, "It was dark when I woke up. I ran the rest of the way. Three miles into the woods with no flashlight and no jacket and no clue what I was going to do when I got there, but I don't think I've ever run that fast in my life."

No one spoke. No one moved. It felt like we were all frozen by something even colder than the ice in James' hands, until the very thought of movement was impossible.

"Her backpack was there. It had been . . . it had been ripped right off her body. The straps were torn in two. There wasn't any blood, but the official report says it was a bear." James' mouth twisted into an entirely humorless smile. "My father wrote it. I told him it wasn't a bear, and he said all the evidence was there, and he wrote it down and he told her parents he was sorry and he closed the case. Like Sally could ever be a *case*. Like she didn't matter."

A tear ran down his face. He swiped it fiercely away. "They gave me her college fund. She didn't have a will in the legally enforceable sense, but she had a list of everything she cared about and who liked it best, or who needed it, and they followed that. I think she knew there was a chance going to the crossroads could get her killed, and she did it anyway. To help me. All she wanted to do was help me."

"Why are you still here?" asked Cylia. "If you have the magic and you have the money, and the crossroads can be anywhere, why stay? You could have gone to school. Learned more about how this sort of thing works."

"Because it wasn't a bear," said James. "The crossroads *took* her, and if there's any chance I can get her back, I need to do it here, where she got lost. Maybe I can do it, if I do it here."

I could hear echoes of my grandmother in his desperation, and they chilled me more than his hands had. She'd believed the same thing: that if she started from the place where my grandfather had gotten lost, she'd be able to bring him home again. That was more than fifty years ago. If he's ever going to come home, it hasn't happened yet.

"The crossroads don't give back what they take," I said.

"You think I don't know that?" James picked up his coffee mug, twisting it between his hands. "I can't find anything that says otherwise. Even when people have offered to trade themselves for the missing party, it doesn't work out. No one comes home. But there's a first time for everything. I'm going to figure out how to destroy them, and I'm going to offer them a choice: give Sally back or die."

"What happens if they give her back?" asked Fern.

James' smile was the rictus grin of a death's-head. "I kill the fucking thing anyway. No more Sallys. Never again."

"Okay," I said. "So long as we're on the same page."

It was late, and we were all exhausted, both physically and emotionally. James rolled his bike to the edge of the driveway and slung his leg over the seat, waving once before he pedaled away. Sam, looming behind me like a very strange bodyguard, scowled.

"Do you believe him?" he asked.

"I do," I said.

"He broke into our house."

"And I lied my way into your carnival. People do messed-up stuff when they're desperate." I turned, putting a hand on his arm. "He'll be back in the morning.

Let's go to bed. I'm tired and I'm cold and I'm a little scared of what all this is going to mean. So if it's cool with you, I'd like to not think about it for a while."

Sam nodded, expression softening, before he turned and started for the stairs, his tail wrapped around my wrist like a tether making sure I didn't lose my way. In the dining room, James Smith's frozen coffee sat on the table, slowly thawing, all but forgotten.

Eight

"Every debt comes due. Given enough time,
every debt has its day."

                                    –Enid Healy

The next morning, behind the house

My knife flew straight and clean, hitting my makeshift target dead center. I had used pieces of plywood from the barn to make half a dozen of the crude things. I was fairly sure our "landlord" wouldn't notice them missing: there were about a dozen identical sheets crammed in there, half of them riddled with mold or cracked down the center. If he had a problem with it, I could always leave him a check.

I took a breath in through my nose, let it out through my mouth, and threw again. This knife landed next to the first, socking into the same groove. My shoulders started to relax. If I could keep throwing clean, I was okay. Stressed and scared and a long way from home, but okay. That was all I really needed to be.

"I'm heading into town," said Cylia. I turned, the next knife already in my hand. She offered a strained smile, her hands tucked deep in the pockets of her jacket. "If we're going to be helping the chief of police's son do something dangerous and potentially fatal, I figure we should show our faces around the place first, so no one can call us 'those strangers at the old Smith house' when they have to explain our corpses to the paper. You want to come?"

I hesitated. James had said he wouldn't be able to come to the house until early afternoon, and while throwing knives was fun and all, it wasn't necessarily as productive as getting a sense of the community. Leaving the wards was fine, as long as I didn't say anything the crossroads wouldn't like while I was away from them. Technically, I was already outside the wards, and nothing bad had happened yet.

You can't hang ghost wards on a person, because a person is just a ghost with a nice Sunday suit of breath and blood and bone. If I wanted to stay warded, I needed to stay in, or near, the house.

Screw that.

"Sure," I said. "Let me get my coat."

"I'll meet you at the car," said Cylia, and walked away.

Sam was in the kitchen when I thundered through the back door. He turned to watch my arrival, eyebrows raised. "Do I need to get unfuzzy?" he asked.

"No one's here, I'm going into town with Cylia." I paused in my journey toward the dining room long enough to lean up and kiss him on the cheek. "You cool staying here and watching for James, in case he shows up early? I don't want him going through those books unsupervised."

"You could always stay here with me," Sam offered.

"Nuh-uh. One, we tend to distract each other, and two, I need to get a sense of the town. You should do it, too, either tomorrow or the next day. We need to rub off this veneer of new and interesting before we attract attention we don't want."

"Fine. Find us a place we can get coffee or ice cream or something, and I'll take you on a townie date. No carnival, no theme park, just footsie under the table and something with too much sugar."

"Deal," I said, and flashed him a grin before darting out of the room.

Dating is difficult when you spend more than half your time dealing with the nonhuman communities of the world, and don't really have the necessary selling points to fill out an OK Cupid profile. There are a few cryptid dating sites—necessary, when you're a member of an endangered species with very specific mating requirements—but the working cryptozoologist population is too small to sustain anything like that, and we wouldn't use one if we had it. Our need isn't as great, and there's too much chance the Covenant would catch wind and decide to try infiltrating it. No.

What that means, though, is that most of us will meet our significant others, whether temporary or long-term, "on the job." My parents met when my father followed reports of an impending Covenant strike to my mother's house, and discovered the "monsters" in the chatter were her adoptive parents and little brother. *His* parents met when Grandpa Thomas was assigned by the Covenant to kill or recruit Grandma Alice. And *her* parents met when my great-grandfather went looking for the Questing Beast that was devouring people in the wake of my great-grandmother's carnival. There's no such thing as normal in the cryptozoological world. There's just a wide, wide range of weirdness.

Sam and I are part of a long line of weird, and I'm not ashamed of that. It did, however, mean that we had yet to have anything remotely close to an ordinary date. So far, we'd done a night at his family's carnival, a roller derby game that ended with him trying to strangle me while I set him on fire, and a day at Lowryland, which ended, if such things are possible, even worse. Sitting down for a cup of coffee or an ice cream sundae would be perfect, and exactly what I needed to take my mind off the fact that Mary was still missing and the crossroads wanted me to commit a murder.

Compartmentalization is a necessary function of the

sapient mind. Every species I've met with human-level—
or potentially beyond human-level—intelligence has
been capable of going "sure, the world is ending, but
what about my soup?" I honestly believe that without
that capacity for self-distraction, we'd all break under
the weight of the world we have to live in.

Cylia was leaning against the hood of her avocado-
colored muscle car, squinting at her fingernails. "I need
to find a place to get a mani-pedi," she said, as I approached. "My cuticles are wasted."

"Is Fern coming with us?"

"She's sleeping in. I think she was more unnerved by
last night's visitor than she's letting on, and this is how
she copes." Cylia looked at me through her lashes. "She
really counts on you to know what to do. That means
she's always going to follow your lead."

"I know." I slid into the passenger seat, waiting for
Cylia to get behind the wheel before I said, "It's a little
terrifying sometimes. I don't know why she believes in
me so much."

"You're a Price." Cylia shrugged and buckled her
belt. "Honestly, if I'd known that sooner, I'd probably be
just as bad as she is."

There it was again: my family name, setting expectations I couldn't live up to since, well, forever. It was
weird, being in a situation where my allies put all the
weight of the family on my shoulders, but my enemies
had no idea what that was supposed to mean.

Well. Not enemies, exactly. James wasn't an enemy yet,
and if we were working together to take down the crossroads, he was never going to have to be. If, on the other
hand, they decided to enforce me doing them the "little
favor" I'd agreed to do . . .

No. They had my magic, and they had the authority
to hold it until I kept my end of the bargain. Fine, whatever, let them keep it. I'd been a sister and a friend and
a cheerleader and a derby girl and a very, very efficient
killer long before I'd started setting things on fire by

laying hands on them. If the crossroads wanted to keep my magic, that was one small piece of who I was. I could learn to live without it. Hell, I already more than half had. It was nice not to have to worry about setting Sam's fur smoldering when we cuddled.

"Do we have an agenda for this trip?" I asked.

Cylia started the engine. "Go into town, find a coffee shop, buy coffee and muffins, praise them to the high heavens, make sure people see us. If anyone asks, my name's 'Celia.' Less chance of it standing out. We're already going to stand out enough."

"If there's a drug store, I'd like to pick up some henna," I said. "My roots are showing off like they're in a beauty pageant."

"I like it when you're vain," said Cylia, a laugh in her voice. "Reminds me that you're a person and not a terrifying battle android sent from the twenty-fifth century to destroy us all."

I snorted and settled in my seat, watching out the window as the woods rolled by.

When we'd arrived in New Gravesend, it had been dark and I had been asleep. That wasn't a great combination for getting the lay of the land. Now, I was coming to realize my assessment of the area wasn't as far off as I'd been afraid it was. Everywhere I looked, there were more trees. They towered, reaching for the sky, transforming the landscape from midday brilliance into a strange sort of quasi-twilight. Everything that lived here had to adapt to living in shadow. The trees wouldn't allow anything else.

It took us about five minutes to make our way out of the winding backroads and onto a broader, better-maintained street that slipped smoothly from the shadow of the trees into a more landscaped setting. The trees here were just as tall, just as old, but they had been thinned, possibly over the course of decades, until they were almost a friendly barrier wall against the deeper, darker forest. Stay in these trees and it would be all gingerbread witches and Halloween specials, rather than the horror movie that lurked a little deeper in.

We crested a ridge, small but deep enough to shape the landscape, and there it was: the town of New Gravesend, Maine, bustling, bucolic, and clearly dreaming of the day when it could be called a city. It looked like a postcard brought to life, all brick and clean wood and comfortable New England architecture. Tourists probably flocked here in the late fall—about four weeks from where we were standing—to count the changing leaves and gasp at their beauty, returning to their cozy little bed and breakfasts at the first hint of evening frost.

The streets were occupied but not crowded, with plenty of parking along what I assumed was the "main drag." About half the shops were the sort of thing designed to appeal to my hypothetical tourists—one selling just candles, another selling nothing but maple syrup and maple syrup accessories, and a third selling the kind of fancy cupcakes that probably cost three dollars and required the eater to spend an hour brushing their teeth. The rest of the shops were more practical, selling home goods, fresh produce, and warm winter clothes. It was like looking at a town that couldn't decide what it wanted to be when it grew up. There was something surprisingly comforting about that. If a municipality could have an identity crisis, maybe the fact that I was still sorting my shit out wasn't so big a deal.

"Yes!" Cylia actually fist-pumped. "Nail salon. Next time Fern feels up to it, we're totally doing nail day. Think Sam would like to come?"

"The whole point of pedicures is getting the foot massage and relaxing," I said. "If he relaxes, he gets fuzzy. So no, I don't think he'd like to come, but he'll probably appreciate the offer anyway." No one likes being left out, even when they know they can't come along.

"He can mow the lawn instead. The very opposite of relaxing." Cylia pulled into an open spot directly in front of what looked like the only coffee shop on the block. I glanced at the window, and fell instantly in love.

The wood was mahogany, polished until it gleamed; the glass was thick, obviously leaded, with the name of the shop—BURIAL GROUNDS—painted in ornate gold letters inside a frame of stylized tombstones. Elegance and creepy trappings, just the way I like it. Inside, I could see multiple overstuffed chairs next to private tables, about half of them occupied, as well as several larger tables. The crowning glory? A group of teenagers had colonized one of the big tables, coffee cups by their hands, clearly engrossed in their game of Dungeons and Dragons.

"I'm not coming home with you," I said in a dreamy voice. "I live here now. If you need me, you can check between the beans and the biscotti."

"I never took you for a coffee girl."

"I'm not a coffee girl, in the 'give it to me if you want to live' sense. I'm more of a 'give me an old-fashioned library aesthetic and a bunch of chairs heavy, big, and comfortable enough for me to disappear into for a week or so and I'll be happy' girl."

Cylia laughed. She sounded light, easy, relaxed—all the things she hadn't been since she'd followed me to Florida. "Come on," she said. "First cup's on me."

The bell over the door was real brass. There was weight to the way it jingled, like even the sound was antique. I smiled, eyes half-closing with the pleasure of it. Everything about this was *normal*. I could have been in Portland, or Seattle, or anywhere else in the world where people enjoy a hot beverage and a comfy chair to drink it in.

Cylia elbowed me lightly. I glanced at her, surprised, and she pointed to the counter, past the gleaming display of baked goods packed with delicious butter, sugar, and calories.

There, standing next to the register and blinking at us

like we had no right to exist outside of our rental home, was James Smith.

Cylia flashed me a quick grin before undulating forward, putting more sway into her narrow hips than I would previously have thought possible. I'd never seen her trying to look seductive before. It didn't quite fit, like the first time I'd seen Verity dance the tango. Yes, she was a lovely woman, and yes, she had the right to shake what her maker gave her any way she wanted to, but thinking of her like that just didn't feel right. She was a widow. She was still in mourning.

You would never have known it by the way she leaned against that counter, beaming at James like she was starving and he was on the menu.

"Hi," she said brightly. "We're new in town. What's good?"

"Try the banana bread," he said, with just enough bored detachment that I could tell he'd caught on to what she was doing. I would have applauded, if it wouldn't have given the game away. "It goes great with seasonal mocha."

According to the whiteboard, the seasonal mocha was maple walnut. The thought alone was enough to make me want to scrape my tongue until the sweetness went away. Cylia didn't appear to share my reservations. Her smile grew broader.

"One of those, large, and a slice of banana bread. And my friend here will have . . . ?" She glanced expectantly at me.

"Black coffee with marshmallows," I said.

James blinked. "What?"

"It says I can have hot chocolate with marshmallows. I don't want hot chocolate, but I do want marshmallows. So, black coffee with marshmallows, please. Oh, and one of those rice cereal bars." I like sweet. I just prefer it on my own terms.

James rolled his eyes, but didn't otherwise comment

as he rung up our order. At least this explained why he couldn't be to the house until later. Most employers won't accept "spending the morning hanging out with strange women, figuring out how to perform an act of large and terrifying sorcery" as a reason for not coming to work. Maybe the world would be a better place if they did.

Cylia paid while I wandered off to find us a seat, studying my surroundings. There were watercolor paintings on the wall, done by a local artist—mostly landscapes and delicate studies of flowers. A bookshelf was shoved into a corner near the bathrooms, with a sign reading "take a book/leave a book" hanging next to it. I kept going, hoping to find an open table with two seats. Finally, I saw one, tucked into the farthest corner of the coffee shop.

It would have been nice to have a better view of the windows, but beggars can't be choosers. I settled in one of the open chairs, curling my legs up under myself, and relaxed into the leather. If I closed my eyes, I could have been literally anywhere. I could have been home.

God, I missed home.

"You look comfortable." There was a clatter as Cylia put our drinks down on the table. I cracked one eye open. Real ceramic cups, on real saucers. "The barista charged me for cocoa, since there's no setting for 'putting marshmallows in coffee like a savage,' and cocoa normally comes with whipped cream. The third mug is full of whipped cream."

I leaned forward, suddenly interested. "So it is. Did you want any?"

"Be my guest." Cylia sipped her own coffee—if you could call it that—before giving it an impressed look. "Okay, I think I could fill a hummingbird feeder with this stuff. I like it."

"Better you than me." I spooned whipped cream into my coffee, stirring until it dissolved. Half the marshmallows dissolved in the same time. When I finally tasted my drink, it was sweet, creamy, and filled with that subtle swampy taste that can only come from incorporating real marshmallow into something.

"Says the woman drinking sludge. That's sludge. I always knew you were abusing your body, but I'm starting to suspect you died of scurvy years ago and haven't slowed down enough to notice."

I toasted her with my cup. "To leaving a beautiful corpse."

"Or something." She took a larger gulp of her own drink, looking around. "This is a nice place. Cozy."

Most of the clientele looked to be about our age—mid-twenties, nothing better to do. Apart from the table of teens with their Dungeons and Dragons and a few retirees sitting near the counter, we could have been part of the daily demographic. That was soothing, too.

"I wonder what people do around here for fun," I said.

"Drink coffee, apparently," said Cylia. "There isn't a roller derby league. I checked. And don't look so concerned—it's not like I was going to suggest we try out. Even though I bet we could have taught the locals a thing or two."

I smirked.

There are three positions on a flat-track roller derby team: the jammer, who goes fast to score points, the blockers, who try their best to keep the jammer from going fast to score points, and the pivot, who can switch between those two roles under specific, carefully controlled circumstances. Some people think jammers have big egos, since there's only ever one jammer per team on the track at a time. Those people are not necessarily wrong. They're not necessarily right, either . . . but it's true that many jammers are not great at sharing. Cylia and I, when we're at home, are both jammers. We were still jammers in Maine, just jammers without a team to jam for. Somehow, this had evolved into a friendly rivalry, in which we both insisted we knew the rules of derby best, and would one day show the world . . . as soon as we had the chance to strap on skates again.

It's amazing what the mind can get up to when faced with the endless tedium of driving across America. Endless, endless America. If I'd tried to focus on one more non-evil corn field, I think I would have lost my mind.

Cylia snapped her fingers. I jumped.

"Hello, and welcome back to the scene already in progress," she said brightly. "I'm about done with my drink. And my banana bread. I was going to walk down the street, see what else there is around here worth seeing. You want to come with?"

"I'll stay here, if that's cool with you," I said. "Let me get a feeling for the way things work around here, and maybe have another cup of swamp coffee."

"Got it," said Cylia. She stood. "If I'm not back in an hour, meet me at the car?"

"Deal."

I sipped my coffee as I watched her walk away.

None of us had a fixed address we could use on a cellphone contract. Even if we had, phones can be tracked. The more sophisticated cellular technology becomes, the more tools there are for using it to find people. We needed to stay out of sight, and so we'd been solidly low-tech since fleeing Lowryland: Cylia had a pay-as-you-go for emergencies, but we kept it turned off to keep it from being traced.

I didn't miss having a phone as much as I'd expected to. Sure, scrolling endlessly through Twitter was a good way to kill a few minutes, but so was reading a book, or watching the people around me.

They seemed pretty normal, as small-town populations went. They came and went with the frequency I expected, and the bathrooms were used often enough that I knew they couldn't be entirely disgusting.

James wandered over with a pot in his hand. "Refill?" he asked.

"It would dilute my marshmallows," I said.

Calmly, he reached into the pocket of his apron and

pulled out a small paper cup full of marshmallows, which he set down in front of me. "Refill?" he repeated.

"I think you may be my favorite," I said gravely, extending my cup toward him. "Don't tell anyone else. They'd all be jealous."

"Right," he said. Lowering his voice, he added, "Especially your boyfriend, who should have been a linebacker. He'd twist my head off like a bottle top."

"He doesn't usually twist heads off, but point taken."

"Are you here to spy on me?"

I quirked an eyebrow. "If we are, that officially makes us the worst spies in the history of spying. And the history of spying includes some very, awfully, *terribly* bad spies. Like, unrealistically bad. So no, we're not here to spy on you. This was the first coffee shop we saw, and we followed the sweet lure of hot caffeine all the way to the door."

"There's a Starbucks by the grocery store."

"Oh, be still my heart, what a terrible mistake we have made, shopping locally, enjoying marshmallow flavored delights," I deadpanned. "Seriously, it's a coincidence. Not everyone who wanders through the door is doing so with malicious intentions. Thank you for the marshmallows."

"Let me know if you need anything else," said James, with the blithe politeness of a professional food service worker.

I saluted him with my coffee mug as he turned to walk away. Then I froze, suddenly finding it difficult to breathe.

The man who'd just walked through the café door was tall and thin, with a pointed chin and sandy brown hair. He was dressed like he was on a lunch break from a local law firm: proper suit and tie, everything fitted exactly as it ought to be. Nothing cheap or off-the-rack for *him*. His wire-framed glasses managed to conceal the color of his eyes, making him pleasantly, attractively generic. He was every act one boyfriend in every romantic comedy ever made; he was every Clerk #2 from every episode of every show in the *Law & Order* franchise.

There was nothing about him that should have made my heart beat fast and my blood run cold, nothing that should have turned me into a suspense movie cliché, except for everything about him. Except for the fact that I knew him.

Leonard Cunningham had found me.

Nine

"You know, given the choice—given the ability to change everything about myself—I don't think I'd have been born into this family. Because I wouldn't only be choosing a better world for myself. I'd be choosing for my children."

–Jane Harrington-Price

Burial Grounds, absolutely trapped

I PUT MY COFFEE DOWN, scanning the room for avenues of escape. What had seemed like a quaint, charming design before now felt like a dead-end alley specifically made to trap me. There might be a fire door on the other side of the bathrooms—why the hell hadn't I bothered to check the bathrooms? Was I really getting that complacent?—but there might not be. Either way, if I went looking, Leonard would see me move. He would *notice* me.

Assuming he hadn't already. As if on cue, he met my eyes and smiled, raising one hand to tap his temple in an utterly polite gesture of greeting. I sank farther into my chair.

I could bolt. The counter wasn't blocked by anything, not so much as a service door, and if I waited for him to place his order and pick up his drink, I could make a break for it. Vault past James and out the door and . . . what? Run? On foot, no gear, no prep, no way of telling my allies that the Covenant was in town? Sam would never forgive me if I ran out on him again. I might forgive myself, if running meant he would live, but that wasn't the case. Not now.

There were sixteen people in the café with me, not counting James, who could take care of himself, but who might not know about the Covenant and the kind of danger he'd be in if they realized he was a sorcerer. I didn't know how good Leonard was in close quarters, or whether he'd be willing to kill innocents to take me down. I wasn't going to bet this many lives on it.

Sometimes, the only thing to do is nothing. I forced my shoulders back and my chin up, sitting as straight as I could. This was a place where my background in cheerleading came in handy as hell: derby girls can snarl and cry and bleed, but cheerleaders are expected to retain their poise no matter what. I've seen girls carried off the field with broken legs, still smiling. I could do this. For them, in their honor, I could do this.

Leonard stepped up to the counter, speaking briefly with James before collecting a mug and accompanying saucer and making his way toward me. I watched him come, and didn't move.

Finally, he was standing in front of me, so close I could have put a knife in his throat before he had a chance to move. He smiled pleasantly, indicating Cylia's abandoned chair with his free hand.

"Is this seat taken?"

"Yes."

He sat down anyway. I hadn't honestly been expecting anything else.

"You're looking well, Annie. The fugitive life clearly agrees with you. Have you been able to keep up your training? It hurts to think of all that physical conditioning slipping away because you've eaten too many gas station pies."

I looked at him and said nothing.

Leonard sighed. "Don't be like that. I swear, women

are so touchy sometimes. If I implied that you'd gained weight, I'm sorry."

"If that were all you'd done, I'd buy bigger jeans and deal with it."

"Ah. Still holding that messy business at the carnival against me, are you?" He took a careful sip of his drink—coffee, by the smell of it—before offering, "I didn't kill you when I had the chance, you know. I think that ought to buy me a little tolerance."

"I could slit your throat before anyone in this place realized I was going to move."

Leonard took another sip. "Mmm. Maybe yes, maybe no, but then you'd be covered in blood—arterial spray is so messy—and that would be a bit difficult to explain. Not to mention you have no idea whether I'm here by myself. I could have an entire team waiting across the street to take you down."

"You'd be dead. That might be a fair trade."

"Not really. You wouldn't still be running if you'd realized that the best way for you to protect that viper's nest you call a family was to come to me willingly." He put his cup down and reclined in his chair, smiling, utterly at ease. "If you were an operative in good standing, we could return to the old status quo, where we leave your people alone except for the occasional observer, and your people understand that if they rise against us, we'll destroy them. It was good enough for Enid and Alexander. I can't imagine it wouldn't be good enough for the current generations."

"We're not living in the fifties anymore."

"No. No, we're not. Sometimes I think it's a pity, other times I'm not so sure. The Internet is a blessing, absolutely. And facial recognition software! My God. Let it advance a little further and we won't need witches. We'll finally be able to purge them from the human population, and won't that be a blessing for everyone?"

"Maybe not for the witches," I said softly.

Leonard looked at me like I was a fool. "Have you ever *met* a witch, Annie? They're beset by demons of their own creation from the cradle to the grave. They never know peace, never know comfort, never know anything more than the torment of their own unnatural abilities, their own unbearable burdens. I know you want us to be monsters, because it would be easier for you if we were, but remember, the Covenant was formed to protect humanity from the things lurking outside the firelight. Sometimes that includes humanity itself."

I looked at him. Then I turned to look at the coffee shop around us. People were going about their business, blithely unaware of the danger. We might as well have been talking about the weather. It was a good tactic. Most people don't pay nearly as much attention to their surroundings—or to the conversations happening around them—as they believe they do, and the Dungeons and Dragons game at the front of the shop was only going to help keep us under the radar, since anyone who *did* overhear us would probably assume we were talking about something similar, some world where all the monsters were drawn on graph paper and all the problems could be solved with a roll of the dice.

"Why are you here, Leonard?" *How are you here, how did you find me, what do you want, how do I make you go away.* The questions were like puppies, tumbling over themselves inside my mind, getting tangled into balls of limbs and waggling tails. I wanted to ask them all. I didn't want to ask any of them.

I didn't have time for this. James would finish his shift soon. He'd leave, and I would be alone with Leo in a way I hadn't been since the carnival, when he had finally seen fit to remind me that he was more than just another Covenant operative: he was their heir apparent, the man raised since birth to one day lead the greatest organization of monster hunters in the world. The fact that he could seem ordinary enough to make me forget that fact was just one aspect of why he scared me so badly.

He . . . *lulled*. He made things I'd hated my entire life seem forgivable, or at least understandable, like there were two sides to the story. Listening to him was like attending a lecture on moving a person's Overton window, making the unthinkable permissible one simple, logical twist at a time.

"Why do you think I'm here, Annie?" He picked his mug up again, turning it in his hand. His eyes remained fixed on me. "It's my responsibility to check on the recruits, to make sure they're doing well. You did an excellent job with that Blight infestation in Ohio. How did you clear the field alone? Oh, of course—you weren't alone. You had the ape with you. How is he doing? Still deluding himself that he could ever hold onto you? I'm sure you'll get tired of slumming soon. Don't worry. I won't hold it against you. You're not the first, and you won't be the last, to think there's value in a little extra-curricular hunting."

"If you ever talk about Sam like that again, I will kill you, and damn the consequences," I said pleasantly.

Leo laughed. "I almost wish I could test that conviction. It would be worth the pain to see you realize how badly you'd messed up."

"Fuck you."

"You know, I prefer you this way: honest." He sipped his coffee. "No pretenses, no lies, just this glorious, untamed killer looking for a place to direct her rage. You could be spectacular with the right hand to guide you. Warriors do better when they have scholars standing behind them and pointing at the target. You'd never have to think again. All you'd need to do was move. Wouldn't that be wonderful?"

I couldn't help myself. I burst out laughing. James looked over his shoulder, frowning when he saw the source of the noise. I couldn't explain. I smiled sweetly at Leo instead, leaning forward.

"See, that's where you show that you don't know me at all. I've never wanted to be the blunt instrument."

That was Verity's job, and she was welcome to it. She enjoyed moving through the world like a knife, slashing and stabbing and cutting away at the foundation of things until they crumbled around her. She didn't *plan*. She . . . choreographed.

I planned. I considered the consequences. And yeah, sometimes I acted impulsively, sometimes I went against my own better instincts and my own precious planning, but I always did it for a reason. The fact that Leo thought otherwise was one more piece of proof that he had never seen *me*, Antimony. He'd only ever been looking at my name, and what it would mean to bring my family back into the fold.

"There are other paths open to you," he said.

"I like the one I'm on just fine," I replied. "Why are you *here*, Leo?"

"You disappeared for quite a while. I was concerned. You're my project, Annie, and I'm going to see you to completion. Your parents might have raised you in hiding—however many of you there are—but once we knew you existed, there was no way you were ever going to get away. You're clever enough to understand that much."

"Go away."

"What, you're not going to ask whether I'm here alone?"

"I know you're not here with Chloe or Margaret, since I'm pretty sure they'd both kill me on sight. I don't know who else you could bring with you without attracting their attention. I *do* know that you've got more freedom of movement than most Covenant operatives, probably because you're going to run the show one day, and they want to be sure you understand what you're getting yourself into. So I figure yeah, you're probably here alone. The best reason not to kill you is that if I did, the rest of the Covenant would come."

"Clever girl." Somehow, from his lips, those words sounded like an insult. Leo stood, putting his mug down.

"I know where you are. I will always know where you are. You're going to choose me, Annie. Believe me when I say that. You're going to choose me, and when you do, I'm going to be generous and let you come directly home. We've been waiting for you so long, a few more weeks aren't going to hurt anything."

He turned his back on me, giving me a perfect target. All it would have taken was one knife between those shoulder blades and . . . well, it's not that all my problems would have gone away forever. It's just that I would have had a different set of problems, one that maybe pissed me off a little less.

I didn't move, not to reach for my knives, not to throw them. I just sat there, perfectly still, and watched him walk away.

Time passed. I don't know how much. I was frozen in place, numb with shock and horror. Not only were the crossroads following me, but now the Covenant was on my tail again—something I'd been expecting since leaving Lowryland, sure, but which I had managed to mostly put out of my mind. It had been a consequence for the future, something to be dealt with when it happened. Something that couldn't be planned for or avoided.

For the first time in a while, I was grateful to the crossroads for syphoning the fire from my fingers. If it had still been with me, I was pretty sure the coffee shop would have been in flames.

"You okay?"

I glanced up. James was a few feet away, no longer wearing his apron, an anxious expression on his pointed face. He indicated my left hand with a quick gesture of his own.

"You've been sitting here flexing your hands since your friend left. Is he also renting from my cousin?"

"*No.*" The word came out with more force than I'd

intended. I took a breath. That didn't seem like enough: I took another, and said, "No. He's not. You shouldn't . . . if you see him, don't come near me. Or any of us. He's not a good guy."

"Ah." James' expression clouded. "I'm a secret friend. There's a game I've played before."

I hated the bucolic little town around me when he said things like that. I'm not always the world's best judge of character, but James was enough like my cousin Artie—enough like me—that I could see the cracks where he'd been struck. The world has a way of grinding down the people it deems different, or less worthy of being loved.

"No," I said, for the second time. The word fell between us like a stone. "That isn't what this is. Please. I'll explain when we get to the house, all right? I'll explain everything."

"You sure do come with a lot of explaining," he said, then turned to walk away.

At least his visit had broken the strange paralysis that had followed Leo's departure. I stood, leaving my re-filled coffee mug, surface slick with melted marshmallow, behind. James had disappeared into the back, leaving me once again surrounded by strangers. That was fine. It's easier to be unwell in the company of strangers, because they don't have any idea what "ordinary" looks like.

The air had warmed while I was inside; it felt like a crisp fall day, the kind that should be spent picking apples and making chicken stock, not sitting in a coffee shop and waiting for the Covenant of St. George to descend. Cylia's car was still snuggled comfortably up to the curb, as visible among the sensible, sturdy cars of the locals as a parrot among a flock of magpies. She was leaning against the hood, munching on something from a white paper bag.

She beamed when she saw me approaching, tilting the bag down to offer me my choice of its contents.

"There's a candy shop that still does penny candy," she said gleefully. "I mean, it's a nickel apiece, but the principle is there, and she has maple sugar candy in the display. Who the hell sells maple sugar candy for a nickel? Someone who either has no business sense or way too many trees, that's who. Want some?"

"We need to go home."

Cylia lowered the bag, seeming to see the distress in my face for the first time. "Honey? What's wrong?"

"I'll tell you when we get home. Please, can we go?"

Cylia nodded, once, and started for the door.

I watched the rearview mirror all the way back to the house. No one followed us. Not that it made any difference. The Covenant—Leo—wasn't following me through anything as simple as visual surveillance.

Blood. Sympathy. There were any number of spells that would let them hone in on me and track me down, following me from one end of the continent to the other. Lowryland had allowed me a brief period of peace by surrounding me with so many people that the spells couldn't latch on, but even without the evil magicians running the place behind the scenes, that could never have been forever. A girl can't spend her life at a theme park, no matter how much she wants to.

James' bike was propped against the porch when Cylia pulled into our driveway, and he was standing in front of the door, arms folded, glowering. He turned at the sound of tires on gravel, and didn't unfold his arms. Great. Now I got to deal with an angry sorcerer as well as everything else. This day kept on getting better.

"If it gets *much* better, maybe Godzilla will show up," I muttered.

"What?" asked Cylia.

"Nothing." I slid out of the car, leaning my elbows against the roof as I called, "Problems?"

"No one's answering the door," said James.

Fear slithered along my spine. What if Leo *wasn't* alone? What if—God forbid—he'd been sent to make sure I stayed in the coffee shop, kept on talking? Sam was incredible in a fight, but his formal training had been for the trapeze, not for staying alive in a pitched battle against seasoned monster hunters. Fern . . .

Sylphs aren't natural fighters. She could put power behind her punches by increasing her density beyond reasonable limits, but she didn't know how to fire a gun and she didn't habitually carry any sort of weapons. Her usual response to fear was to get lighter, and hence faster, and try to outrun it. That wouldn't work with the Covenant.

Being anywhere near me was a death sentence. Had been since I'd allowed myself to be sent to England. How had I been foolish enough to forget that?

"Don't you have a key?" asked Cylia, digging hers out of her pocket.

James shook his head. "I wouldn't have broken in last night if I did. Dad convinced Norbert I didn't need one. Said it would only encourage me to blow off work and spend all my time reading. I usually sneak in through the back door, but it's locked."

"Huh," said Cylia, shooting a quick look in my direction. "Annie?"

"Open the door and wait out here," I said. A quick gesture and my hands were full of knives. James' eyes widened. That trick can take some time to get used to, even though there's nothing magical about it: it's all practice and knowing exactly where the edges are. "If I'm not back in fifteen minutes or you hear screaming, both of you get in the car and drive as fast as you possibly can. We're in Maine. The closest sanctuary I know of is in Gentling. If you go there, they'll hide you. You may need to remind them daily of who you are, but they'll hide you."

The people in Gentling are the result of a meeting of the land and sea, literally. They are, almost all of them, crossbreeds between humans and finfolk, one of the safer, more complicated forms of merfolk. They tend to have issues with short-term memory, but they're allies, and have been since my family quit the Covenant. If Cylia and James wound up there, the citizens of Gentling would make sure they were all right.

"Got it," said Cylia. Her key slid into the lock with a faint click, and then the door was open, revealing the front room. I stepped through, moving lightly, my steps designed to smother noise before it could begin. The sunlight streaming through the door behind me made it harder to see, rather than easier, but I didn't wave for Cylia to close it. I might need the escape route.

There was something cold and assessing in the pit of my stomach, measuring up the house as the site of a siege, trying to decide where the first blows would have been struck, to guess where the blood would have been spilled. Every time I turned a corner without finding the signs of a struggle, another inch of my skin relaxed, until I was walking quiet as a cat, slithering as much as striding from shadow to shadow.

When I was a kid, I used to imagine going to one of my teachers and telling them how I'd *really* spent my weekend. Telling them about learning to field strip and rebuild weapons, how to sharpen knives, how to navigate a field full of traps that had been designed to be nonlethal but could still do a lot of damage if I misjudged, if I stepped wrong, if I was ever careless for so much as a moment. I used to think about the looks on their faces, to wonder how many of them would be proud of me before the urge to call Child Protective Services kicked in.

Walking through the silent house that had gone so quickly from refuge to burial ground, I was grateful that I never had, and even more grateful to my parents for putting me through those casual tests of my ability to stay alive. Some lessons, if taught early enough, work their way all the way down to the bone.

The door of the room I was sharing with Sam stood ever so slightly ajar. I paused outside, taking a deep breath, and kicked it open as hard as I could, twisting so that I was framed perfectly in the opening, a knife in either hand.

Sam, wearing a pair of shorts and nothing else, looked up from the book he was reading and blinked at me.

"Okay," he said. "That's seriously hot, but Annie, what the fuck?"

I dropped my knives, clapped my hands over my eyes, and started crying.

Ten

"I hope you never have to learn what you're not willing to give up. Knowledge like that always costs so much more than you were hoping to pay."

–Alice Healy

In a house, in a bedroom, in tears

"ANNIE? JESUS!" SAM THREW his book aside and was next to me in an instant, moving with the inhuman speed that was his birthright. He folded his arms around me and held me at a slightly awkward angle, hugging and checking for injuries at the same time. It was efficient. I had to give him that much.

The thought struck me as somehow funny. I started laughing through my tears, hiccupping helplessly as the adrenaline racing through my body scrambled my feelings and made them virtually impossible to understand. He wasn't letting go. I slumped, trusting him to hold me upright. I couldn't stay here long, not with Cylia and James waiting outside for me to come back and tell them whether or not everyone was dead, but I could have a few seconds. I'd done enough to earn that much.

"Annie, come on, I need you to talk to me. You're scaring me."

"Sorry." I took a deep breath, in through my nose and out through my mouth, and uncovered my eyes as I turned my face toward Sam's. The panic in his eyes mirrored what I knew he must have seen in mine. That helped me center myself, a little. I wasn't glad to have scared him—far from it—but I was grateful for the fact that I could take that fear away.

Love is complicated and messy, and it sort of sucks because I never used to have to worry about this kind of shit.

"Leo's here," I said.

Sam stiffened, his arms loosening as he prepared to start swinging, his tail, which had wrapped itself around my ankle, tightening like he was afraid I was about to be ripped away.

"Where?" he asked. His voice was low, filled with a quiet and implacable rage. If fūri were like waheela, possessed of both fully human and fully animal forms, I would have found out in that moment, because if he'd been capable of transforming into something more dangerous, he would absolutely have done so.

"In the town, I mean, not here at the house." I took a step back. Sam let me go, his tail holding on for a beat longer than his hands. "I was afraid . . . when we got here and the door was locked and no one was answering, I thought . . ."

"Fuck, honey, if he'd sent a team here to kill us, I won't pretend they couldn't succeed, because the Covenant scares the pants off me, but I can promise you there'd be at least a broken window." Sam raised one hand, fingers folded in a Boy Scout salute. "I solemnly swear that if I'm about to be murdered by bigoted zealots, I'll stop worrying about property damage and make as much of a mess as possible, so you'll know what you're walking into. Okay?"

I giggled, the sound rendered thick by snot and tears. Then I sniffled, wiping my nose with the back of my hand, and nodded. "Okay. I'm going to go check on Fern. Can you get dressed and go let Cylia and James know that the Covenant *hasn't* murdered everyone while we were off having coffee?"

"Sure—wait." Sam frowned. "You were having coffee with James?"

"Only technically. He works at the town coffee shop."

"Oh. I guess that makes sense. I'll see you downstairs." He gave me one last quick hug before starting to pick his clothes up off the floor.

I was actually smiling as I walked back into the hall. It was hard not to read the scene I'd busted into as a charmingly awkward attempt at seduction. I mean, half-naked, in bed with a book, in the middle of the day? Come on.

At least he knew how to get my attention.

The stairs to the attic were narrow and just rickety enough to shake as I climbed them, sending vibrations through the floor above me. Fern's fondness for her chosen room made more and more sense. Out of everyone in the house, she was the only one whose entire defensive strategy was "run." Cylia could bend an attacker's luck against them, making it more likely that guns would misfire or rocks would somehow turn underfoot. Sam could punch them until they stopped coming. Fern . . .

Fern could run. And by putting herself at the top of the house, she had both created an exit that no one else was likely to be able to use, and established a way of hearing if anyone was coming.

The stairs ended at a narrow door. I rapped the knuckles of my hand against the wood, and called, "Fern? It's Annie. Can I come in?"

"Sure." Her voice was faint but audible.

Cautiously, I opened the door to reveal a small, neatly appointed room. The walls were white; the curtains were trimmed in lace. The overall effect was one of sweetness and innocence, like this room had originally belonged to a young girl who couldn't be trusted with unfettered access to the ground.

Fern was sitting on the edge of the bed, staring fixedly out the single barred window. She looked over her shoulder as I crossed the threshold, offering me a wan smile.

"You're scared someone's found us, aren't you?" she asked.

I blinked. "Yes," I said. "How did you know?"

"A car came a little while after you and Cylia left. A man got out and walked around the house. He tried the doors, and when he found that they were locked, he left them."

My chest tightened. "What did he look like?"

"Tall. Really dark hair, like James. Broad shoulders. He was wearing a uniform. I couldn't see exactly what kind, he was too far away for that. I'm sorry." Fern glanced down. "I should have tried harder."

"Did he have glasses on?"

"No."

Not Leo, then. He'd told me a lot of lies, which should have felt like a fair trade for the number of lies *I* had told *him*. That was how it had worked with Sam, anyway. Only Sam and I had both been trying to protect ourselves, while Leo had been trying to subvert me to a cause I had no interest in. There was at least one thing he hadn't lied about, though: his eyesight was worse than my brother's, and Alex can't hit the broad side of a barn when he doesn't have his glasses on. There was no way Leo would have removed his glasses before coming to case the joint.

The rest of the description, though . . . "That sounds like it may have been James' father. The chief of police."

That didn't seem to help. Fern looked, if anything, more alarmed as she asked, "Why would he be here? We haven't done anything wrong."

That was questionable, although we hadn't done anything wrong inside city limits apart from punching James' nose, and he'd deserved it. "Maybe he wanted to get a look at the people renting from his nephew, or maybe he was trying to be neighborly. Have you been locked up here since he left?"

Fern bit her lip and nodded. "He scared me. I figured if I waited for you to come back, it would be okay. You'd make sure it was okay."

Her faith in me was as touching as it was misplaced. "I'll always try," I said. "Come on downstairs."

It was easier to descend than it had been to climb. The shaking of the steps was familiar now. If I went to visit Fern more than a few times, it would become ordinary, unremarkable, and even something I could overlook. The intelligent mind doesn't hold on to novelty very well. That's intentional. If we were constantly being surprised by our surroundings, we would never be able to get anything done. We have to become jaded if we're going to be functional.

It was hard to feel jaded as I stepped into the dining room with Fern at my heels and beheld my motley, self-assembled group of allies. It was strange to realize that, thanks to my exile, I was the first person in generations to go entirely outside the family for help. No cousins, no honorary aunts or uncles—not even Mary, not unless I could get her back from the crossroads. The possibility of that unconfirmed loss was a rock in the pit of my stomach, possible and implacable and painful.

Cylia was leaning against the wall, while James and Sam sat on opposite sides of the table like they were getting ready to start arm wrestling each other. All three of them looked over as we arrived in the room.

"False alarm?" asked Cylia.

"Sort of," I replied. "James, is there any chance your father would have decided to come do a walk-around of the property while you were at work?"

His scowl was immediate and intense. "Absolutely. He doesn't think anyone deserves privacy. If you don't have anything to hide, you shouldn't mind the police sticking their nose anywhere they feel it belongs."

"I have plenty to hide, but aside from that, I still wouldn't want strangers pawing through my underwear drawer," I said. "A reasonable expectation of privacy is not an admission of guilt. Would it put you in a bad position if I asked you to tell him he's welcome to drop by whenever, but we'd really prefer it if he didn't skulk around in the bushes while we're doing the shopping? Because he freaked Fern out pretty badly."

James grimaced. "If I ask him that, I'm as good as admitting that I'm spending time here."

"Who was it that didn't like the idea of secret friends?" I asked, trying to keep my tone light. "That runs both ways."

"Fair." He sighed. "I'll tell him I dropped by to get a replacement chain for my bike and wound up showing you how to reset the fuses or something. Anything to make me sound useful."

"Your dad's sort of a dick, isn't he?" asked Sam.

"Yeah, he is," said James. "I should probably defend him, but why bother? It won't make him any less of an asshole."

"Fun times." I walked over to lean against Sam's chair. I was too filled with nervous energy to sit; I'd wind up carving notes in the table without realizing I was doing it, and I didn't feel like paying for a new one. "To answer the question of what's wrong: Leonard Cunningham, presumptive heir to the Covenant of St. George—as in, he's going to be the man in charge as soon as his grandfather dies, whether of natural or Leonard-induced causes—has tracked me down."

Cylia paled. Fern made a small, unhappy sound. Sam said nothing, but his tail snaked out to wrap around my ankle once again, keeping me anchored where I was. It felt like a tether, like a lifeline. As long as he was holding on to me, I couldn't drift away. "If any of you want to leave, this is the time to do it."

"I've heard of the Covenant," said James thoughtfully. "They're a holy order, right? They hunt monsters."

"Everyone in this room who's classified as a monster by the Covenant, raise your hand," said Cylia.

Four hands went up. James paled. I looked at him steadily.

"Hand up, Iceman," I said. "They'd kill you, too, for the crime of not being an ordinary human. Or, if you seemed dedicated enough to the cause of human ascendency, they'd use you, breed you, and use your kids, right up until the day when you weren't useful enough. Then they'd kill you the way they've killed hundreds of innocent cryptids. Some of them might be sorry."

Some of them. Not many, and even thinking that some of them might understand mercy felt like a betrayal of my family. Still, I've spent enough time with the Covenant that I can't think of them as an unflinching force of hate the way I used to.

Chloe snored. Margaret just wanted to understand her place in the world, when her family and her community were at the kind of odds that could only be resolved with a shovel and a shallow grave. Even Leo had a tendency to hum under his breath when he was focusing on something. They're people to me. Much as I don't want them to be, they're *people*.

"Some of them *would* be sorry," I amended. "Some of them would carry your death for the rest of their lives. But since they'd never be able to put it down, they'd find a way to use it. To say 'see, if it weren't for the monsters, he would have lived,' and not acknowledge that they'd been the ones to pull the trigger. If you're convinced enough that you're in the right about something, lying to yourself gets easy. Don't let the fact that you're human lull you into thinking you're safe."

James had grown, if possible, even paler. "And you brought this to my town? Why?"

"I promise, I didn't do it on purpose," I said. "The full story would take a long damn time to tell."

"I think I deserve it."

"And you'll get it, *after* we decide what we're going to do." I looked to Fern and Cylia. "I don't think he saw you, or if he did, I don't think he's made you. Neither of you was with the carnival, and the population density at Lowryland kept them from getting a lock on me there."

"Plus keeping a tail on me when I don't want it there is virtually impossible, unless you have a blood sample," said Cylia. "Nice try. I'm not going anywhere."

"Neither am I," said Fern. "Teammates stick together."

"You guys . . ." I shook my head. "You could get hurt. *Really* hurt."

"Remember Smashed Potatoes, from the Concussion Stand?" asked Fern. "She left, like, half her face on the track. Her actual face. I think she had to get dental implants. We can get hurt anywhere. It's better to get hurt doing something you love, or helping someone you love, than to get hurt because the world isn't fair. You can't make us leave."

"I have a lot of knives," I said.

"That's nice," said Cylia. "You'll never hit me."

James looked between the two of them, finally cracking a small smile as he turned back to me. "You're so lucky," he said. "You have two Sallys. I can't leave here. Even if I wanted to, even if I had money or somewhere to go, I can't. I have to find a way to save her, or at the very least avenge her, and that's not going to happen if I'm running."

"He already knows who I am," said Sam amiably. "If he touches you, or comes anywhere near me, I'm gonna twist his head off and use it as a basketball."

We were all quiet for a moment.

"Too much?" asked Sam.

"The sad part is, no," I said. "That's actually really sweet. Thank you. All of you."

"Don't thank me yet," said James. "I'll stop coming around if it's not safe. Sally matters more than any of you. I'm sorry."

"It's all right," I said. "I understand."

"We all do," said Cylia. "But you need the books we

have here, and I'm assuming you can't move them to your place without your father figuring it out."

"Yeah," said James. "It's going to be hard enough spending time here without him getting suspicious."

"I could be your girlfriend," said Fern.

We all turned to stare at her. She flushed red.

"I don't mean *really*," she said. "You're the wrong species, and I'm not a pervert like Annie. Um. Sorry, Annie."

"No offense taken," I said. "I like my monkey."

"Ook," said Sam blandly.

"Humans aren't . . . you smell wrong, I'm sorry," said Fern. She was still blushing. So was James. It would have been adorable, if they hadn't both been so clearly mortified. "But I look like a human girl, and I'm pretty, I know I'm pretty, and I can pretend to be into you. Would your dad be okay with you hanging around here if he thought it was because of me?"

"I'm more flexible, attraction-wise, than Fern is, but I'm also ten years too old for you," said Cylia. "I'd take her up on the offer."

"It . . . might work," said James slowly. "My father would be ecstatic if I started seeing someone, even if it was a stranger."

"Oh, if your dad's anything like some of the carnie dads I used to know, he might be even happier to know that your first girlfriend will eventually leave town and let you try again with more practice under your belt," said Sam.

I lifted an eyebrow. He shrugged.

"Grandma never wanted me to date outside the carnival, but she was in the minority," he said. "Dating townies meant things never got serious enough to be a problem. A lot of people did it. I did not do it. I have not been concealing a string of townie girlfriends. Please don't glare at me."

"Nah, I'd just shave you while you slept." I took a

deep breath, trying to let some of my tension go. It wasn't anything like easy. "All right: so we're all staying, and we have two problems. The crossroads, and the Covenant. James, is there anything we can do to help you with the first problem?"

"How are you at taking notes?" he asked.

I grinned.

There's one of us in every class. The kid who takes notes when the teacher sneezes—or worse, who doesn't need to, who views teachers sneezing as so vitally important that it can be remembered without being written down. The one who blows the bell curve to hell and dances on the ashes.

When we started, all five of us were crammed into the library, making the air several degrees warmer and making it difficult to move between the shelves. Sam was the first to give up, after an hour of increasingly frustrated squinting at books he had no interest in reading and didn't fully understand.

"I love you," he said, kissing the crown of my head. "I'm going to go check the woods for more unwanted guests. If I find this Leo guy, I'll bring back one of his arms. Maybe with the rest of him still attached. Maybe not."

"More practical than roses," I said cheerfully as I went back to my book.

Cylia was the next to bow out, muttering something vague about another trip to the grocery store and making a casserole for when we inevitably experienced a massive blood sugar crash. Fern hesitated before running after her, not even saying good-bye, and James and I were alone.

He was a fast reader, taking notes one-handed in a crabbed shorthand that I couldn't understand. That made sense. Most of the teacher's pets I've known, myself included, have had their own way of writing things down. I take my notes in unbroken cursive, with minimal spaces between words, using Russian grammar, since leaving out unnecessary articles means having more room on the page for things that matter, and being flexible with word order means the important words can come first. It also cut way, way down on bullies and mean girls asking to see my work after they'd spent the entire class period whispering and passing notes between themselves, which cut down on my parents needing to make excuses for how those kids had "tripped" and fallen face-first into my fist.

I'd gone through three elementary schools before figuring *that* little trick out.

The books from James' mother's hidden library were as focused on the local history as the more public-facing volumes, but with a distinctly eldritch twist. The handwriting in the margins was hers, of course, adding context and commentary to already horrible situations. After reading the third account of someone using the crossroads in front of the hanging tree to summon a dead ancestor to tell them where the family fortune was hidden, I lowered the book and gave James a sidelong look.

"Is Stephen King *really* writing fiction?" I asked. "Or is he just a small-town historian who somehow got filed in the wrong part of the bookstore?"

"Every serious metaphysical scholar in Maine secretly dreams of climbing in Mr. King's kitchen window and filling his house from top to bottom with centipedes," said James idly, turning a page.

I blinked. Finally: "You're screwing with me."

"Yes." He looked up, offering me a quick, thin smile. "You catch on quickly. You should be proud of yourself."

"Dweeb," I said, and went back to my book.

"Nerd," he muttered, sounding oddly pleased.

We read in silence for a while after that, until I frowned, tapping the page with my finger. "You said you already knew how to hurt the crossroads," I said.

"Yes," said James.

"How?"

James took a deep breath. "They aren't normally subject to the physical laws of this universe. They exist . . . outside it, somehow, like they're on a different channel. When they manifest to make or seal a deal, they become temporarily subject to the same physical laws as anything else. There are spells that can rend a body apart—spells that don't require the presence of actual *flesh* to work. If the crossroads are manifest, and I pour my magic into the casting, I can hurt them. Under the right circumstances, I can even kill them. And if I cast the right binding ritual, they can't get away from me until they give me what I want."

"Sally," I said grimly.

James nodded. "Sally," he agreed. "The main problem is getting the crossroads to manifest when I'm not offering to make a bargain."

"That's the part where you'd been losing me," I said. "Why not say you're there to offer a bargain and then double-cross them?"

"The binding ritual that will hold the crossroads in our reality while I demand they give Sally back won't work if I don't cast it with the purest motivations possible. Revenge is fine. Selfishness is fine. Lying is not fine. I could still pin them down long enough to hurt them, but they might be able to turn things back on me and take me with them. I'd rather not die if I don't have to. Not unless it's the only way to bring Sally back."

"Noble, but I promise you, Sally wouldn't be amused if you died to get her out of magical mystery jail."

James gave me a sidelong look over the top of his book. "You never met her. How do you know?"

"Because while I've never met her, I've been socially isolated, and I've had socially isolated friends, and never once did any of us say 'you know what, I'd be cool if you died for me when you didn't absolutely have to.' We don't work that way. By which I mean *friends* don't work that way."

"Sally may have died for me," he said.

"Yeah, but she may not have, and either way, she didn't *mean* to. She was trying to do something good and she fucked up, which is basically the story of humanity's time on this planet—we're always trying to do something good, and we're always fucking up. I bet if she'd told you she was running off to die for your sake, you would have smacked her upside the head."

"I never hit Sally," said James stiffly.

"I wasn't implying—lighten up, okay? I know you're doing this for her, and I know that when you're trying to save someone, all kinds of self-sacrificing bullshit can seem like a great idea. Can you just breathe for a second? We're getting off the subject."

"I know, but I—" James stopped, took a deep breath, and said, "All right. My current plan is to convince the crossroads to become manifest, cast the binding ritual, demonstrate that I can harm them, and demand they return Sally. If they refuse, I harm them more, until they agree. If they are unable to return her alive, I destroy them. If they return her to me safely, I destroy them anyway. This ends."

"How are you going to destroy them? Just . . . punch them to death with your hurt-stuff spell?"

James looked at me, eyes wide. "You really *don't* have much more training than I do, do you?"

"Nope," I said cheerfully. "Answer the question."

"There's . . . another ritual. My mother was researching it when she died, and I have most of the pieces. Explaining it takes a little background." He paused. I nodded, and he continued, "Like I said before, things changed in 1490. Prior to that, the crossroads were neutral, not malicious. I'm not the first sorcerer to get the idea that the crossroads should be stopped. The trouble is, if you kill them *now*, they grow back. Like a weed.

You have to go back to the root of the problem. To 1490."

I stared at him.

"There's a record from the late 1300s, of a woman going to the crossroads—the old crossroads—with a complaint about losing her mother's locket. She asked them to rewind time for her."

"Um, okay, that's where we're stopping, because if you're talking about rewinding the entire world to 1490 so you can screw the crossroads, I'm going to have to give this plan a hard pass. I like the Internet, and indoor plumbing, and having ever been born. I refuse to Butterfly Effect my way through history."

James rolled his eyes. "Bradbury was exaggerating a simple scientific idea for the sake of drama. We wouldn't actually become strange dinosaur creatures if we crushed a moth."

"Okay, one, we don't have time for me to start in on you downplaying the brilliance of Bradbury, so I'm going to pretend you didn't say that, and two, maybe humanity wouldn't be replaced by something else, but that doesn't mean we'd still be here. Even if we ignore the sheer improbability of any specific sperm and egg combination managing to happen—if we go full multiverse and say that yes, your parents, if they existed, would absolutely have conceived you, James Smith, no question, no chance of you being replaced by somebody else—getting to your parents requires a chain of coincidences and accidents of timing that's about a million miles long. Every living being on this planet is a winning lottery ticket of genetic circumstance, and I'm not interested in having my ticket recalled. Not even for the sake of an innocent girl, since we'd be erasing her, too."

"That's all well and good, and I appreciate your pragmatic approach to survival, but I'm not proposing rewinding reality to the fifteenth century."

"You just said—"

James sighed. "The woman whose bargain ran time

backward didn't *actually* run time backward. The crossroads moved themselves earlier in time, and they carried her with them. She was able to go to the farm, watch where her earlier self put the locket away for safekeeping, and retrieve it. While she was in the past, no one could see her. No one could touch her."

"Okay . . ."

"I have the exact wording of her bargain. I can command the crossroads to rewind me, and just me, once they're manifest, and then—"

It was my turn to cut him off. "Wow, okay, no." I pinched the bridge of my nose. "Now I know you didn't have a sufficient assortment of nerd friends when you were a kid, because you're not thinking like an asshole. Ever heard the phrase 'literal genie'? It means giving someone exactly what they ask for, instead of what they wanted. The 'make me a sandwich' gag."

James frowned. "What do you mean?"

"I mean unless you have a secret squad of lawyers in your hall closet to double- and triple-check the wording of your wish, you're *really* unlikely to wind up when and where you want to be, even if you're using the original bargain. It's best to assume that any plan that depends on time travel to make it work is not *going* to work." I paused. "But it's possible a variation might. You're talking about getting the crossroads to manifest in *this* reality, instead of the reality where they spend most of their time. But there's a third reality in play. The place where the crossroads ghosts take you when you want to finalize a deal. It exists outside of time."

"Really?" His gaze sharpened. "How can you be sure?"

"Because I was drowning when my Aunt Mary took me there, and I stayed there a lot longer than I should have been able to without finishing the job." I shook my head. "If we can get *there*, it's possible something could be done that would disrupt the connection between the changes and the crossroads themselves."

"I told you, I have a plan."

"A plan, and a spell only you can currently cast. Can the plan also involve a lot of C-4? Because if it can't involve a lot of C-4, it might be time to rethink things."

James looked at me, eyes glittering with irritation. "I promise I won't attempt to destroy the entity that has done unspeakable damage to our world without running my plans by you. Now, what have you found?"

"What makes you think I've found anything?"

"You've been hugging that book since I started talking."

"Right." I relaxed my grip. "There's a way to call an audit. If you have a crossroads bargain in your past, and you feel like it wasn't upheld, you can call a crossroads ghost and demand they take you to the crossroads themselves for an audit. I could do it, except for the part where I'm not dead, which means they've kept their side of the bargain so far."

"Ah."

"You could do it."

James stared at me.

"You said Sally's note said she was going to the crossroads to get you out of this town. You said she wanted you to be free. Well, you're still here. They took her away, and whatever they left in her place wasn't enough to get you what she wanted you to have. I'd say that's plenty of cause for an audit, wouldn't you?" I offered him the book. "Read it. Tell me if you think it'll work. If it will, we start figuring out what comes next, and we go for it."

"I . . . okay. I'll read it," said James, taking the book.

I nodded, and stood. "You do that. I'm going to go check on Sam."

James didn't say anything as I walked out of the room.

The house was quiet. Everyone else was off doing whatever they found more enjoyable than sitting in a room with a grumpy semi-stranger and reading. I felt more awake than I had in weeks. I had a problem to solve; I had books to use while I was solving it; and most of all, I had a grumpy semi-stranger. Someone to study with and snipe at was basically my idea of a day at the spa.

Studying had always been the place where my brother Alex and I came closest together, no matter how far apart our interests were. We could sit side by side and argue about things that didn't mean a thing to anyone else, and when we were done, it always felt like we were . . . friends. Like we had found something beyond siblings to be for one another.

As I descended the stairs, I realized I missed him. Really missed him, in a small but painful way. I wanted my big brother. He would have loved this, like a word problem that didn't use math for its solution, but some bizarre combination of philosophy, economics, and applied backstabbing.

When this was all over, I was going to ask him to come over and spend a day learning about something stupid, just to have an excuse to sit next to him with one of Grandpa's journals in my hands and nothing pressing on my schedule.

I was still thinking about how nice that would be—some old books, a few free hours, my brother, and me—when I stepped out the front door onto the porch and froze. Bethany, still in her letter jacket and spirit bows, now matched with blue jeans and a red crop top, leaned against the rail and smiled at me through lips lacquered red as a poisoned candy apple.

"What's shaking, Annie?" she chirped. "What's the news, what's the haps, what's the status of you winding that boy around your finger? Because I gotta tell you, management isn't happy with how fast you're working. And when management isn't happy, *nobody* gets to be happy."

Crap.

Eleven

"Family doesn't always make things better.
Sometimes family only makes it worse."
                                    –Mary Dunlavy

*On the front porch, wishing it were easier to hit
a ghost*

"IT'S BEEN LESS THAN a day," I said stiffly, drawing
myself up to my full height. At least I was taller
than she was. Ghost or not, she looked like she'd been
human before she died, and humans are still primates.
We like to be tall. "No one gives away all their secrets in
less than a day. Tell your 'management' that I'm a sorcerer, not a miracle worker. I'm not even really a sorcerer right now, since they've got all my magic."

"You gave it to them," said Bethany. "They might not
be so cranky if you hadn't spent the morning having coffee with your boyfriend."

"Sam wasn't anywhere ne—ew." I wrinkled my nose,
my disgust causing me to briefly forget the threat Bethany represented. "That's vile. Go tell your bosses that
they have filthy minds, and I'm not my sister. I don't date
Covenant men. The genocide never scrubs off of them."

"Please. Anyone with eyes could see the way he was
looking at you. Plus he's human, so that's got to be attractive, right? No one with options goes for the guy in
the gorilla suit."

"You know, I've always wondered what it would be

like to punch a ghost in the throat," I said, through gritted teeth.

"A lot like punching a cloud," said Bethany. "I don't recommend it. I'm not some stupid hitchhiker who can be frightened with threats of violence. I serve the crossroads, and in case you've managed to forget, they own you. A little civility is in your best interests."

"This *is* a little civility," I said. "More importantly, this is the best you're going to get unless you give Mary back to me. He's here, we're making nice, it's been less than a day. You want his secrets, you have to give me time."

"The more time you have, the more time he has. The more time he has, the more likely it becomes that he's going to do something you're going to regret." Bethany smiled, ignoring my dig about Mary. "Unless you want to find out what happens when you don't give the crossroads what you promised them? Because I don't think you're going to enjoy it very much."

"If your bosses only wanted me to kill him, I wouldn't need any time at all. Knives don't have a waiting period. They want me to be his friend. They want me to know what he knows. People like James don't trust quickly, no matter how tempting it is. I need to go slowly, or I'm going to lose him, and then you're never going to know what he knows, or where he learned it." Not for the first time, I was incredibly grateful that telepaths were rare—and that I'd never, so far as I knew, encountered a ghost who could read minds. If cuckoos leave ghosts, they don't do it often. And thank fuck for that.

"I'll tell them you're not finished. They won't be happy."

"Seems like right now, that's more of a problem for you than it is for me." I looked at her as calmly as I could. "Where's Mary?"

"Mary Dunlavy. You people just cannot let the idea of her go, can you?" Bethany shook her head. "She didn't do her job the way she was asked to. Do you have any idea how long our bosses have been waiting for her to bring one of you people to them? She found her loophole and she exploited it until it closed around her like the noose it was. She's none of your concern."

"She's my aunt."

Bethany's nose wrinkled. "Aunts aren't anything, not even when they're blood. They're people who pretend to be family because they have a relative in common somewhere way back on your father's side, and they never make things better. You should be happy to be rid of her."

"And yet I'm not. Tell the crossroads that. Tell them I'd be working faster if I weren't so worried about her."

"They gave her the kind of leeway they did because she brought them Tommy Price and Bobby Cross, and those two were enough to feed a whole lot of bargains. But leeway doesn't last forever, and Mary-Mary, quite contrary, hasn't been pulling her weight for a long time. You need to forget about her."

Distantly, I realized James and I had the same goal now: we were both tilting at the crossroads like they were our own personal windmill, hoping it would be enough to bring back someone we had never intended to lose. For James, it was the living. For me, it was the dead.

"I don't think that's going to happen any time soon," I said. "You can go."

"Why is your house warded against ghosts?" She tried to make the question sound casual, but it had teeth, and I knew they were poised to crash down and rip me open.

Fortunately, I had an answer. "My family is pretty haunted," I said. "Mary is usually good about keeping Aunt Rose in check, but she's gone, and I don't want to risk waking up to find a ghost sitting at the end of the bed and critiquing my underpants. It's happened before. Forgive me for taking steps to make sure it doesn't happen again."

There was a flash of something dark and unhappy in Bethany's eyes when I mentioned Rose. "How many dead aunts do you *have*?"

"It's amazing how often I hear that question." I

crossed my arms. "Go away, Bethany. You have all the information I can give you, and the more time I spend out here trying to convince you I'm not hiding anything, the less time I'm spending with James. If your bosses want constant eyes on me, they can give Mary back. I'll let her follow me to the bathroom if that's what it takes. You, on the other hand, I don't know and I don't trust and I don't want inside my house."

Bethany looked down the length of her nose at me. "You're going to regret that. You're going to regret that more than you can possibly understand."

"I'm willing to take the risk."

She scoffed and disappeared, not even making the faint sound of air being displaced. She had never been fully solid. That was, oddly, encouraging.

Most ghosts have rules that govern how much time they can spend among the living, and how well they can "pass" while they're here. For example, Aunt Rose is a hitchhiking ghost. As long as she has a coat on, she's functionally alive. She eats, she breathes, she drinks all the soda in the house—when we know she's coming for a visit, Mom buys this really gross old-fashioned celery soda that tastes like bad decisions and fad diets, which Rose pours over vanilla ice cream like that's somehow reasonable. Her coats wear off at sunrise, but she can always put on another one. If not for the inevitable need to go back to the road, she could masquerade as one of the living for years.

Mary—and presumably Bethany—is more of a fringe case. Her job with the crossroads requires her to be able to move among the living without attracting attention or seeming out of place. So she doesn't need a coat, and she doesn't turn transparent at sunrise, and she doesn't instinctively change into the clothes she was wearing when she died every time someone startles her. She has to spend a certain amount of time at the crossroads for every hour she spends with the living, but she's never been willing to disclose the exact ratio.

Bethany could follow me through town if she wanted to. She could sit at the next table over in Burial Grounds, sipping coffee she didn't need and watching every move I made. Suddenly, the ghost wards on the house didn't feel petty or small. They felt essential. This was how I took care of my small, weird, found family.

Shoving my hands into my pockets and trying to shake off the lingering unease of Bethany's visit, I tromped down the porch stairs and started across the yard, scanning the trees as I went. There was a lot of forest, and a lot of vertical space for a fūri to occupy. Make it a logic puzzle, then. Which way would Sam go?

Not toward town. Town meant people, and people meant needing to seem human when he really didn't want to. Not toward James' house, either, not with Chief Smith lurking around the woods. It seemed unlikely for the local chief of police to try to sneak up on us, but stranger things have happened. That left deeper into the woods, or through the narrower patch to the lake. After a moment's indecision, I turned lakeward and started walking.

Tracking something—or someone—arboreal means relying on a whole different set of contextual clues. There weren't going to be many, or any, broken branches at ground level; everything was going to be happening overhead. Unfortunately, I have a healthy respect for gravity, which meant climbing every tree I passed was out of the question, and I couldn't walk with my head bent all the way back unless I wanted to hook my foot on a root and eat ground.

(Verity would have had no such problems. Verity would have taken this as an excuse to play me Tarzan, you lucky, and gone swinging through the woods after him. Verity is human, unlike Sam, and her constant striving toward high places is one more predictor of her inevitable plunge into an early grave.)

In the end, I settled for splitting my attention, scanning the ground for anything out of place—freshly

broken branches, excessively bright, new-fallen leaves—
and looking up to trace them to the place where they'd
started. Sam was fast and strong enough to leave a lot
of distance between traces, but he wasn't the most subtle
person I'd ever tried to follow. Less than ten yards in,
I was confident of his direction. After twenty, I was
moving fast, not pausing or looking back.

My own steps were lighter, placed so as to cause minimal disturbance to the brush. It was unlikely that anyone would have been able to follow me as I was following
Sam. That was a combination of healthy paranoia and
early training coming to the fore: my parents taught me
often and mercilessly that a predator who couldn't find
you is a predator that can't kill you. Since I didn't much
care for the idea of being caught unawares, I did my best
not to leave any trail for potential hunters to follow.

The trees thinned. The broken branches stopped, and
there was a mighty disturbance of the leaves, showing me
where Sam had jumped down. I kept walking. The great
blank disk of the lake loomed up in front of me, gleaming
gunmetal gray in the sunlight. The boat house was visible
to the left, decrepit but holding. It was a horror movie
accessory turned house fixture, and the trail of scuffed
leaves and broken branches led me straight there.

There was a small dock around the side, around fifteen feet in length. It would have been a good place to
tie a boat, if we'd had access to one. As things stood, it
was a good place for Sam to sit, chucking rocks moodily
out across the water, his back to the woods.

I walked over and plopped down next to him, grabbing one of the rocks from his pile and sending it skip-
ping merrily on its way. "Are you trying to give a fish a
concussion?"

"Jesus, Annie!" He flinched away, staring at me.
"Learn how to make noise when you walk, would you?"

"Now, where would be the fun in that?" I sobered.
"You should be more careful, though. If I can sneak up
on you, so can Leonard."

"Leonard. Right." He grabbed another rock and threw it hard at the surface of the water. It didn't skip so much as it tore in a straight line across the lake until momentum gave out and it sank. "Leonard from the Covenant, who's totally obsessed with you and going to kill the rest of us so he can take you home to mama."

"Not me: my family name. He wants to be the one who brings the Prices back to the Covenant, and he doesn't care much about my thoughts on the matter." I bumped my shoulder against Sam's. "As long as we're careful and he's alone, we can take him. Which is good, because we're going to have to do it sooner or later. He can find me. No matter where I go, he can find me."

"Right. Tracking spells."

"Yeah." Maybe there was something about scrambling them in the books James' mother had left behind. I'd have to get my magic back before I could attempt to perform even the simplest ritual, but once I had . . .

A witch is no match for a sorcerer, and so far as I'm aware, witches are all the Covenant has left. If this worked, I could go home. The thought was intoxicating. I could see my parents. Update the mice. Introduce Artie and Sam. I could play roller derby again. It was a wonderful dream. It was worth fighting for.

"That's why you ran away from the carnival in the first place, right? Because they might have tracking spells, and they might find you, and people might get hurt. And that was a good enough reason for you to leave." Sam picked up another rock, weighing it in his hand as he stared off at the horizon.

I sighed, shoulders slumping. "Sam," I said, in a small voice, "if you're pissed at me for some reason, will you say so, so I can start apologizing and we can get whatever this is over with? Please? I came to check on you because I wanted to see you, not because I wanted to get yelled at over something stupid."

"I'm just wondering how long it'll be before you go off with Leonard to 'save' the rest of us. It'd be easier. Sure, he's a genocidal maniac who'd probably skin me as soon as look at me, but at least he's human. Or there's James. You could stay here with him and play small-town witch, and not have to deal with any of this bullshit."

I started to reply. Then I stopped, forcing myself to count to ten.

There were a lot of ways this conversation could go. I could see several of them unfolding, like a terrible Choose Your Own Adventure. There was the version where I let my frustration boil over and started yelling, and we had the kind of fight that we maybe didn't recover from. There was the version where I listened to what he was saying without thinking about why he was saying it, and got hurt, and walked away, turning some of his fears true.

Both of them were versions that would absolutely have won out, once. I was the baby of my family, the one who'd never had any expectations set upon her shoulders, the one who'd been allowed to keep the family babysitter long past the point where it was necessary. I'd been a little mean and a little judgmental and, weirdly, a little sheltered, which is something that can be difficult to accomplish when my parents insisted on dragging me into the woods to meet every damn thing that came along. It had been *easy* to focus inward since the world was big and didn't seem to want me.

Sam had grown up in a community that was larger and smaller than mine at the same time, surrounded by people who loved and accepted him, but who never let him forget he wasn't human, that he could never leave. College had never been on the table for him: he couldn't sleep and stay in human form. Without a degree, most jobs wouldn't even look at him twice. He'd been born into the carnival. He'd expected to stay there forever, no exit, no escape.

And then he'd met me, and I'd been the first girl who *wasn't* from his community who didn't seem to care that he wasn't human, or that he was a rude asshole when he was anxious, which was most of the time when there were strangers around. I'd also been the first girl to kiss him without demanding he turn human first, like the side of him that came more naturally was somehow inappropriate or obscene.

Cryptids like Fern and Cylia move through the world looking like members of the currently dominant species, and if they decided to hook up with a human, no one would bat an eye. But Sam . . . he would always be a little fuzzy, and I suspected, would always be a little insecure about it. He'd been raised by humans, indoctrinated by human stories and human media, and if we weren't exactly a retelling of *Beauty and the Beast*, it was only because we could both be pretty beastly when we wanted to.

"Hey." I touched his shoulder. He didn't turn. "*Hey*."

"What?" Sam finally looked at me, eyes wary. "Are you going to argue with me? Because I don't think—"

I leaned over and kissed him.

Sam stiffened, clearly not sure what he was supposed to do. He'd been expecting a fight, not . . . this. In the end, hormones won out. His hands slid around my waist, pulling me closer, as his tail snaked up to tangle in my hair. I scooted over accommodatingly, letting him pull me as close as he wanted, offering no resistance.

Kissing Sam is basically the same as kissing a human. There are some subtle differences in his bone structure, and his sideburns are fur, not hair, making them dense and soft against my fingers, but apart from that, he has lips, he has a nose, he has a face that's close enough to human that when I close my eyes, I can easily pretend. So I didn't close my eyes. I kept them open, watching as I kissed him. Watching the tension in his brow, and the way the skin around his own eyes crinkled, still tight.

I pulled back, stroking his temple with one hand. "Hey," I said. "No. Okay? Don't go there. There's nothing good, and you don't need to waste your time."

"Really?" He opened his eyes, looking at me solemnly. "Because it sure feels like I need to book a ticket."

"Really," I said, still stroking his temple. "I'm not saying we're going to be together forever, okay? You need to meet my family. You need to figure out what you signed up for when you took me on that Ferris wheel. But I'm not running away with the first human guy who glances in my direction. After you, human guys would seem boring. But maybe more importantly . . . you know, we talked about your dating history—"

"Such as it is," he muttered.

"—but we never really talked about mine. You know I wasn't a virgin when we got together. That wasn't because I'd been in capital-L love before. It was because I fucking hate unicorns and didn't want to be somebody's sacrifice of the week. Even though 'virgin sacrifice' means 'sacrifice whose blood has not been used in a ritual before,' and not 'never gotten laid,' linguistic drift happens and people get confused and I'm babbling again." I took my hand away from his face. "I didn't date before you came along and fucked up my life of voluntary celibacy, okay? I was *happy* not dating. Relationships are a lot of work. They're complicated and confusing, and they never seemed worth it before you. You made this worth the work. Do you get what a big thing that is for me? I love you. Capital-L love, stupid squishy let's write a musical about it love. I've never been able to say that before. I don't fall fast, and I don't fall easy, and I'm not going to run after the first human guy who bats his eyes at me. Okay?"

"I'm trying to believe that," said Sam reluctantly. "I know . . . I know I'm being sort of stupid, and I know you're not going to dump me for some guy just because he has the ability to wax his chest and have it stick. But this is all new to me, too."

"I know," I said, and kissed him again. "It's okay. It's *okay*. I'm in this for the long haul. You and me against the world, right?"

"The world won't know what hit it," said Sam, before kissing me in earnest. I leaned against him, enjoying a moment where nothing was wrong, and nothing needed me to fix it, and I was just a girl with her guy, sitting on the dock while the sun shone.

"That is *disgusting*," said a familiar, British-accented voice. "Genuinely vile. Bestiality, Annie? Really? I knew you were dallying with filth, but this . . ."

I shoved away from Sam, hands going for the knives in my shirt. His tail was in the way, keeping me from getting to my weapons.

"Sam! Let go!" I shouted.

Leonard Cunningham was on the bank not fifteen feet away, a crossbow in his hands and a sneer on his face. He looked as revolted as he sounded.

Sam unwrapped his tail from around my wrist as Leonard raised the crossbow and prepared to fire. There wasn't time to throw a knife, and even if there had been, I knew the consequences of me killing Leonard—heir apparent to the entire damn Covenant—would be much more extreme than the consequences of him killing either one of us. I could kick off a whole damn war. So I took a guess as to which of us he was about to shoot, and I shoved Sam off the dock as hard as I could.

The last thing I saw before Sam hit the water was his face, eyes wide, bafflement giving way to horrified understanding.

A sharp snapping sound and an accompanying pain pulled my attention back to Leo. I looked down. The crossbow bolt was sticking out of my left shoulder, just above the collarbone.

"Thought you weren't going to start attacking me when you still thought you could recruit me," I said, words made thin by shock.

"I was aiming for the *monster*," he spat.

"Oh. Cool. Because so am I." I smiled wanly and allowed myself to topple to the side, following Sam into the icy waters of the lake.

Twelve

"Nothing—*nothing*—is more important than
making it home alive."

—Evelyn Baker

*In a lake, injured, sinking, because that's a great way
to spend an afternoon*

THE WATER WAS COLD.

That doesn't quite cover it. The water was *fucking* cold, the kind of cold that makes a girl think a supernova might be a good time. If there had been any question whatsoever of whether the crossroads had my magic, the plunge would have answered it once and for all, because there was no way I could have stopped myself from involuntarily setting the lake boiling.

The crossbow bolt was still in my shoulder. A numb ache spread out from the wound, one that had nothing to do with cold, and everything to do with whatever tranquilizing agent Leo had spread along the shaft. I wasn't willing to consider the thought that it might have been poison. If it was poison, I was going to drown. Simple as that.

Well, no. Not simple as that. If I died here, there wouldn't be anyone to stand between my friends and the Covenant, or to keep James from letting his hunger for revenge—however justified—lead him into a dead-end attack on a force so much bigger and older than he was that he'd wind up wishing for something as easy as a crossroads bargain. I fumbled for the bolt, hoping I could either pull it out or shove it through.

The water was dark and murky, and the amount of blood I was already losing, even with the bolt to slow it down, didn't help. There was no telling how much bacteria and pollution was getting into the wound. If not for the spreading sleepiness, I would have left it where it was, one more thing to be dealt with later. Unfortunately, my air was running out, and if I wanted to be able to swim to safety, I needed both full range of motion in my arm, and not to pass out from some novel Covenant toxin.

I was still struggling with the bolt when something hit me from the side, shoving me away from the dock, out toward the middle of the lake. I didn't pause to think or assess the situation. I just reacted, producing a knife from inside my shirt and stabbing wildly into the dark.

For a moment, the thing that was pushing me along fell back, grip faltering. Then it surged back, pushing me onward. I tried to stab again, to no avail. The cold and the numbness and the lack of air were getting to me, and the knife slipped from my fingers, to be lost forever among whatever forgotten things covered the lakebed.

I thrashed without breaking free. Another hot gush of blood escaped my shoulder. This was it, then; after everything, this was the way I died. Powerless and pinned and bleeding out from a Covenant crossbow in the middle of a lake in Maine. Would my friends get away? Cylia would. She might not be able to save the others, but her luck was good enough, and she was good enough at using it, that I had faith she would escape. She might even get Fern to safety.

Cylia knew where to find Elsie. Once she had Elsie, she could find the rest of my family. She could tell them what had happened. She could tell them not to go to war over me. She was no Aeslin mouse—God, I missed my mice—but she could still be my black box, and tell them everything that had happened.

I hoped she'd tell them I had finally managed to fall in love and mean it.

The lake was so cold. The water was so dark. I closed my eyes, breathing out, and let the water have me.

What came next came in flashes, separate and distinct, like pieces of a dissolving dream

Sam, staggering out of the lake in human form, his clothes waterlogged and clinging to us both, me cradled in his arms like something out of *The Creature from the Black Lagoon*. I didn't wake up, exactly, but I came close enough to consciousness to glimpse the light slanting through the branches overhead, to feel my frozen clothes sticking to my skin.

Everything hurt. I didn't like it. I slipped away again.

Flash: The ground beneath me, crackling with leaves, sharp with stones, cold, but not as cold as the rest of me. Sam was hitting me on the back, solid smacks between my shoulders, like he was trying to play some kind of drum. I coughed and water flowed over my lips, wet and warm and terrible. It had been part of me and now it wasn't anymore. I felt, paradoxically, like I had lost something. I sank back down to think about it, even though there was no thinking on the other side of wakefulness.

Flash: Sam, no longer human, his hands larger and his skin warmer as he held me against him, his breath coming in short, panicked gasps. His voice was a distant echo, distorted and far away. "Annie? Hey, Annie? Can you hear me? Can you open your eyes, or say something, or do *anything* if you can hear me?"

I could not. I returned to the dark, where the lake was waiting, ready and eager to pull me under. The water was no longer cold, or even really water; it was the light and floating nothingness that had met me at the crossroads when I went to make my bargain. It was a space outside of space, where nothing could hurt me ever again. If I opened my eyes, I was sure I could find Mary, and that she'd be happy to show me where I needed to go. She was waiting for me. I just had to go to her.

But I couldn't see her, and when I did open my eyes, just a little, it was on another flash of the real world: Sam, running through the wood, every step jarring the crossbow bolt in my shoulder, sending waves of pain and nausea crashing through my entire body. It was too much. I closed my eyes again, and the next time I opened them, I was on the couch in the living room, Cylia bending over me, James and Sam hovering, equally useless, nearby.

"I need to get this out so I can clean the wound, and I don't want her bleeding to death," said Cylia. "James, get over here."

I wasn't fully present, but I was close enough to realize what was about to happen, and struggle to dive back into the dark. No such luck: Cylia said something rendered incomprehensible by my own dizziness and the increasing pounding in my ears.

I still have enough of a heartbeat for it to pound, I thought, feeling strangely proud of myself. I stopped fighting, exhausted from this revelation. Cold spread through my shoulder, even deeper and more intense than the cold of the lake. It was like someone had wrapped just that corner of my body in a sheet of ice.

"Hey. Be careful. She needs that arm."

"I *am* being careful."

"She's a cryptozoologist, not a side of beef."

I recognized Sam's voice. That was nice. It was nice that he was here. It was nice that he'd been able to make it out of the lake. I didn't know how he'd done that, not with the thing that had been in the water, that had taken me—unless he *was* the thing. Maybe that wasn't a big revelation, but at the moment, groggy from blood loss and cold and shock, it seemed like a twist worthy of the original *Twilight Zone*. Up was down, left was right, and Sam was the monster in the lake.

Any further revelations would have to wait. The cold stopped spreading, and before it could recede, it was replaced by a pain so intense that I snapped all the way to wakefulness, already screaming.

"Hi," said Cylia amiably, and held up the crossbow bolt she had just removed from my shoulder. "Welcome back and don't move, I still need to get you patched up. James slowed down the blood in your shoulder enough that you're only leaking instead of gushing, but that's still not great."

"Annie?" Sam sounded worried. For the first time, I realized the pillow beneath my head was too warm and too firm to be anything but his leg. "Are you okay?"

"Never ask someone who's just been shot if they're okay." I closed my eyes, hissing through my teeth as Cylia began methodically cleaning my wound. "But I'm alive."

"Thank fuck." He smoothed back my hair with one large hand. His fingers were shaking, the motion traveling across my skin like a subsonic vibration. "I thought . . . fuck. You know what I thought."

"Sorry. You don't get rid of me that easily."

There was a knock at the door. I opened my eyes, staring up at the ceiling.

"I don't suppose Fern took the car and went to the store," I asked carefully.

"No," said Cylia. "She's upstairs, where she can keep a watch on the whole yard and shout if somebody comes walking across the yard with a crossbow."

"Swell."

Whoever was outside knocked again.

Would Leo be knocking? Assuming he knew where the house was—and realistically, he had to know where the house was; there simply couldn't be that many visiting strangers in a town this size—would he come in through the front door, knowing we'd all be pissed off and waiting for him, or would he go around the back and approach us like the low-down dirty snake he was? If not him, then who?

Fern hadn't yelled. If it were Leonard, wouldn't she have yelled to warn us that he was coming? She didn't know what he looked like, but the crossbow was probably a big giveaway on the "bad intentions" scale.

"James, are your hands bloody?" I struggled to sit up. Sam pushed me gently down.

"No," he said. "Not yet. Please stay put so I don't have to make you."

"Kinky," said Cylia, with forced cheer, and kept patching my shoulder.

"There's no blood on me," said James. "It froze and fell off. Why?"

I closed my eyes again. There was nothing on the ceiling for me to see. "Go answer the door. It's either Leo, who shouldn't shoot you when he doesn't know you, or it's your father, and you can tell him you're here to visit your new tourist honeybunch. Buy us time. That's what we need right now."

"Couldn't we just, I don't know, *not* answer the door?" asked Sam. "Is that an option?"

"Not with Leo. Not with James' father. A controlled confrontation is better than a break-in." James' father probably had a key. Dammit.

I needed time. Time and stitches and about a gallon and a half of antiseptic poured into the open wound where my flesh had been violated, rinsing away the risk of infection, leaving the hole behind. There was going to be a scar. Would it be enough to limit my range of motion, to leave me less than I had been before? I didn't know. At the moment, I didn't much care, because regardless of whether or not there was permanent damage, I was going to skin Leonard alive as soon as I had the chance.

"I . . ." James stopped. "Of course. Sam?"

"Just shout and I'll be there." Sam's voice was low,

angry. Out of all of us, he might have been the only one actually hoping it *would* be Leonard, because then he could take the man apart.

It was an oddly comforting thought.

James' steps receded as he left the parlor for the front room and hence the door. I heard it open, the sound faint and distant, followed by voices raised in quizzical confusion. The door shut. James came walking back, faster.

"Uh, Cylia?" he said. "I know Annie's hurt and everything, but I think it might be a good idea for her to come to the door."

"Not until I say she's okay to move," said Cylia.

"Okay, I understand that, but there's a dead woman on the porch who says she wants to talk to her, and I don't think taking down the wards would be a good idea right now."

My eyes snapped open. This time, when I tried to sit up, Sam didn't stop me. I turned to stare at James, who was standing, flushed and flustered, in the parlor doorway.

"What did you say?"

"There's a dead woman on the porch."

Hope bloomed in my chest, hot and bright and unbearable. "What does she look like?"

James blinked. Apparently, of the available questions, that was one he hadn't been expecting me to ask. "Um. I don't know. Late teens maybe, brown hair, blue jeans? She looks dead. I can see through her."

My hope crashed, replaced by realization. "Okay. I know who that is. Cylia, you need to let me up now."

"I really don't," she said.

"You really do, unless you want my entire family descending on New Gravesend to look for my corpse," I said. "We believe in redundancies. We travel with talking mice who never forget anything so there will be a record of what happened if one of us dies, and we adopted a natural psychopomp years ago so we never have to worry about getting trapped in some asshole's spirit jar if we die in the wrong place. She must have felt it when I blacked out. She's here to carry me to the afterlife. Only I'm behind anti-ghost wards, so she can't tell whether I'm living or dead. Which means she's going to get worried, and then she's going to get angry, and then she's going to call my mom."

Everyone, even Sam, blinked at me. Finally, Sam said, "Even for you, that's weird."

"I know." I stood. The room spun. That was the blood loss making itself known. Wincing, I muttered, "I need to eat about a pound of raw hamburger and take a bunch of iron pills. Don't let me forget."

"Spinach salad for dinner," said Cylia.

"Swell."

Even with Sam holding me up, walking to the front door was harder than it conceivably should have been. Every step was heavy, and my head kept spinning, making the room bob and weave in an impossible arc. I felt like I'd just donated blood, only a hundred times worse, and with no orange juice or cookies to lighten the blow.

"I want orange juice," I muttered, and opened the door.

Rose, her hand raised for another knock, stared at me. "Annie?"

"Hey, Aunt Rose." A wave of weariness washed over me. I leaned back, trusting Sam to catch me. He did, uncharacteristically human hands wrapping around my shoulders—careful of the wound—and holding me up. "Got a call on the 'somebody's dying' phone, huh?"

"I've learned to ignore it when you people get minor injuries, but this one didn't feel minor, and right as it was getting really bad, it cut off."

"That was Sam here carrying me through the wards. They're set up to repel ghosts. They must have blocked the signal."

"Fun with unintended consequences, I guess." Rose

aimed a broad, exaggerated wink at Sam. "Hey, hand-some. Still the boyfriend, I see."

"Still the dead lady," said Sam. "Hi, Rose."

Aunt Rose, better known as Rose Marshall, better known as the Girl in the Green Silk Gown, smirked at him. She was wearing what I always thought of as her traveling clothes, blue jeans and sneakers and a white T-shirt with a faded truck stop logo on the front, the letters worn down to ghosts of themselves, so it was impossible to guess whether she was advertising something near or far away or nonexistent. Her hair was cropped short, almost a pixie cut, and swept carelessly away from her eyes. Like Mary, Rose had been in her teens when she died. She still was. Let the stars burn out and the sun explode, and she'd still be sixteen years old. Some things about being a ghost are lousier than others.

Smirk fading, Rose swung around to face me. "I'm guessing by the bloodstains on the boyfriend's shirt that he's the reason you're still among the living. What the hell happened? And why am I the first one here? Mary should be clawing these wards down to get to you."

"She's gone."

Rose blinked. "What?"

"The crossroads took her because they thought she might be more on my side than theirs." Saying it out loud made it feel terribly real—and more, terribly like my fault. If I hadn't made that bargain . . .

If I hadn't made that bargain, Sam and I would both be dead. I'd take guilty over the grave any day. "They sent a replacement, though, which is why we have the wards up. I don't really need a strange crossroads ghost telling me how to manage my business."

Rose frowned. "Does the replacement have a name?"

"Bethany?"

"Of course." She put a hand over her eyes. "Of course it's Bethany. Of course they'd try to use family to fuck family."

I blinked. "Aunt Rose?"

"Bethany isn't your family. She's mine." She lowered her hand, looking at me bleakly. "She's my brother's granddaughter. She tried to . . . well, never mind what she tried to do. She got punished for it, she died, and now she works for the crossroads. She's not a bad kid, but she isn't going to fight the crossroads for the sake of a woman she doesn't know. Especially not if she realizes you know me."

"That's fun," I said, voice flat.

"That's life."

"Excuse me." I turned. James had stepped forward. "Could I get an introduction? Since it seems this is a friend of yours?"

"Right, sorry. James Smith, meet Rose Marshall. Aunt Rose, meet James. Aunt Rose is a hitchhiking ghost. James is a sorcerer. Play nicely with each other, or I'll knock your heads together."

"Hey," said Rose, with a small wave. "Nice to meet you."

"Likewise," said James.

"Now that we've got that out of the way . . ." Rose looked back to me. "I understand, completely, why you're not going to lower these wards. Don't. But do you mind telling me why you almost died, and why I shouldn't be heading for your parents *right now* to tattle on you?"

"Covenant fucker shot her in the shoulder," said Sam.

Rose raised an eyebrow. "Oh, is that all?"

"He shot me in the shoulder with a crossbow bolt that had been coated in some sort of tranquilizer, so I promptly passed out, fell into the lake, and nearly drowned," I said.

"Him shooting you next to the lake was a stroke of luck," said Cylia. "The water was cold enough to slow the bleeding, and it rinsed away most of the tranquilizer. Really, this could have been much worse."

My stomach clenched. I hadn't considered how much

luck had been involved in my survival—or how much of
that might have been Cylia's doing. "Are we . . . ?"

"I like how much faith you have in me, but you have
your own luck," Cylia said. "I'm not keeping things
sunny enough to prevent you getting *shot*. That's the sort
of long-term violation of the laws of nature that winds up
ending when the one doing the bending has a stroke or
gets broadsided by a semi. You got lucky because you got
lucky. Don't count on it happening in the future."

James looked like he needed a footnote on what the
hell that meant. I mouthed "later" at him and returned
my attention to Rose.

"You probably can't stay here without attracting the
attention of the crossroads, which wouldn't be a great
thing right now," I said. "Plus we can't let you in, and we
don't have any coats you can borrow."

Rose waved a hand, dismissing my concerns. "I wasn't
planning to stick around anyway. Maine? Not my scene.
We're near enough to the terminus of the Ocean Lady
that I'll just get someone to drive me to Calais so I can
head down south to visit the routewitches."

"This would be a very enlightening conversation if I
understood half of it," said James.

"Later," I repeated, this time audibly. "Aunt Rose,
are the crossroads going to . . . have they *done* something to Mary? Is she all right?"

"I don't know, kiddo," she said. "I wish I did. One of
the first rules of getting by in the twilight is stay the fuck
away from the crossroads. They don't do favors. They
try to act like they do, but—really—they're all about
taking care of themselves. Maybe she's fine. Maybe they
have her in some kind of spirit jar, or, hell, maybe
they've sent her to broker deals in Puerto Rico while
Bethany chews your ass. They might have done that simply because they know it'll hurt her to be unable to help
you when you're suffering. Or maybe they've cut her off
entirely, and she's . . ." Rose paused, mouth twisting.

"Ghosts can't die. We're already dead. But we all have things we have to do if we want to stay anchored in the afterlife. I don't hitchhike because I want to. I do it because if I don't do it, the twilight doesn't know what to do with me, and I start to fade in and out of the world. It's possible they've severed her from her job. You need to be prepared for that."

For a long, long moment, I didn't say anything. I just stood there, staring at the dead woman who had become my aunt through adoption and inertia—when someone sticks around for decades, it's hard not to make them part of the family—and feeling the dull ache in my shoulder grow stronger.

I had the crossroads breathing down my neck. I had a Covenant asshole *shooting at me*, or at least shooting at my boyfriend, which wasn't actually any better. And now I had to face the possibility that I'd lost my babysitter and constant companion, not because someone was having a baby, but because I had screwed up badly enough to need to call upon the crossroads.

"No," I said. My voice was surprisingly clear. I took a breath, and repeated, "No. That's not going to happen. We're going to get her back. You can't stay, it's not safe for you to stay, but I need you not to tell my parents what's happening. There's nothing they could do to help, and with the Covenant on the ground here, it's not safe for them to get involved."

"Someday you're going to outgrow this need to martyr yourself, and then things are going to get interesting." Rose reached out like she was going to touch my cheek, only to recoil when her fingertips brushed the wards. She managed a weak smile. "Good work on the wards. Keep them up. No matter how much you think you want to take them down, keep them up. You're going to need a place where Bethany can't reach you. You think you've dealt with crossroads ghosts before. You haven't. You've dealt with Mary, and she's not the norm. Stay careful. Stay safe. And, kiddo, please try to remember . . . Mary's as dead as I am. She had her chance. You're still having yours. It's not worth it to trade yourself for her."

She turned to Sam and James, suddenly smiling the bright, easy smile that has coerced generations of truckers to let her into their passenger seats, promising easy roads and minimal traffic ahead. She's had decades to perfect that smile. It was still funny to see the boys trying to deal with the sheer intensity of it.

"Sam, nice to see you again. Remember, every day you keep putting up with our girl is a dollar in the betting pool for me, so I hope to dance at your wedding. James, nice to meet you, always a pleasure to be on a sorcerer's good side, if you ever need a hitchhiking ghost, I'm your girl. Now, all of you, behave, and try not to let Annie get shot again."

Like that, she was gone, not fading out of the world so much as simply ceasing to be a part of it. She had never been fully solid, and so there was no inrush of air, only silence. There wasn't even a coat to leave behind.

I looked at the place where she'd been for a very long moment. Then, carefully, I closed the door and turned to face the others.

"All right," I said. "Let's fix this."

Thirteen

"If you do your job and get out, people will wonder about you forever. If you do your job, ask for applause, and pass the hat, they'll forget you in the morning."

–Frances Brown

In the living room of a rented house, trying to figure out what happens next

"DID THE CROSSROADS *REALLY* turn this lady's husband inside-out?"

Sam sounded so plaintive that I craned my neck to see the page he was looking at, not moving from my place against his side. Cylia didn't want me out of her sight until she was sure there weren't going to be any negative side effects from Leo's tranquilizer, which meant the research party was back on, and had taken over the living room. Fern was upstairs in the attic, watching for trouble, but that didn't mean she'd been spared; Cylia had toted an entire armful of local histories and a sheet of questions from James all the way to the top of the house for her to work on.

Having what was essentially a homework party while wrapped in a mothball-scented blanket and propped against my living heater of a boyfriend shouldn't have been so pleasant, but it really, really was. I felt like several pleasant academic fantasies were all coming true at the same time, and fully expected to be crowned homecoming queen the next time I fell asleep.

"Looks like it," I said. "She asked them to reverse his manner of thinking and behavior, so they straight up reversed *him*. This is why it's best to be careful with your wishes. What year does it say that happened?"

Sam squinted at the page. "Um, 1495."

"That fits with the rest of the reports," said James. "When the change happened, it was followed by several years of deals that weren't just counter to the desires of the petitioner, but destructive in a way they had never been before. I'm guessing it took the new crossroads several years to determine how cruel they could be without driving their potential, er, customers away."

Something about that didn't sound right. I returned to my original position, leaning my head back to rest against Sam's shoulder, and stared up at the ceiling.

Cylia asked James a question. I didn't really hear it. I heard even less of his answer. I was far away, remembering my first weeks as a roller derby trainee, otherwise known as "fresh meat." Roller derby can be dangerous, but it would be a lot worse if not for the training everyone went through before we were allowed anywhere near a bout. We had to learn how to skate. We had to learn how to hit. And most importantly of all, we had to learn how to control our momentum, because once you strapped a reasonably athletic woman into a pair of roller skates, she became a physics-fueled engine of death, presenting a danger to both herself and others. During my first few weeks on skates, the most dangerous thing about the sport had been, well, me.

"No." I sat up abruptly. The motion pulled at my injured shoulder, making it throb in an unpleasant manner. "That's not what happened."

James looked up from his own book and raised his eyebrows. "It wasn't? Because everything I have here seems to imply that it was."

"It's one of those things that looks intentional if you've never been there," I said. "It's like learning a sport. You can hurt yourself if you don't know your own strength."

James looked at me blankly. I realized that an introverted, nonathletic kid with few friends would not have been in much demand for his high school teams, and that's where most Americans learn whether or not they enjoy playing sports. There are things you can do as an adult, but they're fewer, farther between, and they take more individual effort. Time to try another approach.

"Remember when you started freezing things?" I asked. "You probably shattered a few sheets when they got too cold, because you didn't know how strong you were and you hadn't learned to control it. The more you know, the more delicate you can be."

James' eyebrows climbed even higher toward his hairline. It was Cylia who spoke.

"Are you saying the crossroads are being controlled by some sort of cosmic horror in short pants?" she asked. "Because if we're about to fight a toddler from beyond the stars, I'm out. I will pack the car and be gone by sunrise."

"It's good to know you have limits," I said and meant it. "But not quite. I'm saying that whatever moved into this dimension and hooked into the crossroads in 1490 either got stronger when it crossed into our world or found a richer source of power than it expected. Add a language barrier or twenty—I'm betting there was a lot of turnover in the crossroads ghosts when this change was happening—and it's understandable that people were getting turned inside out or whatever. The thing had to adjust to being where it was now."

"I hurt my grandmother once," said Sam.

We all turned to look at him.

His cheeks reddened, and he ducked his head. "I was a kid," he said. "She wanted me to go to bed and I didn't want to go, and I hit her. She fell. There was this awful snapping sound, and she *fell*, because humans are fragile when you're a little kid fūri and you don't know your own strength. I got better after that. I learned how to be careful."

"The crossroads don't care about whether or not they're hurting people," said James.

"Oh, but I think they do," said Cylia. "It's like bending the luck. If everyone who lives near a jink is having nothing but bad luck all the time, no matter what, they're going to get suspicious. Worse, they're going to decide they can't live there anymore because it isn't safe for them. Even if they never know there's a jink on the other end of their losing streak, they'll know the house is cursed, and they'll get out. Which means the jink doesn't have neighbors anymore. No camouflage, no one to borrow luck from. Not a good situation."

"You're saying the crossroads doesn't want to *kill* people because then no one will come to them to make a deal," said Sam slowly.

"I am," said Cylia. "Is there some sort of record of how many people go to the crossroads?"

"Why does this concept make more sense when it comes from someone you like?" asked James. "I already said this."

"Yeah, but she makes me bacon," said Sam.

James sighed. "Right. No, Cylia, there isn't a record of how many people go to the crossroads. They can appear anywhere a crossing exists, streets, cow paths, sidewalks, anything that intersects, which makes it difficult to measure foot traffic. And most people who go to make a deal don't exactly advertise it. The accounts we have are collected from oral accounts."

"Okay, boring but cool," said Cylia. "Was there a big decrease in oral accounts after the crossroads started turning people inside out?"

"Fuck, yeah, there was," said Sam. "It even says it in this book. 'After the sad case of Mr. Wallace, none in the township dared approach the gallows for the better part of seven years.'"

"See?" Cylia looked smug. "The crossroads did too much damage, people stopped being willing to take the risk, so they had to do like Annie said and figure out how to be less hard core, since otherwise they were going to lose all their customers. We don't know what they get out of the deals. Whatever it is, it's something they need, and they didn't want to lose access because they were killing people accidentally."

"On purpose is another story." I frowned, looking up at the ceiling again. "They know James is working to destroy them."

"Not news, hon," said Sam.

"No, I mean . . . they know he's planning to take them down. They know he hates them, and they know why. So why not offer him a bargain of his own?"

"I would never," said James, his voice colder than his hands could sometimes be.

"Wouldn't you? Because there was a time when I said I would never, and then it turned out that 'never' is negotiable. Humans like to survive. We like to win. Maybe more than any other species I've ever met, we like to come out on top. If the crossroads had approached you— probably through Bethany—" And maybe that's why most crossroads ghosts are attractive young women, with the emphasis on *young*. They look harmless. No one's afraid of a babysitter or a pep squad organizer. They have faces people want to trust. "If they'd said, 'Hey, your friend made a bad deal and we're sorry, but you can make a deal to get her back, no funny business,' are you really sure you'd have turned it down? If you got Sally, and maybe a little something nice on the side, would that have been enough?"

James was silent. I'd struck a nerve. That was good. I was about to hit harder.

"I don't think they have the power to return her."

He flinched, visibly, and turned to look at me, eyes wide and cheeks pale.

"Take that back," he said.

"I don't think she's dead, because I *know* my grandfather is alive, and they took him the same way. I also know that if they had a sense of self-preservation, they would have given him back to my grandmother like, five seconds after they realized they had a human hunting dog determined to gnaw their legs off."

"Is she a sorcerer, too?"

I paused to contemplate the sheer horror of Grandma Alice with access to actual, flexible magic, instead of being limited to the static charms she etched on her skin. "No," I said finally. "Let's be thankful for that because I think we'd all be dead if she were. But it shouldn't matter. The crossroads don't like her. She's a nuisance and a danger, and she just wants her husband back. The cost of keeping my grandfather should have long since become too great, and they should have returned him. They didn't, which means they can't. They're actively *scared* of you. You *are* a sorcerer, and you have your mother's books and a grudge. There's no good reason not to give you what you want, even if it's just to make you go away."

James was quiet for a moment. Finally, in a small voice, he asked, "Why are you telling me this?"

"Because the crossroads didn't even *try* to lie. They didn't offer Sally back and dump a corpse at your feet, or anything fancy like that. They know what you're trying to do, they're scared enough of you to want me to kill you for them, and yet they're not lying to you. Why not?"

"They don't lie," said James. "They mislead. They distort. They misinterpret in the worst ways possible. But they don't lie."

"So let's assume they can't, meaning anything in these books," I waved a hand to indicate the piles around us, "that someone attributes as coming directly from the crossroads has about a fifty percent chance of being the absolute truth."

"Why only a fifty percent chance?" asked Sam.

"Authors lie, even if the crossroads can't," said Cylia.

"Someone says 'the crossroads told me this,' and the author thinks 'that lacks a certain gravitas,' and the next thing you know, the crossroads are talking like something out of Dante. If we ask the crossroads something directly, they have to tell the truth."

"That doesn't hold for crossroads ghosts," I said. "Mary lied to me all the time when I was a kid."

"And she's still your friend?" asked Sam.

"She was my babysitter, and my parents wanted me to have a few years where I thought Santa wasn't real."

"You mean where you thought Santa was real," said James.

"I meant what I said," I replied.

Cylia shuddered. "Gift-giving asshole," she said.

Sam and James exchanged a look, united in their confusion. It was nice for them to have something to bond over. If Sam started getting squirrelly again, I'd be sure to drop something about the Easter Bunny into the conversation. That would keep them busy for a while.

"Maybe that's *why* they have the crossroads ghosts," I said, letting the topic of beloved holiday figures who were secretly terrifying slip to the side. "I mean, something had to control the crossroads before the change, but whatever it was would have been making the deals, not brokering them. On the other hand, having something with a friendly, nonthreatening face that can lie to people . . . that's valuable if you're some kind of nasty that feeds off human misery. Or whatever it is that the crossroads feed off of. I wish to hell Mary were still here. She might be able to answer some of these questions."

Or she might not. The crossroads had always kept a tight leash on what she could and couldn't talk about, and she had tried so hard to be careful. Well, look where that got her.

"I don't like being the designated ignorant person, but I'm going to step up and take one for the team," said Sam. "What does any of this matter? Why do we care whether or not the crossroads can lie?"

"We care because if they could lie, they'd be offering James a way to get Sally back if he promised not to hurt them. Hell, maybe they'd be making him a new Sally. My maternal grandfather was dead for a while, and he got better, but he's not the man he was before his murders." Resurrect the shell of Sally and shove Bethany inside; trust James to ascribe any strangeness to the aftereffects of trauma. It wasn't an elegant plan. It was a functional one *if* the crossroads could lie. "That also means when they told Mary—and then Bethany—that he scared them, they meant it. The answer is here." I waved a hand, indicating the books around us.

"Okay, but . . . where?" Sam scowled at the book in his hands. "We've been going over these for hours. There's nothing here but a lot of desperate people making stupid deals and getting lectured about it by whoever wrote the thing down."

"Good question." I sat up to get a better view of James. "Are you sure all the books are here? Your mom didn't keep a private library at home?"

"My parents were basically a redneck *Bewitched*," said James grimly. "My father never wanted to hear a word about magic, not even when she was trying to warn him that it can be hereditary. There's no way she would have kept things at home. He would have found them."

I frowned.

My family is big into taking notes. We have the mice to recount what they see and experience, providing an absolutely invaluable service, especially when you're on the road and it's not safe to write things down. But nothing will ever replace the journal as a source of wisdom for future generations. My grandfather, like most sorcerers of his generation, even created his own grimoire, recording as much as he could about who he was and what he knew how to do.

Of course, he did most of the writing while he was still working for the Covenant, which meant he was creating a written record of all the reasons they should really burn him at the stake. So he'd learned how to do things in code, and how to hide them.

James' mother had been a sorcerer.

"Change of plans," I said and stood. "Fern isn't going to be the make-believe girlfriend."

"Oh?" said Cylia.

"Oh, no," said Sam.

I flashed him a wry smile as I leaned over and kissed him on the forehead. "At least it's not Leonard?"

Sam groaned.

Fern took the news of being released from her pretend relationship with relief, since pretending to date James would have involved leaving the house—something she wasn't currently inclined to do. She also took her share of the research seriously, producing several pages of tightly-spaced notes that didn't tell us anything we didn't already know.

Sam leaned against the doorframe as I laced my skates, arms folded, scowling. He really was excellently suited to looming.

"Is this a jealousy thing?" I asked, keeping my eyes on the knot I was attempting to tie. "Because if you're going to be the kind of boyfriend who gets cranky every time I look at another guy, we may need to have a conversation that's going to make us both really, really unhappy."

"It's not a jealousy thing," he said, and he sounded like he meant it. "I'm not going to pretend to *like* it, but you took a crossbow bolt to the shoulder rather than let me get hurt. I think I'm an asshole if I ask for more proof that you're sticking with me."

"So what is it?"

"It's a 'some Covenant fucker is out there with a crossbow, and he might shoot you again, and when you're pretending to be some other dude's girlfriend, I can't come with you to keep you safe' thing." Sam's scowl deepened. "You can ask me to do a lot of things, and most of them I'll probably go along with, because I know you do what you do for a reason. But you can't ask me not to worry about you."

I tied off my skate with a tight knot and stood, testing my balance before gliding over to Sam and leaning up to press a kiss to his cheek. "I won't ask you not to worry about me. I'll ask you to spare a little worry for anyone who decides I'd make a good target. I'd hate to go to prison for murder."

"We'd break you out," he said, a small smile working its way through the scowl.

"My hero." This time, when I leaned in to kiss him, he turned, making it into a proper kiss. He wrapped his arms around my waist, joining his hands at the small of my back, and so I slid my own hands around to loop around his neck, keeping myself stable.

He kissed hard and hot and like he was afraid this might be the last time he got the chance. I responded in kind, and for a few seconds—not nearly long enough—everything else ceased to carry any real importance. We were together. We were going to figure out a way through this.

Someone cleared their throat behind us.

"Sorry to interrupt, but if we want a chance of beating my father to the house, we should go," said James.

I leaned back, hands still linked behind Sam's neck, and twisted to look toward James. He was standing in the doorway, cheeks flaming red, looking like he wasn't sure which of us he was allowed to be focusing on. Finally, he met my eyes.

"You're really going to roller skate all the way to my house?" he asked.

"I don't drive, and even if I did, we only have the one car; this is better." I let go of Sam's neck. He reluctantly took his hands from my waist. "Do I look respectable enough?"

Cylia had packed my injured shoulder with gauze and topical painkillers, creating a bulky distortion in my silhouette. I was compensating with a heavy cardigan that put an unfortunate amount of pressure on the wound, but also concealed it completely, and would hopefully slow any further crossbow bolts enough to give me time to react. Wool isn't the *best* armor out there. It still has Old Navy polar fleece beat, hands down. My jeans were dark and crisp and new enough to be respectable, while also being unlikely to show any bloodstains that happened to arise from the day's work. Really, the most disreputable thing about me was my bag, a battered leather thing Cylia had found for me in a thrift store in Oklahoma.

"You look fine," admitted James, after an overly-long pause for consideration. "My father will definitely believe you're my type."

"Nerd?" I asked.

"Yes," he said. "Let's go with that."

I smirked. Even while pretend dating, James was doing his level best to act like my breasts didn't come into the room ahead of the rest of me. I respected that. It's impolite to stab your allies.

His bike was propped against the porch. I stepped down to ground level, using my toe stops liberally to keep myself from rolling, and started stomp-skating along the gravel driveway. Each step jarred the hole in my shoulder, making me question my life choices and the efficacy of the painkillers in my system at the same time. I knew I couldn't take anything stronger if I wanted to be any use for the rest of the day, but oh, how I longed for a numbing agent free of all side effects.

James walked down the driveway to join me, holding his bike by the handlebars, a twisted smile on his face. "I'm starting to feel like the lead in a teen detective story," he said.

"Neither of us has been a teen for a while," I noted.

"Yes, but if we were in a movie about adults, we'd

have a car. And we're in our mid-twenties, which is basically the same as being sixteen in Hollywood years."

The gravel twisted beneath my wheels as I trudged along and considered his depressing pronouncement. "I have way too much sex to be in a teen movie."

"CW show, then."

"And what, we'd be a modern-day *Buffy* spin-off? No, thanks. If someone popped up and told me they were the chosen one, destined to save the world from darkness, I'd ask them very nicely to get away from me, in case it was catching."

James laughed. We came around the final curve in the driveway, and there, blessedly, was the street in all its poorly-maintained glory. Sure, it was a typical Maine country road, meaning there were potholes as big as my torso every few hundred feet, but it was a hell of a lot better than gravel. Whooping, I skated on, feeling the tension drop from my shoulders as my wheels met pavement.

Allowing myself a few seconds of peace, I skated a wide circle, feeling the muscles in my thighs tense and relax in the familiar dance of derby. James slung his leg over his bike and pedaled after me, catching up in short order.

"You're pretty good on those things," he said. "Think you can keep up?"

I didn't have any protective gear, not even a helmet, which meant he could see my grin in all its feral glory. "Try me," I suggested.

He did.

The average human, on the average, nonracing bicycle, can sustain a speed of twelve to fifteen miles an hour if not pedaling hard enough to be a danger to themselves and others. The average human, on the average, properly-fitted roller skates, can sustain something similar. James was someone who rode his bike for convenience and speed, not necessarily as part of an actual exercise program. Whereas I was someone who rode my skates for the sole purpose of being faster than everyone around me. I wasn't passing blockers or scoring points, and I didn't get too far ahead of him, since he was the one who knew where we were supposed to be going, but speed? Oh, I had speed on my side.

After his initial surprise at how fast I could move had faded, James laughed and settled into coasting alongside me. When cars approached, I moved behind him, trusting him to understand the flow of local traffic better than I did. When the road was open, which was more often than not, we rode as a pair.

My shoulder ached, but skating works a different set of muscles, and it wasn't like I was actually playing roller derby, for all that if I let my eyelids drift to half-mast I could hear the rattle of wheels on the track and the distant cheering of the crowd. I missed my teammates more than I would ever have thought possible before this little adventure, and I couldn't wait for the day when it was safe for me to go back to them. They'd give me hell for my long unannounced absence, but I was confident there was some loophole somewhere in the rules that would let me start skating again, once they saw I was sincere. There's always a loophole. If you look long and hard enough, there's *always* a loophole.

The road, which had been briefly almost decent, became more pitted and cracked as we swung back into rural territory, having traveled less than two miles overall. We turned up a driveway as long and winding as the one back at the rental house, although this one was paved and better tended than the road. No gravel here.

No smile on James' face, either. The levity he'd displayed during our ride disappeared, replaced by a look of grim determination. He didn't look like a man marching toward his own death, quite: more like someone heading for a dinner where they knew the menu wouldn't include anything they could eat.

Going home shouldn't be the sort of thing that makes

a person look like that. I glanced at him, sobering, and followed him up the driveway to the house.

It was a larger, better-tended version of the house where I was staying. The windows were clean, the paint was fresh, and the shingles were in excellent repair. It could have been on the cover of a magazine about rural living in modern Maine.

James slowed as we neared the house, hopping off his bike and walking it alongside him. "I have to leave it in the back," he said. "It's unsightly."

"It's a *bike*."

"Yeah, well." His laugh was small and tight. "I don't make the rules. I forgot to ask before: did you bring any shoes? Because you can't wear those skates in the house. If my father came home and found you tracking up his hardwood floors, I'd be moving in with you over at my cousin's place after he threw us both out on our asses."

That might not have been such a bad thing. James needed something in his life to change. Being thrown out of his house wasn't ideal, but it would be a start. "I always have shoes with me."

"Good. I mean, you can't wear those in the house either, since they'd still track up the floors, but at least this way, they'll be next to the door and my father won't think you're some weirdo who runs around the woods barefoot."

I couldn't imagine anyone looking at their son's new girlfriend and immediately starting to assess her footwear, at least not outside of some messed-up retelling of *Cinderella*. I didn't say anything. James looked genuinely worried, and no matter how silly or overblown I thought that concern might be, he deserved better than to be teased about it.

"Got it," I said. "Any other house rules I need to know?"

James stopped, looking me frankly up and down. I resisted the urge to squirm.

"That kind of sweater isn't quite a coat, so you don't need to take it off. Your hair should be fine. If he comes home, try not to squirm, don't swear, and don't say anything that might make him suspect something's up."

"What's going to make him assume something's up?"

"Everything," said James grimly, and propped his bike against the back porch. He waited long enough for me to remove my skates and place them in my bag before unlocking the door. Silent, I followed him inside.

Some houses always feel like homes. Maybe they're clean and maybe they're not, but they're lived-in in a way that makes it clear their residents enjoy living there, or at least don't mind it overly. Other houses feel more like waystations, a place to stop for a little while before continuing on to whatever comes next.

This wasn't either one of those. This was a house that felt like a museum if I was being charitable, and like a prison if I wasn't. Oh, it was nice enough—nicer than the house where I'd grown up, which had always shown the signs of being home base for multiple cryptozoologists, their spouses and children, and whatever pets we'd all dragged home that week. The floors were polished mahogany, the walls were lined with beautiful, antique-looking shelves and small, decorative objects, and everything radiated class in that unique New England way. I could have filmed a period drama there and no one would have questioned my set design.

But the air was cold, and the smell of floor polish and mothballs dogged our footsteps, clinging to the inside of my nostrils. Sorcery is hereditary. I still couldn't shake the thought that if I'd grown up here, I would have manifested ice over fire as well. This was a place for freezing by inches, where nothing burned bright.

There was only one picture on the hallway wall: a man who looked somewhat like an older, sterner James, albeit with broader shoulders and a handlebar mustache, standing next to a devastatingly lovely dark-haired woman in a white lace wedding gown. She was smiling for the camera, but I could see the etched-in lines of sadness around her eyes.

James put his shoes on the rack next to the door. I followed his lead, and he followed my eyes to the portrait. "She really did want to marry him," he said, voice soft. "Everyone agrees about that. No one's ever been able to tell me *why*, but it's not like I could go around quizzing relatives at her funeral. She loved him. She loved me. She left us anyway."

"Sometimes people don't have a choice," I said. The words were useless; I could tell that even as I spoke them.

"People should try harder," said James, and resumed making his way down the hall.

It ended in a small foyer, light breaking into rainbows as it cascaded through the decorative stained glass around the front door, painting the stairs in patterns of prisms. He went up. I followed, silently charting escape routes and things that could be used as supplementary weapons if the knives hidden inside my clothing didn't prove to be enough.

Sometimes I wish I were more comfortable with firearms. And then I remember that I spend most of my time either on roller skates or hanging from a trapeze, and consider how easy it would be to shoot myself, and that reconfirms my desire to be the girl with all the knives, rather than the girl with the sucking chest wound. Although as Leo was so happy to demonstrate, sometimes it's possible to be both.

Asshole.

The stairs extended upward for three stories, marking each transition with another landing, another turn. James took them fast enough that I only got glimpses of each respective floor, until we finally reached what I assumed was the top, stepping onto a floor that was a little less polished than the others had been, where the wallpaper was a little more faded. There were signs of ongoing upkeep—no dust on the baseboards or cobwebs in the corners—but it seemed perfunctory, especially compared to the rest of the house.

I gave James a curious look. He shook his head.

"My room is up here," he said. "My father thinks it will encourage me to get a better job if he doesn't pay the maid to come to the third floor. I either do all the cleaning myself or find a way to stretch my paycheck enough to cover her expenses—which, mysteriously, he claims would cost what it currently costs him to pay her to clean the rest of the house. She's a lovely woman, taught me how to wash windows without streaking when she realized what he intended to do, but I'm not willing to empty my savings for the sake of having a floor I can see myself in."

"What kind of better job does he think you're going to get without leaving your small town and without a college education?" I asked. "I mean, is he one of those people who thinks big paychecks with full medical and dental grow on trees, and we're all just lazy?"

"Essentially, yes," said James. "What do you do?"

"Play roller derby, mostly. Hunt. Try to negotiate peaceful coexistence between human and cryptid communities. It's not what most people would consider 'gainful employment,' but it's fulfilling, and I'm good at it."

"And your parents approve?"

"They tolerate the roller derby. The rest of it is a pretty classic case of 'I learned it from watching you.'"

"Ah." James stopped at the end of the hallway, where a hatch had been cut in the ceiling. "Hang on a moment. I'll get the hook."

"Attic?"

"Yes." He opened a closet, producing a long wooden pole with a metal hook at the end. Deftly, he pulled the hatch open, releasing a rickety ladder to descend into the hall. It looked like it had last been given a thorough inspection for termite damage and rusty nails sometime around, oh, never. I eyed it dubiously.

"Ballpark figure," I said. "How many times have you nearly died using that thing?"

"Only five or six," he replied, and propped the hook against the wall. "Come on."

He started up the ladder. My shoulder throbbed, as if to remind me that I was in no condition to be climbing anything, much less a death trap masquerading as a useful household fixture.

I hate it when my injuries tell me what to do. I followed him.

The attic was about what I expected: small, cramped, and crammed with junk, to the extent that it no longer seemed to matter whether the house had any insulation, since the boxes and chests and old furniture would serve as a no doubt excellent windbreak. James couldn't stand upright without whacking his head on the roof. I had maybe a half inch of clearance, less if I moved toward the back, where the wall sloped down until no one older than five or six would have felt genuinely comfortable.

"You could rent this place out to a whole family of bogeymen and be able to afford a cleaning service," I said.

James blinked at me. "The Bogeyman is real?"

A life spent in the company of Aeslin mice has left me sensitive to capital letters where they don't belong. "No, the dude in your closet who wants to eat your baby is a myth. Bogeymen, on the other hand, are completely real. You probably have some living in the local sewer system, assuming they were able to get in there early enough to partition off some of the larger tunnels. They like to be subterranean, they don't like to be bathed in the smell of other people's shit."

"That's . . . huh." James shook his head. "The more time I spend around you, the stranger the world becomes."

"Says the cut-rate Bobby Drake. Call me when you figure out how to make those nifty frozen slides,

Iceman." I turned slowly, letting the light of the attic's single bare bulb show me my surroundings. "Where are we even supposed to start here? And where's the rest of it?"

"My father had all Mom's things moved up here after she died. I've found a few other books throughout the years, although they've been—wait." James suddenly frowned at me. "What do you mean, where's the rest of it?"

"I mean, this attic is like, maybe half the size it should be." I knocked on the ceiling, triggering a cascade of dust and splinters. "The house is bigger than this. There's a window visible from the outside that isn't visible from the inside. Did you never notice that?"

"Don't be stupid. I would have noticed a *window*." James was trying to sound arrogant, but he looked unsure. Almost confused.

"Would you?" I can be a steamroller when I get going. I know that, and I've learned to be gentle when I have to. It's simple self-preservation: sometimes being gentle is the only thing that keeps the people I'm trying to talk to from turning and running for their lives. "When we know what something looks like, sometimes we stop seeing it. We make assumptions based on the things we *know*, and we don't go looking for proof, because we don't need it anymore."

"This is the only attic I've ever seen."

"All right," I said. "Wait here."

Going back down the ladder was no easier than going up it had been. If anything, it was harder, since now the wound in my shoulder was awake and aggravated and wanted me to know that my behavior was entirely unacceptable. I ground my teeth and plotted terrible things to do to Leonard Cunningham as I descended, until my shoulder was throbbing and my feet were firmly on the hallway floor.

Bastard was going to pay for shooting me. I can put up with a lot of nonsense in the course of doing my job, but shooting me? That was a step too far, and I was *not* going to tolerate it. As for the part where he'd been aiming for Sam, well . . .

If I thought about that too hard, I'd go from justifiably annoyed to outright angry, and that wasn't going to do any of us any favors. One thing at a time. Figure out what was wrong with James' attic, find the missing piece of the crossroads puzzle, discharge my side of the bargain without getting myself killed in the process, find Leo, kick his smug bastard teeth all the way out of his ass. Priorities.

The hall hadn't changed: it was still dusty, shabby in a way that would have been anathema anywhere else in the house, and lined with logical, reasonable doors leading to logical, reasonable rooms and storage spaces. James' bedroom was the closest door to the stairs. The door next to it led to a linen closet, and the door on the other side led to a currently empty bedroom, only a few faded cardboard boxes shoved up under the window.

The window. I paused to give it a longing look. Under normal circumstances—i.e., without a hole in my shoulder, and without the need to worry about either James' father coming home or Leo showing up with another crossbow—I would have gone straight out *that* window and up the side of the house to the *other* window James swore wasn't relevant. Easy peasy. Only not so much when I couldn't be sure of maintaining my grip, and double not so much when I didn't want to go to jail for breaking and entering.

(There isn't much Verity and I agree on. Marshmallow fluff being an awesome sandwich topping is one of them. A dismaying willingness to climb things in order to find out what's at the top is another. I just believe in doing it safely, with a net whenever possible, while she seems to find joy in the plummet.)

The hallway furnishings, such as they were, gave the distinct impression of having been booted upstairs after failing some downstairs quality check or other. The shelf between the linen closet and the bathroom had chips in its finish; the curio cabinet under the window had a thin cobweb of cracks in one corner. Nothing that would have drawn a second glance in my house, but here, those were sins that might never be forgiven.

I looked at the cracked curio cabinet, and thought about home, where glass got cracked and tile got chipped, but everything was filled with light and life and joy. We loved each other, even when we hated each other. That was what family was *for*. I couldn't let James keep living like this, especially not when he was the only other sorcerer my age I'd ever met. He needed training. He needed people who could understand him, and who wouldn't get mad if he froze the pipes every once in a while.

Half my family isn't actually related to me, aunts and uncles and cousins and even siblings we've acquired somewhere along the way and refused to put back where we found them. I wondered how well Alex was going to take the news that he was no longer my only brother. Hell, I wondered how well *James* was going to take the news.

Given that being part of my family came with parents who gave a fuck and houses that didn't feel like punishments, I was pretty sure he'd be okay with it. And Sam might throw him a parade. I may be weird, but even I'm not going to start dating my adopted brother.

One bookshelf didn't fit the rest of the hall aesthetic. It was solid mahogany, built to last, with a warm, almost rosy varnish over the wood, which had been lovingly carved and sanded, making it look like the good kind of museum piece, the kind that got preserved because it was loved, not because it was valuable. The glass fronts of the doors were leaded and unbroken, and there was nothing about it that should have seen it banished to this hall. So why was it here?

I approached the bookshelf, studying the way it met the wall—without so much as a crack to slide a sheet of paper through—and the apparent weight of the books inside. They were thick, hefty tomes, enough to have caused even the sturdiest shelf to eventually bow a little, but there was no bend. Everything looked exactly like it was supposed to, which was the problem. It was like someone had crafted the perfect dollhouse bookshelf, only to realize that it was built to human scale and stick it here instead.

There was a cleaning service. Even if they no longer came upstairs, this thing had been cleaned once. Keeping that in mind, I got up onto my tiptoes, extended my uninjured arm, and felt carefully around the decorative molding of the very top, the places where the dust would have been impossible to get at, and where many services would never even have tried.

There was a click. The bookshelf shuddered as it swung out from the wall, revealing a plain, slightly undersized door on the other side. I smirked, turned the knob, and stepped through, onto a narrow staircase that might be rickety and choked with cobwebs, but was at least better than a ladder.

The bookshelf swung shut behind me, casting the entire stairway into absolute darkness, and behind me, in a pleasant voice, Bethany said, "There aren't any wards here, Annie. I was just waiting until we could have a moment alone."

Shit.

Fourteen

"Always know where your exits are. If you
don't have any, be prepared to make one."
                                                    –Enid Healy

*Locked in a secret passage with a dead woman,
where no one is going to hear the screaming*

"GO AWAY, BETHANY, I'M WORKING," I said, voice low
and tight.

"Mmm . . . no. I don't think so." Ghostly fingers caressed the back of my neck, cool and clammy. That was
a choice. Assuming the rules governing Mary were universal to crossroads ghosts, Bethany could be as warm
as the living when she wanted to. If she wasn't, it was
solely because she wanted to mess with me.

I hate being messed with. "I'm serious. Go away, or
first chance I get, I'm finding someone who can craft a
spirit jar, and I'm putting you on time out."

"Oh, because that's a proportionate punishment for
bothering you? Locking me in solitary confinement until the great Antimony Price decides I'm worthy of my
freedom? I didn't know much about your family before
I died, but I've been doing my homework, and you people are a real class act. You're still Covenant in your
bones. You may have changed what windmill you're
willing to die defending, but that doesn't do anything to
take the swords out of your self-righteous, hypocritical
hands."

"That argument would work better if I thought you believed any part of it, and weren't just repeating buzzwords—oh, and getting your metaphors wrong. Get out. I can't win his trust if he doesn't trust me, and boys don't go for haunted girls."

"Please. Mary's been haunting your family for what, three generations? If boys didn't go for haunted girls, you'd have died out like the relics you are."

I couldn't see a damn thing. I pinched the bridge of my nose, wishing I hadn't been so quick to give away the fire in my fingers. "What do you want?"

"We want to know what the boy knows."

"I told you, I'm working on—"

"Not good enough."

"All right, how about this: he knows the crossroads ate his best friend."

Silence. I couldn't tell whether I'd startled her or whether she was gone. That's the trouble with ghosts. Sometimes, they make things unnecessarily complicated.

Finally, Bethany said, "The bargain of Sally Henderson was sworn and witnessed before my time, but I'm assured she got what she asked for. What she paid for."

"That's cool and all, but still. Ate his best friend. I don't care whether she did it so she could have a pony, that's going to be upsetting for the people she left behind, which is to say, James."

"That's why he wants to hurt us?"

I paused. Something about her voice . . .

"I'm not talking to Bethany anymore, am I?" I asked.

In response, a hand grasped my wrist and yanked. I stumbled, falling forward—

—and landed on my feet on an endless country road. Fields of corn stretched out toward eternity on either side. The sky was the color of a worn-out dishrag, so stained with other people's dirt, with other people's crimes, that it would never come clean again. Bethany stood in front of me, looking suddenly small and young and bewildered, like she had no idea how we'd gone from the stairwell to the outside.

I had some idea. I'd been here before, after all, although the last time, I'd come willingly, and to save my own skin. I focused on the empty air behind Bethany, and spoke like I knew what was going on.

"I'd rather skip the intermediaries, if you don't mind."

"That sounds like a request." The crossroads—the entity that shared the name of the physical place—coalesced out of shadow and dust, becoming a hole slashed in the fabric of the world. I couldn't focus directly on it, couldn't say anything about it other than that it was roughly human-shaped, with a head and arms and torso made of the same nothingness as the rest of it.

It cocked that head, and I had the disconcerting feeling it was looking at me.

"What will you pay?" it asked.

"Nothing," I said. "I haven't asked for anything. 'If you don't mind' meant it was your choice, and you chose to appear, presumably because you know how creepy it is to talk to a hole in the world." I crossed my arms, only wincing a little as it pulled on the wound in my shoulder.

A little was more than enough. "We can fix that for you," said the crossroads. "We can make it as if you were never hurt. A small thing. A token, really, requiring only the smallest of payments."

"I'm good," I said. "Dudes dig chicks with scars." Half-true. Sam didn't exactly "dig" my scars, but he appreciated the work I'd put into acquiring them, and he was willing to celebrate the fact that no matter how many times the world had tried to gut me, I'd persisted in surviving. "Why am I here?"

"You haven't killed the Smith boy."

"That wasn't what I was told to do," I said, as calmly as I could. "I'm supposed to make him trust me, learn everything he knows about how to hurt you, and *then* kill him."

"We don't want you to know how to hurt us." The

crossroads sounded sullen. No small trick for an anthropomorphic personification of making a shitty deal at the flea market. "If you learn everything he knows, you'll know how to hurt us."

"If I don't learn everything he knows, I won't know where the books I need to destroy are being kept. Someone else will be able to figure out how to hurt you."

"And we'll kill them, too."

Who could have guessed that arguing with an unknowable force of the cosmos would be so much like arguing with a toddler who had stayed up past bedtime? "I haven't killed the Smith boy because right now, it isn't safe to kill him. There are too many variables. You told me to befriend him, to make him trust me, and then to kill him. I'm still on step one."

"Or you're stalling."

I said nothing.

The shape made of absence took a step toward me. "We think you're stalling. We think you don't want to kill a human being who has, by your standards, done nothing wrong. He's a threat to us, but we've never been something your *family*," it said the word like it was filthy, like it was blasphemous, "wanted to protect. You people, with your little idealisms and your little ideas of what it is to be good or evil or in-between. We think you've decided he might be right. That's why you've locked our eyes outside. You don't want them to see you plotting."

"I locked Bethany outside because she's not Mary," I said. "You want me to drop the wards, give me back my babysitter. I'll let Mary watch every damn thing I do, and I'm pretty sure she can't lie to you, or you would have lost track of my family the second Grandma gave Dad and Aunt Jane to my great-aunt Laura."

Great-Aunt Laura had been an ambulomancer and a magnet for the dead, just like her mother, which had led to her becoming the best ghost-wrangler in North America, at least for a while. She'd been able to weave a ghost cage from a piece of newspaper and a tattered cobweb, and her wards had been the stuff of legend. Literally. People had come from all over the world to look at them and learn how to improve their own wards. It would have been easy for her to ward her charges from the eye of the crossroads, if not for Mary, who had come with the children—babysitter and trusted friend and keeper of so much of their history. Without Mary, we would still have had the mice, but they don't understand human things the way she does. Without her, we might have lost what it meant to be a Price.

My stomach twisted, a wave of nausea washing over me. Without Mary, we might also have lost the focus of the crossroads. Had anyone ever realized that exchange was being made? It seemed like the sort of thing that should have been a choice, not a fait accompli presented to each new generation as unavoidable.

"Mary is too involved," said the crossroads. "She tries to put your interests above our own. She has to be taught who she belongs to. A ghost is only as good as its manners."

The nausea abated somewhat as I realized the crossroads had—however accidentally—given away one very important piece of information.

They were talking about Mary in the present tense. Whatever they'd done to her, she still existed. There was a chance, however slim, that I might be able to save her.

"Then we're at an impasse," I said. "I'm not going to lower the wards for a ghost I don't know, who has been nothing but rude to me since she appeared, and who's already shown herself to be perfectly willing to assault me. You get one favor. You can ask me to kill James Smith, or you can ask me to let your spy into my house. Who knows? Maybe I'll learn enough to make killing him seem like a good idea even if you're not making me do it."

"Yes," said the crossroads. "We are, indeed, at an impasse. You think you have a position to bargain from. You forget we have already bargained. We have already struck a deal with you, and you are refusing to adhere to our agreement. We promised your life would not be taken from you, no matter what happened, and we hold to the compact. We did not, however, promise to take disobedience lightly."

"What—" I began.

That was as far as I got before the world caught flame around me. No: not around me. Inside me, burning every nerve and every fiber of my muscles, until I felt like a bonfire wrapped around bone, consuming myself without being consumed. I screamed, the sound ripping out of me in an agonized wail as I dropped to my knees on the impossible road. I didn't even feel the moment of impact. The pain was too great. The pain was the entire world. Electric fire beat me down until I was on my hands and knees, gasping and choking, trying to force myself to keep breathing when my lungs were full of ash and ember, smothering me.

"We seem to have struck a nerve," said the crossroads, and giggled—actually giggled, a high, tittering sound that rubbed across my already-aching nerves and somehow made them even rawer, giving the pain new and innovative ways to work its way into my body. "Feel that, little miss negotiation? That's the price of failure. You gave us fire. We're allowed to let it burn. Best of all, because it sparked in you, it can never kill you. You can burn together forever, you and the flame. It won't cleanse. It won't clean. It will just hurt. Always, and always, and always, until you decide the pain has to stop somehow. How long do you think you can burn before you decide your family's considerable skill at killing things needs to be turned inward? We promised not to kill you ourselves. We made no promises about your own hand."

The fire was everything. The pain was enormous, screaming, swallowing every thought I tried to have, until the world was a handful of crushed glass shards, each of them containing nothing but a single word wrapped in a veil of pain. I couldn't breathe. I had to breathe. If I stopped . . .

"Poor thing. Now. Let's see if you're ready to be good."

The pain stopped.

I promptly vomited on the road, gasping and shaking from the shock of having the agony ripped away. I felt like I'd run a marathon, naked, through a field of barbed wire. The pain in my shoulder was almost incidental, something fleshy and easily ignored behind the worndown ache that filled my entire body.

"Suffering exhausts a person. So many of the people who come to us are looking to be relieved of pain. We've had so much time to study what it does to the psyche of a human being, to suffer without cease. We can give you a lifetime of scholarship on the matter."

There was a soft scuff in the dirt as the shapeless shadow of the crossroads moved into my field of view and knelt, showing me its absence.

"Is this what you want, Antimony? Do you care so much about a man you just met that you would burn for him forever? Because that's what waits for you, if you don't do as we say. Do you understand? Nod if you understand."

Choking back bile, I forced myself to nod.

The crossroads had no face. It couldn't smile. Still, it seemed pleased as it rose.

"Good girl. Now, as we finally understand each other, do you want to change anything about your earlier answer?"

I wanted to say "yes." I wanted, in the craven, cowardly pit of my soul, to tell the crossroads that I'd go back to the real world and snap James' throat as soon as they released me. Anything to put the fire back into my hands where it belonged and keep the crossroads from using it against me. Anything to get away.

And I couldn't. Maybe the crossroads hadn't let me burn long enough to break me, but my stubborn streak has always been a mile wide, and I *hate* being told what to do. I swallowed hard, the muscles of my throat protesting the motion, and whispered, "No. He doesn't trust me enough to let me that close."

"Are you *sure*?" There was a warning note in the figure's voice.

Again, the answer rose in my throat, burning like acid. *Tell it what it wants to hear*, I thought, and "Yes," I whispered. "He needs to trust me, or all this was for nothing."

"We can hurt you any time we want to. You understand that, don't you? We can hurt you, and there's nothing you can do to stop it. We're always with you because you belong to us. If you died right now, you'd be as much ours as Bethany is, and we'd burn you until the stars went out to punish you for refusing to behave."

It didn't take any effort at all to whimper. A hand caressed my hair.

"Good girl. You're learning. We'll see you soon."

The world blinked, like I had closed my eyes for a long, terrible moment, and the empty road and the corn and the crossroads were gone, replaced by the blackness of the hidden stairwell. I was crumpled on the stairs, not on my hands and knees, but on my side, like a child's discarded toy.

The exhaustion was still consuming my muscles, making sure I understood that the pain I had suffered at the hands of the crossroads had been very real, and the threat of its return was equally sincere. I pushed myself, shaking, onto my hands and knees, feeling around the wall until I found the rail. There was no smell of vomit. Wherever I'd thrown up, it hadn't been here.

That was terrifying. The crossroads existed at least partially outside our reality, and they could apparently take me there whenever they wanted to. Was that a forever thing, or a "just until you finish fulfilling your bargain" thing? If it was the former, I was screwed. I could easily see them snatching me off the track or out of my own bed, throwing me into the dirt and setting my nerves aflame.

Which was just one more reason to destroy them. I pulled myself to my feet and resumed climbing the stairs, closing my eyes to make it easier to move through the dark. It's a psychosomatic thing. People who navigate by sight expect to, well, *see* where they're going . . . unless their eyes are closed. Take sight out of the equation and they move with more confidence, like they've already decided that a few stubbed toes are a foregone conclusion.

The rail was surprisingly solid, holding my shaky weight with ease. I climbed until my outstretched hand found another door. Those windows again. If there hadn't been a door at the top of the stairs, the light would have been able to shine into the stairwell. I opened my eyes. I opened the door.

The missing half of the attic was as open and airy as the half where James was presumably still looking for clues was cobwebby and cramped. I stepped through the door, careful to close it behind myself, and looked around.

Someone had been using this space as a private office once, a very long time ago. A layer of dust covered everything, from the small rolltop desk situated across from the window to the bookshelf positioned to keep it safe from the worst of the sun. There was a filing cabinet old enough to be used for a 1950s period piece, and the usual assortment of knickknacks: a few framed pictures, covered in a layer of dust so thick that their subjects could no longer be seen, a letter opener, and a long-dead plant, its wilted remains draped over the side of a clay pot. The door through which I'd entered was behind me. Another, smaller door was on the wall ahead of me, the base of it raised more than a foot above the floor.

There was nothing about the room to indicate that anyone had been in it for more than a decade. I took a cautious step forward. The last thing my day needed was the sudden discovery of dry rot.

I did not plummet back down to the second floor, or into whatever mysterious oubliette this room's owner had established to deter intruders. I took one more look around before walking over to the second door, knocking briskly, and pulling it open, revealing what looked like the back of some large, solid piece of furniture.

No handy secret entrance on this side, then. Crap. Voice muffled by the wood, I heard James say, "Hello? Annie?"

"I am a magical talking wardrobe," I said, too exhausted to do a good spooky voice. "Move me and all your questions will be answered."

A series of thumps and small noises of complaint marked James' progress across the attic. The wooden panel blocking my view rocked once before he complained, "It's too heavy."

"I have faith in you."

James scoffed. "That makes one person."

"Look, I can clap my hands and say I believe in fairies, if that's what it's going to take to get you to exert yourself, but I can't exactly help. Crossbow bolt to the shoulder, remember?" I didn't feel like explaining my encounter with the crossroads. It already seemed hazy, like a dream I would have been better off forgetting.

There was nothing hazy or dreamlike about the ache filling my body, making it difficult for me to stay steady on my feet. There was a chair at the desk. Fond visions of sitting down filled my head, nearly luring me away from the wardrobe. It wasn't like I was helping *anyway* . . .

And it wasn't like James deserved to come into his mother's private study and find me sitting at her desk, wiping away what few traces of her presence might remain. It was that thought alone that kept me on my feet, while the wardrobe rocked and shuddered and finally shifted a few inches to the side, revealing a slice of James' pale, pointed face.

His eyes widened as he saw the sunlit room behind me. "What in the . . ."

"I found the other half of the attic," I said, reaching up with my good arm, weak as it currently was, to help him keep on pushing. The wardrobe was heavy, the kind of furniture built to pass down through generations like some sort of cursed idol or unholy artifact. James' grandkids might be living on a space station in orbit around Sirius IV, but they'd have this wardrobe with them, taking up half their available space, looming disapprovingly.

"I see that." The opening was finally large enough for him to squeeze through. I stepped to the side. He didn't seem to notice. He was too busy staring at his surroundings, turning in a slow, mesmerized circle.

Finally, in a hushed tone, he said, "Mom used to say she was going to get some writing done while I went out to play, and promise to be downstairs by lunch. Only one day, she wasn't. I was seven. I searched the whole house for her, and I was getting really scared when there was a bang and she came down the stairs. She told me she'd been in the bathroom and hadn't heard me calling. But she wasn't in the bathroom, was she?"

"Nope," I said. "Surprise."

"How . . . ?"

"She was a sorcerer. There are lots of tricks to make things boring. Too boring to investigate, even for a smart guy like you." That also explained his father's willingness to abandon an entire floor of his otherwise perfect home. Yes, he was punishing James, but that didn't mean giving the spiders a stronghold from which to attack the lower floors. A minor distraction charm, however, especially one that was intended to eventually let James find what she had hidden . . .

He was turning in a slow circle, eyes wide, drinking in every dust-covered inch. He bit his lower lip, cast a glance in my direction, and started for the bookshelf.

"Her diaries," he said, grabbing the first volume. He opened it to a random page, and blinked. "It's blank." He flipped frantically through the book before grabbing another, and another, finally turning to me and saying despondently, "They're all blank."

I heaved a sigh of relief. "Finally," I said. "Something I can help with."

Fifteen

"Some skills are essential, no matter what your future holds. Never assume that knowledge is useless."

–Jane Harrington-Price

In the private attic office of a dead sorcerer, playing intrepid detective

"IT'S A FORM OF invisible ink," I said, sitting cross-legged in the middle of the office floor across from James, an open book between us. It was a relief to be seated. I wasn't sure I would be able to stand up again, but hey, one thing at a time. "All kinds of magic-users use it to keep their notes from being discovered by people who might want to hurt them."

It's a testimony to Grandpa Thomas' love for his magically-deficient wife that most of his notes—at least the ones written after his arrival in Buckley—had been taken in ordinary, ever-visible ink. But there had been a note, tucked at the back of one of his books, that mentioned more information might be found by someone who looked the right way.

I like to think he'd suspected his genes would assert themselves somewhere down the line, winning out over bubbly blondness to produce, well, me. A descendant who'd have fire in their fingers and would need a way to learn what that meant. Not that he could leave much in the way of useful instruction—very few sorcerers are self-taught, because very few "spells" have clear, coherent steps that take well to being written down—but at least he could reassure that potential grandchild or great-grandchild or whatever that they weren't losing their minds or starting fires the normal way, with matches and lighter fluid, and then forgetting about it. No sleep pyromania here! Just a good clean dose of Jean Grey syndrome.

James looked at me dubiously. "Invisible ink," he echoed. "Are you going to suggest we get a hair dryer to make the words appear?"

"Okay, one, that's lemon juice, two, you're making fun of me, and three, this is way more like one of those fantasy novels where the writing only appears by moonlight than some kid's science project. I want you to put your hands above the page. About six inches up. You don't want to freeze the book."

The dubious look intensified. "Freeze the book."

"Look, I make fire, not ice, so I am very safety-first. I had to do this part with a bucket of sand in easy reach." Not a fire extinguisher: that would have been too difficult to explain to my parents, and too potentially destructive for the books. Any time something started to smolder, I'd just thrown fistfuls of sand over it until the smoldering stopped. Low-tech but effective, that's the family motto.

James sighed. "All right. You found the room, we'll do things your way." He squared his shoulders and extended his arms, palms down.

He clearly resented my continued presence, and I couldn't blame him, because this room . . . this was a piece of his mother he had never seen before. I couldn't imagine what that felt like. I didn't *want* to imagine what that felt like. I knew I was lucky to have both my parents. I was even luckier to have two parents who genuinely loved me and wanted what was best for me, even if we didn't always agree about what that was. James . . .

He'd lost the one person who should have been there

to love and understand him from the beginning, and then he'd lost the one person who had volunteered to try filling the gap, until he was left with only a father who viewed him as a burden and an embarrassment. Any questions I might have had about how accurate that view of the situation was had died when we'd climbed the stairs to the second floor. The charms around the hidden door might have contributed to Mr. Smith's neglect of the cleaning, but they wouldn't have caused him to mistreat his only son.

"What do I do?" asked James.

I snapped out of my introspection. "Focus on your hands. Try to call the cold without allowing it to happen. You want to touch the potential, not the actuality."

The temperature in the attic dropped several degrees. I wrinkled my nose.

"Dial it back, Iceman," I said. "The idea, not the real thing. Think about what the magic feels like when it answers you. Think about the way it hums."

I've never had the kind of training James needed—or that I needed, quite frankly. Magic-users are rare. Sorcerers, being wholly hereditary, recessive, and hunted by assholes like the Covenant of St. George for centuries, are even rarer. There's no way to advertise for a teacher, and the people who'd answer an advert like that are usually not the sort of folks it's a good idea to trust. But I've had access to my grandfather's books, and for a little while at Lowryland, I had Colin, who may have been syphoning off my powers and using them to fuel a malicious luck-theft spell that would eventually have gotten a lot of people killed, but who also knew what the hell he was doing.

"Breathe," I said. "Settle into the magic. Think of it as choosing to sing instead of scream. Screaming hurts your throat. So does singing, if you don't warm up properly, but it can be so much easier, and it can last for so much longer. Pull back the cold. You don't need it like you think you do."

The air around his hands glittered, filled with power and potential. The air began to grow warmer, thawing as he pulled the cold back into himself.

The blank pages under his hands shimmered, and letters began to appear. They were faint at first, but quickly grew in visibility, until both pages were packed with slanting letters in rust-colored ink, as real as any diary had ever been.

James gasped.

"Is that her handwriting?" I asked. I already knew the answer: it matched the writing in the margins of the books back at our rental house.

He nodded. There were tears in his eyes.

"Great." I leaned forward, trying not to flinch from the chill still radiating from his palms, and slammed the book shut.

"What?!" James glared at me, the air growing colder around us once again—this time with irritation. "Why did you do that?"

"We need to take these books back to the house."

"Why? We can read them here!"

"Well, one, here, your father could come home any time, which would put a damper on research, and two, we promised the others we'd come back." We'd done no such thing, only implied it. James was a smart guy. I hoped he'd catch on soon, since doing charades to say "there are no wards here" was a bit beyond my skills.

Instead, he glowered. "They're my mother's diaries."

"Yes, and she clearly hid them here figuring that if you inherited her powers, you'd find them and figure out how to read them. But the others are waiting." Silently, I mouthed, "Please."

James started to object again. Then he caught himself, visibly course-correcting, and asked, "How much room do you have in your backpack?"

"Enough," I said.

Thank God.

It took about ten minutes to get the diaries into our respective backpacks. Lifting mine was difficult, to say the least; between the injury in my shoulder and the ongoing weakness of my body as a whole, I felt like I was trying to attend a weight training course after a six-hour derby bout. Not good.

Worth it. Whatever was in these books was enough to scare the crossroads, which meant we needed to decode them while behind the closest thing we had to a locked door. Once the crossroads knew what James' mother knew, they would not only be able to defend themselves, they'd be a lot more likely to demand I kill him on the spot. They were already pushing that agenda hard enough to be concerning if I wanted to undersell the situation in a way James probably wouldn't appreciate. "Hey, the eldritch nightmare you're devoting your life to wiping out sort of wants me to get on with slitting your throat, but sure, we have time to argue about where your mother's diaries belong" is concerning, right?

"Be careful with those," said James, as he squeezed through the opening into the main attic. It made the most sense to get the wardrobe back into position and then meet each other in the hall, where I could show him how to access the office. I had the feeling he was going to be spending a lot of time in there.

Good. He deserved a safe place in his own house, somewhere his father would never think to look for him. Somewhere to decide what happened next.

"I'll treat them like they're those weird egg babies we had to take care of in social studies," I said, and flapped my hands in a "go on, then, shoo" gesture. "Get moving. I want to get back to the house."

James, who still hadn't twigged to the fact that it was the lack of wards that was distressing me, gave me a curious look. He didn't know about Bethany attacking me in the stairwell, and why should he? It wasn't like I could say her name without the risk of summoning her. Stupid ghosts.

I flapped my hands again. James began wrestling the wardrobe into place.

There wasn't much I could do from my side of things. I stayed where I was, watching to be sure he got it close enough to the wall to restore the seal and prevent anyone else from stumbling on the hidden room. It took a while, and when the wardrobe was once again snugly positioned, I closed the door and started for the stairs.

The absolute blackness of the stairwell was as unsettling on my repeat visit as it had been on my first one. At least this time no unwanted ghosts appeared to haul me off to meetings with the crossroads. I took the steps as fast as I dared in the dark, one hand clutching the rail and the other stretched in front of me, waiting for the moment when my fingers would brush against the door. There was still no smell in the air, of vomit or otherwise. I'd been half expecting it to appear after the fact, making my story harder to believe.

Harder for anyone else to believe, anyway. I had no doubt about what I'd been through, and if I'd been inclined to start questioning, the continued twitching of the muscles in my neck would have been enough to convince me not to. I'd been tortured. I hadn't been tortured here.

James was waiting in the hallway when the bookshelf swung open and I stepped through. He shook his head, looking impressed and almost offended at the same time.

"I never tried to move that shelf," he said. "I never even thought of trying."

"That was your mom," I said. "She put protections up, and I guess she figured either they'd break down faster than they did or she left you something you haven't found yet that would have told you where to look."

"I suppose," he agreed, eyes still troubled.

Impulsively, I reached out and squeezed his shoulder. "You've got her diaries. You'll have time to find out." Assuming I could keep the crossroads from forcing me to kill him before he had the chance.

How much of that pain would I be able to take before it broke me? It was a question I had never wanted the answer to. I still didn't . . . but I was afraid I was going to get it before all this was over.

We closed the bookcase and descended the stairs to the first floor together, James a few steps ahead of me. While I hadn't dared say as much to him, it was so if my legs gave out and dumped me on my ass, he'd be there to catch me.

Skating back to the house was going to be a *lot* of fun, I could see that already.

"If you have snacks you want during the study party that's about to get underway, I'd suggest picking them up now," I said, moving to retrieve my unworn shoes from the rack next to the back door.

James opened his mouth to answer, and froze as the sound of a car's engine rumbling to a stop washed through the room. He paled. That alone was enough to tell me this wasn't the day the cleaning service came, and this wasn't the kind of house where door-to-door solicitors dropped casually by.

There was no way we were getting out of here without being seen. I dropped my shoes back on the rack. James lunged for the fridge. Neither of us said a word, but we both knew this drill. I'd learned it trying to steal a little privacy from two older siblings. James had learned it in a much harder setting, and was thus faster and more efficient in his motions. By the time my ass hit one of the chairs at the kitchen table, there were two glasses of milk and a plate of Chips Ahoy waiting, creating the impression of a wholesome, bucolic afternoon.

I took a big gulp of my milk, only wiping half of the ensuing mustache away as James took his own seat. He blinked.

"Authenticity," I said, by way of explanation. There wasn't time to say anything else. We both heard the key turn in the front door, and the door itself swinging open, followed by a heavy boot tread on the floor.

"I saw your bike, boy," called a man's voice, almost disdainfully. "Where are you?"

James sat up a little taller, shoulders squaring, chin coming up, like he was preparing to be judged. Which might not have been so far from the truth, all things considered. "I'm in the kitchen, sir."

I reached out like I was going to take a cookie, waiting until the footsteps grew closer before pulling my hand back. My timing was good: James' father appeared in the doorway in time to catch the movement, and his eyes flicked to me, drawn like all good predators to the impression of something trying to run away.

"Jimmy?" he said. "Who's this?"

"This is Annie," he said, and gave me a besotted smile that spoke well of his future with the local theater group. "She and her friends are renting Cousin Norbert's house for the fall."

"Hello, sir," I said, standing and smoothing the hem of my shirt like I was suddenly anxious about its appropriateness. "You have a lovely home."

James' father said nothing as he looked me up and down.

The wedding pictures had been enough to prepare me for the ways in which he was like and unlike his son, and I was grateful to have seen them. What they hadn't prepared me for was the sheer weight of his presence. He filled the room like a thundercloud, dangerous and fascinating at the same time. He was still in uniform, dressed to protect and serve.

Finally, he asked, "Where are you from, Annie?"

"Vancouver," I said. West coast accents are fairly interchangeable to the east coast ear, and being Canadian seemed like a good way to cover for any mistakes I made. I hadn't been born in a barn: I had just been born in another country.   .

"Huh," he said. His gaze flicked to the milk and cookies on the table, and then back to me. "You've got a little something on your lip."

"Oh!" I raised my hand to cover it, like I was ashamed, and reached for a napkin. James was already in the process of handing me one. Our fingers brushed. Quick as I could, I pictured Sam naked in my bed, then pictured my grandmother walking into the room. That did it. Heat rose in my cheeks as I jerked my hand away. To the nonpsychic observer, it would look like the mere act of touching hands had been enough to make me blush.

James' father was not, thankfully, psychic. He lifted his eyebrows, then looked to James. "A word?"

"Yes, sir." James stood. "Annie, I'll be right back to escort you home." *So please don't move.*

"All right," I said. "It was nice to meet you, sir."

"Likewise, young lady." That seemed to be enough to serve as a good-bye: James' father turned and walked out of the room, and James hurried after.

Moving seemed like a bad idea, especially when the chief of police was interrogating his own son on his intentions toward the tourist girl in the next room over. I took a cookie instead. The fact that Chief Smith had somehow failed to notice that James and I were apparently having the kind of date more appropriate for sixth graders was almost irrelevant. He didn't know his son. I wasn't sure he'd ever taken the time to try.

The cookie was store-bought but tasty. I ate another one, and drank about half my milk. It felt good enough on my scraped-up throat that I finished the glass before looking thoughtfully at James'. He hadn't touched it. I was on the verge of making the swap when James himself came storming back into the kitchen, head down and shoulders hunched.

"Ready?" he asked.

"Ready." I stood immediately, grabbing the backpack from where it rested next to my chair. "I just need to get my skates on and we can go."

"Good." James made for the back door without another word, not even pausing to clean up our "snack." He grabbed his shoes on the way out. I did the same, although I stuffed mine into the bag before sitting down and starting to lace up my skates.

James didn't stop. He went to the bottom of the porch and got his bike, hands white-knuckled on the handlebars. I gave him a concerned look, but I didn't hurry. There are things in life that shouldn't be rushed. Lacing up a pair of skates is one of them. When your mode of transport is attached to your feet, the last thing you want is for a knot to give way.

Eventually, I felt secure enough to stand, slip my arms into the backpack's straps, and walk carefully down the stairs to join James. "I know the way," I said softly. "If you need to go ahead, you can."

"He's probably at one of the windows, watching us go," James replied. "If he sees me pedal off without you, the game is up."

"Is that all?" I asked, and leaned in to kiss James on the cheek. Only the cheek. It was suitable to the length of our supposed relationship, and more, given what he'd said about his life so far, I was willing to bet he hadn't kissed many girls.

The startled look on his face when I pulled away was enough to confirm my guess. I offered a sideways smile.

"Veracity," I said, and started skating.

My legs were sore and tired enough that I hadn't managed to get very far by the time he caught up with me. He coasted along, matching my pace, until the house was out of view around the curve of the driveway and there was no way his father was still watching us.

"Veracity?" he echoed, in a strangled tone.

"If we just met, we wouldn't be making out on your lawn yet—and if we did, your father would probably decide I wasn't the kind of girl you ought to be hanging out with. I'm not calling him sexist. My father would make the same call if he saw me making out with someone I barely knew." Heaven only knew what he was going to make of Sam. At least, I wasn't the first one to go out on an assignment and come home with a shiny new significant other. Hopefully, he was still annoyed enough about Verity bringing home an ex-Covenant operative not to mind that Sam wasn't human.

"Insufficient kissing wasn't my objection!"

"I'm sorry if I crossed a line, and I should have asked first—consent counts, even when you're undercover. But if he was watching us, selling the bit was more important. I sold it."

"You must have been the pride of your Girl Scout troop," said James scornfully.

"Never joined. Something about them being nosy Nancies kept my parents from signing the paperwork. My cousins and I formed our own scouting organization. We called ourselves the Danger Scouts and went camping in the woods behind the house and annoyed the local Bigfoot population something awful." I smiled fondly. "I'm pretty sure Mom threatened every cryptid within a hundred miles with the consequences of what would happen if we got hurt, because those were the nicest camping trips ever."

James looked at me blankly. "Your family sounds very strange."

"Oh, you have no idea. You're going to love them." I winced as one of the muscles in my right thigh objected to my moving. "I'll explain why when we get back to the house, but do you think you could pull me for a while? I think my legs are about to give out."

James' blank look morphed to one of genuine concern. "What's wrong?"

"Again, I'll explain when we get there."

"All right." He didn't sound like he believed me. "Grab on."

There was a little metal grid at the base of his seat, designed for clipping on wagons or other accessories. I threaded my fingers through it as I fell in behind the bike, focusing on locking my knees rather than pushing myself forward. It helped. I closed my eyes in relief, letting my legs take a much-needed rest. James kept pedaling, more slowly now that he had my added weight to contend with.

This wasn't good. If the crossroads could catch me any time I set foot outside of the wards, I was going to wind up like my grandfather had been in the last years of his life: locked into a steadily narrowing space, unable to go outside or fight back. It was a chilling thought. More chilling was the question of whether the wards *mattered*. The crossroads had sent Bethany to collect me, but nothing said that was necessary. They weren't ghosts. As far as I could tell, their only connection to the so-called "spirit world" was their habit of using ghosts as their messengers. The fact that they could pull me into their liminal space without killing me was another vote for the rules being different for them. Mary and Rose could move back and forth between the lands of the living and the dead, and could even carry things with them, but they couldn't transport living beings— like me or the mice—without consequences.

The only consequences I was experiencing came from being tortured, not from visiting the crossroads, at least as far as I could tell. If I was going to catch ghost tuberculosis and die on top of everything else, I was going to be *pissed*.

James kept pedaling, and I kept holding on, letting the road roll by under my wheels, trying to put together a plan for what was going to happen next. Chief Smith might be a problem if he decided to start running background checks on us. Then again, he might not; Cylia was the only one who could be easily found in any official records, and so far as I knew, she'd never had so much as a parking ticket. Sure, we'd been pulled over a few times when her luck fizzled or snapped back on us, but she'd always been able to charm her way out of actually receiving a citation. If she and my cousin Elsie ever decided to start hanging out together, they could take over the world with a smile and a wink.

Honestly, that might not be such a bad thing.

"You okay back there?"

"I'm fine." I cracked an eye open. "Getting tired?"

James scoffed. "Please. I've been riding my bike everywhere since I was nine."

"You don't drive?"

"No." There was a long pause as he considered his next words. Finally, he said, "When I turned sixteen my father told me if I wanted a car I'd have to pay for it myself. But Sally had a car, and I was putting everything aside for college, so it didn't seem important. After Sally disappeared, he said it was time to stop letting girls drive me around everywhere. He said it made me look like a—forgive me, this is his word, not mine—like a pansy who couldn't take care of himself. So I decided my bike was more than good enough for me, thank you very much, and I swore not to learn how to drive until and unless it was time to watch this town getting smaller in my rearview mirror."

Oh, I was definitely taking him home with me. "I get it," I said. "I don't drive either."

"Really? Why not?"

"Never seemed like something I wanted to do. I mean, I know *how*—I passed Driver's Ed, and I passed Driver's Dead, which was my Aunt Rose and a big, empty parking lot and a whole bunch of screaming." That had been a fun series of nights. Fun, and terrifying, and enough to firmly cement the idea that driving was something best left to people who didn't want to be able to grip the dashboard with both hands. "I can usually get by on public transit, roller skates, and cadging rides from people. Plus no one suspects you of being a heavily armed survivalist when you're taking the local light rail. It's a sort of camouflage."

"Lots of weirdoes ride the bus," said James approvingly.

"And we are among the weirdoes."

He turned off the main road and onto the gravel drive that would take us to the house. I regretfully let go of the back of the bike.

"Hang on a second, okay? I need to put my shoes on." The thought of roller skating over gravel, whether or not I was being towed, was enough to make me want to sit down and refuse to move. I didn't think my legs had ever been this tired. Pain is not the same as damage, but it exhausts the body all the same.

James watched me with concern as I sat down in the gravel and went through the process of swapping skates for shoes. When I was finished, and stood, he asked, "Are you all right? Do you need . . . I mean, is there . . ."

"There's nothing medically wrong with me," I said. "I'll explain once we're inside."

He didn't like that answer—I could see it in his eyes—but he accepted it, and held his tongue as we walked the rest of the way along the driveway to the house.

Leonard was on the porch.

I stopped dead, my hands going to the knives at my waistband. "Get behind me, James," I said, voice low and dangerous.

James, to my surprise, did as he was told. It's always nice to work with people who can take directions.

"What the hell are you doing here, Cunningham?" It didn't take much effort to pitch my voice loud enough for Leonard—and hopefully everyone inside the house—to hear. If anything, the effort was keeping myself from screaming. "We don't want you."

Leonard turned from his study of the door, eyes widening with surprise and, yes, relief when he saw me. "Annie!" He started forward.

I pulled the knives from under my clothes. He stopped, raising his empty hands.

"I'm not here to fight, and I don't want to hurt you," he said. "I wanted to find out if you were all right. I swear on my honor as a Cunningham that this isn't a trick."

"You're a Covenant man," I snarled. "You have no honor." My shoulder ached and throbbed, reminding me of exactly what he was capable of.

"I have more honor than you think I do. Annie, please. If you'd just hear me out . . ."

A curtain twitched in one of the upstairs windows. My stomach unclenched a bit. The others were inside, and safe, although Cylia and Fern probably had their hands full trying to restrain Sam. Leaving Leo locked outside was a decent way of dealing with him, at least until some poor fool—like say, me—came walking up the drive.

"I don't want to hear you out, Leo," I said. "I have things to do, and you *shot* me."

"In my defense, I was aiming for that beast you keep company with."

For the first time, James spoke. "I've only met the lady recently, and I admit I'm no expert, but it seems to me that shooting her boyfriend is not a good way to endear yourself to her. Maybe apologize, instead of insulting him?"

"*Thank* you, James," I said.

Leo frowned. "I think you'll find this doesn't concern you."

"Fascinating." James moved to stand next to me. "I always assumed the Covenant of St. George would be made up of smart people, from the way it was described in the old books. I never guessed it would be made up of pompous assholes."

"Now, now, be fair," I said. "They can be smart pompous assholes."

Leo's frown blossomed into a full-fledged glare,

which he directed at the two of us without hesitation. "Who is this, Annie? Tell him to leave."

"This is James, he's a friend of mine, and I won't be telling him to leave, thanks, since I want somebody here to see if you decide to shoot me with another crossbow." I kept my knives up, ready to throw. I wasn't sure how good my aim would be, but hey. Sometimes you can only learn by doing. "I want you away from here, Leonard. Don't come near me, or my people, ever again. And do *not* insult Sam."

"He's not even human!" Leo took two steps forward, agitated. I raised my knives. He stopped. "What kind of future can you have with an animal? He'll never understand you the way I would. He'll never be able to give you the things you deserve. A home, a family—"

"Oh, *now* you're about family? Because last time I saw you, you were super okay with sedating your sister and lying to my cousin about who I really was. You're not trying to make sure I'm okay. You're trying to make sure I'm yours."

"Can you blame me?" He lowered his hands. "There's a war coming, Annie, a war *your* sister started. You're a valuable asset, and more importantly, I'm fond of you. I want you to survive when the Covenant takes back this continent. The only way that's going to happen is if you're on the right side."

"The right side being your side."

"Yes." Leo looked me in the eye. "It is. We have the numbers. We have the training. We have every tactical advantage it's possible to have in a situation like this one."

"Interesting," said James. He turned to face me. "Are all Covenant operatives this dishonest, or did we get a good one?"

"Be quiet," snarled Leo.

"Don't be quiet," I said. "What do you mean?"

"I mean if they had all the advantages he," James flapped a hand at Leonard, "wants to claim they have, why is this happening? Why is *any* of this happening?

You're one woman. Granted, you're faintly terrifying, and I'm not sure I'm going to survive knowing you, but you're not worth delaying an invasion. He's either exaggerating his position or downplaying yours."

"There's a third option," I said. "He's doing both, and he doesn't have the authority to be here."

Leo stiffened. I'd hit a nerve. Slowly, I smiled.

"That's it, isn't it? You're the one who brought me into the recruiting center, even if you didn't realize you were doing it, and once you realized who I was, you were so excited by the idea of bringing a Price back into the fold that you kept it a secret because you wanted all the credit. Only you lost me, and there were too many witnesses you didn't want to kill—at least, I'm assuming you didn't kill your own sister—for you to bury it completely. You're supposed to be back in England getting punished for your hubris right now, aren't you?"

Leo didn't say anything.

I glanced at James. "See, what Leo here doesn't like to remember is that he's our age. He's the new generation, still under supervision, and he's not supposed to scheme and plot and try to do things without running them through the chain of command. I got away because he wanted to see how much rope I needed before I hung myself."

"That's not entirely fair," said Leo tightly.

"None of this is entirely fair," I said. "Why should my version of the story be any different? You don't have any backup, Leo, and it's pretty clear that while you're willing to take potshots at innocent cryptids because . . . fuck, because you're an asshole, because you're jealous, whatever. It doesn't matter why you're doing this. You don't have any authority. The Covenant isn't coming to back you up or solve your problems. I want you out of here. I want you to leave me alone."

"That's never going to happen," he said, and smiled. "I own you. Whether or not you've admitted it to yourself, you're mine. One day, you're going to see how foolish it is to resist the inevitable, and you're going to come back to the fold."

He could do this all day: he'd prepared his supervillain speech, and all I was doing was giving him the material to play off of, allowing him to keep belching forth proclamations about his superiority and predestined victory and blah, blah, blah. Under other circumstances, I might have humored it. People who've already mapped out the conversation in their heads can frequently be tricked into giving things away if you let them keep talking long enough. But I was tired, and I was irritated, and I wanted to be safely behind the anti-ghost wards on the house as soon as humanly possible.

I had one injured shoulder and two hands. I threw the knife in my good hand, enjoying the brief second of shocked realization in Leo's eyes before the blade hit the porch support half a foot from his face with a satisfying *thwock* sound.

"That could have been your throat," I said calmly. "I have more knives, and you seem to have misplaced your crossbow. Leave."

"You're making a mistake."

"You shot me."

"I wasn't aiming for you."

"You keep saying that, and you keep not understanding why it doesn't actually help your case." I took a step forward, proud of the way my knees failed to knock. "Get out of here, or the next knife goes into your eye."

I could do it. Maybe not with my bad hand, but I always have more knives, and I could draw and throw again before Leo had the chance to do anything other than stand there and get impaled. He knew it, too; with a final frown, he finished descending the porch and started toward the small car parked behind Cylia's.

"This isn't over," he said. "You *will* understand why I'm the better choice than this menagerie of misfits and monsters before we leave this town."

"Maybe I'll also bleach my hair and learn how to walk in heels," I said. "Go."

He went. James and I stayed where we were, watching as he peeled out of the driveway and back to the street. Only when he was gone did James look at me.

"Would you really have killed him?" he asked.

"I don't know." I made the knife in my hand disappear. "He's set to inherit leadership of the Covenant. Killing him means this never ends. But unless I can find and confiscate whatever it is he's using to track me, maybe this never ends no matter what I do. So I don't know. Aren't you glad we didn't have to find out right now?"

I started toward the house. After a moment's stunned silence, James followed.

Sixteen

"There's nothing like moonlight and monsters to remind a girl why she loves her job."
–Alice Healy

The front room of a rented house in New Gravesend, Maine

S AM WAS WAITING JUST inside the house. He wrapped his arms around me as soon as I was through the door, pulling me into a tight, borderline frantic embrace.

"I'm sorry, I'm so sorry," he said, voice muffled by my hair. "Cylia said it would be better if I didn't go out, and I listened because I thought she might be right, but then you were there and I didn't help, and I'm so sorry."

"It's okay." He had my arms pinned against my sides. I squirmed until I could reach up enough to awkwardly pat his elbow. He didn't let go. It wasn't the most comfortable hug I'd ever experienced, but he was shaking and I couldn't find it in myself to push him away.

Sometimes I felt genuinely bad about what being close to me was doing to the people I cared about. Not enough to want them to leave me. Just enough to not complain when they hogged more than their fair share of the popcorn.

The door closed behind James. Cylia locked it, glancing out the curtains one more time to be sure Leo was gone. I gave Sam's elbow a final, awkward pat.

"It's really okay," I said. "I'm a big girl. I'm used to

taking care of myself. And if he'd tried anything, I would have put a throwing knife up his nose. Now can you let me go before I need new ribs? I don't want to fight the crossroads in a body cast."

"Sorry." Sam stepped back, tail curling anxiously around his ankles. He continued staring at me, surveying for imaginary injuries. "I'm going to kill that guy. I hope you're cool with it because every time he messes with us, it gets a little more inevitable."

"Just wait until we can make it look like a non-cryptid-related accident, please," I said. "The last thing we need is the entire Covenant descending on our heads because we killed their fearless leader-to-be."

"I swear joining you people has been like tuning in to a program already in progress," muttered James.

"I'm sorry reality doesn't come with a recap at the top of every hour," I said, and slid my arms out of the straps of my backpack. It made an impressively loud thump when it hit the floor. "Fern?"

"Here." The diminutive sylph appeared at my elbow as if by magic, although I knew it was much more likely to be connected to her fondness for lurking in corners and keeping out of the way when not actively involved in whatever was happening. "What do you need?"

"Clear the dining room table. Get notepads for everybody. We're about to do a speed transcription project."

Fern rushed off while Cylia turned to me, eyebrows raised. "I'm assuming there's a reason for this, and we're not just working on our handwriting?" she asked.

"James' mom did most of her serious research in witchletters, and right now, he's the only one who can make them appear," I said. "It'll go faster if he activates multiple books at once, but that means the writing's going to start fading almost as fast as it shows up."

"Meaning we transcribe as quickly as possible," said Cylia. "All right, got it. Any additional complications?"

I opened my mouth and hesitated, looking around the group. Things were already so bad. Did they really need the added burden of knowing the crossroads could hurt me whenever they wanted to, possibly to the point of incapacitating me?

Hell, yeah, they did.

"If I leave the ghost wards James set up on the house—say, to go to his place, or to deal with the crossroads, or to buy a cup of coffee—Bethany can find me," I said. "She found me at James'. And once she finds me, the crossroads can find me. It turns out they have ways of making sure people don't back out on their side of the bargain."

"Can they take back whatever you bargained for?" asked James.

"Thankfully, no," I said. "Aunt Mary made sure of that during the negotiation process. Since what I bargained for was not drowning, and Sam not drowning," and I was still sure, deep down, that he'd already drowned when the crossroads answered my request; that I'd lost him, possibly forever, before I decided to barter myself against the tempo of his heart, "they can't take that back. They're not allowed to kill me over a debt. But they took my magic as collateral against my doing them a favor."

"Killing me," said James.

"Yes, killing you." I looked at him levelly. "I didn't know when I made the deal that it would be a commitment to play assassination games, and honestly, I would probably have done it regardless, because I wanted to live. Where there's life, there's hope. Where there's death, there's . . . well, there's still hope, if my dead aunts are anything to go by, but it's a different kind, and not one that would have given my parents any comfort."

"If I'd died in Lowryland, I'm pretty sure my grandmother would have gone into necromancy so she could bring me back and shout at me." Sam paused. "Is necromancy real? Annie, is necromancy real?"

"I don't know, I don't want to know, and if people are raising the dead for recreational reasons, they need to stay way the hell away from me."

Cylia put up her hands. "I feel like we're getting away

from the point again. Something we're incredibly good at, especially when the point is unpleasant. What are you saying, Annie?"

"I'm saying the crossroads can force people who owe them to go along with paying our debts. They . . . hurt me." I paused, feeling suddenly awkward. Words weren't enough, and this whole thing sounded ridiculous. A bodiless force of chaos and capitalism hurt me? Sure it did.

Taking a sharp breath, I continued, "The crossroads used Bethany to pull me into the space they usually occupy, and they used my own magic to make every nerve in my body ignite at the same time. I can't resist something that came from me in the first place. I don't think there are any wards that could keep it from coming home—and once it does, it's in someone else's control, and it burns."

God, how it burned. Like acid, like fire, like every regret in the history of the world all rolled up into a single striking sword, slicing through me over and over again without leaving any marks behind. It was the kind of pain that broke people. It could easily have broken me. If I had to experience it again, I was direly afraid that it *would* break me.

James stared at me, a stricken expression on his face. "Where did this happen?" he asked.

"In the hidden stairwell. I think she was watching. Waiting for a moment when I wouldn't have anyone around who might try to interfere." I suppressed a shudder. Something brushed against my ankle. I looked down to see Sam's tail wrapping itself loosely around the curve of my calf, holding on without holding too tight.

It helped. Maybe I'm too weird to consider myself a part of polite society anymore, but it helped. I looked back up.

"I threw up when the crossroads stopped hurting me," I said. "It happened while I was still in the in-between space where they take you to make a bargain. There wasn't any vomit on the stairs when they dropped me back into the real world. I think that's the proof we've been waiting for that the crossroads really *do* exist in some other place."

"That is a terrible way of proving a point no one was contesting," said Cylia flatly. "Do not prove any further points in this manner, all right? I don't want to explain any of this shit to your cousin when we get back home."

Home. There was an idea. I'd been happy there. I'd been *bored* there, and suddenly boredom seemed like the very pinnacle of the human condition. If we could figure out how to get me out of my bargain with the crossroads, and get the Covenant off my ass, maybe I could bring Sam home to meet the family. He'd like them. They were weird enough to appeal to his idea of normal.

And that was never going to happen, because no matter how optimistic Cylia tried to be, I was never going to go home. There were too many obstacles in the way.

"James." I turned to face him. "When you go home, I want you to apologize to the air and say you're sure any ghosts who happen to be listening are lovely people, but that you need privacy. Tell them you need to masturbate. Whatever. And then get some damn wards in place, as fast as you can."

James flushed red. Sam snorted. I glanced in his direction. He was fighting not to laugh.

"I'm sorry," he said. "It's just . . . can you imagine what the mice would do with that?"

"Yes, and since I don't want to celebrate the Festival of James Smith is a Wanker for the rest of my life, we're leaving this part out when we tell them about the whole situation." James turned even redder. I shot him an apologetic look. "Aeslin mice. I'll explain more later."

"I'm not sure whether I want you to," said James.

"Too bad," I said. "To get back on track: pain. The crossroads can hurt me any time I'm not behind wards—maybe even when I *am* behind wards, but I'm trying to think positively—and that means they can keep me from acting. If they have enough time, if we don't stop them, they might be able to hurt me so badly that I'll agree to do anything they ask. I can't . . ." I stopped and swallowed, overwhelmed by the enormity of what I was about to say. It went against everything I believed in, everything I knew about myself and my place in the world.

We all—my siblings, my cousins, and me—know a certain amount of self-defense, because any weapon that can be taken away from you is not a perfect weapon. Alex is great at punching people, enough so that even Grandma Alice says he's impressive. She doesn't impress easily. Verity is more of a kicker, and when you're talking about someone who thinks extending a leg over her head is easy, that means something. Elsie likes to go for eyes and throats, while Artie was the star of his school track team.

And then there's me. Little Annie, isn't it cute how she lays traps and digs pits and sets blasting caps and never wants to hurt her hands. Isn't it funny how she sleeps with a knife under her pillow and a pair of brass knuckles in the pocket of her flannel pajama pants, where they leave a bruise on her thigh every morning that looks like she's been punching herself for hours.

Little Annie, who puts her faith in weapons over flesh and bone. Who doesn't even go to the shower unarmed.

"You're going to have to take my weapons away any time I need to leave the house," I said haltingly. "If I go out without them, then even if the crossroads compel me, there's only going to be so much damage I can do. Especially with Fern and Sam ready to put me down."

"I don't know if I can do that," said Sam quietly.

"I can," said Fern.

We all turned. She was standing in the kitchen doorway, expression grim. The stern line of her mouth melted into a faint smile as she looked at me.

"If I dial my density as far up as it can go, my skin gets harder to break, too, because otherwise I think my bones would explode it or something," she said. "So all I need to do is become super heavy, knock you down, and sit on you. Then you won't be able to hurt anybody, even if the crossroads really wants you to."

"I knew I liked you for a reason," I said.

Her smile turned, briefly, more sincere, before fading away entirely. "If we're going to fight the crossroads, though, I think there's something we have to think about, maybe. It could make things easier."

"Fern, no," said Cylia.

I frowned. "Someone want to fill me in?"

"I was just thinking the same thing," muttered James.

"She wants you to offer the Covenant asshole a truce," said Cylia.

I blinked.

"Not a truce," protested Fern. "Offering him a truce makes it sound like I want us to be friends. I don't want us to be friends. But he already knows our faces, and the Covenant probably doesn't like the crossroads any more than we do. If we can get him to come be on our side for fifteen minutes, or at least stop trying to shoot us every time we go outside, we can focus on one problem instead of two, and then maybe we'll *all* stay alive for a little longer. I want to stay alive, Annie. I'm sorry if that's selfish or something, but it's true. There aren't enough sylphs left for me to just . . . just run off and get myself killed."

She sounded genuinely distressed. I sighed and tugged my ankle away from Sam's grasp before walking over and folding her into an awkward hug. I'm not good at physical displays of affection. Maybe that's why I like Sam's need to have a hand, foot, or other appendage on me at all times; it takes the burden of performing comfort off of me. Fern made a small choking noise and sagged in my embrace.

"I'm sorry," she said. "I'm sorry, I'm sorry I don't want to be selfish, I don't want to be bad, but I don't want to die either. I want to prove I'm smart and strong and clever enough to have babies of my own. I want to have adventures, but I want to live."

"You will," I assured her, and I didn't think I was

lying, except in the greater "the grave comes for us all" sense of the idea. "You're going to find another sylph and have lots of babies that bob against the ceiling like so many balloons, and it's going to be wonderful. I'll even babysit for you."

"Creche childrearing," she reminded me, with a small hiccup in her voice that could have been either a laugh or a sob.

"So I'll come to the creche and do a shift there. Imagine me covered in babies. I don't even *like* babies. It'll be hilarious. All we have to do is get through this mess and we can do that, okay?"

"Okay," she said, and pulled away enough to wipe her eyes. "You'll think about it?"

"I'll think about it," I promised. "Now let's get to work."

You know what's boring as hell? Transcription, which is why court stenographers and the people who do captions for television should be paid substantially better than they are. Typing what someone else is saying is no fun at all. Copying someone else's manuscript, also not fun. Copying someone else's handwritten diaries that were never exactly designed for public consumption may well be the least fun of all. Doing it when the writing keeps trying to disappear, well . . .

"This is like the *American Ninja Warrior* of homework, and I hate it," said Sam.

"No contest here." I squinted at the page in front of me. "James!"

"Coming!" James rushed around the table and placed his hands above the book, fingers spread, face screwed up with concentration. The temperature dropped precipitously and the wavering, indistinct letters flared back into solidity.

"Thank you," I said, and paused, assessing him. Most

of the color was gone from his face; his eyes seemed shadowed, and there was an odd chapped quality to his lips, like he'd been walking outside in the freezing cold long enough to have all the moisture sucked out of his skin. "Are you okay?"

"Are we done?"

"No." James' mother had been a thorough documentarian, recording every scrap of data she could beg, borrow, steal, or observe about the crossroads. That was good. She had also been using the books to keep a diary of her daily activities, and while she never quite crossed the line into TMI—no lurid accountings of her sexual exploits or descriptions of James' father in the nude—she was perfectly willing to go on for paragraphs about the woman who'd shorted her change at the grocery store. Which still would have been fine, if she'd been writing on the front of the paper and using the back to record her more sorcerous observations.

That would, apparently, have been too easy on her eventual offspring, and thus had been dismissed as cheating. Her invisible writing was tucked into margins and on the open lines between the more mundane observations, and since it was all the same color once James had witched it into visibility, I had to keep forcing myself to focus on "the crossroads, on being thwarted, stripped the skin from Goodie Martha's body," and not "Jimmy was fussy again this morning, poor mite; he takes too much after my side of the family."

I was suddenly tempted to go home and find a way to witch the words out of Grandpa Thomas' diaries, and also terrified that if I did, I'd find a lengthy accounting of the places he and Grandma Alice had had sex in the house back in Buckley. Sticking two narratives in one book was *exhausting*.

"I'm done with this one," said Cylia, holding up a notebook. "How many more do we have?"

"Too many," said Sam glumly. "Can't we just nuke the place from orbit?"

"It's the only way to be sure, but no," I said. "I don't think the crossroads are something you can nuke."

"Not unless you want to make the dimension adjacent to our own radioactive for the next millennia, and probably still hostile," said James, as he hurried to refresh the writing on Fern's book. "Has anyone found anything that seems useful?"

"Your mom wrote down crop yields for like, three years, and I'm still not sure why," said Sam.

"Oh, I have an account of a local farmer trading his youngest daughter to the crossroads in exchange for a decade of good harvests," said Fern. "If the dates match up, maybe she was making sure the crossroads kept their word."

"Did the daughter die?" I asked.

"Disappeared," said Fern. "Like, um." She cast a sidelong look at James.

"Like Sally," he said grimly. "Yes, they're quite fond of that trick. Pull it all the time."

"Which is possibly a good thing," I said.

Slowly, he turned to stare at me. The temperature dropped again, the writing on the pages in front of me growing darker and crisper as his magic filled the room. Goosebumps formed on my arms. I fought the urge to pull back in my chair, remembering—not for the first time—that there are reasons people are, on the whole, afraid of sorcerers and the things we can do.

"What, exactly, do you mean by that?" he asked. His voice was even colder than the air around us.

"I mean that if they do this frequently, and we're not finding anything to indicate the crossroads have been handing out corpses, or brainwashed slaves, or fresh new bodies, then there's a good chance a lot of these people may still be alive somewhere. Someplace on the other side of the pocket realm where they do their bullshit business. There's a lot of reality on the other side of our dimensional wall. My grandmother has been exploring it for decades. Once we have an idea of where the crossroads might have been putting all these people . . ."

Once we had a scrap of information, a sliver of a clue, I could set Grandma loose on all the dimensions that had ever existed, and she would find all those people, and she'd bring them home. She'd bring Sally home.

She'd bring *Grandpa* home. Grandpa, who knew what it was to understand the Covenant and reject them anyway, who understood what I was and what I was becoming better than anyone in our shared family. We'd never met, but I had absolute faith that he'd be able to help me, because I was, in so many ways, his mirror. He could help me.

He had to.

James' eyes widened, the cold fading as my words sank in. "You really think . . . ?"

"I am making no promises, but I think they'd be stupid not to be keeping those people alive. They're a horrifying eldritch construct that doesn't belong here. They're not vampires." I tapped the page. "We read. We learn things. And once we know stuff, we fix things."

"Hear, hear," said Cylia.

And so we read, and as we read, we wrote, pulling a dead woman's secrets into the light for the first time since she'd tucked them away in her hidden room, banking on the hope that her son—who she already suspected was going to be like her in more ways than one, whose fingers were always cold and whose eyes were always focused on something past the horizon—would one day find them and make them his own. We read, we wrote, and we hoped to find the answer.

Until finally, impossibly, there it was. I stared at it, the writing in my own hand, black lines on white paper, answers and questions combined, and my mouth was dry, and I didn't know what to say.

Perhaps predictably, it was Sam who first noticed that I wasn't writing anymore. "Annie?" he asked, putting down his pencil. "You okay?"

"No," I said. I took a deep breath. "Okay. First, James, I apologize: your stupid time travel idea wasn't all that stupid after all. Second, we're going to need to go through the rest of the library to see whether there's anything there on summoning ghosts."

"Why?" asked James warily.

"Because we're going to need my Aunt Mary for the next part." I picked up my notes and read, "'The crossroads are a place and an idea at the same time, which is both their strength and their weakness. Because they are both physical and not, an attack on one aspect which does not address the other will never be sufficient to guarantee their destruction.'"

"This is making my head hurt already," murmured Sam.

I ignored him. "'It is my belief that, based on the following accounts'—and she has a list of names here, of people who made bargains; I recognize a few of them, so I bet we've transcribed all their stories—'the weakest point of this contradictory existence can be found at its origin. A spell which carried a petitioner back to the moment of the crossroads' creation would also enable the crossroads to be sundered into their component parts. The echo of this sundering might then weaken their grip on the world, and allow a simple exorcism of the spiritual force powering the crossroads as we know them now to be effective.'"

"That's . . . that's a really fancy way of saying 'throw the TNT and pray,'" said Cylia dubiously. "It can't be that easy. If it were that easy, somebody would have nuked the crossroads the first time they exploded a herd of cows, and we wouldn't be doing this now."

"The first problem is access," I said. "It says . . . okay, so it says in order to get to the point where an attack can have any chance of working, you must first bring someone who has been wronged by an unfair bargain to the crossroads. They have to get all the way to the deal point without changing their mind. And they need a crossroads ghost to basically play mediator. I don't think Bethany is going to volunteer for a plan that ends with her not having a job anymore."

Of course, that was only the first problem. I had to hope that "first" wasn't the word they'd focus on.

It wasn't. "Would Mary volunteer?" asked Sam dubiously.

I paused. Mary, my Mary, Mary Dunlavy, who'd become a babysitter after her body was already cold in the field. Mary, who'd always done her best to protect her family, *my* family, from the clutches of the crossroads, who had only become a crossroads ghost because it was that or disappear into the afterlife, leaving her father alone. He'd died shortly after her deal had been made, and he hadn't lingered, not like Mary, but he was still the reason she'd decided to stay.

"There's that awful saying, blood is thicker than water," I said. "At least that's how we say it now, hundreds of years after it was originally written. Some people say the whole phrase should be 'the blood of the covenant is thicker than the water of the womb.' The family you make is as important as the family you're given. Maybe more important. When you choose someone, it's because you have a choice. Mary chose my family. She's one of us, and she wants us to be safe. I think . . . I think if we can get her back, she'll help us challenge the crossroads."

Cylia nodded. "So we take you, because you've been wronged, and we get Mary back, and—"

"No." I shook my head. "I *haven't* been wronged. That's the problem."

Silence. Everyone blinked at me, briefly united on Team Missing the Point. That was okay. It wasn't like I'd exactly drawn them a flow chart to work from.

"Annie, they want you to *kill James*," said Sam carefully.

"I noticed," I said.

"It's just that that sort of feels like they're wronging you."

"They're not." I shot James an apologetic look. "I agreed to a favor to be determined later. I knew they could ask me to do something awful, something I'd have to find a way to get out of, and I said I'd do it, because I wanted to live more than I wanted to know that I was dying with clean hands. If anything, I'm wronging *them* by refusing to do what I promised."

"I appreciate your rebellious streak," muttered James.

"Hey. I didn't know for sure that they were going to ask me to kill a person. I didn't know what they were going to ask for. I just knew I had a lot more options if I wasn't dead, and that if I didn't get to my friends, they were *going* to be dead."

"As one of the people she saved, I want to go with 'yay Annie's flexible morality,'" said Cylia. "If I get a vote."

"Um, same," said Fern.

James—the only person in the room who hadn't been at Lowryland, who didn't understand the pressure I'd been under when I'd agreed to sell myself to the crossroads—flung his hands up in a gesture of disgusted defeat. "Fine," he said. "I'm the one who's been wronged. We can get your ghost and we can get ourselves to a potential bargain site, but how do we reach the actual liminal space where the bargains happen? The crossroads are malicious, shortsighted, and occasionally ignorant of human nature, but they're not stupid. They'll know something's up."

"Oh, that part's easy," I said. "We just have to convince them I'm there to kill you."

And then I could deal with the second problem. Because I had the spell, the words and gestures that would hopefully, if performed in a liminal space like the crossroads, use their questionable relationship to reality to rewind time to the point where all the trouble began. The only question was who would cast it, since none of the others had or knew how to use magic, and James was going to be playing witness in the trial that would determine his own future.

That left me, and my magic was currently in the custody of the crossroads. Which meant I needed to find a way to access it while it was being held captive. No pressure or anything. It was just that if I got this wrong, we were all going to die.

Seventeen

"Lord save me from the living."
                                        –Mary Dunlavy

The dining room of a rented house in New Gravesend, Maine

MY PRONOUNCEMENT FELL INTO the room with all the grace and buoyancy of a lead balloon. If we could have tied it around the crossroads' metaphorical ankles, our problems would have been over—or at least temporarily confined to the bottom of the lake.

Finally, with a surprising amount of delicacy, Fern said, "So, um, you want us to take you and James to the crossroads at the same time, where you're going to stab him or something?"

"I shouldn't need to stab him very much," I said.

"That's encouraging," muttered James.

"Oh, don't be such a big baby," I said. "I'm good at stabbing people. I can make it look very violent and impressive without puncturing a kidney or anything."

He stared at me. "Is this meant to be reassuring? Because if it is, you're doing it wrong."

"If we do this right, I shouldn't have to stab you at all," I said. "Although stabbing you a little would help, since it would mean I had a knife. Which you could then take away from me, leaving me unarmed." Unarmed, and going to confront an unspeakable horror on its own turf.

There was a time when I thought I was the smart one in my family. Now I just think I'm the one who was saving up all her stupidity to use it in one gloriously impressive display of What Not To Do.

"I have so many problems with this plan that I don't think I could list them all even if I wanted to try," said Sam. "On second thought, no. I really want to try, because this isn't so much a 'plan' as it is the Rube Goldberg version of a suicide attempt."

"Do you have a better idea?" I asked.

"Yeah. We ward the fuck out of the car and we get out of Maine." Sam glared at me. "This doesn't have to be our fight. This *shouldn't* be our fight. This is a bad fight, and I don't like it, and I don't want you getting hurt."

"See, that's the important word here. 'Hurt.' Mary's hurt. Whatever the crossroads are doing to her, it's not pleasant. Maybe it's not pain like the living experience it, but it's not good. So someone I love is already suffering because of all this. James is hurt. When the crossroads took Sally, they hurt him, and he has a right to be angry, and he has a right to want to make them pay for what they did. And while I'm pretty sure you don't care about either of those things as much as you would if you didn't feel like I was in danger—and I really love you for caring about whether or not I'm in danger—here's something you should care about: I can't live my life behind wards. I can't be locked in some shiny cage and told that you'll take care of me."

I waved my hands, indicating the room around us, the safely warded house with its strong walls and sturdy windows.

"My grandfather made a deal with the crossroads to save my grandmother's life," I said. "I don't know the exact terms he agreed to. No one does except for Mary, and she's never been allowed to tell us what they were. What I *do* know is that after he made his deal, he stopped going outside. Not right away, but slowly, staying a little closer to home every day. His world narrowed inch by inch, and by the time the crossroads carried him away, he couldn't even go down the stairs. Grandma had to carry his meals up to him, because he'd lost everything below the second floor. They crushed him like a rat in a trap, and when that wasn't funny anymore, they came for him anyway. There aren't wards to keep the crossroads out. All you could do is break me, so that when they showed up and said, 'Hey, kiddo, time to pay for fucking with us,' I'd be grateful for the chance to see the sky again." I took a breath. "Also, warding a car isn't like warding a house. I'm not sure it would work, and even if it did, we'd have to take James with us and have him recast the wards every hundred miles or so, which wouldn't work out for long."

Sam stared at me for a moment before he shoved his chair away from the table, rose, and walked out of the room. I watched him go, fighting the urge to run after him. Not so I could promise to stay out of danger—that was never going to happen—but so I could put my arms around him and hold on until he realized we were doing the right thing. It was terrible and it was dangerous and it was *right*.

He was going to be really thrilled when I went looking for Leo.

"This is so much fun, gosh, why did it take me this long to completely fuck up my life," I muttered.

"I'm the one you're planning to stab," said James, a note of wry sympathy in his otherwise dry tone. He was trying to distract me.

I've always been happy to be distracted with the idea of stabbing someone. "True enough," I said, gathering the shreds of my composure into something that could almost pass for cheer. "I bring one knife, I stab you to show the crossroads I'm serious, then you take the knife away. They won't expect it to be my only weapon. It's too far out of character."

James gave me a dubious look. "How many weapons do you customarily have?"

"The family record is fifty-three, currently held by

my mother, who is absolutely terrifying and also really good at hiding darts in her hair without scratching herself," I said. "I mean, we have some apocryphal numbers on Grandpa Thomas, but he's been missing for decades, and no one is willing to believe anything in triple digits until we've seen actual proof."

"Is disarming the traps a mating ritual for you people?" demanded James, aghast.

I winked broadly. "Indiana Jones ain't got nothing on someone who successfully dates a member of my family."

James put his hands over his face and groaned. I turned my attention to Cylia and Fern, sobering.

"Cylia, do you have enough good luck to add a little extra oomph to the summoning ritual we use to get Mary back, as soon as we figure out what that ritual is going to be?"

She hesitated before nodding. "Yes, but if that's what you want me to do, that's *all* I can do. We have Covenant operatives, we have a malicious hole in the world, and I love you, but that doesn't mean I'm dying for you, got it? I need to hold back enough to make sure I get out of here in one piece."

"Does that include getting Fern out of here in one piece?"

"It does."

"Then fair, and good, and absolutely right. You help us recover Mary and then you're in the clear. You don't have to do another thing if you don't want to."

Cylia made a sour face. "I don't want to do any of this."

"Don't I get a vote?" asked Fern. "What if I don't want to get out of here without you?"

"Sorry, sweetie, but you're the endangered species in the room, not me," I said.

"That's not true," she said. "You and James are both sorcerers. Isn't that hereditary and like, super-recessive? You're endangered, too."

James and I exchanged a look.

"In the alternate universe where Sam didn't exist and we were somehow compatible—"

"Which we're not: I prefer women who are marginally less likely to puncture my internal organs over a minor spat," he muttered.

"—maybe that would be a concern," I finished. "Sorcery is super-recessive, yes, but I'm not currently planning to have kids, and we're trying to keep James from being murdered. I think for us, running away is the greater risk. For you, it's the way you get clear of what's about to happen. Take the exit, Fern. Please. For me. Let me go into this knowing that you're safe."

She looked at me, blue eyes wide and pleading. It was hard to meet those eyes and not agree to do anything she wanted, if she'd just stop giving me that look.

"What about me?" she asked. "You want me to run away knowing that you're *not* safe. You're my best friend, Annie. I don't want to leave you."

"Maybe you won't have to," I said. "I mean, we still have a plan that depends on you knocking me down and sitting on me if the crossroads get too far into my head. That hasn't changed."

Fern looked slightly mollified. That was okay. If I was my friend, I'd look forward to the chance to hit me, too.

"After we have Mary back, we can ask her nicely if she'd be willing to climb into a spirit jar for us," I said, leaving the topic of who was leaving who behind. "They're a kind of ghost prison. It's cruel to leave a ghost in them for long, or to imprison them without consent, but once a ghost is confined, if they're not struggling to escape, they're undetectable."

James caught on first. "Meaning we could carry her with us to the crossroads without them realizing she's there."

"Exactly. They'll probably feel it when we free her, but if they assume she ran as soon as she was free, we'll be able to get the drop on them. I haul you down there, threaten you, stab you a little, get the crossroads to manifest in order to gloat—"

"At which point we free the ghost to demand a renegotiation of the deal that wronged me." He was starting to get excited. "That might actually work."

"Assuming the crossroads doesn't seize control of you and make stabbing him a little into stabbing him a lot," said Cylia. "How are we going to prevent that?"

"He'll freeze my hand to make me drop the knife," I said. "I won't have any other weapons, and I'm not that great in a hand-to-hand fight. Sam can take me easily." Barring that, Leonard could subdue me. The idea of having my ass kicked by a Covenant operative wasn't appealing. The idea of having my ass kicked by *that* Covenant operative was even less appealing.

If Sam wasn't willing to go along with this, Leonard might be my only option. I was pretty sure I'd be able to talk Leonard into helping us fight the crossroads, which were, after all, a threat to all humanity, and hence the sort of thing the Covenant *should* have been fighting.

In a better world, that's what they would have been doing. In a better world, the Covenant would have listened when my great-great-grandfather went to them with evidence that slaughtering intelligent creatures wasn't the only way to make things better for humanity, and they would have started to conserve and protect, as well as kill. Leonard and I could have been on the same side all along. In a better world.

Too bad this was the world we had to live in.

"When Mary forces the renegotiation, what happens?" asked Cylia.

"We get pulled into the liminal space where the exorcism can be effective," I said. "It's not a true exorcism—no priests, no demons, no holy water or pea soup. It's more of a banishing ritual tied into the innate power of the crossroads themselves. They don't have *time* there, not the way we have it here, and we should be able to reach all the way back to the root of what they did and sever the connection."

"Wait," said Fern, a sudden frown on her face. "Doesn't the crossroads have your magic? That's how they can hurt you the way you said they can. What happens if we break the connection before you get it back?"

I shrugged, trying to sound like I didn't feel strongly one way or the other as I said, "I never really liked setting things on fire anyway. If it gets rid of the crossroads, it's worth it."

I tried not to remember the way my fire had clung to me when I reclaimed it in the hidden room at Lowryland, the feeling that I'd betrayed something essential about myself when I gave it away in the first place. I tried not to dwell on how hollow my bones felt, like there was an empty space inside them where the magic should have been. I'd never wanted it. I'd never asked for it. But that didn't mean I was ready to lose it.

And none of that mattered. If giving up my magic was the only way to make sure the crossroads stopped ruining lives and destroying families—if it was the only way to keep them from turning me into a murderer— that was what I was going to do.

"We have a plan," I said, and was proud of the way my voice didn't shake, not even a little. "Now if you'll all excuse me, I'm going to go find my boyfriend and shake him until he stops being an asshole."

I turned and walked out of the room before any of them could object.

Not that any of them did.

The door to the room I was sharing with Sam was open, giving me a clear view of him sitting on the edge of the bed with his head bowed and his hands between his knees. More unnervingly, he was in human form. No tail, no fuzzy cheekbones. Just one Chinese-American man, alone, looking like his heart was breaking.

He didn't react when I stepped into the room, or when I sat down next to him on the edge of the bed. I bit my lip as I looked at him, unsure of what I was supposed to do or say. This was new territory for me. None of my past relationships, such as they were, had reached anything like this point.

"I sort of hate you right now," said Sam, voice dull.

"Okay," I said.

"I was happy with the carnival. I mean, I had to pretend to be human almost all the time, and it was hard to meet girls, and the ones I *did* meet always freaked out when I got fuzzy, and one chick said kissing me when I had a tail would be bestiality and she didn't swing that way, but I was happy. I had my grandmother, and the trapeze, and if things weren't perfect, it wasn't like they could get any better."

"Okay."

"I figured I'd take classes in business management and accounting through one of those predatory online colleges and sell one an old Ferris wheel to pay my tuition debts, and then I'd take the whole thing over when Grandma retired, and she'd sit outside her trailer and yell at me while I tried to work with townies who wanted to be racist assholes because they'd never seen a Chinese person before. And when she died, I'd keep the show going until I found a cousin or something who I could leave it to, and I'd die on the trapeze in front of an audience who'd come to see the oldest flying man in the world, and I'd be happy. I thought I was going to be happy."

"Okay," I said, for the third time, because there wasn't anything else I *could* say. All the other words were behind a wall of assumptions and costs and consequences, the little realities of moving from his world into mine. He had always been a cryptid. He had always been a target. But before me, he had never known just how big a target he was.

"I was so wrong." He kept looking at his hands. "I thought I knew what happy was, and I guess I did because I wasn't miserable. People liked me. My grandmother loved me. She still loves me. She'll die loving me, even if she never sees me again. I love the trapeze. I did good stuff with the carnival, and I'm not sorry I did it, but I wasn't happy the way I am when I'm with you."

I said nothing.

"Even when I'm mad at you, or you're mad at me, or you do something stupid, like when you ate that gas station sushi and I had to hold your hair back while you threw up in the ditch, even then, I'm so happy it hurts. This isn't happiness. This is weaponized joy. I'm going to die from loving you too much, and I'm not even sure I'll be sorry. How is that fair? You didn't mean to and I don't blame you, but you've ruined me for being happy without you. I can't do it. I can't go. I want to, and I can't."

"Okay," I said, one more time, and placed my hand over his.

He was still for a moment before he tilted his palm up to meet mine, his fingers wrapping tight, holding me in place. He still looked human. I knew how tense he had to be to be holding human guise for so long, and it hurt.

"I gave up the carnival for you," he said.

"I never asked you to. I sort of remember asking you not to."

"I know." He was quiet for several seconds. "Could you really not learn to be happy inside the wards? At least for a little while?"

"It wouldn't be for a little while. It would be forever, or for the rest of my life, anyway, until the crossroads decided to tear them down and kill me. I couldn't do it forever. I'm not that kind of person. I need to be able to run once in a while if I'm going to enjoy being still. I need to know that when I open the door, there's going to be a whole world on the other side, not just a linen closet I've already seen a thousand times."

Sam sighed heavily. "I guess I already knew that."

"Could you be happy if I said you had to stay human for the rest of your life? Not just a few hours when people could see you, but forever? Could you have loved me if I'd looked at you when you weren't so tense you wanted to scream and said I liked you better the other way?"

"No," said Sam, in a small voice.

"That's why I'd never ask that of you." I allowed the rest of the sentence—the fact that he'd asked exactly that of me—to go unsaid.

The fingers wrapped through mine grew longer, the skin changing texture in a subtle, not unpleasant way. A moment later, his tail wrapped around my ankle, holding me in place. That was all right. I hadn't been trying to run.

"I hate this," he said.

"I know." I leaned over, resting my head against his shoulder, and closed my eyes. "I hate it, too."

"Do you really think it's going to work?"

There were so many possible variables that trying too hard to think about them made my head spin. If we could get Mary out of whatever void the crossroads had cast her into. If we could convince Leonard he wanted to watch our backs, or at least didn't want to keep trying to kill us while we were dealing with something unspeakable and awful. If we could get James to the crossroads without anyone getting more than lightly stabbed. If, if, if. There were too many "ifs" and not enough definite objectives.

Alex would have told me this was a terrible plan. Uncle Mike would have insisted I needed so much more backup that it was better to just wait until he could get here from Chicago. Even Verity would have looked at this idea and written it off as flimsy and half-cocked. But it was what we had, and time was running out; if I didn't want to add "mystically compelled shut-in" to the list of ways in which I took after my grandfather, we needed to move.

"I have no idea," I said.

There was a pause. "I thought you'd lie," said Sam.

"Yeah, well, if this doesn't work, I don't want you telling everyone how I lied to you right before the crossroads decided to make my head explode." I squeezed his hand, eyes still closed. "I love you a lot, you know. I'm not going to be sorry about that, no matter what happens next. I got the chance to meet you, and that would never have happened without everything else. I'm grateful."

"I'm not," said Sam. "I'm pissed. I would never have missed you if I hadn't met you. I could have been too ignorant to know that I wasn't really happy up until the day I died."

"Would that have been enough?"

"Maybe," he said, and pulled his hand out of mine so he could put his arms around me, and he held me. Not for long; not for nearly long enough. But he held me, and I held him, and for a few more minutes, we were okay. We were together. We were going to win.

For a few more minutes, we were both liars, and that was all I wanted in the world.

Eighteen

"A parent's greatest fear is the idea of burying their children. Everything else is a distant second, and worth forgetting in the face of that unbearable loss."

–Evelyn Baker

Burial Grounds, about to do something very, very foolish

WE'D ALL AGREED, AFTER I managed to lure Sam out of the bedroom and back to the table, that speaking to Leonard was best done in a public place, since he was less likely to whip out a crossbow and start shooting people—aka, me—for ideological reasons when there were witnesses. I enjoyed not being shot. Any time I felt like I was in danger of forgetting how much I liked not being shot, all I had to do was move my arm and I remembered.

I did *not* like the feeling of impending panic that had been hovering over me since the moment I stepped outside the wards. My chest was tight, my jaw was tighter, and I had to keep fighting not to hyperventilate. I was going to need therapy when all this was over. Panic attacks whenever I went outside were not on my list of "useful souvenirs."

But that would have to wait. I was tucked into the deepest, darkest corner of Burial Grounds with a coffee mug in my hand and my eyes on the window. I hadn't been subtle about my approach: Cylia had dropped me two blocks from the shop and I'd taken my time walking to the door, waving to passing cars along the way, pretending everything was fine. Bethany couldn't snatch me off the street without being seen, which sort of went against the whole idea of being secretive, and if Leonard had me under any kind of surveillance, there was no way he could have missed me making the trip. All I had to do now was wait.

And wait.

And wait.

I was starting to think my time would have been better spent staying safe at the house and helping James figure out what sort of summoning ritual would work for a crossroads ghost who'd been punted into some sort of spectral jail by her employers when the door swung open and Leonard Cunningham stepped cautiously inside. He was tense, looking from side to side like he expected to be attacked at any moment.

A hot jet of satisfaction scorched through me, forcing me to bite the inside of my cheek to stop myself from grinning in a decidedly unfriendly manner. He was scared? *Good.* He had reason to be scared, starting with the fact that he was only still alive because I needed him that way. His death would summon way too much of the Covenant down on our heads, and that was one complication too many for an already complicated situation.

His scan failed to find any likely attackers and he approached the counter, ordering a mug of something and waiting for its delivery before collecting it and making his way down the length of the café to my table. He stopped just shy of the available chair.

"I'm assuming this was an invitation," he said.

I pushed the chair a little farther out with my toe. "You're not wrong."

He settled warily, cup held between us like a highly inadequate shield. I gave it a disdainful look. Leonard shrugged.

"I have little means with which to defend myself in public without violating the traditions to which I am sworn," he said. "Allow me the small comfort of knowing I could douse you in scalding liquid if you gave me sufficient cause."

"After the McDonalds lawsuit, coffee shops don't keep their water all that hot," I said.

Leonard looked at me blankly.

I sighed. "What, do you not have greedy corporations and medical bills in England? Look it up. Yes, I'm here to talk, and no, you shouldn't need to throw hot coffee on me. I'm here under the flag of truce." I picked up a napkin and waved it back and forth. "Behold the flag. How whitely it waves."

"You are a very strange woman," he said, pursing his lips. "How you passed initial screening, I may never know."

"I had someone changing my scores when everyone else's backs were turned because he wanted to keep me," I said.

Leonard flushed red and turned his face slightly away. Score one for the annoying American.

"Charming," he said.

"I'm not here to make friends, I'm here to win," I said, and waited a beat for his reaction. None came. I sighed. "You need to watch more reality television, or my tendency to talk entirely in pop culture references when stressed isn't going to make this easier. Look, we need to have a serious conversation about what you're doing here, and what you're *going* to do to make up for shooting me."

"I told you, I'm observing—"

"Observing me, right. I assume you have some sort of blood-based tracking charm, right? Something that lets you keep a solid lock on where I am? Well, first off, I'm going to need you to give that to me. And I want your word, on whatever it is that passes for your sense of honor, that you don't have the materials to make another one."

He turned enough to scowl at me. "What makes you think I'd tell you the truth?"

"Well, again, you want to recruit me. You let me live because you want to be the Covenant operative who brings the big, bad Price family back to the table." I leaned forward, smiling my most feral smile. "You can't lie to me and hope to bring me home with you at the same time. It's one or the other, and I'm banking on your self-interest telling you the bird in the hand is going to peck the crap out of you if you don't put it back in the bush."

Leonard's scowl deepened before he said, in a tightly controlled tone, "I was able to collect enough of your blood to make a single tracking charm. Margaret and Chloe have been persuaded to keep their silence."

"How?"

No reply.

"*How*, Leonard?"

"Chloe . . . had no actual evidence of your malfeasance," he said slowly. "I was able to convince her you'd been taken against your will. She believes, and is convincing our parents, that I'm trying to recover you from a kidnapping. I lack backup because retrieving one half-trained agent is less important than recovering from Robert's death and bolstering our resources against the coming conflict."

It was surprisingly easy to believe that. Chloe Cunningham was a smart woman, skilled enough to stay alive in a fight and canny enough to see which way the wind was blowing. She was also a Covenant girl, trained from birth to take orders and believe her superiors. Leonard was their grandfather's heir apparent, and one day he was going to run the entire enterprise. Assuming he didn't end up disappearing into a shallow grave first. Plus, Chloe and I had been roommates back in the training facility. If I was a double agent, that reflected poorly on her. If I'd been kidnapped, on the other hand . . .

"What about Margaret?" I asked. "She knows damn well that I'm not a patsy."

For the first time, Leonard looked uncomfortable. "Margaret has been . . . pliable since her first mission in the States. I wondered whether something might have happened to her there. Regardless, she's been easy to convince, under any form of hypnosis, of almost anything I needed her to think."

I stared at him. Finally, stiffly, I said, "Only the fact that you don't look happy about this is keeping me from stabbing you right now. If I find out you've put a finger on her—"

"What? No!" Leonard recoiled, looking honestly appalled. "I would never abuse the trust of another Covenant soldier like that. What kind of monster do you take me for?"

"A murderer and a liar, mostly, but that's another conversation." I shook my head. "You're willing to manipulate her mind for your own gain. Why should I believe you're not willing to do the same to her body?" My words came out even sharper than I'd intended, powered by the strength of my guilt and dismay.

Margaret Healy was my cousin. Distant, yes, and from a branch of the family that hated mine and wanted to see us all dead, but still, she was blood. She'd been raised in the Covenant, told from birth that the Healys—now Prices—who'd left to go to America were traitors at best, and villains at worst. Sure, she was an adult and could technically make her own choices, but it can be hard to go against the dominant philosophy espoused by literally everyone in your life.

She had been on the Covenant strike team that tracked down Verity and Dominic in New York. They'd managed to capture Verity. They would have been able to use her to learn everything about the family. We would all have been lost . . . if my cousin Sarah hadn't used her natural telepathic powers to basically melt Margaret's memory and rewrite it into something more convenient.

Doing that, using her powers that way, had hurt Sarah

badly enough that she'd spent more than a year unable to manage even simple arithmetic, wandering in a fugue state while her adoptive parents and my brother did their best to keep her from hurting herself. I'd been angry with Verity for a long time after that. No: that didn't cover it. I'd been *furious* with Verity for a long time after that. I'd been angry and unforgiving, and I'd blamed her for the fact that one of our cousins might be lost inside her own head forever.

Then Sarah had started getting better. She still wasn't what she'd been before, but she was well enough to have confirmed that she'd acted of her own free will, and that made a difference, at least to me.

I had never really considered what the long-term effects for Margaret might have been.

"I thought you'd be happy," snapped Leonard. "If I hadn't convinced her she'd seen you taken by that beast you continue to call a boyfriend, she'd be here with me—and she wouldn't be aiming for recruitment. You're playing a dangerous game, Annie Price. It's going to end badly for you, one way or the other."

"My freedom or my life, you mean?" I shook my head. "It's going to end badly for one of us. I want you to stop fucking with Margaret's head."

He raised an eyebrow. "I'm not seeing where you have the grounds to make that request."

"How about she's my family, and I owe her at least that much?" I leaned forward. "Also, how about someday I'm going to be coming back to England to tell your leadership where to stick it, and I bet they'd be real interested in hearing how much you've been messing with that poor woman. She deserves better than your bullshit. Leave her alone."

Leonard leaned back in his chair. "I think I liked you better when you were playing at being Timpani."

"And I think I liked you better when I thought you were a brainwashed foot soldier instead of a would-be mastermind, but here we are, and this is what we have to work with," I said. "I came here because I wanted to sit down with you. I have a proposal."

He took a careful sip of his coffee, savoring it, before he said, "You are always welcome in the arms of the Covenant. You know that. I'm even willing to spare—"

"Okay, I'm going to stop you right there, because you can't help us if I'm busy stabbing you," I said. "I'm not coming back. Not now, not tomorrow, not ever. I am not your good little Covenant girl, and I'm never going to be. I hate you. I hate everything you stand for. All your ideals, all your ideas about what this world is supposed to be, everything. It's vile. It's disgusting. It's archaic, and not in the fun Renaissance Faire kind of way."

Leonard narrowed his eyes. "I see. Well, then. If I'm so revolting to you, why are you here?"

"I could say it was because I wanted a cup of coffee, but we both know I'd be lying." As if the desire for caffeine could have lured me out into the open with Bethany still lurking around, ready to deliver another "reminder" of my duty to the crossroads. "Do you know what the crossroads are?"

His lip curled in clear disgust. "Witchcraft."

"Not quite, and since you're using a tracking charm to follow me, I'm not sure you get to complain about honest witchcraft right now." I picked up my own coffee, turning the mug between my hands. The heat seeping through the ceramic was soothing, like it was slipping the fire back into my fingers a little bit at a time. "I'm guessing you know what they are, though."

"Foul places, used for the making of the devil's bargains."

I didn't bother to swallow my sigh. "If you're going to be like this, we may as well call this finished right now. I need to *talk* to you, not feed you quarters so you can spit out excerpts from the Covenant training manual like some sort of fucked-up vending machine. Will you *listen*?"

There was a long, dangerous pause as Leonard considered his options. I stiffened, waiting to see which way he was going to go.

There was no way he'd managed to conceal a crossbow on himself. That was good. But there are a lot of weapons smaller than a crossbow, and he could be carrying any number of them. I, on the other hand, was not, for James' safety: I'd have to improvise, which meant smashing a lot of innocent furniture. If he decided we were done talking and it was time for him to attack me, we could destroy this place. That would attract attention. Win, lose, or draw, I'd have a lot of problems if he turned this physical, and that would complicate getting James down to the crossroads to sort things out.

"All right," he said finally. "I'm listening."

"You have access to the Covenant library. Have you ever really looked at the history surrounding the crossroads?"

"I did a research project when I was in primary school." He said it so calmly, so reasonably, that it made me want to laugh until I cried.

What would the world have been like if my ancestors had been able to make the Covenant see sense about changing their tactics, about learning to live with the cryptids and yōkai and ghosts instead of working to destroy them at every turn? I could have grown up doing school reports about things I actually cared about, rather than pretending I thought Christopher Columbus was a good man and not a colonialist bastard. I could have been so much more *prepared*.

We build our presents on the ruins of our pasts, and we hope the foundations we construct from the dust of bad ideas and painful choices will be strong enough to hold up our futures. They have to be.

"So you know the crossroads changed in the 1400s," I said, like there was no question of his knowledge. It was out there to know: he'd done his research: of course he knew it. I wasn't challenging his authority, not at all, only reminding him of something that anyone who'd bothered to open a book would have seen.

Leonard blinked. "Er," he said. "Yes."

Of course he hadn't known. The Covenant wrote things down, but they didn't care about the reasons those things happened, or what they'd been before they turned hostile. That was why the Covenant had been able to become such a force for destruction, and why they'd always been doomed to stagnate and fail. If you don't understand what you're trying to fight against, you're inevitably going to be defeated.

"James—the local man you've seen me talking to—found a way to undo that change. The crossroads used to be a natural thing."

"Nothing that encourages good men to make deals with devils can be natural."

I rolled my eyes. "There we go again. Okay, look, no. Whatever the crossroads were when they started, they were created in this world, by this world, to be a part of this world. They're *supposed* to be here. Maybe they're the noosphere's nervous system, or maybe they're a pressure valve for all the little, unavoidable magic that builds up around living creatures, or maybe they're a big cosmic zit. Whatever. They're *natural*. The world would suffer if we destroyed them." I wasn't entirely confident about that last part—most people get by just fine without ever going down to the crossroads—but I didn't want to give Leonard the idea that we could, or would, destroy the crossroads completely. Mary wouldn't survive losing the source of her tether to this world.

Was I willing to risk actual, living people for the sake of saving my phantom babysitter?

Hell, yes, I was, and anyone with a heart would have done the same thing.

Leonard frowned. "What are you saying?"

"I'm saying the malicious 'I want to kill your cattle and eat your firstborn because I'm an evil entity from beyond time and space' crossroads we all know and hate *aren't* natural. They're some kind of parasite that's managed to take over the space the real crossroads are supposed to occupy. If we can get to them without being stopped, we can hurt them. Maybe even kill them. The real crossroads, the one that *doesn't* eat people, comes back. You look like a hero for being there when it went down. Hell, you go back to England and take all the credit. Now you've proven yourself. You went to America to recover an agent, and you fixed a problem that's been plaguing people for centuries. Gold star you, pat yourself on the back, and never darken my door again."

"It's not possible." Leonard put his coffee cup down, the better to gesture vaguely with both hands. "If the crossroads could be destroyed—or even rendered less dangerous—we would have done it centuries ago."

"Except no, because you'd have to be willing to work *with* people, not against them," I said. "We have a plan. It requires a sorcerer, a crossroads ghost, and someone the crossroads believe they have a hold over. Can you honestly say the Covenant would be able to put together the same kind of group?"

Silence.

"I didn't think so. We have a plan and we have a team, and now we need you."

"Me?" Leonard sat up a little straighter. "What do you want from me?"

"First, we want your word that you won't try to attack us again while we're dealing with this shit. The crossroads are bigger and nastier than you are, but that doesn't mean we're magically immune to cross*bows* while we're dealing with them." I allowed myself the luxury of a scowl. "What the hell is it with your family and crossbows, anyway? First Chloe, now you. I'm getting real tired of Cunninghams trying to shish kebab me."

"They're convenient and easier to dispose of than firearms."

"Maybe in England. Over here, we're all about the unregistered handgun. Anyway, the point stands: I want your word that you won't try to attack me again, or any of us. We need to be able to work without fear of some kind of messed-up sneak attack."

Leonard gave me an assessing look, clearly searching for the catch. "For how long?"

"See, where I come from, 'please don't attack me anymore' isn't the kind of request that comes with a time limit. I'd really prefer it if you never attacked any of us again. If you can't bring yourself to promise that, how about we do this: you give me the tracking charm and you promise me a year."

"A year."

"A year," I repeated. "One year, during which you won't follow me, you won't look for me, you won't do anything to disturb me. You said you were preparing for war back in Europe? Well, you stop it. For a year, you stop it. When the clock runs out, either we'll have found a way to make peace, or we'll pull the whole world down with us."

Leonard hesitated. "What you're asking . . ."

"You already have a narrative that fits. I'm your sweet little recruit, stolen by beasts during a mission I should never have been sent on, a mission that claimed the life of a senior agent." An agent whose face I still saw when I slept—and probably would for the rest of my life.

My parents raised me to defend myself and protect the world around me, a world of magic and monsters and people who deserved the chance to live. That doesn't mean I'd been prepared for the impact of killing a human being. I wasn't sure anything, ever, could have prepared me for that.

"Yes," said Leonard slowly.

"You were looking for me, and you stumbled across, fuck, I don't care. A coven of like-minded wizards who were planning to set magic aside as soon as they'd managed to use it for one great good. A big red button labeled 'erase crossroads forever.' Whatever. It doesn't matter, and you know what your grandfather is going to believe. You stopped to take care of the greater evil, and my captors whisked me away while you were distracted. You couldn't find me. You needed to make your report. I'm sure once you're back at Penton Hall, you'll be able to come up with plenty of paperwork and administrative bullshit to keep you busy until the year runs out and it's fair game again."

"You'd have me look like a fool for losing track of you."

I scoffed. "A fool who just got full credit for *destroying the crossroads*, much? Maybe you'll look a little heartless for letting poor me get eaten by ghouls or whatever while you were distracted by cleaning up an actual threat to mankind, but I'm pretty sure your superiors will forgive you. The Covenant has always been willing to make sacrifices for the greater good, right? Gryffindor bullshit."

"Are you making Harry Potter references because I'm British and you assume that's the way to reach me?"

"No, I'm making Harry Potter references because I'm an enormous nerd and it amuses me to remind you of that," I said. "One year, Leonard. Your word that you don't attack me or any of my friends for that time, and that you don't try to track us, either."

"Why should you believe me?"

"Oh, that's easy." I smiled sweetly. "We learned about this concept in school, called mutually assured destruction. So here is what I am assuring you. If you come near me before that year is out, if you send one of your strike teams after me, if you inconvenience me in any way or with any intent to do me harm, I will come back to England, knowing everything I know about your resources and your security, and I will kill you. The question thus becomes: do you think you can completely redo your security, without blowing your own 'I was trying to get her back, I absolutely didn't encourage a spy to nestle in our midst' cover story, before I can come there and start making you understand why it was a bad idea to cross me? Because I don't think you can. I think I'd do a lot of damage, and yeah, you'd probably put me down, but I'm okay with that if it means you find out that choices have consequences."

Leonard paled. "You're bluffing."

"I'm a Price, Leo. Do Prices bluff?"

He didn't answer me.

"Your word, and you get to be a hero. Or tell me no, keep fighting us, and you get to be a corpse. One way or another. If I were you, I'd take door number one. It's a pretty sweet deal, and it means you still have the chance to bring me back to the fold, as you so charmingly put it, assuming you still want me. I don't want you, but hey, that's always been beside the point as far as you're concerned, right?" I picked up my mug. Took a sip. Set it down. "One year, your word, and you make the world a better, safer place for humanity. I thought that was your mission statement."

"I'm beginning to question the wisdom of recruiting you," he said sourly. "You're more trouble than you're worth."

"I've been telling you that for a while," I said brightly. "You in?"

Leonard hesitated.

"I asked you a question."

"Yes," he said.

My smile became genuine. "Great. Let me get a to-go cup and we're out of here."

Cylia watched in the rearview mirror as Leonard and I climbed into the back seat. The front passenger seat was open, but I wasn't leaving Leo alone, and I wasn't seating him next to Cylia. That left treating her like a taxi, at least in the short term. I would have felt bad about that, if I hadn't been transporting a potentially armed

Covenant operative. Patting him down in the coffee shop would have been suspicious.

"Hello," she said, voice cool. "If you even reach for your wallet, I'm running us off the road."

"Charming," said Leonard. He turned his attention to me. "Are all your friends this hospitable?"

"You've made a lot of endangered species over the years," I said. "Maybe you should expect a little justified hostility."

"Hmm." He gave Cylia a more thoughtful look. "Dragon princess?"

"Go with that," said Cylia, slamming her foot down on the gas.

Dragon princesses are nothing more nor less than female dragons, evolutionarily adapted to pass themselves off as attractive human women for the sake of staying safe from men like the one next to me. That isn't common knowledge, and there was no reason for me to whisper a word of it to Leonard. Let him be the ignorant one for a change.

Cylia kept her eyes on the road as she drove, her hands white-knuckled on the wheel. "I assume Annie already gave you the speech about shallow graves and no witnesses if you hurt a single one of us."

"It was largely implied," said Leonard coolly. "I'm not a monster, Miss . . . ?"

"You could have fooled me," said Cylia. "I know a lot of broken families because of men like you. I know a lot of unfinished stories. You don't get my name. You don't get to offer me the hand of friendship just so you can pull it away when you decide I'd be better off dead. You get a ride in my car, and you get me not killing you yet. That's all I'm willing to give."

Leonard gave me a look, smirking faintly. "You have charming friends," he said.

"I have friends who have very, very good reasons to hate you, and since you're pretty proud of those reasons,

I don't think you have the moral authority to get angry at them," I said. "You have a lot of blood on your hands."

"Hundreds of years of it," Leonard agreed. "Only a century's-worth has been washed from yours. What does that make you, do you think?"

"Deep in debt, but at least aware that I'm there," I said. "Now give me the charm."

Leonard blinked. "Excuse me?"

"Part of our deal was that you give up the tracking charm you've been using to follow me. I want it."

"The crossroads—"

"Successfully destroying them wasn't a condition of getting my life back." I held my hand out. "The charm, Leonard. Now. Or I tell my friend here that you clearly have no interest in keeping your word, and we do that 'shallow grave' thing she's so into. I haven't gotten her a birthday present yet."

"A little murder would improve my day immensely," said Cylia.

Leonard scowled as he reached inside his jacket—a gesture that caused Cylia to tense even more behind the wheel—and produced a small, flat glass disk that gleamed red as rubies in the light. The blood contained inside had somehow remained bright and fresh, captive of the magic that kept it from clotting. I snatched it out of his hand and made it vanish into my pocket.

"Will you give it to your new keepers, so they can keep tabs on you?" he asked, a sneer in his voice.

"I'll destroy it," I said. "And then, assuming you're smart enough to keep your word, I'll be able to go home. Don't you want to go home, Leo? Because if you try to double-cross us, you won't. Ever. You'll die here, in a foreign country, and leave your parents and sister to mourn you."

"Remember that mutually assured destruction?" he asked. "If I disappear, my family will not rest until they know what happened to me."

"See, in England, you think a hundred miles is a long

way," I said. "In America, we think a hundred years is a long time. It's funny, when you stop to think about it. We have a lot of empty places where your body could disappear. Sure, your family might figure it out eventually, but I promise you, you'd be missing a lot longer than you think, and we'd have plenty of time to get a head start. Play nice. We can all get out of this alive."

Cylia snorted but didn't say anything. Under the circumstances, that was probably the best I was going to get.

"I'm not sure why you think I'll want to work with you when you insist on threatening me at every turn," said Leonard.

"Our sparkling personalities," I said. "Also the part where you're getting the credit for this, at least as far as the Covenant is concerned. You're going home a hero. A big, successful, awesome hero. No one's going to care that you lost me because you'll be the man who killed the crossroads."

Leonard didn't have to look tempted for me to know that I had him. He wouldn't have been in the car otherwise. Hopefully, he hadn't thought through the rest of what this meant.

He was going to be working *with* us. Even if he tried to double-cross us—which let's face it, he was almost certainly going to do—he would still have worked with us, and we would still know the truth. We'd know the hero of the Covenant of St. George had teamed up with his ancestral enemies to help us finish a job that was already almost done, and would have been finished with him or without him. Knowing meant we could document every damning step of the process.

Talk about "mutually assured destruction." Maybe a Covenant soldier like Dominic had been, like my grandfather had been, could have handled the sudden revelation that he'd voluntarily teamed up with a pair of sorcerers and a bunch of cryptids to fight an eldritch horror, but Leo was supposed to be their next leader. He was the proverbial chosen one, meant to usher the

Covenant of St. George into their bright and genocidal future, and if I could use this to undermine his authority, I would. In a heartbeat.

Of course, so much was contingent on me *having* a heartbeat when all this was over. The air outside the car pressed in on us, until it was like we were driving through the deep, unseen sea, surrounded by creatures that had never seen the light of day. I knew it was my paranoia speaking—the crossroads had no need for that kind of fancy special effects, and if Bethany had been lucky enough to be paying attention during my brief field trip outside the wards, she would already have come to say howdy and remind me about all the homicide I was supposed to be committing. I hated to depend on luck. I hated knowing that one slip and I'd be burning again, with a fire that should have been my friend.

"I am so much more like my grandfather than I want to be," I muttered.

"What's that?" asked Leonard.

"Nothing." He could find out about my specific issues later. Or not at all. I liked option two better.

No ghosts appeared to trouble us as we finished the drive to the house, and if I hustled for the front door a little faster than was seemly, whatever. Let Leonard think I was desperate to get to the bathroom after hanging out in a coffee shop for the last hour. Everybody pees.

Fern and James were in the front room, Fern filing her nails with the careful nonchalance of someone who wanted to be just about anywhere else, James making notes in a small, leather-bound notebook that looked like it had seen better days. The couch had also seen better days. Books covered every square inch that wasn't occupied by James, and he had enough books piled on his legs that I wasn't sure he was making a difference in the overall burden.

While the air no longer held the brutally frigid snap of artificial winter, it was still cooler than it should have been, like we'd been running the air conditioning. Sam was nowhere to be seen. I looked around, frowned, and returned my attention to Fern.

"Is he in our room? Because I don't have time to do another heart-to-heart right now." Being in a relationship was *hard*. I still liked it—especially the parts where I got to have sex on a regular basis—but wow was it more work than I had ever realized it was going to be.

Fern shook her head and pressed a finger to her lips, signaling me to be quiet. Oh. I turned, watching as Cylia and Leonard made their way toward the house.

Cylia was in the lead, probably because he assumed she'd know where the traps were. That was why she made it over the threshold while he was still climbing the porch steps, and was safely inside when Sam dropped soundlessly, like something out of a horror movie, from the awning to land behind Leonard.

I'll give Leo this much: Sam might not have made a sound, but whatever small displacement of the air he'd caused had been enough to clue Leonard to the fact that he was in danger. He stopped walking, back going very straight as he considered his options.

He didn't have many. Unless he wanted to treat those of us in the house as the "safe" option, which hey, maybe we were. Or maybe this had all been a very complicated murder plan.

"Mutually assured destruction, I thought," he said.

"Yup," I agreed amiably. Sam was coming out of his crouch, unfurling behind Leo inch by inch in a manner that would have been unbelievably menacing if I hadn't found it so ridiculously hot. There was something very wrong with me. I welcomed it.

Cylia grinned. Fern continued filing her nails. James glanced up from his notes long enough to make a disapproving face—less "oh no, a threat to human life is happening where I can see," more "if I get blood on my book, I'm going to be pissed"—and went back to writing.

"I came in good faith."

"This time," I said. "I don't think I'm your problem, though."

Finally, slowly, Leonard turned and considered the fūri behind him. Sam was standing completely straight, lips drawn back to show teeth that were thicker and stronger-looking than the human norm, the hair-slash-fur atop his head bristling in a clear threat display. His tail was curved in the high angle that meant he was angry, rather than the relaxed curl of comfort. I took a moment to appreciate all the research I'd done into his semi-unique body language. This little scene would have been a lot less fun if I'd been guessing at whether my boyfriend was *really* ready to commit murder on my behalf.

He was. He so, so was. All I had to do was say the word and Leonard would be one ex-Covenant member, mostly because they seem to require their members to have heads attached to their bodies.

"Er," said Leonard. "Hello. I don't believe we've been properly introduced."

I was impressed. Given how incredibly dedicated to the idea that all cryptids were monsters that needed to be destroyed most members of the Covenant were, I had expected a less civil response. Then again, maybe the fact that Sam looked willing to answer incivility with violence was doing something to temper Leo's natural instincts.

"No," said Sam curtly. "We haven't been."

"Leonard Cunningham." Leo stuck his hand out like he fully expected Sam to shake it. "If you kill me, you'll bring the wrath of the entire Covenant of St. George down upon your head, and the heads of your companions. As you seem reasonably fond of them, I assume you're not intending to do anything foolish."

"Nah. Nothing foolish." Sam's hand engulfed Leonard's, long fingers wrapping around it and overlapping onto themselves. Leonard's back stiffened further as he realized how strong Sam's grip was.

"I wish I had popcorn," I muttered to Cylia.

"You and me both," she said.

"See, you're right: I like my friends. They're pretty cool. Even the asshole on the couch isn't as annoying as I thought he was going to be when I first met him. And you're right that I don't want to make trouble for them, since that's not really friendly-like. But there's something you're wrong about." Sam tugged. Leonard stumbled toward him, unable to break free of the stronger man's grasp.

I'll give Leo this much, if nothing else: shaken as he clearly was, he maintained a scrap of dignity as he asked, "What's that?"

"Annie's not my friend." Sam's smile widened, becoming even more threatening. "You shot her. You *shot* her with a *crossbow*, and she fell into the lake. She could have died. You get that, right? She could have died. You did that."

"I was aiming for you," said Leo.

"And maybe I could have forgiven you for that—I mean, probably not, but maybe—only you didn't hit me. You hit *her*. She could have died." Sam let go of Leo's hand so abruptly that the other man stumbled backward, thrown off-balance. Sam looked at him dismissively. "If you ever threaten her again, I'm going to rip your spine out and beat you with it until you stop twitching. If you ever actually hurt her again, you're going to wish I'd done something as friendly as removing pieces of your skeleton. Got it?"

"Unfortunately, yes," said Leonard.

"Great," said Sam. "Welcome to the party."

Nineteen

"Find out what people expect and then do
as close to the opposite as your conscience
and the laws of physics will allow. Gets 'em
every time."

–Frances Brown

*The front room of a rented house in New Gravesend,
Maine, getting ready to make some really impressive
mistakes*

LEONARD LOOKED AT JAMES' meticulously written and
organized notes, a small frown on his patrician face.
He'd been reviewing our work for the past twenty minutes, and I was starting to twitch. Who knew I could get
test anxiety from watching a member of the Covenant
go over my plans to either change the world forever or
get myself and everyone who trusted me utterly, irre-
deemably fucked? What a fun voyage of self-discovery
I was on.

If Leonard was aware that we'd arranged ourselves to
box him in, he wasn't saying anything. James was still in
his original position on the couch, having moved a few
books but otherwise not acknowledging that Leonard
might like to be comfortable. That was part of the plan.
If Leo tried to bolt, James could grab him and present
him with a nice case of frostbite to slow him the hell
down. Cylia was leaning against the front door, Fern
was sitting cross-legged at the entry to the hallway, and

Sam and I were sitting on the stairs, me with my back against his chest, him casually playing with my hair while shooting nasty looks in Leo's direction. He was as tense as I'd ever felt him when not in human form, and his tail was wrapped around my left ankle tightly enough to hurt a little. I didn't object.

"There's a flaw in your reasoning," said Leonard finally, looking up and scanning the room until he met my eyes. "A fairly large one."

I raised an eyebrow. "And what's that?"

"Your plan hinges on you having access to your original crossroads ghost, the one you say is well-inclined toward your family," he said. "If you can't leave the wards without risking exposure to the second ghost, the one that *isn't* well-inclined, how are you planning to get the first ghost back?"

I smiled slowly. Sam's body was warm behind me, chasing the last of the lingering chill from the air. I felt like I was starting to thaw for the first time since Bethany had appeared to tell me what the crossroads wanted me to do.

"I'm sure you must have asked yourself why we'd need another warm body when the party was already pretty full," I said. "I mean, it's not that we didn't *want* to run around wondering if we were going to get stabbed in the back at any moment, it's just that five is the usual sweet spot for any sort of superhero outing."

Leonard looked at me warily. "I'm sure you're speaking English."

"All that snobbery and you don't even read comic books. Man, I really dodged a bullet getting away from you people."

"You didn't dodge the crossbow bolt," said Sam.

"Point," I said. Looking at Leonard, I said, "We need you to go to the crossroads—not the main one, not the one by the hanging tree, we're saving that to visit with Mary—and indicate that you're ready to make a deal. We have summoning charms that should work to get

Bethany's attention. Then all you need to do is hem and haw enough that she stays focused on you while we get Mary back."

"And what, pray tell, am I to claim to want?" asked Leonard.

"Simple." I felt an echo of Sam's smile in my own as I bared my teeth at the man in front of me. "Say you want me. Say you can't go home without me. Say you can tell the crossroads have some sort of claim on me, and you've come to buy it back. All you have to do is avoid sealing an actual bargain while we get Mary out of wherever she's been banished to. Once that's done . . ."

Once we had Mary, we'd be able to petition for a re-assessment of Sally's deal. We could get to the crossroads where they lived, if that was even the right term. And then things would really get interesting.

Leonard looked at me levelly. "You're trusting me a great deal."

I rolled one shoulder in a shrug. "You're not going to make a crossroads bargain over me. You don't want to win by cheating, and those bargains always have loopholes in them. Your control over the Covenant is going to depend on not having any of those loopholes in your past, waiting to strike. Also, you pretty much think the crossroads are literally the big-D Devil, and you're probably not wrong. So yeah, I trust you, but only because I know I can. You fake it. You flirt and you fluster and you keep Bethany busy, and in exchange, we give you the world. Think you can manage?"

Slowly, almost reluctantly, Leonard began to smile.

"You only needed to ask," he said.

Finding a local crossroads manifestation point was easy. Too easy: while every crossing potentially *could* be a breakthrough for a bargain, most municipalities don't have more than one spot that has actually been used recently enough to have the necessary resonance. Maybe two. In New Gravesend, it seemed like every possible crossing point had been used. Several times.

"It's always been like this," James said. "I tried to research it at the beginning, when I was trying to determine what mattered. In the end, I had to stop because it doesn't matter *why* the crossroads pay so much attention to a little town like this one. They do. That's enough."

I thought of how few sorcerers there were left in the world—fewer, even, than could be accounted for by the rabid way the Covenant hunted us, because sorcerers can hide. They're masters of tucking themselves away, out of sight and hence out of mind. I thought of the way the crossroads had gone for my grandfather, and how eagerly they'd gone after me once the opportunity arose. They couldn't be that hungry for every possible bargain, or there'd be no way to keep them a secret from the wider world. The fact that they'd pursued him, pursued me, and even pursued James . . . they didn't like sorcerers. They didn't like us at all.

James' mother had been a sorcerer. This had been her town. And the talent ran in families. It might be difficult to tell which had come first, but I was willing to bet if we really went digging, we'd find that the number of bargains began to climb right around when the first of James' ancestors had moved to New Gravesend.

I was right. I was sure that I was right. Looking at James' face as he earnestly explained where Leonard was going to go to bait the crossroads—where the rest of us were going to go while Bethany was distracted, to get Mary back—I knew I could never tell him. He was a smart guy. If he'd wanted to consider the possibility that his family had brought this down on their hometown, he would already have done so. The fact that he hadn't told me it didn't matter and, more, that he needed to stay at least a little bit in denial.

"What do I do if the crossroads decide to have done with me?"

"Come back here," said Cylia. "There's a key under the mat at the back door. Let yourself in, have a cookie, and wait to see whether we survive."

"If you don't?"

"Run," said Fern. She wrinkled her nose. "The crossroads will probably still be hungry after it eats us."

"How encouraging." Leonard stood, looking at the window, where the sun was dipping ever lower. "What happens if you succeed at your task?"

"Bethany probably freaks out and disappears," I said. "You run. We'll be at the hanging tree at midnight. You can help us destroy the crossroads if you show up before we go into the final battle against the eldritch terror."

Leonard turned to stare at me. Finally, he shook his head, and said, "You would have fit in so much better with our number than you believe is true. You could have been the best of us."

"Instead, I'm going to be the best of the opposition," I said. "Good luck out there."

"I won't need it," he said, and walked to the front door, letting himself out.

"That man is either very brave or very stupid," said Sam. "Or both. Can I vote both? I'm going to vote both."

"Maybe he'll die," said Cylia hopefully. "I bet the crossroads could turn him inside out if they wanted to. There's no way the Covenant could blame that on *us*."

"The Covenant doesn't need a specific target when they start pointing fingers," I said grimly. "If he gets turned inside out, that just makes it harder for us to hide the body. I'm sure he'll be fine. He's a snake, and snakes always slither out of trouble." I turned to James. "How long would it take you to walk to the crossing you've directed him to?"

"About twenty minutes, assuming I didn't get lost," he said. "Give him thirty minutes, just to be sure."

"Is that enough time to set up the ritual circles?"

"I hope so." He put his book aside and rose. "If you'd

all come with me, we can get started. Not you, Annie. You need to stay inside until we're ready to begin."

"I know." I didn't bother trying to keep the bitterness out of my tone. I wanted to help. I wanted to be there to check every line and analyze every curve, to squabble with James over the placement of candles and semiprecious stones. Summoning the dead can be very simple or very complex, depending on what kind of spirit you're trying to call, and while we could normally snag Rose with a handful of dirt and a gas station hot dog, Mary was going to be harder. The fact that we needed to call her back without attracting the attention of the crossroads was just one more layer of difficulty on top of an already sticky situation.

I stayed seated on the stairs as the others rose and followed James to the back door. Sam was the last to go, pausing long enough to bend over and press a kiss against my temple.

"You going to be okay in here?" he asked.

"I'll watch from the kitchen window," I said. The boathouse, which had seemed like the best place to set up a summoning circle without either violating the wards or attracting unwanted attention, wouldn't be exactly in view, but if someone needed me, they could run back and wave until I opened the window. Summoning via semaphore.

"It'll be over soon," he said as he stepped away, already back in human form, just in case someone saw them. He grabbed his jacket from the back of the couch, not bothering with any kind of shoes.

It only took a few seconds for me to be left entirely alone. I stayed where I was, looking at the empty room, strewn with books and notes and nothingness, before I finally rose and started toward the couch, beginning to collect our research materials. Anything to keep myself moving, to keep myself busy while they got started setting things up.

"I can't do this," I murmured, and that was the

complete, achingly honest truth. I didn't know how my grandfather had been able to do this, to handle the borders of his world narrowing until they weren't even large enough to encompass his entire house. I'd read his journals, of course—we'd all read the journals—but they showed a level of "stiff upper lip" that I guess we should have expected from a Covenant-trained British man. Grandma might have been able to tell me more, if we'd ever felt like it was safe to ask her.

That was a fun thought. We could kidnap James and ask him to transfer the ghost wards to Cylia's car if this didn't work. She could drive me to Michigan, all of us peeing in bottles and trying not to yearn for showers, James recasting the wards whenever they ran down. We still owned the house where Thomas Price had become a captive of the crossroads. Grandma Alice went there all the time, and we all tried to pretend it was healthy for her to spend her time on Earth in a house that might not hold any ghosts but was absolutely haunted all the same.

We could put me there. Fix up a bedroom and leave me like a cork in a bottle, one more Price for a house that had already tried and failed to protect our family.

"Morbid much?" I muttered. I kept picking up books, stacking them on the coffee table with their spines turned away from the door. That was a little piece of habit I'd picked up when I was a kid, a way to keep Verity from commenting on the books I was reading. Privacy had never been plentiful in our house.

I missed it. I missed knowing there was a good chance any open door would reveal a member of my family, sharpening knives or making out with their latest significant other, or even folding laundry and waiting to dragoon the first person too slow to get away into rolling socks. I missed *home*.

In that moment, it was incredibly hard to believe I was ever going home again.

I was stacking James' notes in a tidy pile when the

doorbell rang. I whipped around, a cascade of papers accompanying the motion, and stared at the door. The doorbell rang again before someone started hammering on the wood.

Swell. Cylia's car was in the driveway and the lights were on; there was no way I could slink back to the kitchen and pretend no one was home. Bethany wasn't likely to ring the bell. Even if she did, she couldn't get me as long as I stayed behind the wards. I took one quick look around the front room, confirming that nothing *really* weird was visible, and moved, cautiously, toward the door.

I pulled it open just as Captain Smith raised his hand to start another round of hammering. He blinked at me. I blinked at him.

"James isn't here," I blurted.

"May I come in?" he asked, and pushed past me without waiting for an answer, sweeping his eyes over the book-strewn living room. He didn't seem to realize that most of the books had come from his house: his gaze skipped straight over them, lip slowly curling in a sneer. "He's *been* here," he said.

"Well, yes, because we were making out for like, an hour, but I don't see why that's any of your business." I crossed my arms, glad Sam wasn't in the room to hear *that* particular lie. Although it would have been nice to have the backup. "He's not here."

Belatedly, I realized his bike might still be outside. Oh, well. Too late now.

"Good." Captain Smith turned back to me. "I want to talk to you."

"And I want you out of my house. Isn't it fun how we're both being thwarted today?"

"You need to stay away from James."

"My house. Out of." Belatedly, it occurred to me that I was speaking not only to the local chief of police, but to the father of the man I was supposedly dating. I added a grudging, "Please."

"He's a delicate boy. He doesn't need some loose

woman coming from out of town and getting him all confused."

I blinked. "I . . . what? I don't know whether to be more offended by you calling James 'delicate' or you calling me 'loose.' I assure you, I am the opposite of a loose woman. I'm a tightly-wound, sort of prickly woman. Hermione Granger is my Patronus."

From the look on Captain Smith's face, he wasn't entirely sure I was speaking English. "I don't think you understand how unpleasant I can make things for you."

"I don't think you understand how little I care." Rage washed through me, crisp and chemical and oh-so-welcome. Here was a distraction. Here was something I could sink my teeth into. I stepped forward, jabbing a finger in the direction of his chest. "We've broken no laws. We're both adults. Holding hands and kissing is none of your concern. Maybe you should be asking yourself why you've never sent him to college. He's a smart guy. He deserves better than whatever the hell weird obsession you've got with keeping him nice and captive and—"

"He's never been outside of New Gravesend in his life," snapped Captain Smith.

"Whose fault is that?"

"His mother's!"

We both froze, staring at each other. He didn't look like he'd intended to say that. Interesting.

"I thought she died," I said.

"She did," he replied. "She became very sick, and then she passed away, and he's been delicate ever since. He doesn't need more stress."

"College—"

"Would have been stressful for the boy. He hasn't even tried to leave town since he was eleven. School field trip. He collapsed at the city limits. He doesn't understand how fragile he is."

I opened my mouth to answer, then stopped, cocking my head and looking at him. Really *looking* at him, not at James' idea of him, not at the chief of police, but at the man. The man who'd married a sorcerer and buried her when she should have been in her prime. The man who'd raised a son he didn't seem to understand or want, but who'd refused to let that child go, when the logical thing would have been to ship James off to the first boarding school that was willing to take him.

The man who lived in the most crossroads-touched town I'd ever seen, who tried to keep the law functioning there, and who couldn't possibly be as oblivious as his son assumed he had to be. There was just no way.

"You knew she was a sorcerer, didn't you?" I asked.

He looked away. That was answer enough.

"What did you do?" I asked, in a very small voice.

"It's not what I did," he said. "It's what James' great-great-great-great-grandfather did."

Dammit. "James' mother," I said. "She got sick when James was a kid. Did she know she was going to get sick?"

He nodded.

"Did she know she was going to die?"

He nodded again.

"Did the same thing happen to one of her parents?"

A third nod. "She was an only child. They're always only children on her side of the family, and they always see one of their parents die when they're eleven or twelve years old. Old enough for it to hurt."

I was pretty sure losing a parent would hurt no matter how old somebody was when it happened, but I didn't say that. "Why?"

"Because some ancestor of hers decided his magic," there was a bitter twist to the word that was almost more shocking than hearing the word at all, "was more important than his family, and he made a deal to make sure it would always breed true. Apparently, it doesn't a lot of the time, for magic folks."

"It skips generations," I said, in as neutral a tone as I could manage.

"It does," said Captain Smith, and frowned. "You don't seem surprised."

"Because I'm not," I said. "One of James' ancestors made a deal with the crossroads to guarantee all his descendants would be sorcerers and had worded it in such a way that when each new member of the family began to come into their magic, the previous member of the family would die a sudden and unavoidable death. That's pretty straightforward. What keeps him here in town?"

"The bargain included the phrase 'that New Gravesend should always be protected against the dangers of the unseen world,'" said Captain Smith.

I pinched the bridge of my nose. "Of course it did. All right. First, you should talk to your son, because he has no idea you know any of this, and he's a sorcerer, so telling him you know magic exists wouldn't be the *worst* idea you ever had. And you don't break a crossroads bargain by making sure someone is ignorant of the fact that it affects them." Was he ignorant? Truly?

He had to be. He would have said something if not, or recognized that he could be contesting his family's bargain, rather than Sally's: there's nothing like an old family debt that you didn't volunteer for and can't get away from to make a case for systemic unfairness.

Captain Smith's cheeks reddened. "I didn't come here to be told how to raise my son."

"Uh, you already raised him. He's an adult. The only reason he hasn't been clawing the walls down trying to get out of this town is because he's been trying to get justice for Sally, but one day he's going to give up, or he's going to decide he needs to consult with somebody who knows more about this shit than he does. He's going to take whatever he's been able to save from his shitty job and buy a bus ticket for anywhere but here, and then what? He crosses the city limits and dies of a massive coronary? You're doing him no favors and a lot of future harm by keeping him in the dark. So no, I will not stay away from your son, and no, I will not help you do a better job of lying to him, and I would like you to get out of my house now, please."

Captain Smith regarded me levelly for several seconds. "I could make life in this town very difficult for you."

"Life in this town is already difficult enough. Leave, please."

He started for the door. Then he paused, turning to give me a thoughtful look. "How do you know all this about magic?"

"Oh, didn't I mention? I'm a sorcerer, too." I raised my hand, fingers poised like I was going to snap and, I don't know, blow us both to Kingdom Come. "Leave, please. I don't want to explain why you're here when James comes back."

Captain Smith gave me a look that was half anger, half fear before bolting for the door. I ran after him, slamming it so hard the windows rattled and flipping the deadbolt home. My heart was pounding; my skin felt two sizes too small.

"Get it together, Annie," I whispered, leaning my forehead against the doorframe and forcing myself to breathe. "Get it *together*."

The crossroads hated sorcerers. That wasn't a surprise. But how many of us had it destroyed, limited, confined, all for the sake of avoiding the confrontation I was trying to help kick off? This was too much. This was too big. We weren't going to win. The crossroads had destroyed generations of people just like me, and it was hubris to think we were going to be any different. James wasn't going to get away. I wasn't going to get away. It was over. We'd lost.

I looked longingly toward Cylia's purse, still sitting on the floor by the end of the couch. She had a prepaid burner cell. I knew she did because I'd been there when she bought it. Having a phone number was essential if she wanted to set up and pay for things like utilities.

I could call home. One last time. I could tell my mother I loved her. I could tell my father I was sorry. I could tell my mice they were going to need to prepare a new set of catechisms soon, rituals I was never going to be a part of, because we were going to lose bad. We were all going to die here, so damn far away from home, and I hated it, and it wasn't fair, and it wasn't right, and I could call home if I wanted to. I could say good-bye.

Or I could win. I could tell the odds and the crossroads to go fuck themselves, and I could win. It seemed impossible. It seemed more than impossible. It was still the better option.

Reluctantly, I pushed away from the door and walked toward the kitchen, leaving Cylia's purse alone. The curtains were drawn across the kitchen window. I pushed them aside, and shouted in dismay as Sam's face appeared, all but pressed against the glass.

"There you are," he mouthed, words silenced by the thick, storm-ready pane. He disappeared. The door opened a moment later, and he stuck his head inside.

"James says the circle is close enough to perfect as makes no difference, and he wants you to come have a look before we get ready to start the summons," he said. "Leonard should be at the crossroads by now. Think they'll eat him? Could we get that lucky?"

"Talk to Cylia if it's luck you're looking for," I said, and took a deep breath before muttering, "Here goes nothing," and stepping out the back door.

Bethany didn't appear. I allowed my shoulders to unlock.

Sam nodded. "See? We're doing this." Then he grabbed my wrist with one still-human hand and tugged me off the porch, heading across the field toward the distant shadow of the boathouse.

I've never been the most outdoorsy member of my family, but I've never been on the verge of losing everything outside my bedroom walls before. The world seemed to have become supersaturated during my short time inside, the colors growing brighter, the smells growing more intense. I looked around as much as I dared as we trotted through the field, not quite running, but more than walking fast.

Fern was waiting just outside the boathouse. "What took you so long?" she asked.

"I got distracted cleaning up." I could tell them about Captain Smith later, when Mary was back and we were going up against the crossroads directly. James would need to know. He didn't deserve to be blindsided by the news that one of his ancestors had guaranteed his mother's death, or that his father had been lying to him for his entire life.

Sometimes, good intentions do more damage than all the wicked plots in all the world.

Inside, someone—probably Cylia—had strung a bunch of white hazard lights around the edges of the boathouse, casting a cool white light over the circle sketched in chalk, salt, and little white feathers across the majority of the floor. I stopped, frowning.

"Where did you get that many white feathers?" I asked. "Did somebody kill a goose?"

"No, we killed a pillow," said Cylia. "Our landlord has good taste in linens. James did most of the work of drawing the summoning circle. The rest of us just handed him feathers when he asked for them."

That was good. Anyone can draw a summoning circle, but they work best when drawn by someone with actual power. I walked a slow loop around the edge, checking for breaks, checking for places where the lines were narrower, or shallower, or anything else that could lead to us getting something other than what we bargained for. To his credit, James watched me but didn't say anything about the inspection. It's a fool who argues about a second set of eyes on a complicated problem, whether you're talking calculus or demonology.

The candles were placed with precision. The semiprecious stones, which were mostly quartz and appeared to have been gathered from the edge of the lake, were properly nestled in their cradles of salt. I bent to adjust a few of them, moving their angles more into alignment with the rest of the scene, and didn't say a word. This was going to work or it wasn't. We were going to get one of our allies back—one of our weapons back—or we weren't.

Only one way to know for sure.

I straightened, looking slowly around the room. My motley crew of allies and oddities looked back, waiting for the word.

"All right," I said. "Let's do this."

Twenty

"People who say that right and wrong are all
about absolutes are usually getting ready to
stab someone for looking at things differently. Try to stab them first."

–Enid Healy

*In a somewhat decrepit boathouse, preparing to do
something genuinely foolish*

WE ARRAYED OURSELVES AROUND the circle, standing
as evenly spaced as possible, our hands outstretched and our fingers splayed, not quite touching one
another. Sam's arms were long enough in his fūri form
that he could have reached the people to either side of
him—me and Cylia—but that wasn't the point. We were
sketching a phantom connection as part of our snare to
catch a ghost, and actual contact would have interfered.

The rules of magic are complicated, confusing, and
sometimes contradictory. Magic is basically the English
language of universal constants.

"Mary Dunlavy, we call to you from across the void,"
I said. "You have duties yet unfinished and promises yet
unfulfilled here upon this mortal plane, and you will
answer me, or give good reason why."

"Wouldn't giving good reason be an answer?" Fern
asked, sounding faintly baffled.

I didn't answer. It didn't matter if she spoke. Cylia
and Sam were similarly unlimited. Only James and I

had to stay completely on task. We were the ones who supposedly knew what we were doing. And hey, James had never called a ghost before, and I was distracted by the fact that the fresh new wards on the boathouse were of necessity less complete than the ones on the house, since we needed to be able to pull Mary through them, but at least we'd read the back of the cereal box. Or something.

"Mary Dunlavy, you are needed," said James. "Your work is not yet done. Your time is not yet finished. Your allies call to you, and will not go unheard."

The air in the boathouse began to chill. Whether that was because the calling was starting to work or because James was nervous enough to be freezing the air around him was anybody's guess.

"Mary, come to me." I let some of the solemnity slip from my voice, replaced by raw pleading. "I'm not done with you yet. You're not going to be my babysitter forever, and that means I should enjoy the time I have left."

"Everybody should have a dead aunt," said Sam.

I resisted the urge to glare at him.

The candles flickered. The air kept getting colder, chilling around us degree by degree. I glanced at James, who shook his head while mouthing "not me." Okay. *Something* was coming to answer our summons. Whether it was Mary or something worse had yet to be determined.

Perhaps belatedly, it occurred to me that if the crossroads could monitor me through her, maybe they could also answer a summons intended for her. Maybe we'd just triggered the final showdown well ahead of our intentions, and we were about to face the consequences.

Oh, well. Too late now, and at least we were surrounded by things we could use as makeshift weapons, if it came down to it. Things could have been a lot worse. We could have been doing this skyclad and empty-handed, for example. I tried to hold onto that flash of optimism as the air chilled even further, until—with no flash or fanfare—Mary, or something very much like her, appeared in the middle of our circle.

She was naked, folded forward in a bestial crouch, with her face shrouded by the cobweb sheet of her tangled white hair. Her skin wasn't her usual Welsh pallor, betraying a life spent avoiding the sun and a possible vitamin D deficiency but not much else: it was the chalky, bruised blue-gray of the grave. I could count every one of her ribs and every knob along her spine.

"Uh," said Sam. "Is that . . . did we get the wrong ghost? Because I'm not really into the idea of a possession right now."

"Mary?" I whispered.

The girl in our circle didn't respond, didn't move so much as a muscle in answer to my question. She was still as only the dead can be, not even breathing as she crouched.

It was the hair. No one was left who'd known her when she was alive—she hadn't become my grandmother's babysitter until after her death, although my great-grandma hadn't known that when she hired her—but I was pretty sure she hadn't had waist-length white hair as a living teenage girl. That sort of thing tends to get remembered. She'd probably been some shade of blonde, only to get sun-bleached by the endless country road that lingered, haunted, in her eyes.

Maybe her human face was a pretty façade she put on for the sake of the living people she adored. Maybe this was what she looked like. But she was still Mary.

"Stay here," I said, and stepped over the salt line, entering the circle.

Summoning circles are tricky things. People like to brag about using them to catch demons, but I'm not actually sure demons exist, and if they did, they'd be too big and too scary to catch with salt and candles. Mostly, summoning circles are used to call and contain ghosts. The people doing the calling have to know, for sure, that the ghost is out there: have to know the ghost's name and as many details as possible about who they were when they were alive and who they've become since death. Get a few things wrong, get nothing. Or worse, get the wrong ghost.

Sam started to follow me. James motioned sharply for him to stop.

"It's too late," he said. "She's over the line."

Sam frowned but didn't argue. I was quietly relieved. All Sam could have done was join me in the circle or tackle me out of it, and both those options had their serious downsides. If this was Mary, I didn't need help. If it wasn't Mary, I didn't need him breaking the salt line and letting her out.

It only took a few steps to put me in front of the crouching spirit. I knelt, resting my hands on the floor so she could see I wasn't armed, wasn't holding salt or glass or anything else I could use to hurt her.

"Mary?" I whispered.

Slowly, she raised her head and looked at me.

I did not recoil. If I never do anything worth doing again, at least I'll always know that I did not recoil: in that moment, when Mary needed me to be strong for her sake, I didn't pull away from her. I wanted to. My muscles locked and the hair on my arms stood on end and every instinct I had screamed for me to get away as fast as I could, to put some distance between myself and the terrible thing now looking at me.

Her face belonged on a mummy dug out of a bog, some twisted, unspeakable horror that had been marinating in the muck and slime for a thousand years. Her skin was leather and slime at the same time, simultaneously drawn tight across her bones and sagging like it was going to slough off and puddle to the floor. She was a creature from a child's worst nightmare, too twisted and terrible to exist outside the lands of the dead.

And her eyes were a hundred miles of open, empty road.

I didn't hesitate. I leaned forward, wrapping my arms

around her skeletal shoulders and pulling her close to me, bracing myself against the expected scent of the grave. It never came. She smelled, if she smelled of anything, of sunlight on green corn: sweet and dusty and alive.

"I'm sorry," I whispered against the shriveled flesh of her shoulder.

Mary held herself stiff for a few more long, agonized moments before slowly, creakily raising her left hand and patting me on the back. The gesture started off awkward, like she was a puppet that hadn't quite figured out how her strings worked, but loosened up quickly, until it was the familiar, comforting feeling of being soothed by my babysitter.

"... sorry ... baby ..." she said. Her voice was a distant hiss.

"What can we do?" I kept her close. Part of it was selfish: I never wanted to let her go again. Part of it was the desire not to see what the crossroads had done to her. Punching an ancient force of terrible magic in the face is rarely as good an idea as it seems.

"... don't ... know ..."

I paused. What I was about to try seemed ridiculous, the real-world equivalent of one of those stupid kiddie shows where everything can be fixed with the power of love and friendship and wishing really hard. It was still the only idea I had. Whether this was what Mary looked like behind the friendly human façade she worked so hard to project or whether this was something the crossroads had done to her didn't matter: she was in pain, she was being punished, and this needed to stop.

"You're two kinds of ghost at once," I said. "Whether you were supposed to be or not, you are. You're a crossroads ghost, and I guess that's how they have enough power over you to have done this to you. But you're also my babysitter, and I need you. I need you to be ready to protect me. I need you to be ready and able to stand up on your own in case I try to, I don't know, drink bleach or something else stupid as hell. I'm just a kid. I can't do this without you."

My voice broke on the last word. There was a low noise behind me, like someone stifling a gasp. I didn't turn to see who it was. I didn't do anything but stay where I was, and wait.

Finally, in a tone that was weary but amused—and more amused than weary—Mary said, "You're not a kid, Annie. You're old enough to drink, drive, and destroy other people's property."

"I'm still younger than you." I finally pulled away enough to look at her.

My babysitter looked back.

She was dressed in the peasant blouse and jeans that were her default—and I wondered, for the first time, whether part of that "look" might not be her matching my mother's subconscious expectation of what a babysitter was supposed to look like. When she took over watching the next generation, would her default shift to something more modern, seamlessly jumping over decades to settle on the nineties or the aughts? Still charmingly old-fashioned by the standards of the so-called modern world, but comforting enough to parental eyes to add an air of responsible respectability to someone who looked far too young to be trusted with an infant?

"What," said Sam clearly, "the *actual* fuck."

"Language, young man," said Mary, not taking her eyes off me. "I'll tell your grandmother on you."

"She'd probably appreciate it," he replied. "At least then she'd know I was alive."

Mary ignored him, choosing instead to reach for my hands and stand, pulling me along with her. She was shorter than me. She had been for years, but in this moment she was radiating "responsible adult" fiercely enough that our heights suddenly seemed like a parsing error in the universe.

"That was not a safe or clever thing to do, but I am so proud of you," she said, and pulled me into another hug.

This time, she was warm and solid and *safe*, just like she'd been when I was a kid and couldn't imagine ever wanting another babysitter to watch over me.

"No, I'm serious here," said Sam. "What just happened? Small words, please, and remember that I'm strong enough to twist your heads off, so maybe try to explain before the urge to do some twisting overwhelms my patience."

"That's very violent," said Fern.

"It's been a violent sort of week," said Sam.

"Ghosts are flexible when they're new; they're also, as a rule, weak," said Mary, letting me go and turning toward Sam. "They have one big flash of power, and then they fade. That's why most hitchers start by getting themselves a ride home, and most ever-lasters start by finding their way back to campus, but then no one sees them or hears about them for years. It's because they're lost in the twilight, gaining strength, deciding what kind of ghost they're going to be."

"Wait," I said. "That's not how Aunt Rose tells it. She says she was a hitcher the second her neck snapped."

"She was. But saying she was a hitcher only gives you the broad shape of the spirit. There are a million different ways to be anything."

"Like how a derby player can be a jammer or a blocker or a pivot, and still be a derby girl," said Cylia slowly.

Mary nodded. "Exactly. Rose is the kind of hitchhiking ghost she is because of choices she made after the road shoved her into a category."

"Still not understanding," said Sam.

"I am a crossroads ghost," said Mary. Her words were calm: her expression was not. Rage and resignation warred for ownership. "Nothing's going to change that. The first bargain any crossroads ghost makes is with the crossroads proper. They offer us what we think we want, and we take it, and then we're stuck. They offered me the chance to go home and take care of my father. He wasn't well, you see. I was all he had. So I died, and I rose, and I went home, and the crossroads left me there, because they wanted me to see that all mortal flesh decays. They wanted me to lose him and turn bitter and be truly theirs. Maybe I would have. Maybe I should have. But Frances Healy needed a babysitter, and she asked me, and I was human enough to say yes, and so—during my malleable period, when my choices could still change me—I went home with her. I started taking care of her daughter."

"You were already a kind of caretaker," I said. "You were supposed to take care of the crossroads. Now you're . . . you're a babysitter ghost. Like, literally. God, that sounds ridiculous."

"As a wise woman once said to me, it only sounds ridiculous because you're not used to hearing it," said Mary, with a hint of a smile. "You're a girl who throws fire, lives with talking mice, and loves a shapeshifting monkey. I think 'ridiculous' is a concept for other people."

"Who controls you, if you're a babysitter and a crossroads ghost at the same time?" James asked.

"In this circle, I control me," said Mary. "Take me outside and it changes. I don't know why you called me back from the void, and don't think I'm not grateful, but I don't know what good it's going to do. As soon as the crossroads realize I'm here, I'm gone."

The void. That was why she'd looked so terrible when we pulled her out. Without access to the power of her connection to the crossroads—and presumably, her connection to my family—she had become a spirit with nothing to haunt, and started consuming herself. It was a chilling thought. What would have happened to her if we hadn't called her back when we did?

Nothing good, that was for damn sure.

"We need you," I said.

She looked at me. "Why? I can't tell you anything

you don't already know. The crossroads may not know where I am right now, but they will, and their rules still apply."

"We found a loophole."

Mary blinked. "Go on."

"Sally went to the crossroads because she wanted to make a deal that would get James out of New Gravesend," I said. "They took her bargain. They took *her.* But she didn't get James out of town."

"I've never even been to Bangor," said James.

"That may be intentional," said Mary. She hesitated before saying, "The crossroads don't . . . they don't *like* sorcerers very much. They'll do what they can to keep them contained."

"So we've gathered," I said, fighting the urge to look at James. I needed to tell him what I'd learned from his father—but not here. That was a conversation that could happen inside the house. "If the crossroads took payment without giving him a bus ticket or something, the deal wasn't fair. That means James can appeal. We need a ghost if we're going to make that appeal, however. We need someone who can represent us when we make our claim."

Mary went very still. Finally, in a low voice, she asked, "What are you planning to do?"

"Stop this. Stop *all* of this." I walked back to the edge of the circle and stepped out, bending to retrieve the jam jar James had prepared. The ragged edge of a label clung to its side; the glass smelled faintly of strawberry.

I held it up for her to see.

"Will you help us?" I asked.

Mary bit her lip as she nodded.

I leaned over the edge of the circle, put the jam jar down, and pulled my hand back. The air shimmered as Mary dissolved into a thick mist and flowed through the jar's open mouth, filling it with what looked like a slow-moving dust devil made of glitter, like the sparkle of broken glass on pavement. I leaned in again, this time to put the lid in place.

"Thank you," I said, and the room was silent.

The wards on the boathouse were good enough to keep Bethany from finding me, but there weren't any seats, and the air was already getting cold. We couldn't stay out there forever, no matter how convenient it might have been. In the end, the best solution was for Sam to swing me over his shoulder, shift into fūri form, and cross the yard at a speed some motorcycles couldn't match.

By the time we hit the porch, the wind had been knocked out of me from jouncing up and down, my hair was a wind-swept disaster, and I wanted nothing more than to go for another run. When Sam dropped me back to my feet, I was grinning broadly. He raised an eyebrow.

"You are *so* weird."

"Nice way to talk to your girlfriend, monkey-boy." I took a step away from the door, putting myself more firmly in the kitchen, and patted my pocket to be sure that the spirit jar hadn't been dislodged. Cylia, Fern, and James were trudging across the lawn toward the door, all of them looking solemn and more than a little dispirited. What we were doing . . . it was big, it was stupid, it was relatively untested, and it was likely to get one or more of us killed. At the very least, it was going to get James stabbed, and while I knew I was telling the truth when I said I was only planning to stab him a little bit, *he* didn't know that. Not for sure.

"Speaking of talking . . ." I said, and took a deep breath. "I need to talk to James. Alone."

Sam blinked at me, nonplussed. "Mind if I ask why?"

"His father was here," I said. "While you were getting the ritual circle ready. I learned a few things, and James needs to know them, but they're . . . they should be private. *I* shouldn't know them."

"Family secrets," said Sam. "Yeah, I can understand those."

"I figured that might be the case."

"Yeah. I mean, my family has plenty. I just . . ." He shook his head. "Is it always going to be like this? Are we always going to be just . . . just lurching from one disaster to the next, like some sort of fucked-up horror franchise in slow motion?"

"Maybe," I said. It felt like a great admission, like I was betraying myself and my family in a single word. "I mean, I do stuff. I've gone months without anyone or anything trying to kill me. We have fun. We have lives. My sister had time to go on a reality dance competition, and my brother flies to Australia twice a year. But still, maybe. I sort of have an addiction to wandering past the warning signs in order to poke the potentially dangerous things with a stick. Is that a problem?"

"I don't know." Sam shook his head. "I want to say it isn't. I want to say this isn't exhausting. But it sort of *is* exhausting, you know? It shouldn't have to be you all the time."

"It isn't," I assured him. "It's just that this sort of thing happens a lot more often than anyone realizes. There's not a chosen one. There never was. There's just people, all over the world, trying their best to make sure the sun comes up tomorrow. We do the job because we know the job exists, and once you know the job exists, it's hard to pretend it doesn't matter. Does that make sense?"

"Yeah," said Sam, his tail sliding around my waist and pulling me closer as he spoke. I went without resistance. "I guess it does."

"Is that okay with you?"

"I don't know, but I'm going to find out."

He leaned down and kissed me. He was still kissing me when the others reached the back door. Fern giggled.

"Oh, my sweet Lady Luck, can you people get a *room*?" asked Cylia. "Should you be making out with the monkey while you have your babysitter in your pocket? Because I'm not human, but that feels wrong to me."

"We have a room," said Sam, breaking away in order to turn and smirk at her. "It's upstairs, remember? I just figured you wouldn't want us running off when there's work to do."

James looked back at the boathouse through the open back door. Then he grasped the knob and pulled it shut, bowing his head, not looking at any of us.

"We're actually doing this," he said. "This is actually going to happen."

"Tonight," I said. I stepped away from Sam. He unwound his tail, letting me move freely. "Are you ready?"

James laughed. The sound was thin and strained, the laughter of a man who didn't know what else to do. "Does it matter? This is happening. This has *been* happening for my entire life and longer. Someone has to do it."

I glanced at Sam. His expression was grim. He was hearing the same thing I was, the echoes of our earlier conversation spreading through the room from other sources, from lips other than my own.

"When a thing is right, and you know you have the power to do it, backing down is wrong," I said, and touched the spirit jar in my pocket. It was cold against my fingers, colder than it had any right to be, chilled by the circling spirit of a teenage girl who had never been given the chance to grow up. "Can I talk to you? Alone?"

James gave me a startled look. "I—why?"

"I'll explain upstairs."

Sam waved. "If you're worried about that head-twisting thing I mentioned before, it's cool. I'm not in a decapitating mood."

"All right," said James warily. "Annie, lead the way."

Cylia and Fern frowned in eerie unison. It was Cylia who spoke, asking, "Annie? Is this something that should be shared with the entire class?"

"That's up to James," I said. "We'll be back downstairs as soon as we can."

"All right, then. Who wants waffles?" Cylia spread her hands. "I can twist our luck until it screams, I can do as much as I can to make sure things fall our way, but I can't make any promises. I don't have knives, or magic. I can't fly. I can't move faster than a speeding bullet."

Sam rubbed the scar on his forehead left by a Covenant bullet, and said nothing.

"What I *can* do is make sure we're all fed and fortified before we go off to tangle with a deathless eldritch force from another reality. So I ask you again, who wants waffles?"

As it turned out, everybody wanted waffles. James and I slipped away while she was whipping up the batter. Hopefully, we'd be back downstairs soon.

Hopefully, this wasn't the straw that broke the sorcerer's back.

Hopefully.

Twenty-one

"Nobody's chosen. Everybody gets to choose. Make the choice that brings you home. We're not being paid to save the world, here."

–Jane Harrington-Price

In the upstairs library of a rented house in New Gravesend, Maine, getting ready for an uncomfortable conversation

I'LL GIVE JAMES THIS much: he'd grown up in a house with a father who resented him for existing, had developed sorcery without spilling the beans to any of his classmates or coworkers, and had fallen begrudgingly but completely into our weird little world, and he had done it all with a closed mouth and an open mind. He waited until we were in the library with the door shut before he rounded on me.

"Well?" he demanded. "What *now*? Are we secretly blood relations, or have you discovered that the ritual to summon the crossroads requires us to get married before we conjure the dead? Or have you decided to kill me after all, and this was your way of getting me alone before you do the deed?"

I blinked. Then, helplessly, I began to laugh.

This seemed to annoy James further, thus proving that he was a sensible man who'd simply had the misfortune to fall in with a bunch of weirdos. I flapped a hand, trying to get my laughter under control. It had a hysterical edge that I didn't like, especially under the circumstances.

Finally, tears rolling down my cheeks, I managed to make it stop. "I'm sorry," I gasped. "This isn't funny, it's just—the *look* on your *face*—" It was all I could do not to start laughing again.

To my surprise, James quirked a small, somewhat wan smile. "Sally said something similar the day she informed me of her intention to be my new best friend. Apparently, I looked like a deer in front of a train."

"I can't wait to meet her." I wiped my tears away, sobering further. "Really, though, I need to talk to you, and I need you to listen to me until I'm done. Okay?"

The smile vanished, replaced by more familiar wariness. "All right. What do you need to say?"

"Your father dropped by."

James scowled. "I assure you, whatever he told you, it wasn't on my behalf."

"I figured, since he started off by telling me not to have any further contact with you. I thought about telling him you were in the boathouse, naked, waiting for me to show up with the maple syrup and the handcuffs, but I was afraid he'd take me seriously and go storming out there to make you put your pants back on."

James said nothing as his cheeks and ears flared beet red. Laughing at him would have been unkind. I settled for patting him on the hand.

"Don't worry. I didn't say it."

"Thank God," said James, in a strangled voice. "I think he'd lock me in the attic for a month."

I paused to eye him. "Do you mean that seriously?"

He turned his face away.

Fuck. "Just so you know, I had already decided I was adopting you and taking you home to meet the rest of the family. I really, *really* hope you wanted siblings, because you now have two sisters, a brother, a sister-in-law, a brother-in-law, and assorted cousins, aunts, uncles, and other such familial detritus."

James looked back to me, blinking in slow bewilderment. "Ah," he said finally. "I suppose I'll have a busy Christmas."

"You better believe it." I took a deep breath. "Look. He didn't just tell me to stop seeing you. He told me some things about your mother."

"As if he knows anything—"

"He knew she was a sorcerer."

That silenced him. James stared at me, eyes wide, cheeks pale enough to make his earlier blush seem like a mistake.

"She told him before they got married, because she wanted him to know . . . and because there's sort of a curse on your family line." This was where I had to tread carefully. If James started blaming himself for his mother's death, dealing with the crossroads was going to become one hell of a lot harder. "One of your ancestors was afraid the family would lose the magic. Sorcery is sort of the ultimate recessive gene, at least as far as human magic-users go. Even sorcerers marrying sorcerers won't guarantee it gets passed along. So he went to the crossroads, and he asked them to promise his line would always breed true. I guess the crossroads ghost who was supposed to help him word that request was a little less diligent than Mary, because he used the phrase 'that New Gravesend should always be protected against the dangers of the unseen world.'"

"Meaning what?" asked James, in a small, strangled voice.

"Meaning there's a reason you've never been outside the municipality. His crossroads bargain is still in effect, and it won't let you leave. You have to stay here because you're the town's official protector." Untrained, untested, and unprepared. Some protector. It was an elegant trap, one that would probably have finished snapping shut the first time something that actually needed to be protected *against* wandered into the city limits.

"And my mother knew?" he asked.

This was the hard part. I took a deep breath. "According to your father, she knew, and she also knew that as soon as you were old enough for your magic to stabilize—as soon as the bargain was kept—she'd get sick. Only one descendant at a time. The crossroads don't like sorcerers. They weren't going to allow your family to breed an army against them."

James was silent for several seconds. Then, jerkily, he stood, and punched the nearest wall. Frost clung to the wallpaper where his knuckles hit. I took a step back, watching silently as he struck it again and again, until he stopped and slumped, leaning forward until his forehead hit the wall. He was panting.

"I'm sorry," I said. "I know this is a lot."

His laughter was bitter. "A lot? I killed my mother."

"No, you didn't. She knew, James. She knew she'd only get a few years with you, and she decided it was worth it. You don't get to say that she was wrong. Okay? She wanted you to exist. She wanted to know you."

He turned to look at me bleakly. "What do I do now?"

"Now?" I shrugged. "Now you do what you've been working toward all along. You kick the crossroads until they beg for mercy, and you do it for Sally, and you do it for your mother. And then you come home with me, and I introduce you to the rest of the family."

He hesitated. "Will they . . . do you think they're going to like me?"

It was no effort at all to smile at him. "I think they're going to love you, new brother. I really think they will."

The waffle party was in full swing downstairs. Cylia had piled several plates high and set them in the middle of the dining room table, surrounded by an assortment of toppings both predictable—maple syrup and powdered sugar and strawberry jam—and a little bit surreal—bacon bits and chicken nuggets and candied cauliflower. She saw me eyeing the chicken nuggets, and shrugged.

"Chicken and waffles is a time-honored tradition," she said. "I wasn't going to fry chicken, so you get the next best thing."

"Plus no bones," said Fern gleefully. "The best meat doesn't have any bones."

"Sylphs are natural insectivores," I said, for James and Sam's benefit. Their mutual horrified looks were simply a bonus. Fern giggled. The bonus wasn't just for me.

Sam was perched on the back of the couch with his plate of waffles, eating with both hands while holding his coffee with his tail. I settled on the cushion in front of him with my own smaller portion, watching the room as I cut the waffles into bite-sized pieces.

Looking at Cylia, it would have been easy to tell myself she was completely at ease with the situation, ready to deal with whatever the world wanted to throw at her. The platters of waffles put the lie to that idea. She was as tightly wound as the rest of us, and dealing with the situation the only way she could: by taking care of us now, before she couldn't anymore.

She didn't think we were going to make it through this. That was almost reassuring, in a messed-up way. I might be stubbornly willing to keep telling myself I could find a route that saved everyone I cared about, even if I couldn't necessarily save my magic, or even myself, but if she was accepting the depth of the shit we were in, that meant she wasn't deluding herself. And if Cylia had accepted the reality of our situation, Fern had, too. Sam might think I could handle anything, but he was enough of a realist to know things might not go our way. As for James . . .

He'd spent years planning a way to get his revenge on the crossroads and bring Sally home. Alive or dead. Alive would be better, of course, but at least having a corpse would give her family freedom, even as it broke his heart forever. Sometimes closure is the only gift worth giving.

We'd been in town for less than a week, and he was on the cusp of finally getting what he wanted—possibly even including his freedom, if he survived the confrontation. If this went the way we were hoping, when it was done, he'd be able to put New Gravesend behind him forever. He could walk away from the father who'd never understood him, from the shadows on his mother's grave, from the people who had been perfectly happy to live in the safe harbor of a sorcerer's protection, without remembering what that meant for the sorcerer.

(Maybe that was unfair. James hadn't known about the crossroads deal, after all, and if the sorcerer didn't know, how could the people he was ostensibly forgetting understand what he'd given up to stay with and watch over them? The problem with bargains that span generations is that they can be forgotten without being invalidated. It's not right and it's not fair, but it's the world we live with, and it's the only world we've got.)

Everything was changing. All we could do was try to keep up.

The doorbell rang. Sam shifted back to human form without getting off the back of the couch. I stayed where I was, continuing to inhale waffles. Everyone else had had the chance to get a head start on me and James, after all. Cylia looked around the room, saw that no one was moving, rolled her eyes, and moved toward the door.

"Think she needs backup?" asked Sam, swallowing.

"I think she needs a target for her pent-up aggressions," I said, and ate a bite of waffle paired with chicken nugget. It wasn't bad. It wasn't great, either, but my culinary preferences have always been more about convenience than quality. "If it's James' dad again, he's never coming back."

"If she scares him off the property, I'm moving in with you," said James.

I laughed, and was still laughing when Cylia returned, now trailed by a ruffled-looking Leonard Cunningham.

He fixed me with a steely-eyed gaze that was probably meant to be impressive, but really made him look like he'd eaten something unpleasant.

"Want some waffles?" I asked.

Whatever he'd been expecting, it wasn't that. He paused, blinking at me.

"Yes, please," he finally said. "I'm starving."

"They're on the table, help yourself," I said. "We're carb-loading before we head for the crossroads. Everything go okay?"

"He's not inside out, so I'm assuming yes," said Sam.

"Everything went . . . reasonably well," said Leonard. "I feel the need for a stiff drink, or perhaps five, but no one died, and I was not badgered into accepting any bargains."

For the first time, I noticed how pale he was, and the faint tremor in his hands. He had been genuinely shaken by the encounter. I set my plate aside and stood.

"Drinking is probably a bad idea right now," I said. "Are *you* okay?"

"I don't know." Leonard shook his head. "I'd heard stories, but I always assumed . . . I thought the people who let themselves be taken advantage of were weak, somehow. That they'd earned the fates the crossroads cast for them. But I . . ."

He stopped, waving his hands for a moment before he looked at me helplessly.

"I could have fallen to temptation," he said. "You are my enemy. I know that. I may never convince you that my side is the right one. But with God as my witness, it is my duty to help you stop this thing. This is an abomination. It should never have been."

I smiled and extended one hand. After a beat, he took it, expression turning quizzical.

"All right," I said. "Now that we're all on the same page, let's get this party started."

Twenty-two

"Nothing is too much to pay to bring the ones you love safely home. Remember that when the time comes to pay the last thing you wanted to lose."

–Alice Healy

Crossing New Gravesend, moving toward a confrontation

IT TURNED OUT LEONARD didn't have an American driver's license: he'd been getting around town via a local taxi service. Good for the economy, not so great for the part where we had one car and six people. Cylia's fondness for ridiculously roomy classics meant we could cram five people into the car we had, as long as the folks in the back didn't mind getting *real* friendly, but six was a step too far. Worse, we were hoping to come back from the crossroads with seven. The laws of physics said cramming Sally in with the rest of us wasn't going to happen.

When in doubt, remember that there's more than one way to get anywhere. James had his bike. He was the one who knew the way, which made it important for him to stay in the car with Cylia, but I, in addition to never learning how to drive, had been riding my own bike since I was nine years old.

"You're sure you're okay with this," said James, for the fifth time. "I could write the directions down, and you could ride with Cylia."

"I'm fine." I checked the strap on my helmet. Roller derby safety gear and bicycle safety gear are basically identical, at least for our current needs. "Just make sure she goes slow, and I'll be able to keep up without crashing. We get there, we get Sally back, everything is awesome, we all go out for donuts."

"I like donuts," said Fern, stepping up next to me with her own helmet in her hand.

I raised an eyebrow. "Am I missing something?"

"Only the part where we're riding doubles to the hanging tree," she said and dimpled. "I'm the lightest, remember? I don't want to be squished in with a Covenant boy. And you're stupid if you think we're letting you out there alone. There's too much that could go wrong."

"Did Sam put you up to this?"

Fern's smile lost a few watts, dimming into something more reasonable. "Sam's not the only one allowed to worry about you. I was here before he was, and with the way you humans date, I'll probably be here when he's gone."

She wasn't trying to be hurtful. Sylphs have a different approach to relationships, prizing friendship over romance. Whether they operated that way before humans killed off so many of them that being willing to live alone became a survival strategy is anyone's guess. We've left a permanent mark on this planet, and not only because of our fondness for digging holes.

"I'm not alone," I said. "I have Mary."

"She's in a jar." Fern rolled her eyes. "Can we pretend we've had this whole fight, and skip ahead to the part where you admit I'm right and we get on the stupid bike? I want this over with. I want to go *home*."

I opened my mouth and paused. "You're right," I said finally. "Let's do this."

Fern looked relieved. James nodded.

"Be careful," he said and walked to the car, sliding into the back with Leonard. Cylia and Sam were in the front, the one because she was driving, the other because if something happened and he had to change forms, it would be much easier for him to shove himself through the window from the front.

I swung my leg over the bike, barely feeling the frame shift as Fern settled herself behind me, her mass dialed as far down as it would go. She wasn't going to slow me down. If anything, her ability to get heavier and add a little bit of ballast when I went around corners would keep me from losing control and hence speed me up.

"Ready?" I asked.

Fern slid her arms around my waist. "Hope so," she said.

I waved to Cylia, signaling for her to start the car. She did, rolling out slowly at first, then gathering speed as I began to pedal, sliding smoothly into position behind her. Fern held me tight, and the road was open, and we had so far to go, and we were almost finished. God help me, we were almost done.

New England is the place to go for tiny, creepy towns that look like they belong in the latest Stephen King made-for-TV movie. The trees along the highway shielded us from most of New Gravesend, but what I glimpsed between them was more horror cliché than anything else: tiny, mismatched houses with artfully shabby yards, lived-in but abandoned at the same time. The occasional child at play made things even worse, standing next to trampolines or holding red rubber balls as they considered their next moves. If any of them had been close enough to talk to us, I would have had no trouble believing they'd invite me to come play with them—or worse, tell me that everyone floated in this terrible town.

It was my imagination working overtime, taking the fact that I was on my way to challenge the crossroads and had allied myself with the Covenant and using it to turn my natural suspicion of the unknown up to eleven. Even knowing that didn't make me more comfortable, especially when Cylia turned off the main road, down a narrow, twisting lane so lined with trees that even the

moonlight couldn't find a way to shine through. I pedaled as hard as I could, unwilling to risk losing the faint
illumination of her taillights. This was an ordinary road,
part of an ordinary town that certainly didn't deserve
the thoughts I was throwing in its direction, but everything felt shadowy and terrible and like it was going to
come crashing down at any moment, leaving us trapped.

"I need better hobbies," I muttered, and pedaled
onward.

I'd never seen the infamous "hanging tree" before, but
I knew it when it came into sight. No other label could
have applied. It was a monster, skeletal and spidery at the
same time, with branches that spread wide to claw the
sky, forcing other trees to grow away from it lest they find
themselves denied the opportunity to grow. Its trunk was
a vast, gnarled thing, roots bursting through the ground
and the roadway alike, shattering the pavement. It was
easy to understand why settlers in the area might have
looked at this tree above all others, and thought, "Yes,
this is a good place to start killing people."

A second road—barely wide enough to be worthy of
the name, although it was paved, which was more than I'd
been expecting—ran across the first, creating a small but
distinct crossroads. Cylia pulled off to the shoulder, putting her hazard lights on. An unnecessary precaution: this
didn't look like the sort of place that got a lot of traffic.

I stopped the bike behind her, lowering the kick-
stand. "Here we go," I said.

Fern unlooped her arms from my midsection. "Are
you nervous?" she asked.

"I'm terrified," I said, sliding off the bike and turning
to face her. She blinked, clearly surprised. I shook my
head. "Lying never got us anywhere. We're about to bait
a force that's bigger than any of us into pulling us out of
this level of reality, and once we're there, we're going to
try something monumentally stupid. If this doesn't
work, we could all be lost forever."

Would Grandma Alice add me to her list of people to

look for? Or would the crossroads shunt me off to wherever they'd been keeping my grandfather, giving him someone to talk to for maybe the first time ever? It was a surreal thought. I didn't want to learn the answer.

"I just didn't expect you to say it, that's all," whispered Fern.

I put a hand on her shoulder. "You don't have to do this. This isn't your fight."

"You're my friend," she said. "It's always been my fight."

A car door slammed. I turned. The others were climbing out of Cylia's car, Sam in human form and looking cranky about it, Leonard scowling, and James looking like he was just shy of throwing up on his shoes. Given what was about to happen, I couldn't blame any one of them. I removed my helmet and slung it over the handlebars. We were isolated enough that I wasn't as worried about someone stealing our shit as I was about never coming back to get it.

Fern by my side, I walked over to join the others. James looked at me. I looked levelly back.

"You ready?" I asked.

He nodded, lips thin, utterly silent. That was fine. If he'd tried to talk, he probably would have started coming up with reasons why we needed to change the plan, and so he was biting his tongue because he understood there wasn't another way. We needed the crossroads to manifest. Everything else depended on that.

I held my hand out to Sam. He reached into his shirt and produced one of my throwing knives, dropping it into my palm. The feeling of relief that washed over me was indescribable. I was armed again. Even if it was only long enough for me to stab an ally.

"What's that for?" asked Leonard warily.

"You'll see," I said, and grabbed James' arm with one hand. "Come on."

James didn't help me, but he didn't resist as I hauled him to the place where the two roads converged. The others followed at a safe distance, waiting for the shit to hit the fan. I stopped at the dead center of the crossroads, noting that the leaves under our feet were undisturbed. No one had come this way in a while.

Nothing happened.

I didn't want to go straight to the stabbing: I was only planning to do it once, and I didn't actually want this encounter to end with an unnecessary corpse. "Fight me," I hissed.

James' eyes widened in understanding, and he began struggling to get his arm out of my grasp. "Let *go*, you lunatic!" he snapped. "I don't know what you're trying to do here, but you're going to regret this!"

His voice was high and shrill, the performance of a man who'd never done theater in his life. It shouldn't have fooled anyone. But as he went on, the air around us grew thick and electric with something that wasn't pressure, yet managed to have weight all the same. The eyes of the crossroads were upon us, watching, waiting to see what we were going to do. We had their attention.

"Sorry," I mouthed. James, realizing what was about to happen, stopped yelling, true panic slipping into his eyes. He might have been preparing a protest, an excuse, anything to keep me from moving on to the next part of the plan.

He didn't have the chance. The knife was already in my hand, and it slid into his side with the soft, characteristic slicing sound of metal meeting meat. He gasped, panic melting into shock. The air around us chilled as he called his magic, instinctively flailing for a way to make the hurting stop.

I'd promised to only hurt him a little, and I'd meant it, but that didn't mean I was going to stand by and let him deliver another case of frostbite. My knife was embedded in the muscle of his side, positioned to stay well clear of his internal organs. I gave it a small twist anyway, causing more damage. More importantly, having a knife twisted inside your body *hurts*. The cold broke as James lost his concentration.

The weight of the watching crossroads grew even heavier. *Come on, Bethany,* I thought. *Be a good girl and do your job, we're counting on you to do your job—*

The air shimmered, growing hazy as a summer day in the middle of the desert, even though the sky was dark and the wind was cold. Bethany didn't appear. That didn't mean she wasn't going to, but for the moment, when we spoke, we were speaking directly to the dark.

"Here you go," I said loudly, and shoved James away from me, away from the blade of my knife. He fell in the dirt in a tangle of limbs, one hand clasping his side. Blood trickled between his fingers, thick and red. He was practically panting from the pain. He'd probably never been stabbed before. Amateur.

The others were arrayed behind me; I could hear them breathing, hear the soft scuffs of their feet as they shifted their weight. Otherwise, the wood was silent, as if the world itself was holding its breath.

"Well?" I demanded. "I'm not killing him if no one's going to witness it. I refuse to let you say I didn't do it because you didn't see it. I'm not letting you weasel out of this."

"We weasel out of *nothing*," said a voice from the air, as affronted as a child accused of stealing cookies. "How dare you accuse us of cheating? Flesh cheats. We *deliver*."

"Prove it," I said, and flung the knife into the dirt by James' head. It landed less than an inch from his ear, causing him to recoil in genuine surprise and no small trace of fear. "Manifest."

"You are not our master," hissed the voice of the crossroads. Then, in a tone of smug sadism, it said, "But we can show you what it means for us to be yours."

The air twisted. In the time it took to blink, the night sky was gone, replaced by a golden twilight that stretched from one side of the sky to the next. The trees went with the sky, replaced by endless cornfields and a horizon that seemed so far and open that human hands could never hope to hold it. Not all the trees: the hanging tree remained, looming in bleak and terrible judgment over all.

I was standing on the well-worn pavement of an endless country road, at the point where it was crossed by a gravel farmer's trail. This was where the thresher would have gone, if this field had ever been intended for harvest. The knife I had thrown at James' head was still there. So was James. I glanced to the side, not quite daring to turn.

"We're here," said Leonard, voice low. "Wherever 'here' is."

So I wasn't doing this without my backup. That was good. My friends were still in danger. That was bad. Leonard was in danger, which was a little more good than bad, but wasn't ideal. Worst of all, the presence of the hanging tree told me we weren't entirely in the pocket dimension where the crossroads "lived," if the term could be considered applicable. The so-called real world surrounded us on all sides, only inches away, covered by an overlay of the unwanted and obscene.

James could perform his exorcism here and accomplish nothing. We needed to go deeper.

"We see you now," said the voice of the crossroads, coming from everywhere around us at the same time. The smugness was still there, now underscored by a note of greedy anticipation, like a spoiled child on Christmas morning. "Finish it."

"If I do, I get my magic back? I need to be able to protect myself from Leonard." I gestured toward him. I didn't have to work to put a quiver into my voice. That part came naturally, and I hated myself for it, just the slightest bit. There was every chance destroying the crossroads would mean giving that part of my soul up forever. It was a small price to pay, especially when measured against the lives the crossroads had claimed or destroyed over the years. It still stung.

"Yes, yes," said the crossroads impatiently. "You will be restored, only *kill him*."

"Right," I said, and reached into my pocket as I turned toward James.

His eyes widened, and in that moment, I could see the fear there, clear as day. He carried frost in his fingers. He knew—or could guess—how much it would hurt to have it stolen away, and he knew what he'd give to get it back. What was one life against everything I should have had, everything that was already mine by right? My friends would forgive me. I could say I'd lost control, or that the crossroads had somehow forced me to do it, I could claim to be Jean Grey in the grasp of the Phoenix, and they'd believe me, because it would be so much better than the alternative. I could have my freedom and my fire back, and all it would cost was the life of one measly little self-taught sorcerer.

Bethany flickered into existence only a few feet away, eyes even wider than James'. She knew. Somehow, she knew. "Stop her!" she squealed.

"Catch," I said, and threw the spirit jar containing Mary at James' chest.

He didn't catch it, quite: it bounced off his open hands and onto the pavement, where it cracked. It didn't shatter, but it didn't need to. A ghost can fit through any opening. A broken vessel can't contain a spirit that doesn't want to be contained. Smoke snaked through the crack, glittering in the twilight air, coming faster and faster until it shaped itself into the semblance of a teenage girl, solidified, and dissipated, leaving Mary in its wake.

I clapped a hand over my mouth, tears rising to my eyes. This was Mary as she was meant to be, without any interference from the crossroads or influence from the kids she agreed to babysit. Her hair was a streak of bone-white down her back, and her eyes were no color at all, but the shadowed hollows of a skull granted the illusion of life by a trick of the light. She wore a winding shroud, like something I might have expected to see on the Grim Reaper, and all she needed was a scythe and a strictly pointing finger to complete the illusion that she was the Ghost of Christmas Future come to deliver a major ass-kicking.

"Fuck. *That*," said Bethany, and disappeared again, back to wherever crossroads ghosts go when not summoned.

"Why am I here?" Mary asked, before any of the rest of us could react.

James, gaping, said nothing.

She turned to look over her shoulder at him, giving a small "well, hurry it up" nod of her head at the same time. "*Why* am I *here*?" she repeated urgently.

"Uh," said James.

Cylia stepped forward. "Our friend wishes to contest an unfair crossroads deal," she said, voice loud and carrying. "He has that right."

"Only if he does so of his own free will," said Mary, still looking at James. "Well? We haven't got all night."

"I do!" he gasped, staggering to his feet. "I mean, I am. I mean, yes. I'm here to contest an unfair crossroads bargain."

"You have made no bargains with us," snarled the voice of the crossroads. "What trickery is this? Do you think to *cheat*?"

"It's not a cheat," said James. "I didn't make the bargain, but Sally did. She came to you to find a way to get me out of this town. Well, she didn't get me out. She didn't get me anything but left alone. The deal that keeps me in New Gravesend is still in place, and Sally's gone, and that means the bargain you made with *her* wasn't honored. You're a liar and a cheat, and you didn't give me what Sally paid for, and I demand recompense!"

"Oh, you'll have it," said Mary, and smiled like the sun before she clapped her hands together and the world, such as it was, flashed corn-gold and blight-black in the same moment, and then everything was gone, and we were gone with it.

Twenty-three

"Family is more than what's in your blood.
Family is what's in your heart, and who you
reach for when the sun goes down."

                      –Mary Dunlavy

*In the liminal space between worlds . . . because
that's a great idea*

THE FLASH FADED, and we were standing on a new road.

The corn still surrounded us, but where before it had been ordinary, even pleasant, the sort of corn that can be found in any farmer's field, this corn was threatening, almost predatory, if that word could be applied to a plant. It grew higher than my head, and as the wind whispered through it, it *rustled*, a sound like the gnashing of a million terrible teeth, like the sharpening of a thousand cruel claws.

The road under our feet was hard-packed dirt, and the twilight was gone, replaced by blazing midday sun. Everything smelled of heat-baked earth, of rust, and the distant, unmistakable taint of long-dried blood.

Mary had moved during the transition, and was on the other side of me now, putting herself between us— all of us—and the shape that had suddenly been sliced out of the flesh of the world. It was a person and it was a void at the same time, more of an absence than anything else. It hurt my eyes if I tried to look directly at it. It was *wrong*, an offense to everything that was good and right and true, and I was suddenly, horribly grateful Leonard was here. Maybe now that he'd had a look at a true abomination, he'd start chasing those and leave the innocent cryptids of the world alone.

Or maybe he'd run screaming and kill anything that frightened him twice as hard. People are complicated and difficult and hard to predict.

"My God," whispered Leonard. I'd never heard a member of the Covenant of St. George sound so afraid.

"A complaint has been raised," said Mary, voice clear and carrying. "I did not arbitrate the bargain in question, but I am here now. I will speak for the man James Smith, who carries such complaints against you."

There was something lilting and old-fashioned in her voice, like the modern world was falling away from her one syllable at a time. She had lived and died in the 1930s, but the sound of her now was much older.

James stepped up behind her, one hand pressed over the wound in his side. "Yes," he said. "I have a complaint."

The crackling, impossible shape of the crossroads somehow managed to get across the impression that it was snarling at the pair of them. "Dead men can't carry complaints."

"But he's not dead yet, and Antimony brought him to the crossroads," said Mary. "Sally made her bargain before Annie did. It takes priority, and that means the complaint against it takes priority. You must resolve this before he becomes touchable again. Those are the rules. You want to follow the rules, don't you?"

There was a thin edge of warning in her voice, like failing to follow the rules would have consequences. Maybe they would. This place . . . this wasn't a *real* place, not like Earth, not even like the various dimensions where my grandmother searched for her missing husband. This was a gap hewn out of the space *between* worlds, and if the rules dropped away, there would be nothing left to keep it standing.

Break one of the rules here, break them all. The crossroads had created their own prison when they seized a place that seemed impermeable to outside attack. Sure, they were almost untouchable from the outside, but once someone was able to get *in* ...

I took a step backward, away from the brewing confrontation. Sam gave me a curious glance. I nodded, and he mirrored my movement. Cylia, Fern, and Leonard did the same, until all five of us were backing carefully away, moving inch by inch down the road, away from Mary, and James, and the terrible fury of the crossroads.

Finally, we were far enough away that it felt safe to turn and run, paralleling the corn, which continued to rustle like the world's greatest graveyard.

"I do *not* want to go into that!" shouted Sam.

"None of us do!" I replied.

"Where the fuck are we going?" asked Cylia.

It was a valid question. It deserved a serious answer. I considered as I ran, and finally called back, *"Away."*

She glared at me. Under the circumstances, I couldn't blame her. We were, after all, running down an endless unpaved road under a blasted summer sky, in a pocket dimension wholly owned, operated, and controlled by an unspeakable eldritch terror with a thing for being an asshole wishing ring.

That was the point. Not the asshole thing: the pocket dimension. We kept running until figures appeared on the horizon and I stumbled to a stop, motioning for the others to do the same. Fern, her density dialed down too far to make stopping easy, shot on a few more feet before Sam's tail whipped out, wrapped around her middle, and jerked her back.

"What the hell?" Leonard demanded.

"Look." I pointed at the figures up ahead.

He squinted for a moment. Then his eyes widened. "Is that . . . ?"

"Yeah." Three figures, one a shape cut out of the air, one white-haired and standing in front of the third. They were too far away for us to pick out fine details, but it didn't take fine details to recognize Mary, James, and the incarnate crossroads. There was no one else they could have been.

Leonard and the others turned to stare at me. I shrugged.

"My grandmother says there are two kinds of dimensions: real ones, like Earth, and artificial ones. The fake dimensions never extend as far as the real ones. Most of them don't want to. They're there to fulfill a purpose, and they don't waste energy having things like 'distance' or 'geography.'"

"What kind of foolishness have you people been getting *up* to?" demanded Leonard.

I ignored him.

"There are lots of crossroads," said Fern. "People all over the world make bargains like you did. How can there be lots if their whole world is so small that we can run through it without running out of breath?"

"I'm not a dimensional physicist," I said. "I have no idea."

"So we ran away for the sake of not running away," said Cylia. "Why?"

I took a breath and looked her directly in the eye. Here went everything.

"We're in the crossroads," I said. "Everything here is the crossroads. The sky, the ground, the corn, even that weird cut-out fucker arguing with Mary and James. That means the things they've taken from people are here. Not my grandfather or Sally—I don't think anything human can live here for very long—but the *things*."

Cylia nodded slowly. "Things like your magic."

"Things like my magic," I said. "I can't reclaim it with the bargain unfulfilled. What we're about to do may mean I never get it back. But at Lowryland, when I was close to it, my fire knew I was there. If I'm close enough to the magic, and if I'm very, very lucky, I could use it. Not enough to start a fire or something like that. Enough to cast a spell."

"Annie . . ." said Sam.

"What kind of spell?" asked Cylia.

"The kind that throws us backward through time to the point where everything went wrong, and lets me try to stop it." James' plan. James' idea. Just a slightly different execution.

"You would need to be . . . very lucky," said Cylia carefully. "Even then, odds are good the luck would snap back on you after the spell was cast. You could die."

"I'm against any plan where Annie dies," said Sam.

"As am I," said Leonard. The pair of them paused to glare at each other.

"I'm hard to kill," I said.

"That's not the only thing that could go wrong," said Cylia.

"I know, but James is busy, and none of the rest of you have any magic at all, not even in someone else's jar." I offered her a wan smile. "It's a bad plan. It's a dangerous plan. It's the plan we've got, and we're doing it."

"Annie?" Fern sounded uncertain.

"Yeah?"

"You knew before we came here that James would be busy. Was this the plan the whole time?"

Everything went silent. I took a breath, turning to fully face her before I reached out and grasped her shoulders.

"You are my best friends," I said. "You're the best friends a girl like me could ever have. You get that, right? I'm a Price. I grew up thinking all I'd ever have would be my family, and maybe the occasional flash of gratitude from someone I saved because we're still trying to pay off a karmic debt that started centuries ago.

And I got you. All of you. You're amazing. You're strong and clever and *good*. God, you're good. So yeah, this was the plan all along, and it's not because I have a death wish, and it's not because I owe anything. It's because no matter how much else changes, I'm still a Price, and we're like cockroaches. We don't die."

"Except when you do," said Leonard.

I had almost forgotten he was there. I glanced at him and frowned. "Except when we do," I said. "But that's not going to be here, and it's not going to be today. So how about you wish me luck and watch my back, okay?"

I waited for them to nod before I pulled the folded piece of paper from my pocket, opening it to reveal the spell I had meticulously copied from James' mother's journal. Seeing it in my own handwriting made it make more sense. That always happened. Making a thing your own made it more comprehensible, and hence easier to manage.

Please let this be easy to manage.

Sitting cross-legged on the hard-packed dirt of the road, I leaned forward and used my pointer finger to inscribe the beginning of a circle around myself. Finishing it took some twisting, but I was careful to keep my butt firmly on the ground. The simpler a spell, the more important it is to follow it exactly, and this one was as simple as they come. If it wanted me sitting while I drew my circle, I was going for the full sit.

I looked up. Cylia and Fern were watching James and Mary as they faced down the crossroads. Leonard was watching me, a scowl on his face. So was Sam, although he wasn't scowling, just staring at me with open-faced longing. His tail was wrapped around his left ankle, squeezing so hard it had to hurt. It was taking everything he had not to grab me and book it. I could see it in his eyes, and I loved him for wanting to save me, even as I loved him even more for staying where he was.

"It's going to be okay," I said, with a confidence I didn't entirely feel. "Trust me. I'm a professional."

"Professional pain in my ass," he muttered.

I flashed him a quick, strained smile, and looked back down at the paper in my hands. Lowryland had done me few favors, but my training there had given me this much, at least: I had a better sense of what the spell was meant to do, and how to craft and control it. Now all I needed was the magic.

"Come back to me," I whispered, bowing my head until my chin almost grazed my chest and closing my eyes, straining for a flicker of fire anywhere around me. "The deal was you'd go to the crossroads until I paid for your release. Well, I'm at the crossroads now. We're in the same place. The deal didn't say anything about keeping your distance while we were in the same place."

Was there a hint of heat in my fingertips, or was that wishful thinking? If I was lucky—and Cylia was here to make sure I was lucky—it was my magic straining to get back to me. It wasn't much. It would have to be enough.

Spells come in two major varieties. One type imposes the caster's will on the world, creating something out of nothing or mending something that's been broken. Those spells are pretty clear violations of the laws of physics, many of which have unkind things to say about people who go around summoning extra mass or setting things on fire all willy-nilly. If a physicist ever acquires the power to cast those types of spells, and the underlying forces that make them possible, I expect the human race will have access to faster-than-light travel inside of the *week*.

(Honestly, it's sort of a terrifying miracle that no sorcerers have decided to go into physics. It takes someone who really understands gravity to figure out how best to turn it off. Then again, maybe that's why it hasn't happened. No one with the sense God gave the little green apples is going to want to combine the peanut butter of physics with the strawberry jam of sorcery into one big, delicious sandwich of ending reality as we know it.)

The second kind of spell is subtler. It's the sort of

nasty working that the coven controlling Lowryland used when they tailored their tickets to steal luck from their clientele. It draws its power from the thing it focuses on, rather than from the caster. That means the caster's strength isn't the limit on what the spell can do. It also means the target the spell is linked to can wind up seriously hurt, depending on how skilled the sorcerer doing the casting is.

The real world is big and complicated and unforgiving, and we don't get the luxury of pretending there's "good magic" and "bad magic." This isn't Harry Potter. But if it were, the spell I was about to attempt would definitely have been verging on the Dark Arts.

Carefully, I sketched the shape of it on the ground in front of me, pressing down until I left layers of skin behind. I didn't need to bleed for this specific spell, but pain is always good fuel for the kind of magic capable of chewing people up and spitting them out again. Sam made a wordless noise of dismay. I kept my eyes on the ground. He *really* wasn't going to like what happened next.

Exorcisms can be performed by anybody. There's nothing magical about them. They're more like antivirus programs for the universe, and they don't have anything to do with demons, or faith, or any of the other trappings of the Catholic church. They're just an ordinary person who belongs in the dimension where they're standing, looking at something that *shouldn't* be there and saying, "Yeah, you need to go the hell home."

Time travel is another matter.

"Tick," I said, and focused on the days that had passed since I'd left my home. All my stuff was there. My bedroom, packed with everything I'd ever wanted to be in love with, the carcasses of a hundred hobbies, the still-breathing bodies of a dozen current obsessions. Would they continue to hold the same appeal for me when I finally made it back to Oregon? Or would I have become someone so different that I no longer knew how to be in love with the things that had made me who I was? Everything that lives can change. Change isn't always a good thing.

"Tock," I said, and focused on the carnival, the days I'd spent—however briefly—as Timpani Brown, last survivor of a dead show, orphan and drifter and newest member of the Spenser and Smith Family Carnival. That was where I'd met Sam, where he'd somehow managed to turn an antagonistic dance into a courtship into the closest thing I was ever likely to experience to a fairy-tale romance. Sure, it was more Shrek and Fiona than anything by Disney, but honestly, that suited me. I would have looked silly in a ballgown anyway.

"Tick," I said, and focused on Lowryland, the time I'd spent there, wishing each day away, content to sink into mundanity and bland security. I didn't regret those days. I mean, I regretted the ones that had led to me getting tangled up in a coven of sort of evil assholes who were happy to use my magic to boost their own nasty plans, but that was less about the time and place and more about the people involved. Lowryland had given me the space to recover, the time to breathe, and a place to heal. For that alone, I would always think of it fondly.

The air was getting thicker and more opaque around me. I could barely see Sam's feet through the growing barrier. If I'd dared to look up, I probably wouldn't have been able to make out any of the details of his face. That was unnerving, if not unexpected. He existed in the here and now of the crossroads. I was trying to use their own power to take myself somewhere else, somewhere older and deeper and less *here*.

The heat slipped out of my fingertips, slowly at first, growing faster and faster as the air continued to blur, now becoming then becoming now becoming nothing, every time and anytime all tangled up together. The Doctor would have been proud. Of course, the Doctor would also have come equipped with his very own time machine and rendered this entire exercise functionally moot. Who needs an untested, unpredictable act of sorcery when you have a big blue box?

"Tock," I said, and the air exploded outward in a shimmering wall of razor-sharp shards, passing through the place where my friends should have been before dispersing into a field of shining golden wheat. I stared.

The landscape had shifted without changing a bit. I was still sitting in the middle of a lonely dirt road, stretching from one end of the horizon to the other like an unbroken string, ready to carry the travelers home. The sky was still midsummer blue, the sun still too bright to look at directly . . . but there were clouds there now, white and puffy and breaking the glare into smaller, more manageable pieces. They flitted almost playfully across the sun, and while it was warm, it wasn't so hot that I felt the need to run for cover.

The corn was gone, replaced by harvest-ready wheat, each head heavy with grain. It was enough to feed a family, a township, a world, if it was managed correctly. There was movement far out in the field, like someone was reaping even now, gathering the goodness of the season to fill their belly.

There were no footprints in the earth around me. My friends hadn't disappeared: they'd never been here in the first place. I was far away from them, in a time so far before my own that it might as well have been another country, breathing air that had never been intended for me. I rose on shaky legs, trying to focus on the wheat, the road, on anything apart from the question I hadn't allowed myself to ask before attempting this particular feat of foolhardy heroism.

If I was here to stop the thing we knew as the crossroads from latching onto and replacing the *actual* crossroads—whatever that was or meant—and I had managed to use the parasite's power to come back this far, how was I going to get home?

Twenty-four

"We make our choices. We live with their
consequences. That's what it means to walk
in this world, whether we like it or not."
                                    –Evelyn Baker

*In the liminal space between worlds, having a minor
panic attack*

THE ANSWER TO THE question I hadn't asked came
from an unexpected place: behind me. "You can't go
home," said a voice, familiar as waffles on a Sunday
morning and cold as the wind blowing through a graveyard. "You're already there. Antimony Timpani Price,
do you have any idea what you've done?"

Some of the tension left my shoulders, replaced by a
yawning exhaustion that felt big enough to reach up and
swallow me whole. "Hi, Aunt Mary," I said, turning. I'd
always known, on some level, that when I finally died,
she would be the one who'd come to carry me down into
the twilight, down to where the ghost girls go.

Rose claims the position of primary psychopomp for
our family, and that's all right, really. She's earned it. But
for Mary, the youngest member of the family is her responsibility until they're not, and that meant if—well, if—

"Am I dead?" I blurted. "Because that wasn't supposed to make me dead, but I don't really see how you
can be here if I'm not."

"You're not dead," she said. She wasn't smiling. That

wasn't a good sign. "You *did* just break about a hundred rules of dealing with the crossroads. We're standing five hundred years in the past. Do you understand how much trouble you're in, young lady?"

"Are you going to ground me for irresponsible time travel?"

"I might!" She stomped her foot, glaring at me. "You don't seem to understand how serious this is! What were you trying to do?"

"Travel five hundred years into the past. Give or take a few decades."

Mary stilled. "Why?"

"How are you here? The spell only covered me. Are you still arguing for James? He's defenseless if you aren't there to stand between him and the crossroads."

"He has his sorcery, which is more than I can say for you," she countered. "And he has a group of cryptids who've already said they want to keep him alive, and a foolhardy knight of that damned Covenant looking to prove himself against a greater foe. James is *fine*. As for your first question, I'm here because you're mine, and anywhere you go, I can always follow. Whether I want to or not, apparently. Annie, what are you doing?"

I took a deep breath. "Hopefully? An exorcism."

Mary stared at me for a count of ten, empty highway eyes wide with confusion that slowly transformed into horror. "Annie."

"It's the only way."

"*Annie.*"

"It's not really time travel. I'm not going to create a paradox or rewrite the past or anything stupid like that." Or was I? If I broke the hold of the faux-crossroads before they could clamp down, would the crossroads ever have the chance to take my grandfather? Maybe I was about to create a timeline where I'd never been born, one where I either didn't exist or was the last shipwrecked survivor of a world that had never been given the chance to become.

It was a pretty horrifying idea. Although if there was any consolation, it was also pretty cool.

"Are you sure? Absolutely *certain*? You're talking about fighting a force powerful enough to claim and corrupt all this." She waved her hands, indicating the pastoral landscape around us.

"About that," I said. "Where is the current crossroads?"

"There isn't one."

I blinked.

"There never was." Mary sighed. "It was only us, in the beginning. Ghosts like me, who'd died where the roads converged, who listened and helped people tap into the power of this place. It's the anima mundi, Annie. It's the spirit of Earth. This is where all the magic and all the will that doesn't get used by the living goes when they become the dead. It's a lake. People could drown here if they weren't careful, and that's why guardians were posted around the edges, to keep the ones who found their way this deep from losing themselves entirely. The bargains are part of keeping the water levels high—or they were, until things changed."

"Why did they change?"

"I don't know." She turned her face toward the sky. "But I think we're about to find out."

I looked up. The clouds, no longer fluffy and white, were gathering in what looked suspiciously like a hurricane funnel. It was obscene, a stain on the previously perfect sky, and I hated and feared it in immediate equal measure. I took an involuntary step backward, as if I could run away from something that looked wide enough to swallow the entire world.

"What you did, whatever you did, undo it," hissed Mary. "Get out of here while you still can."

"Can you get out of here?"

She said nothing.

I paused. "Mary?"

"Yes?"

"You're not really you, are you? You didn't know all that stuff about the crossroads. You only knew what the parasite was willing to tell you, and I'm betting it didn't start with a 'how I ate the world yum yum yum' history lesson. And you *never* told me things I hadn't earned. You're still—I mean, Mary's still—in the present, helping James fight with whatever's using your name now."

"My name?" asked the figure with my babysitter's face.

"Yeah. Yours. Because you're the anima mundi, aren't you?"

Slowly, Mary's lips curved upward in a smile. She blinked, and the empty road in her eyes was gone, replaced by a starfield, specks of light scattered across an endless velvet blackness. They were beautiful, and terrifying, and they had no place in Mary's face.

"Oh, you *are* a clever one," said the anima mundi. "You're not here using my strength. You're riding the one who comes to usurp me. You can't stop it from happening. You said so yourself. This has to be, because it has already been."

"But you're not dead," I said. "You survived whatever it's going to do to you."

"I'm the ghost of the dreams of a living Earth," said the anima mundi. "I'm the layer that connects the twilight and the daylight. No one sees me unless they come here, to my crossroads, and then they pay for the privilege, because there have to be mysteries, and there have to be costs. I'm not the great work you think of when you say 'crossroads.' That comes after and before me."

"And that's great, if a little crunchy granola for me, but the thing that controls the crossroads when I'm from is *bad*," I said. "It hurts people because it can. It makes cruel bargains. It hurt my family, and it hurts the ghosts who're supposed to be helping people understand the deals before they finish making them, and I'm pretty sure it started by hurting you. It throws power around like it's never going to run out. But it is going to run out, isn't it?"

Silently, the anima mundi nodded.

"The crossroads are using the power of the living Earth to fuel their bargains, and they don't replenish it, and they're draining it dry." It was a horrifying thought. It also explained a lot of things, like why the "age of magic" was supposedly over, and why the birthrate for magic-users had declined the way it had. Even with the Covenant hunting down and killing practitioners, magic was something I would have expected to see cropping up with enough regularity that hiding it from the world would be a lot more difficult, if not outright impossible. Instead, only the routewitches seemed to be maintaining their numbers, and according to Aunt Rose, they drew their power from the ghostroads and the twilight, not the living Earth.

It was like a piece had been missing from my understanding of the magical world, and now everything was starting to make sense. And that meant I had to make it home alive. If I hadn't already been planning on it, now I *had* to, because my family needed to know what we'd been ignorant of. We needed to write this down and document it, so it wouldn't be lost again.

"Yes," said the anima mundi.

"So I'm going to stop it."

"How can you, future girl? You gave your own power away. This isn't how you bring it back to you."

"Maybe not. And maybe this is a problem my family didn't help create, since we're not the ones who decided to mess with the way the crossroads operate. But that doesn't mean I'm not going to try to fix it. Fixing things is my *job*." I turned my eyes back to the stain across the sky. The parasite, the thing that would replace the crossroads for five hundred years, was coming. "Do you know what it is?"

"It comes from outside," she said, voice little above a whisper. "It was me, once, or something very much like me, the living spirit of a world that needed to be cared for, that needed to care. It lost its way. It lost its world. Now it lives by feeding on worlds that have never learned to defend themselves. I was turned so far inward that I never once looked outward."

"Time is sort of a negotiable concept for you, huh?"

The anima mundi looked at me wearily. "My death approaches, child. You should not make light of what you'll never know."

"I think I liked you better when you were pretending to be Mary." I reached into my pocket. The salt was still there, soothingly solid under my fingers. "Right here, right now, before it comes, do you have the power to make bargains?"

For the first time, the anima mundi looked surprised. "Yes, but I can't give you back your magic. That happens so far after me that it might as well have happened on another planet."

"If you're the anima mundi, and you're about to be replaced by something from another world, I think it sort of *did* happen on another planet." The invaders from Mars weren't coming. The Martians were dead in their beds, quietly rotting, while their entire world had come to swallow the Earth.

Metaphorically. I was pretty sure the crossroads weren't being possessed by the anima mundi of Mars, if only because this—whatever it was—didn't feel like a local. It had come from outside. Was coming from outside. The bruised streak in the sky was getting wider and deeper and rawer looking, like a wound that was never going to heal. Streaks of corrupted yellow and green spilled from its center, slashing through the sky, tainting everything they touched. The clouds that hadn't joined the growing maelstrom had dissipated, leaving the bleakly empty horizon that I was used to seeing when I came into contact with the crossroads.

"I suppose," she said uncertainly. "What do you want from me?"

"Permission to go into the field without your wheat eating me, or whatever it is supernatural wheat likes to do to intruders."

She lifted an eyebrow.

"Hey, I come from a time where killer corn is all the rage," I protested. "I like to ask."

"That boon I can grant without charge," she said. "Go into the wheat. Do as you like, but try not to damage anything. Agriculture is among the greatest of humanity's achievements."

"Got it," I said, and turned my back on the force of nature with my babysitter's face, taking one last, wary glance at the bruised sky before diving into the waving field of golden grain. I had work to do.

Like I said before, exorcisms aren't about magic, and they aren't about religion. They're about knowing and maintaining the natural order of things. Most bodies are only meant to play host to a single soul at a time. Casting out the one that doesn't belong isn't the *easiest* thing in the world, but it's less about power than it is about ritual, preparation, and will.

Exorcising the crossroads in the modern day, when they'd had five hundred years to strengthen their hold on this world, was next to impossible. Doing it in the past, even if the past was an illusion, might work. It had to work.

If it didn't work, I was going to be in a world of hurt.

I plunged into the wheat, walking fast, until I found a place where the stalks had been cut down and the ground had been stomped flat, preparing for another planting. I took the salt out of my pocket and drew a circle around myself, letting it trickle between my fingers as I turned. I opened my mouth to begin the ritual . . . and stopped.

Church has never been my family's thing. I could recite Bible passages all I wanted, but they wouldn't mean anything to me, not really. When it comes to liturgies and catechisms, there's really only one faith that's been completely available to us, offered freely and without the expectation that we'll join in. We've never needed to believe. We've only ever needed to *know*.

"In the days when the faith in the Feathered Lords was waning, came Elizabeth Evans, called Beth, the Kindly Priestess, who did find Us gathered in her yard, and say, Why, Look At You, You Must be Starving. And she did gather Us in her apron and carry Us into her Home, which would be our Home thereafter, and say, You Are Safe Here, If You Will Follow the Rules I Set—"

The bruise in the sky became a gaping, rotting wound, and the summer shattered, the air going cold. Wind whipped through the wheat, chilling and killing it. How long did this field lie fallow before the corn came pushing its way through the earth, already ripening, already aware?

I shivered, and continued, "Her child, Caroline, the Well-Groomed Priestess, did come to us with open hands, and say, My Mother Is Old, and The Covenant Does Not Understand; Come With Me, For Any Husband I Will Have Will Have You Also. She did marry Peter Carew, the God of Hard Work and Sunshine, and they did raise four children in hope and in glory, hidden from the Eye of the Covenant by the strength of their affections—"

The sky . . . tore. The sky *broke*, like a plate dropped from a great height, and there were shards of sky falling all around me, terrible, impossible shards of sky, which shattered again when they hit the ground, becoming an oily, sticky film that danced with diseased rainbows before sinking into the earth. In the distance, the anima mundi shrieked, fear and rage and agony blurring into a single heartrending sound.

I wanted to go to her. I didn't know her, for all that she looked so much like Mary, but something in her scream tore at my heart and made me want nothing more than to break the circle I'd drawn and run to her aid. Whether that was the incoming crossroads trying to lure me or the spirit of Earth calling for help didn't matter. I had to stay where I was. I had to finish this.

I took a steadying breath, and said, "Her eldest daughter, Agnes, refused us, but did not break her mother's Confidence, saying, You Ask Too Much of Me. But her second daughter, Enid, the Patient Priestess, did say, Mother, I Love You, and I Love the Mice, and I Will Keep Them Safe. She did marry Alexander Healy, the God of Uncommon Sense, and on their wedding night—"

Something fell from the broken, breaking sky, something made of angles and reflections and wrongness. Everything about it was wrong. It was obscene, offensive to the eye: it had no business here, or anywhere near here. It didn't *belong*.

It howled, and its voice was the voice of the void. The anima mundi screamed, agony and anxiety. I pulled a handful of salt out of my pocket, cutting the catechism short as I flung it into the air.

"In the name of Beth Evans, I cast you out! In the name of Caroline Carew, I refuse you passage here! In the name of Enid—"

A hand made of crackling static and absence grasped my wrist, jerking me off my feet and out of the circle. I found myself dangling, toes several inches above the ground, looking into the emptiness that was the face of the crossroads.

"You don't *belong* here, human child," it hissed, like static, like nothingness, like the act of being erased. There was no fire in my fingers. There had never been fire in my fingers. I was vibrating apart, my component atoms becoming nothing but dust and the opposite of memory. I would be the déjà vu that haunted my family for a hundred generations, the girl who should have been but never was born.

(*and a carnival burned before a Covenant strike team, and a screaming fūri died with his grandmother's body in his arms, howling rage, howling misery*)

(*and a jink tried desperately to stop a feeding mara from destroying a roller derby league one skater at a time, until her own luck ran out from the strain of*

manipulating everyone else's, until her neck snapped in
a bad fall, and she was still, so still, so still)

(and a sylph died at the business end of a manticore's
tail, eyes open and startled, staring into nothing, not sure
why she thought she could be saved)

(and they died, and they died, and they died because
I wasn't there, because I had never been there, because I
had never existed at all)

"In the name of Enid Healy, I deny your power," I
whispered. The words were harder than I expected them
to be. I had never been touched by a force of entropy
before.

I didn't like it.

"Stop that, and I'll show mercy," snarled the
crossroads—only it wasn't the crossroads yet, was it? It
was fighting me instead of attacking the anima mundi.
Flakes of light were starting to appear in the shattered
sky as the world struggled to reassert itself, becoming
hazy and unclear.

It hurt, oh, fuck, it hurt. I felt like my entire body was
fizzing at the edges, dissolving and reforming at the
same time. "In the name of Frances Healy, I cast you
out," I whispered.

The thing shook me like a limp rag. I scrabbled to get
a better grasp on the hand that held me, using the strength
it had and I didn't to keep myself as close to upright as
possible.

"I could have been merciful," it snarled, and I was on
fire.

Not literally: literal fire would have been a problem
for both of us, considering we were surrounded by dry,
flammable wheat. This was the fire that burned in the
center of my cells, the fire that should have been mine,
before I had given it away to save myself from drowning.
The anima mundi might not have been able to reach
forward to the things her replacement had claimed in
bargain after bargain, all the long and awful days of its
ascendance, but the parasite had no such problems.

I screamed. Burning hurt no less here than it had in the future, when Bethany had been the one to pour pain into my palms and pretend it was a gift. Bile rose in my throat. I swallowed it back down, forcing myself to keep breathing. Pain is pain. I'd been in pain before.

"In the name . . ." I rasped. "In the name of . . . Alice Price-Healy, I tell you that you have no place here."

The parasite snarled and shook me again. The fire burned higher, hotter. That was almost a good thing. The pain was reaching the point where it hurt so much that it didn't hurt at all. Parts of me were shutting down, going into shock. In the long run, that was going to be a problem. Right now . . .

"In the name of Evelyn Price, I refuse you any place here," I whispered. All the Priestesses, all the generations of Aeslin mice who believed, truly believed to the bottom of their souls, that we were connected to the divine, that we could shape the world with our actions—and we had, we had, every one of us had. We had become a pantheon in their eyes, and we had fought so hard, for so long, to be worthy of what they saw when they looked at us.

"I will *not* be exorcised like some common *spirit*," spat the parasite.

It hurt. It hurt so much that there was nothing to me *but* the hurting, nothing to the world but pain. I somehow found the strength to force a smile, despite it all.

"Our world," I whispered. "Our rules. In the names of Verity Price, Elsie Harrington, and myself, Antimony Price, the Precise Priestess, I command you to leave this place and never come here again. This is not yours. You are not wanted here."

The parasite howled. The anima mundi screamed. I screamed, and I was burning, I was burning, the flames were higher than they had ever been, so high that they were breaking through my skin, and everything was fire, everything was fire, and there was nothing left for me but to burn, to burn, to—

Twenty-five

"Oh, baby. Rest now. Rest, and remember that I love you."

–Frances Brown

Burning

IT DIDN'T HURT ANYMORE.

That was the first thing I noticed. Nothing hurt: nothing even ached. For the first time I could remember, everything was perfect. I was cradled in warmth, like I was sleeping next to the heater in the middle of December, safe and comfortable and protected from anything that might want to hurt me. I couldn't see, but that made sense, since my eyes were closed. I didn't know what was out there, and I didn't *want* to know, because there was one thing I was pretty sure of:

I was pretty sure I was dead.

I'd traveled through time—technically—through a loophole in the laws of temporal physics, to stop an eldritch force of incredible power before it could displace the anima mundi and become the terror we all knew and hated. A spell simple enough to be cast by someone with virtually no magic couldn't be powerful enough to cause an actual paradox: maybe I'd traveled through time, but I'd only done it within the confines of the crossroads themselves. Even if I'd succeeded, I couldn't succeed until the crossroads returned to the present day. The thing I'd just gotten into a slap-fight with would still have five hundred years of torturing humanity before my exorcism caught up with it.

Maybe that was why it had always hated sorcerers so much. Maybe it had targeted people like James' family—like my own grandfather—because it remembered a woman with the ghost of fire in her fingers breaking its hold on the world before that hold could become strangling. I wasn't causing a paradox. I was preventing one.

And now I was warm, and not in pain anymore, and probably dead. It was interesting, really. I'd always assumed death would be cold.

"—hear me?"

The voice was distant and broken, like I was hearing it across a crackling fire. I didn't turn. Whoever it was, they could wait until I was damn well good and ready to stop catching my breath. Did the dead breathe? Rose did, but she was usually wearing a coat and temporarily alive when she hung out at the house.

"—burning, she's burning, how do we *stop*—"

The second voice held a thin edge of hysteria, audible above the crackle of the flames. It sounded familiar, although I couldn't quite say why. I tried to open my eyes, and found, to my dismay, that they wouldn't budge.

Oh, man. If my afterlife was going to be sitting around impersonating a charcoal briquette, I was going to get really bored, really quickly.

"Annie, *can you hear me*?"

Mary. The first voice was Mary. I tried again to open my eyes. I failed again.

"Is she even breathing?"

Cylia.

"She's *still on fire*, can we deal with the part where she's *still on fire*?"

Sam. Oh, Sam. He sounded like he was on the verge of beginning to punch things for the sake of having something less confusing to deal with. Violence isn't always the answer, but sometimes it's a good stopgap until the answer can be found.

"Killing her would be a mercy. This is unnatural."
Leonard. Swell.

"Touch her, and I will rip your lungs out through your throat, I swear to Jesus I will."

Sam, I love you, I thought, and wished that he could hear me.

"Let me through."

It took me a moment to place the fifth voice. James. James Smith. He sounded tired, almost exhausted, but level. I couldn't tell whether that indicated success or failure. Was Sally back? Did we win? I wanted to ask, but I couldn't open my mouth, either. I was silent and stuck, unable to do anything at all.

Death, from what I could tell so far, really sucked. Clearly, I hadn't managed to pick up one of the deluxe packages like Mary or Rose. Maybe I needed to die in a more easily-categorized way. "Fried by parasitic invader trying to consume the living spirit of the Earth" probably didn't come with a clear type of haunting.

"If you touch her—" Sam again, voice low and tight and filled with a barely-contained menace. Between Leonard and James, he finally had something to focus his anger on. I hoped he'd reserve most of it for Leonard. Poor James had been through enough.

"I have to touch her if I want to put the fire out! Let me through, you asshole, before she explodes or something."

Was I going to explode? Apparently, I was on fire, which was sort of unsettling, but I hadn't considered the possibility that "on fire" could lead to "exploding like a car in a bad action movie." Jean Grey spent, like, half her time on fire, and *she* never exploded. Then again, Jean Grey was a comic book character, and this was real life.

Pity, that. I could have used a little bit of the Phoenix Force to get me back to the land of the living.

"If you hurt her, I'll kill you."

"Understood," snapped James.

There was a soft thudding sound, as if someone had dropped to their knees next to me, and then a wave of coolness washed through the warmth around me, chasing some of my comfortable cocoon away. I tried again to open my eyes. I failed again.

"Has she ever done this before?" asked Cylia. "Do humans *usually* catch fire when under stress?"

"Don't you know?" asked Sam.

"Kid, I have gone out of my way for most of my life to have as little intimate contact as possible with humans. I play roller derby because everybody needs a social life, and nobody's going to report you for being weird when you spend all your time with women who call themselves 'Elmira Street' and 'Princess Leia-You-Out.' I do administrative work when I need a paying job. Just me, a computer, and a bunch of big, important people trying to pretend they couldn't be paying me more to deal with their bullshit. Annie here is the first human I've ever allowed in my car, much less in my house."

"No, humans don't usually catch fire when under stress," said Leonard. "How can you avoid humans? We're the dominant species on this planet."

"Believe me, I'm aware," said Cylia disgustedly. "Any chance she's secretly a dragon with a dye job? Is she a natural blonde?"

"I feel like she would probably smack me for answering that question, but no, she's definitely not secretly blonde," said Sam.

I should have been annoyed by the way they were nattering on while I was burning. All I actually felt was relief. There was a thin, strained edge to their voices— they were scared, and trying to cover it up by talking about dye jobs and human behavioral quirks. That was normal. That was natural. They were okay.

The people I cared about were okay. Whether I had succeeded or not, they'd get to bury me and walk away from this, as soon as they figured out that people who are actively on fire are usually dead, and hence do not need to be consulted about future plans. Even if I was lingering on this mortal plane like Rose or Mary, I wasn't going to follow them. Sam deserved better than a dead girlfriend, and my parents deserved to believe I was resting in peace, not condemned to a shadowy existence on the edges of the living world. The only ghosts in my family were Mary and Rose, and both of them had died a lot younger than I had, while they were still in their teens, and neither of them was a blood relative. Prices rest. Maybe it's because we run so hard and so fast while we're alive, but when we die . . .

Prices rest.

The cooling sensation spread, getting stronger—strong enough, in spots, that I was actually getting cold. I made a small sound of protest, not audible above the flames. I didn't want to be dead *and* cold. I was tired. I was so damn tired. I was ready to rest.

"Really? Is that what you *really* want?"

This was a new voice, female, unfamiliar. Without thinking about it, I opened my eyes.

There was no fire. There were no friends. I was alone, sprawled in the middle of a great field of harvest-ready wheat. The sky above me was midsummer blue and perfect as a portrait, marked here and there with the skidding streaks of fluffy white clouds, moving briskly along in a wind I couldn't feel. I sat up. The landscape didn't change.

"Guys?"

There was no response. I stood, turning in a slow circle. There was no one there. I was totally alone. But the voices . . .

"They're still at the crossroads," said the female voice, from behind me.

I spun, reaching for a knife, and stopped dead. The anima mundi looked at me, amused and exasperated in equal measure. I stared speechlessly back.

She looked . . . nothing like Mary. Her skin was smooth and brown; her lips were thin and her nose was broad and her eyes were soft and sad and the color of the wheat blowing all around us. Her hair was black and blonde and red and brown and silver at the same time, falling to her shoulders in streaky corkscrew curls. Some of them were tipped in blue or purple or pink, like even the fashion colors were a part of the living spirit of the world. She still wore the belted shroud she'd had on when she appeared with Mary's face, dressed like she was going to produce a scythe and go reaping souls at any moment.

She was beautiful. That was nice to know. The composite of every human woman in the world was beautiful.

"Why are you a woman?" I blurted.

"Why do you assume I'm a woman?" she countered. "I look like this for you because your life has been filled with friendly ghosts. You were a haunted house before you knew what it was to be more than just a room. Your friends would all see something different when they looked at me. I don't have a specific gender, any more than the thing that tried to destroy me did. I'm just more invested in being kind to the people who walk my path."

"Oh," I said, cheeks flaring red. "Sorry."

"It's all right. People have always assumed. It's only recently that they're realized they should also regret, when those assumptions are wrong." The anima mundi shook their head. "I'm still filtering through all the changes to humanity that have come in the last five hundred years. You've made such progress for a silly, self-centered little species, and yet you haven't changed at all. It's going to be amazing learning what you can do now."

"Will the magic get stronger? Now that you're back?"

"The magic never left. Magic is a constant force of the universe, like gravity, or time. It could grow thin as that thing consumed and spent it, but it could never disappear."

"That isn't what I asked."

"I know. But this is still the crossroads, and questions asked here are difficult things. They have consequences. You still have a question unanswered."

I hesitated. "I don't remember asking a question."

"But you did. You asked yourself whether you were going to die here, and since you're still at the crossroads, you asked me." The anima mundi looked at me solemnly. "That means I get to offer you a bargain."

"Wait, I mean, just hold on a second here," I said, alarmed. "I already have one outstanding deal with the crossroads."

"No, you don't. For this one moment in time, *no one* has a deal with the crossroads, because the parasite that took my place, that used my power to harm my people, has no authority here. Some of the things it gave were good, even if they were in the pursuit of an evil: I doubt your lover would be pleased to find his lungs filling with fluid, or your grandmother would be delighted to find the flesh rotting from her bones. I'm not taking back its gifts. I'm also not taking on its debts. The slates are clean. The books are balanced. We begin fresh, here, to-day, and you, Antimony Timpani Price, will be my first new negotiation. Shall we begin?"

". . . crap," I said, before I could catch myself. "I . . . okay, no, *crap*. Is there any way we could not do this? Like, I just performed an exorcism, I'm pretty sure I'm going to be jet-lagged for the next decade, I really, really don't want to deal with semi-cosmic forces right now."

"Unfortunately, you stand balanced on a scythe's edge, and you have to fall one way or another. Living or dead. Choose."

"Again, that debt thing. I don't want it. I just want to go home."

"Where is home?"

I hesitated. Home was Oregon, safe in our compound, surrounded by trees, where no one could find us, or get past the fences, or cross the yard when they didn't know where the traps were located. But home was also the carnival, stealing kisses with Sam atop the Ferris wheel, everything spread out beneath us in lights and music and the empty midway, and it was the backseat of Cylia's car, and it was . . . it was . . .

"Home is where my heart is," I said. "It's a cliché, but sometimes things become clichés because they're too damn true not to. I want to go home. I want to see my family again. I want to be the reason my friends are smiling, not the reason they're crying. I . . . maybe I want too much, I don't know, but I want it anyway."

"I thought you wanted to rest."

I shook my head. "I'm exhausted, yeah. This has been a pretty shitty year, you know? But I sleep better with a knife under my pillow and a fūri at my back than I will six feet down."

"I could offer you a lot, if it meant you'd stay," said the anima mundi. "I could promise you that everyone who came to save me with you would be safe, and comfortable, and spared from danger for the rest of their days. They wouldn't even have to pay for it. They'd miss you, and that would be payment enough. But you could serve as the first of my new guardians, and help the others adjust. Some of them will have to move on, you understand. They were not the sort of people I would have trusted to represent me, in their lives, and the force they've served has done nothing to change that in their deaths. I'm going to need spirits I can trust to ease me into this age."

"That doesn't sound like rest," I protested.

"No. But it's calm and comfort for the people you have chosen as extensions of your heart, which means it's calm and comfort for your home. Three of them don't belong to the currently dominant species. Calm and comfort would be a great boon to them."

I stared. The anima mundi looked back at me, utterly serene.

"You could still see Mary. She'd be here with you, showing you what to do, how things work, how to negotiate the world on my behalf. As for James, the bargain that kept him in New Gravesend is discharged. He can go wherever he likes, and carry my promise of peace with him. The Covenant will never find him. Leonard will find another way. He could change the organization that made him from within, could reform them, make them what they were always meant to be. Your death would be life for so many."

"I . . ." I paused. "Does this offer cover my family? My actual blood family, I mean?"

The anima mundi shook their head. "No. The Prices are what they are. They court danger like a lover, and seem surprised when their affections are returned. I couldn't grant them calm without remaking them completely, and that would cost more than I currently have to spend. My bargains will be small things until the magic strengthens around me, and even if it were at its greatest, you're a single life. You can't buy that much."

That was almost a relief. I wasn't sure I could have called it a choice, if I'd known that staying would have meant my entire family could be safe, forever. "Okay. I have one more question."

"Ask, and I'll answer, if I can."

"What about Sally?" What about my grandfather, and all the other people the records indicated had disappeared over the centuries? They had to have gone somewhere. They had to be lost, and even if some of them were long, long dead, there had to be at least a few—like Sally—who hadn't been gone long enough for age to have caught up with them.

Now that we understood what had been happening, we owed them the chance to come home. Someone had to at least go looking. And Mary probably still couldn't tell my grandmother that my grandfather might still be alive out there after all.

"She is not here," said the anima mundi. "The parasite cast her, and the others, very far away, and could not return them."

"That's sort of what I was afraid of."

"Then your choice is made?"

"I want to rest," I said slowly, "but I'm not ready yet. I think, right now, what I need is to go back to the others. I need to stay alive. Can I . . . can I do that? Am I allowed to wake up?"

"Don't come here again," said the anima mundi. "There are better ways."

"Not always," I said, thinking of a dark tunnel filled with water where I had almost drowned, where all of this trouble had started. Sometimes the deus ex machina was the only solution you had. "But I'll try to stay away."

"Good," said the anima mundi. They snapped their fingers, and they were gone, replaced by a wall of flame, and I was burning, I was burning, I was—

"—so try *harder*!" Sam was shouting. That was rarely a good sign. But hey, I could hear him, and I hadn't been expecting to do that again.

Shout away, Sam, I thought, struggling to open my eyes. That strange sense of all-encompassing warmth had returned, wrapping itself tightly around me, preventing all motion. The cooling sensation was continuing to spread, making parts of my body actively cold, but the overall warmth remained.

"I can't try harder unless I want to freeze you all solid," snapped James. "Why don't you try something, if you're such a smart guy?"

"I have fur! Fur is flammable!"

"Everything is flammable if you try hard enough," said Fern. "Annie, you need to wake up. I don't know how long Mary can keep us here. The creepy crossroads thing went away, and now everything is empty. We need to go home."

Home. I wanted to go home so badly. I wanted my bed and my things and to talk about comic books with Artie and to skate again. I wanted to introduce my boyfriend to my roller derby team. I wanted to introduce him to my *parents*. And I wanted to make sure Sally, and the people like her, had the chance to do the same.

I opened my eyes. Everything was fire, dancing around me, not consuming me. It was lower in places, like something had stolen its heat away, and I knew if I lifted my head, I'd see James working to chill it, to force it down. I also knew where it was coming from, because the anima mundi had said that all bargains were released: all debts were discharged.

Welcome home, I thought.

My fire purred and roared, so glad to be back that its joy couldn't be contained.

I missed you, too, but you're scaring people, I thought. *Rest. I won't give you up again.*

Was magic always this argumentative? I didn't remember it fighting me like this before the first time I'd agreed to give it away. Not that it mattered. It was back now, safe with me, and I was never letting it go again.

The fire hesitated. Then, slowly, it began to flicker and recede, pulling back into my skin where it belonged. I blinked at the suddenly clear sky above me. It was softening already, moving more into alignment with what it had been before all this happened, before everything went wrong.

Someone gasped. I sat up.

The others were standing about where I'd assumed from the sound of their voices. Cylia had her hand over her mouth. Fern was beaming. Sam's tail was wrapped so tightly around his leg that he was at risk of cutting off the circulation. Leonard was gaping, open-mouthed and bemused. James was the only one kneeling, his hands stretched out above my left leg, the palms covered in a thin layer of frost. Like the others, he was staring at me.

I lifted an eyebrow. "You can put those away now," I said. "I'm good."

"You were on *fire*," he said, in a tone that implied I might not have noticed.

"Yes." I smiled. "Isn't it wonderful?"

That was the last thing I had time to say before Sam slammed into me, wrapping his arms around my torso. I laughed, wrapping my arms around him in turn. Cylia and Fern were close behind him, and I held on to all of them for dear life, and this was good, this was right, this was the way home.

Epilogue

"You can always come home. No matter
what you've done, no matter where you've
been, you can always come home, and we'll
be waiting."

–Enid Healy

***The living room of a rented house in New Gravesend,
Maine, trying not to hit anyone***

LEONARD NARROWED HIS EYES. "There's something
you're not telling me. What happened after you disappeared? Why did you come back on fire?"

"There's so much I'm not telling you that I could
open a whole bookstore called 'Things Leonard Cunningham Doesn't Get to Know,'" I said. "We had a deal,
remember? The crossroads have been defeated. The exorcism was a success. Now's the part where you run
back to England and tell the rest of the Covenant that
you lost me."

"You'll be a black mark on my record that I may
never live down."

"Should've thought of that before you decided to
keep my family name a secret." I folded my arms. "We
had a deal, and you need to get the hell off this
continent."

"You'll join us one day," Leonard persisted. "You're
too smart and too human to throw in with these . . .
things. I *will* be the one to bring your family back where

they belong, and you *will* understand why I've been right all along."

"Whatever," I said. "We'll have people watching for you—specifically you—at all the international airports and major border crossings. If you come back to this country, we'll know. And next time, I don't send you home a hero."

Leonard looked at me for a long moment before he sighed. "We're going to be so good together when you finally come around," he said. "You'll see." Then he was gone, turning and disappearing through the open front door.

I counted to ten. He didn't come back. "You can come out now," I said, without raising my voice.

Immediately, Fern's head popped around the stairs. "He's gone?"

"He's gone," I said, as arms slid around me from behind. I tilted my head back to look at Sam. "Where were *you* hiding?"

"Kitchen," he said. "Cylia's finishing making lunch. We'll be ready to hit the road in like, twenty minutes, if you're packed."

"Since this morning," I said. "You hear from James?"

"He's got his mother's car, and Cylia says it's safe to drive, now that she's fixed the carburetor. He'll be here in ten minutes. Fern's going to ride with him."

Caravanning across the country was an awkward solution, but it was better than trying to cram five people into Cylia's car for more than an hour, and I had faith that we'd pull into a rest stop somewhere and find a perfect little camper-trailer suitable for hooking to James' car, owned by someone who'd always wanted to swap it for an avocado-colored monstrosity. That's how things work when you're traveling with a jink. Sometimes the cards just fall your way.

Sally was still missing. The anima mundi either didn't know where she was or couldn't tell us—and I suspected the former, given how willing they'd been to put everything else back to normal. Mary was helping them with the transition, and if they resented the fact that I'd chosen to walk away, well. I'd helped to save them. They could learn to live with the disappointment.

Sally was still missing, but so was my grandfather, and Grandma Alice was going to be very interested in what James had to say. Maybe they could help each other. Even if they couldn't, James was going to help *me*. Between his mother's books and my grandfather's books, we were going to start our own homeschool Hogwarts and get this shit under control. And we were going to do it safely behind the compound walls, in Oregon, where my family could keep an eye on us.

They were going to love him. Bringing home new family members is a time-honored tradition, and a new sorcerer might be enough to distract from the part where I was enthusiastically dating a monkey. Maybe.

Probably not, though.

The Covenant wasn't looking for me anymore. Oh, they would be again someday—I was absolutely sure of that—but Leonard no longer had his tracker, and without that, I could stay hidden for as long as I needed to. Rose was going to be following him to the airport and reporting back once she had seen him safely loaded onto the next available flight to the United Kingdom. There was time to put things back together. There was time to figure my shit out.

"What are you smiling about?" Sam asked.

I tilted my head backward until I could see his eyes, and said, "I've got so much to tell the mice."

"Weird," he said, and kissed me, and everything was good, and I was finally going home.

Read on for
a brand-new InCryptid novella
by Seanan McGuire:

THE MEASURE

OF A MONSTER

> "The amount of damage humanity is willing to do to prevent tragedies that 'might' someday occur is astonishing, especially since many of those tragedies would be a response to things we had already done."
>
> –Thomas Price

A nice, if borrowed, bedroom in an only moderately creepy suburban home in Columbus, Ohio

Now

SHELBY LAY ON HER back, one arm draped across her stomach and the other thrown across my chest, snoring softly. The pollen count had been stratospheric for weeks, and her allergies were making it difficult for her to breathe. It was a tiny, mundane problem, the sort that could be treated with over-the-counter medication, and maybe it was weird of me, but I was loving it. Most of our problems spent way too much time trying to kill us. It was nice to have something less potentially fatal to contend with.

(Shelby didn't think so, of course, but Shelby was the one with the allergies. No one enjoys being filled with mucus—and I do mean *no one*. I've met cryptids who revel in everything from raw meat to pulling their own teeth out, and not a single one of them has revealed an odd fetish or lifestyle obsession with having stuffed-up sinuses.)

The sun had been up for more than an hour, making this the local equivalent of staying in bed until noon. Coming back from our Australian vacation with a ring on Shelby's finger—opal, naturally, both to play to cultural stereotypes and because she thought it was pretty—had finally convinced management at the zoo where we both worked to synchronize our days off. Shelby liked to say it was because they had seen reason. I was pretty sure they were afraid of her. Same difference, really.

Breaking the lease on her apartment had taken almost two months. By the time she turned her keys in, she'd been sleeping at my place five nights a week, and the majority of her stuff was stored in the attic, waiting for the day when we'd be striking out on our own, whatever that meant. Her parents wanted us to move to Australia; my parents wanted us to come back to Oregon; my grandparents didn't care what we did, as long as we remembered to keep our anti-telepathy charms on us whenever we were planning to have sex.

Oh, right. Whenever I say "my place," you should really replace that with "my grandparents' place," since the house belongs to them. Martin and Angela Baker, good citizens of the Columbus metro area. Businesspeople, former members of the PTA, parents of three adopted children—including my mother—and generally the kind of neighbors everyone dreams of having. The part where he's a construct made from multiple reanimated corpses and she's a form of highly evolved pseudo-mammalian telepathic wasp is sort of beside the point.

Well, no. It's not. For most of the humans I've known, the fact that my family includes a lot of what they'd call "monsters" *is* the point. If they ever found out that their sunny suburbs hosted things like us, it would be time for the torches and pitchforks. No matter how advanced humanity gets, it seems like we're always just a few steps away from becoming an angry mob.

That's why there are people like me and Shelby. We help keep the "monsters" hidden, and we try to keep the world safe for the rest of humanity until the day arrives when they finally realize that we're all just people. We're all just trying to do our best.

Living with my grandparents, my cousin Sarah, and my fiancée all in the same house should probably have been weird, but it was turning out to be surprisingly normal. The family expectation had always been that my siblings and I would eventually go out, find spouses, and bring them home to the sprawling, multilevel house that my parents had constructed for exactly that purpose. This was the same idea, in a slightly different location. The only potential problem was Sarah, and the anti-telepathy charms took care of that.

(Sarah and Grandma Angela are members of the same species. We call them "cuckoos," because they're brood parasites, replacing human infants with their own offspring. On the whole, the species is a nasty piece of work that raises a lot of really unpleasant questions about evolution, biology, and whether some things actually *deserve* the torches and pitchforks. So far as we're aware, Sarah and Grandma are the only exceptions.)

Even with her edges blurred by my lack of glasses, Shelby was beautiful when she slept. Tall, tan, blonde, and perfect, like an Australian ordered straight from Central Casting. We met when we both started working at the same zoo, me as a visiting herpetologist, her as a visiting big cat expert. We'd started dating about three months later, which had been a massive shock to me, since Shelby was way out of my league by any rational measure. Of course, things hadn't stayed rational for long, and she'd tried to kill Sarah not long after we'd started getting serious. Thankfully, Sarah didn't hold a grudge.

Somehow, Shelby hadn't broken up with me over the number of cuckoos in my family, or the fact that I'd lied to her about my name when we first met. It's not safe to be a Price in public, not with the Covenant of St. George constantly looking for a way to solidify their secret stranglehold on the world. The first time I'd seen her in the field had been like a dream come true. First, she'd ridden an injured lindworm like a bucking bronco, grinning like Athena herself, and then, when we realized how it had been injured, she had switched smoothly to sympathizing with it. I'd proposed almost involuntarily.

At the time, I'd believed she'd dismissed it as a joke. The joke was on me: she'd just been biding her time until the perfect moment came along for her to accept, which she'd done while we were in Australia, helping her family deal with a lycanthropy outbreak. Happy endings all around, right?

Except for the part where shortly after we'd come back to the United States, my sister Verity had declared war on the Covenant of St. George live on network television. We still didn't know how the broadcast had managed to go on that long without being cut off by standards and practices. Our best guess was that they had been so busy watching for wardrobe malfunctions on the part of the female dancers that they hadn't paid any attention to the giant snake eating people. American ideas of censorship do not always make much sense.

Except for the part where the only thing my family could think of to do in response to Verity's hotheaded declaration was to send my other sister, Antimony, to England to go undercover with the Covenant. Maybe she could learn something about the way they operated, something she could use to keep the family safe while we weathered this. Everyone had agreed. Even me. And maybe someday, I'll stop feeling guilty about that, because Annie had gone to England and disappeared, dropping off the radar so completely that the only reason we knew she was still alive was the fact that our family ghosts had yet to tell us otherwise.

She was lost. She was lost, and she was alone, and she was my baby sister, and there was nothing I could do to save her. There was nothing I could do to even let her know I was worried about her. So no, life wasn't perfect, and happy endings only happen when all parties involved are safely dead and buried and resting six feet down.

Shelby yawned and rolled onto her side, facing me. Then she opened her eyes and smiled.

"Lazy boy," she accused softly. "Still in bed when the sun's been up for hours."

"You're one to talk," I replied. "I couldn't get up without waking you."

"Ah, but you see, I'm antipodean. My natural rhythms are the reverse of yours. Trying to get me out of bed early is a denial of my culture."

I rolled my eyes. "There you go again, blaming everything on Australia."

"It's convenient. A whole continent, and it's not here to defend itself. Why, if I do this often enough, the tourism board will send me my gold 'Confusing the Americans' badge, and then I'll have fulfilled all my childhood dreams."

"Brat," I said, and leaned closer, intending to kiss her.

Instead, I got a face full of feathers as Crow, my resident Church Griffin, dove onto the bed from somewhere in the vicinity of the ceiling and stretched out on his back, all four legs in the air, croaking and creeling his demands for attention. Shelby laughed. I groaned, beginning to scratch the spot on his belly where the feathers of his upper body gave way to the fur of his lower body. Somewhere in the distance, the mice began drumming, signaling that everyone in the house was finally awake.

Just another ordinary day in Ohio. And I wouldn't trade it for the world.

Sarah was sitting at the kitchen table when I came downstairs, yawning and trying to smooth my hair down with one hand. She had a book open in front of her and was eating a bowl of what looked like Lucky Charms. I paused and looked again. Lucky Charms, yes, but they weren't in milk. Instead—

"Sarah, are you eating your cereal with tomato soup?"

"Yes." She didn't look up from her book. "I like it better than V8. It's not as spicy. I don't mind the spicy, really—it's mild—but it clashes with the little marshmallows, and I like the little marshmallows."

I paused, contemplating that. Like most things about Sarah's faintly horrifying and idiosyncratic diet, it made sense. That didn't make it any less disgusting to my human palate. "Okay," I said finally. "What are you reading?"

"Fermat's Last Theorem. It's about a really famous mathematical puzzle and how it was eventually resolved." She finally looked up, blinking vast, blue eyes at me. "You can borrow it when I'm done, if you want."

"Will I understand it?"

Sarah shrugged. "Maybe."

"I'll pass. I have a lot to read."

"Okay."

For reasons yet to be discovered—mostly because we can't exactly interview cuckoos who don't belong to the family without having our minds telepathically hollowed out and taken over—cuckoos are obsessed with math. It's a species-wide trait, one shared by Grandma Angela and Sarah. Even when Sarah couldn't reliably remember her own name, she was still enthralled by simple equations and endless viewings of an old PBS kids' show called *Square One.* Her recovery has been marked by increasingly complicated equations, and the day she started doing theoretical calculus again was the day my grandparents threw us a spontaneous pizza party.

(Sarah hurt herself trying to save Verity from the Covenant of St. George. She succeeded, which is why I am currently short only one sister, not two. But, in the process, she did the telepath equivalent of throwing her back out and wound up functionally spraining her entire mind. There was a time when we weren't sure whether she was ever going to be herself again. I'm still not completely sold . . . if I'm being honest. She's alert and aware and consistently knows who she is and what she's doing. That's good. She's also shyer, more timid, and less willing to take risks. That's bad. Cuckoos often trend toward cowardice, preferring to hide when possible. It took Sarah a long, long time to learn not to flee when things got bad. That's a lot of ground to lose.)

"Are you and Shelby staying in today?"

"Maybe." I opened the fridge, pulling out the orange juice. "Dee and Frank are hosting a barbeque tonight; I thought we might go down and see them. Frank grills a mean goat. You're welcome to come, if you like."

Sarah's answering smile was quick and wry. "No, I'm not, but I appreciate you inviting me."

"Suit yourself." She wasn't wrong. Most sensible people have a healthy fear of cuckoos. It's hard not to be scared of something that can literally get inside your head. But Frank, Dee, and the rest of the local gorgon community had a lot of experience dealing with unusual people, and Dee liked Sarah.

"Morning," chirped Shelby, sashaying into the room. She looked fresh as a daisy, and not at all like she'd tumbled out of bed not ten minutes previous. I would have hated her, if I hadn't loved her so desperately. "What's good today, Sarah?"

"An abstract philosophical concept meant to guide the actions of people who would really rather be doing whatever they want without concern for repercussions," said Sarah solemnly.

Shelby nodded, pausing to kiss my cheek on her way to the fridge. "Don't know what I expected, but that's pretty good," she said. "Got a plan for today?"

"Read my book, eat my cereal, get online and argue with Artie for an hour about why he can't come to visit yet," said Sarah.

I frowned. "Why can't he? I mean, apart from the

whole 'distance' thing." My cousin Artie is half-incubus on his father's side and got all the upsetting pheromones without any of the control. His life is mostly defined by the size of his bedroom. When he has to go out, he douses himself in the kind of cologne that sears mucus membranes and destroys the sense of smell of everyone in a ten-foot radius.

Maybe that was a good argument against him coming for a visit. The TSA would probably designate his cologne a kind of chemical warfare and refuse to let him on the plane.

"I'm not . . . ready." Sarah waved a hand helplessly in front of herself, indicting as much of her body as a single gesture could encompass. "I'm okay sometimes. I'm okay right now. But last night I forgot your name again, and if you hadn't been wearing an anti-telepathy charm, I would have just gone right into your head looking for it. I'm not safe around people. I could hurt myself. I could hurt *them*."

I looked at her solemnly and didn't say anything. There was nothing I could say. I'm human. Shelby's human. We've got problems, mostly related to our families and their chosen professions, but we're always going to have humanity on our side: for better or for worse, we belong to the dominant species on the planet. Everywhere we go, the world is built to suit our needs, to make us comfortable and safe. Sarah . . .

Cuckoos are terrifying predators. I won't pretend they're not. But Sarah isn't like that. She's clever and she's kind and she worries about losing control of herself. All her telepathic ethics have been carefully self-taught from X-Men comics and old episodes of *Babylon 5*, and she is far, far too aware of how easy it would be to let them all go and give in to the urge to follow her instincts and make the world conform to her own needs.

Sarah shrugged and looked down at her tomato-soaked cereal. "I want to see Artie. I miss him really bad. But his mind . . . he's soothing, you know? He thinks soothing thoughts. If he came here, I'd want to listen to him think-ing soothing thoughts, and I'd forget how careful I have to be, and I'd hurt him. I don't think I could live with myself if I did that. I don't think—"

She froze, head snapping up and eyes going wide as her attention shifted to the back door.

"Someone's coming," she said, and shoved her chair away from the table, running out of the room just before there was a knock at the door. The motion knocked the spoon out of her bowl and sent it clattering to the floor, where it left a smear that was distressingly like a bloodstain.

In sitcoms, people are always knocking at each oth-er's back doors, like it's totally normal for someone to just be in your yard uninvited. It's a lot less common in the real world, and in the kind of suburban neighbor-hood where everyone keeps to themselves and trespass-ing is more likely to get you a visit from the local police than a wacky laugh track, it's unheard of. Shelby and I exchanged a look.

My family has a reputation for being a little overzeal-ous in the weaponry department, and it's true, my sisters and my mother always have at least three knives on their persons. It helps them feel secure. My eyesight isn't good enough for me to be comfortable carrying that many knives before breakfast, and my revolver was safely upstairs in my bedside table. Shelby touched her left hip, signaling that at least one of us was properly armed.

The person outside knocked again. I adjusted my glasses with one hand, slipping into what Verity liked to call my "professor posture": right foot slightly back, arms loose, hands free and open above my waist. An untrained attacker wouldn't notice the slight rise in my right shoulder or the bend in my right knee, ready to absorb shock and turn it into momentum if I had to. A good martial artist might recognize it as a passive neu-tral stance, but most people would look at me and see another man born to a life of tweed, tea, and long lectures about English literature.

I looked at Shelby and nodded. She nodded back, all ease gone. I opened the door.

Dee lowered her hand and stared at me through the rose-tinted lenses of her glasses. Her eyes were wide, and her pupils were dilated. There was something wrong with their shape, a slight point at the top and bottom. Seeing me, she surged forward and grabbed my forearms, heedless of the fact that I could easily have responded by punching her.

"Alex," she gasped. "Thank Medusa." Her hair was askew, like she hadn't been able to get her wig seated properly before rushing out of the house, and it was hissing. The sound was agitated. I'd rarely heard her snakes that upset,

I had *never* seen her this upset. As I pulled her farther into the kitchen, I realized that she was missing a shoe, and wasn't wearing pantyhose. The small scales on the side of her leg that she normally took such careful precautions to conceal were totally visible. A casual bystander might have taken them for psoriasis, but there's no way to tell a casual bystander from a Covenant spy.

"Dee? What's wrong?" Shelby moved past us, closing the door. I shot her a grateful look.

Dee didn't even seem to notice. She continued clinging to me as the hissing from her hair grew steadily louder.

"You have to come," she said. "You *have* to."

"Come where? Dee, what's going on?"

"You have to come home with me." Dee pulled back enough to look at Shelby. "To the colony. Right now."

"Last I checked, they didn't like us much there, on account of how we had that little spat with your half-brother," said Shelby carefully. "Pretty sure Hannah would be happy to have us both decorating her yard."

Hannah was the matriarch of Dee's community, half Pliny's gorgon, half greater gorgon, and all terrifying.

Hybrids like her are rare in nature, and hybrids who survive to adulthood are even rarer. Hannah had managed to hit the genetic jackpot on three levels: she'd been born, she'd grown up, and she'd proven to be fertile enough to have a son of her own, Lloyd. Unfortunately, that was where the jackpots ended. Lloyd had been angry at the world, embittered at his inability to fit in among either his own kind or the humans that surrounded them, and in the end, that anger and bitterness had twisted him into a killer.

I had shot him to save Shelby's life, along with Dee's and my own. That didn't mean his mother had forgiven me.

Dee shook her head so vigorously that her wig slipped and the hissing from beneath it grew even louder. "She said. I asked her, and she said. She said you could come."

Shelby and I exchanged a look. I returned my attention to Dee.

"Why?" I asked.

She sniffled and stepped back, letting go of my arms. "It's the children," she said. "They're gone."

Dee's information, while sparse, was as much as we were going to get. Sometime in the night, strangers had come to the gorgon settlement in the woods outside city limits, and they had left with more than half of the community's children. Gorgons aged two to twelve, all disappeared without a trace—along with over a dozen unhatched eggs, at least two-thirds of which were assumed to be fertile. It had been a professional job, in and out without waking any of the adults, which made me suspect that something other than stealth had been used.

The ages of the children taken honestly concerned me more than how it had been accomplished. Ages two and up. Old enough to listen when someone demanded that they stay silent. Eggs. Too young to make a sound. Babies would have been less likely to fight back—and more importantly, babies didn't have fully developed venom sacs yet, making them less of a risk to their kidnappers—but there's no way to tell a baby not to cry. Whoever had done this, they'd come in with a plan and left with exactly what they were looking for.

Dee had driven herself to the house; her car was parked unevenly at the foot of the driveway, where it was doubtless already attracting the prying eyes of nosy neighbors. None of them would do anything; it wasn't that kind of neighborhood. But they'd sure be happy to gossip about it when they heard that we'd all been murdered in our beds.

Shelby was in the kitchen with Dee, trying to calm the other woman down and get her to take a drink of water before we got going. The road to the gorgon community was protected with illusions and compulsion charms to keep people like us from just stumbling past the borders. It would be a lot easier if we could follow Dee's car, so we needed Dee to calm down enough that she'd be safe to drive. And I . . .

I had something else to take care of.

Getting dressed had only taken a few minutes, even factoring in the time it took for me to get my weapons safely secured about my person. Taking an extra thirty seconds to check your holsters means never needing to say, "Hang on, I just accidentally stabbed myself." Shelby would need about the same, once I went back downstairs to relieve her. We're nothing if not efficient.

Sarah's bedroom door was closed. I knocked lightly. "Sarah? I need to talk to you."

"Closed doors mean I don't want to talk."

"Not necessarily. Closed doors can mean a lot of things. Sarah, please, it's important."

"There's someone in the *house.*"

"That's not someone, it's Dee. You know Dee." At least, I hoped she knew Dee. If she had managed to forget my administrative assistant, what I was about to ask for was pointless.

When I'd first shown up at the West Columbus Zoo, management had allowed me to bring an assistant. I had chosen Dee—Deanna Lynn Taylor de Rodriguez—both because she had excellent credentials, and because she was the only nonhuman applicant for the position. Since "species" isn't a protected class, I had been pretty sure none of the other hopefuls were going to sue me, and I had genuinely needed someone who knew the ins and outs of the local cryptid community. I had gotten more than I had bargained for. I had gotten a friend, one I trusted implicitly. Sarah had met her on several occasions, and the two had gotten along reasonably well . . . I thought.

I knocked again. "Come on, Sarah. You know I wouldn't be up here if this weren't important. Can you please open the door?"

There was a long pause before it cracked open, just enough for me to see one wary blue eye through the gap.

"What do you want?" she asked.

"When Grandma gets home, I want you to please tell her that Shelby and I were called to an emergency with the local gorgon community, and that if we haven't checked in by sunset, we probably need help. Tell her we left with Dee. Can you remember that?"

The pause was even longer this time. Finally, in a small voice, Sarah asked, "What happens if I forget?"

"I don't know," I said. "Can you try to remember?"

She bit her lip and nodded. "I'll try."

"Thank you. Will you be okay here by yourself?"

To my relief, Sarah cracked a very small smile. "The mice will be here with me," she said. "If I start forgetting who I am or anything like that, I'll go ask them to remind me."

Aeslin mice never forget anything, and they're always delighted to have the opportunity to recite their private and remarkably accurate catechism. Sarah's life would never be completely forgotten, not as long as there were Aeslin mice around to remember it for her.

Too bad we couldn't bring them with us to the gorgon community. Sadly, mice are mice, whether or not they can talk, and it simply wasn't safe to expose them to that many snakes. "Okay," I said. "Call if you need anything."

"I will," she said and closed the door. That was that: I was dismissed.

I took the stairs two and three at a time in my rush to return to the ground floor. Shelby was leaning against the counter, sipping from a glass of orange juice, when I rushed back into the kitchen. Dee was sitting at the table, hands folded between her knees and wig discarded next to Sarah's cereal bowl. The snakes that topped her head were twining anxiously around each other, still hissing almost constantly, their tongues flickering in and out as they tasted the air.

It took years of human-gorgon interactions before anyone realized that gorgons instinctively view all humans as deceitful, because from their perspective, we have the best poker faces in the known universe. Our hair isn't expressive, and to them, that's as strange as having snakes growing out of our scalps would be to us.

"Right, that's me up, then," said Shelby, and put her juice aside. "Give me five and we can roll, all right?"

"All right," I agreed, and watched her rush out of the room before returning my attention to Dee. "My cousin's going to stay here, and let my grandparents know what's going on. Are you safe to drive?"

"Does it matter?" There was a dull note in her voice that I didn't like at all. "I need to take you home with me. You have to find the children. You have to . . . how did this happen? We've always been so *careful*."

I refrained from pointing out that not that long ago, their version of "careful" had included a serial killer using a cockatrice to attack innocent bystanders. Even if I'd wanted to be the kind of asshole who blamed an entire community for the actions of one bad egg, I wouldn't have been able to blame the children.

"I don't know, but I'm going to do my best to find out," I said. "Shelby and I both. You're our friend, and we're going to help you."

She looked at me solemnly, tears rolling down her cheeks to drip from her chin. "Megan is home from school this week. She's supposed to be hanging out with her friends and discussing suitors with me and her father, not trying to calm a bunch of panicked parents. How are we supposed to convince her that our community is a safe place to raise a family when we can't even believe it ourselves?"

It took me a beat to catch up. Megan is Dee's adult daughter: she had been away at medical school for the entire time I'd been in Ohio. Gorgons live in secluded communities all over the world; Pliny's gorgons, like Dee and her family, like to settle near human cities, where they can get groceries and other staples without giving up their culture and traditions. Sort of like the Amish, if the Amish were therapsid cryptids capable of turning people to stone. When the kids grow up, they either settle permanently in the community where they were born or move to a new community, and probably never see their parents again. It isn't safe. Even with all the new technological advancements linking the world, it just isn't safe.

"Breathe, Dee. Just please, for me, breathe."

"Sorry about that." Shelby came bounding back into the kitchen. She was dressed like we were heading to the zoo, in khaki shorts and a matching button-down shirt, the sleeves rolled past her elbows. It was incredibly *hello, I am a stereotypical Australian* of her, which made it incredibly clever at the same time. If we ran across any human hikers in the woods, she could just dial up her accent and start asking me to explain what a squirrel was. The fact that she looked like she'd just escaped from an Animal Planet documentary would do the rest.

"It's fine; we were just talking." I flashed Shelby a quick, tight smile before returning my focus to Dee. "Well? Can you drive?"

"I can." She stood, grabbing her wig and jamming it back on her head with one hand. The snakes around the edges withdrew, voluntarily hiding themselves. They had minds of their own, but they were capable of responding to Dee's emotional state. How that works, no one has ever been able to figure out, and until we get access to a lot of scanning equipment and a few neurologists who won't ask awkward questions, we aren't going to.

"Great. We'll be right behind you."

Dee nodded tightly before heading for the back door. Shelby followed, and I was close behind.

Shelby paused at the threshold, giving me a concerned look. "How bad do you think this is going to be?" she asked.

"On a scale of one to ten?"

She nodded.

"I honestly don't know. But I think we should probably be braced for the worst."

Shelby nodded again and stepped outside.

I locked the door behind me.

"You all right?" I glanced at Shelby as I drove. She was still too alert-looking for anyone who'd been awake as short a time as she had, and it wasn't entirely adrenaline—she was actually *conscious*. I've always envied people who could go from sleep to functionality that quickly. "You didn't have time for coffee before Dee came busting in."

"I wasn't in the mood for coffee anyway," she said, waving a hand vaguely. "Not feeling like being wired today."

I opened my mouth, then paused, frowning. "I haven't seen you drink coffee in a couple of days."

"I like to wean myself periodically. Remember what it's like to live without a chemical dependency."

"Huh. Maybe I should try it."

The corner of Shelby's mouth quirked upward in a smile. "You do that." She sobered. "But seriously. How bad is this likely to be?"

"Bad. There are three main scenarios to worry about here. The first—and honestly, the one I'm hoping for—is that another gorgon community is following some old-fashioned customs and raided them last night."

Shelby whipped around to stare at me. "You're not *serious*."

"Unfortunately, I am. Look at it like this: you're a member of a species that's having trouble keeping your numbers above extinction levels. Too big to hide easily from the dominant predators, too dependent on certain resources to withdraw completely from their civilization, but too different to pass as one of them without a lot of work. Your family group is on the verge of dying out due to a lack of new blood and an inability to settle down long enough to meet fairly extensive breeding requirements. But there's another family group that's stable. Secure. They have the resources and the necessary space to breed. Which is more important? Respecting the fact that they love and want their children, or the survival of your species?"

"You don't mean that," she said, still staring at me. Her expression had shifted to something akin to horror.

"I don't approve of it, no, and I don't think it's a good solution for anyone involved. It's still the way some gorgon families did things for centuries after the Covenant of St. George burned their settlements and drove them from their homes. Survival of the species forgives a *lot*." I shook my head. "Humans have done similar things, across history. Gorgons abandoned those traditions more than a hundred and fifty years ago, at least here in North America, but there are always people who think the old ways are the best ones."

"Bastards," muttered Shelby.

"No contest here. At the same time . . . that really would be the best-case scenario. It would mean the children were taken by people who want them and are prepared to care for them and could possibly be convinced to give them back if we're able to provide them with other options. There are always other ways to do things." Gorgons aren't human. They're still people, and they still grow up in the complex stew of cultural expectations that simmers all around us. I couldn't imagine even the most traditional family group would feel good about becoming kidnappers just for the sake of their own survival.

"All right. What's next on the list?"

"Covenant." I shrugged. Dee's car was the only one on the road ahead of us, but that didn't mean I could take my eyes off her for long. As soon as we started hitting the protections intended to keep humans from stumbling into the local gorgon community, losing sight of her car had the potential to mean never reaching our destination. "This could be the start of a purge."

"Wouldn't it have been easier to just go in and . . ." Shelby ran a finger across her throat, making a guttural slurping sound at the same time.

"Classy," I said.

She beamed. "You adore me."

"No question there. But no, it wouldn't have been easier. We're talking about a whole community of Pliny's gorgons—and remember that the fringe, at least, is really dug-in and defensible. The children are wary of strangers, with good reason; at the same time, because they have such good defenses on the approach road, they tend to assume that anyone who's actually inside the community itself is a friend. So their guards would be down. If you want to start by killing the adults, you need a huge amount of manpower. You need to be *absolutely sure* that you can kill them all before anyone sounds the alarm. Kidnapping is easier, and now everyone's out of their minds with worry for their kids. Even if they're more alert and aware of the danger, they're also off-balance and likely to slip up. Tactically, this isn't a bad move."

"But you don't think that's what's happening here."

"No, I don't." I shook my head. "We have people watching the major airports and border crossings. Even the ones who don't like my family are working with us on this because no one wants the Covenant here. I honestly don't think they could have gotten a strike force large enough for this kind of operation into the country without us hearing about it—and if they somehow managed it, I wouldn't expect them to start with a gorgon community in the middle of Ohio."

"Even though that community has ties to your family?" The question was mild. The meaning behind it wasn't.

I took a deep breath. "The fact that we've had dealings with this community before could be a factor, but I think you're assuming a level of intel that we've never known the Covenant to have. They rarely think of cryptids as having relationships, or histories, or anything other than the need to taste human flesh."

Shelby wrinkled her nose. "That's graphic."

"That's the Covenant. If they *knew* that my great-grandfather had been instrumental in the founding of this community, yes, it would be a massive target. Given that even *I* didn't know until Hannah told me, I really don't think they have that kind of detail on what's going on around here."

My great-grandfather, Jonathan Healy, had been the one to help Hannah's parents find a place where they could settle down without being judged for the fact that they belonged to two different, socially incompatible species of gorgons. Without him, this community would never have existed. Without him, Hannah would never have existed. Which also meant that without him, Lloyd would never have existed, and several people would still have been alive.

Every deed, whether intended for good or for ill, has its repercussions. Forgetting that is never a wise idea.

"All right," said Shelby slowly. "What's the third option?"

"Poachers."

She scowled. "Oh, I was afraid you were going to say that. I bloody hate poachers. Cowardly, craven arseholes. But . . . you can't poach *people*. Can you?"

"No, you can't. Normally, that's called kidnapping or abduction, and it's viewed very poorly. Unfortunately, you don't have to belong to the Covenant to think that only humans count as people, and there are humans out there who will pay a lot for 'exotics' like young gorgons."

Shelby looked at me, utterly aghast. "How could you even . . . it's not safe! There's no way you could keep a young gorgon alive without endangering yourself!"

"That's where you're wrong. There are ways. We're just not going to discuss them when we're this close to the parents." Dee had guided us safely through every layer of illusion and dissuasion, easily enough that either I was becoming desensitized to the wards, or someone had managed to adjust them to let us pass. We were driving along the curving private road that led down into the valley where the gorgon community stood, temporary and permanent at the same time, as much of a contradiction as its occupants.

What looked like a small trailer park waited at the bottom of the road, the trailers arrayed in a circle that would easily unwind if the residents ever needed to hook up their wagons and go looking for a new place to live. Not that some of those supposedly "mobile homes" were designed to be moved: as with any long-term trailer park, the residents had settled in, building porches and brick steps, installing aboveground pools and planting vegetable gardens. Most of the occupants, like Dee's husband Frank, had been born in those trailers, and had every expectation of dying there.

They had an apple orchard, corn fields, and enough

planted, carefully plotted land to sustain a community almost twice their size—and that was without going into the fringe, the subcommunity of gorgons where Dee herself had been born. *They* had permanent homes, of brick and wood and drywall. *They* were planning to be in Ohio forever, even if it meant eventually running out the human occupants.

It wasn't the worst plan ever. They had guns and venomous snakes growing out of their heads. They were probably going to be fine, assuming no one showed up with a tank. As gorgon communities went, this was one of the largest, healthiest ones I'd ever heard of.

Which, unfortunately, made it all the more likely that we were dealing with poachers. A community of this size couldn't avoid having contact with the outside world, and even if they were careful, rumors spread; people see things. The Internet added a whole new layer of possible gossip. All it would take was one bored teen posting a few supposedly harmless pictures on their Instagram. Let the wrong person see them, and—suddenly—we had a problem.

And we definitely had a problem. There were gorgons everywhere, standing in front of the trailers and arguing, their body language tight and terrified. The few people whose children hadn't disappeared were keeping them close, sometimes literally by holding onto their arms or shoulders. No one was wearing a wig. I parked a safe distance away and leaned over to open the glove compartment, pulling out two pairs of smoked goggles. I offered one wordlessly to Shelby.

She smiled as she took it, fondness and frustration mixed together in equal measure. "How I thought you were a harmless nerd at first, the world may never know."

"To be fair, I *am* a nerd," I said, fitting the goggles on over my glasses. "If I weren't, I wouldn't have goggles in my glove compartment."

"Point stands," she said, and got out of the car.

Pliny's gorgons aren't mammals, which means their growth patterns don't follow mammalian norms. They don't stop growing when they reach their twenties: they just slow down. Some of the people turning toward us were seven or eight feet tall, towering over their more human-height neighbors.

Dee flung herself out of her car and raced toward one of the taller men, yanking her wig off as she ran. He leaned down and wrapped his arms around her, the snakes on their heads twining together in affectionate greeting. It was a sweet moment, made sweeter when a slightly shorter, slimmer version of Dee joined their embrace.

Shelby and I followed at a more sedate pace. The goggles would protect us from the petrifying gaze of the gorgons, but they wouldn't protect us from being bitten by agitated snakes. Humans really are remarkably fragile in the greater scheme of things.

An even taller woman appeared from the back of the crowd. The snakes atop her head were long, dangling like arboreal vipers instead of curling and twisting like rattlesnakes. The other gorgons moved politely out of her way, allowing her to approach us. I stopped walking. Shelby did the same, and the three of us met in the open space in front of the rest of the community.

"Alexander Price," said Hannah. Her voice was mild, with a Saskatchewan accent that a lifetime in Ohio had yet to ease or erase. It was utterly at odds with her appearance: she sounded more like the nicest waitress at the local diner than a terrifying, nine-foot-tall gorgon matriarch.

"Hannah." I said her name as respectfully as I could, inclining my head in a solemn bow at the same time. If she had a surname, I didn't know it. Greater gorgons don't live among humans as frequently as Pliny's gorgons do, and some of our habits have yet to catch on in their communities. Hannah took after both her parents.

"I didn't think to see you here again nearly so soon,

and if there were any other choice, I would have taken it," she said. Her tongue flicked out, human-seeming but supple as a snake's, and she squinted briefly at Shelby. "Still, our need is great, and you are our best chance of bringing the children home. You understand how precious children are."

The last part of her statement—"even though you killed my son"—went unspoken. It was still there between us, inevitable and unavoidable.

This is why I hate fieldwork. I'm much happier doing conservation and breeding projects with nonsapient cryptids. We owe them just as much as we do their larger cousins, but they're so much less likely to hold a grudge. I didn't say any of that; it wouldn't have done any good. We were in the situation we were in, and now we just needed to survive it.

"We do," I said. "Do you have any idea who might have done this?"

"It's my fault."

The voice was unfamiliar, high and agonized and heavy with guilt. I turned, as did Hannah and Shelby.

The girl who looked a little bit like Dee had pulled away from what I presumed were her parents and was looking directly at me, chin up, snakes coiled tight in obvious distress. She was wearing jeans and a Lowryland T-shirt, and she looked so young and so afraid.

"My name's Megan," she said. "I just got home. This is my fault."

"It's not," Dee said firmly. "You didn't do this."

"It is, Mom. Stop trying to defend me."

"Why do you think that?" I asked. "What do you think you did?"

She took a deep breath. "I've been doing my residency at the Lowryland hospital in Florida," she said. "The semester just ended, so I drove home."

I nodded slowly. "Okay," I said. It made sense that she had driven: flying hasn't been safe for gorgons since the enhanced security measures went into effect. All it would take was one TSA agent trying to pat down a gorgon's wig for things to get very bad, very quickly.

"Only I couldn't drive . . . I couldn't drive straight through without stopping. It's fifteen hours if you do it in one straight shot. I *couldn't*." Megan kept her eyes on me—partially, I realized, so she wouldn't have to look at anyone around her. "I stopped a couple of times. For gas, mostly, and at a motel for the night."

"What happened, child?" Hannah sounded surprisingly gentle. Megan was still a part of her extended family, even if she'd made some sort of mistake.

"I think someone saw me," said Megan.

The gorgons around us exploded into shouts and protests. One woman rushed for Megan, hand raised to strike the younger gorgon, and was dragged back by two others. Megan cringed, snakes hissing and writhing in abject misery.

"It was an accident!" she cried. "The curtains were closed, I swear they were, but when the air-conditioning came on, it blew them apart, just a few inches, and I was getting out of the shower, and—" She stopped, holding her hands up helplessly.

"What did they see?" I asked. "Who saw it?"

"I wasn't wearing my wig," said Megan. "You can't really towel-dry snakes. So they saw my . . . everything."

"They who?"

"Two men. I closed the curtains, I put my wig on, I opened the door—I figured I could explain, or . . ." She stopped again, biting her lip.

I shook my head. "I'm human. That doesn't mean I'm going to judge you." Gorgons are endangered. Humans aren't. It's harsh logic. It still matters. Every death hurts someone, and I'm sure the families of those men would have been heartbroken if Megan had managed to catch them and do what she didn't want to say she'd been intending to do, but the species wouldn't have noticed. Megan, on the other hand, was a female Pliny's gorgon of breeding age. Losing her would be much more of a blow.

"Right. Price." She took a shaky breath. "I was going to kill them if I'd managed to catch them, but they were gone by the time I got outside. I didn't see their car."

"And you think they followed you here," I said grimly. She nodded.

"How *could* you?" Hannah was suddenly looming over Megan, the snakes on her head standing to terrible attention and making her seem even taller. I took an involuntary half-step backward. Humans are only a few millennia removed from monkeys, and part of us will always remember why it's a good idea to be afraid of really enormous snakes.

Megan stood her ground, but the snakes on her head coiled tight and drooped in clear submission.

"You should have gone the other way as soon as you realized you'd been compromised," said Hannah, several of her snakes mock-striking toward Megan. "You should have led them as far from us as possible."

"I thought they were gone," said Megan. "I had no idea I was being followed."

"How far away were you when you stopped?" I asked.

Both of them turned to look at me, and I had to fight the urge to step back again.

"Why?" demanded Hannah.

"Because there's still a cockatrice on the loose out there," I said. "My basilisks would have a hunting range of up to twenty miles a day in the wild; they're happy in their habitat at the zoo because I feed them, but if I let them out, they'd keep walking in whatever direction they could find food. I don't know what a cockatrice's range is. If it's been hunting, petrifying small animals or even things like deer, there could be rumors. Hunters talk."

North America has a big problem with Bigfoot hunters. Never mind that of all the cryptids out there, Bigfoot and Sasquatch are the most closely related to humans, which you'd think might buy them a little respect from their short, fragile, comparatively hairless cousins; there's always some asshole with a big gun who thinks the way to prove how awesome he is involves shooting and stuffing a sapient being.

The trouble is, Bigfoot are good at going undetected—surprisingly so, given their size. Teen Bigfoot enjoy challenging each other to follow hunters through the woods while pretending to be trees any time there's a chance they might be seen, and very few of them are ever spotted. Great fun for the Bigfoot, not so much for the hunters, who have a tendency to get frustrated and decide that they should widen their interests. Sadly, this never seems to mean going home and taking up needlepoint. No, it means going all "I want to believe" and striking out to find something new and endangered to shoot at.

The Covenant of St. George has never had a monopoly on so-called "monster hunters." They just have the best organizational structure and the most dedication to playing weekend extinction event.

"Have *you* heard those rumors?" asked Hannah.

"No. But my family doesn't talk much with hunters. They don't like us because of the way we keep breaking their noses and taking their toys away." Grandma Alice, especially, hates them with a focused, burning passion. People were a lot more willing to believe in the existence of the unknown when she was young, and the distance between belief and bullets is never as far as we would like.

"Also we were sort of busy going to Australia, fighting werewolves, and trying to keep the Covenant from showing up in your backyard, so maybe go a little easy on him, hey?" said Shelby. Her tone was deceptively mild. She was annoyed. "We didn't let the cockatrice loose in the first place, and if we haven't found it, well, you haven't found it either. Fact is, it being out there means the rumors of a petrifactor could easily be spreading, and now we get to do the cleanup."

"I'm sorry," said Megan again.

Dee stepped up next to her daughter, putting her arm around Megan's shoulders and looking at Hannah with flat defiance. The snakes atop her head drew back, assuming a rearing position.

"What's done is done," said Shelby. "We can stand here pointing fingers, or we can get on with finding your kids. Does someone want to show us where they were taken from?"

A low murmur spread through the gorgons. Finally, a woman with white snakes banded in buttery yellow stepped forward.

"I'll show you," she said.

"Good," I said. "Lead the way."

The crowd parted to let us through, and the three of us walked on, leaving Hannah and her anger, and Megan and her guilt, behind.

The gorgon community wasn't large enough for the walk to take long: the woman led us to a small trailer with curtains printed in bright geometric patterns and raised garden beds all around the outside, growing tomatoes and strawberries and various wildflowers.

"That's their window," she said, pointing. "Billy and Marigold. They were safe in their beds when I went to sleep. When I woke up . . ." She stopped and buried her face in her hands.

Shelby patted her on the shoulder, keeping a careful eye on the woman's snakes as she did. "It's not your fault," she said. "It's not Megan's, either. We should make sure to tell her that."

"How can you tell?" I asked.

"The curtains."

I blinked, giving the trailer a second look. Then I swore softly under my breath.

"They're the same in all the windows," I said.

She nodded.

In a surprising number of nonfamilial kidnapping cases, it's possible to identify the children's room from outside. They have cartoon curtains, say, or stuffed animals on the windowsill inside, something that tells kidnappers where to enter the house. When my sisters and I were young, our parents had Mickey Mouse curtains on their bedroom window. The one time someone had tried to come into the house to do us harm, they'd gotten a big surprise, and Mom had gotten a broken orbital ridge. Fun times.

If there was no visual way to know which window to pry open, the kidnappers must have had another way to locate the children. That meant they couldn't possibly have been the men Megan had seen.

Unless we were going about this the wrong way.

"Start looking for tracks," I said, to Shelby. "I need to go ask Megan a question, and then I need to go home and pick something up."

"You've got that 'maybe I know what's going on' look," said Shelby. "Do you?"

"I almost hope not," I said and turned, breaking into a brisk jog as I went back the way we'd come.

The crowd of gorgons had dispersed somewhat, with people going off to take care of things that couldn't be avoided any longer. Most of the ones I assumed were parents were still there, looking utterly lost. So was Dee, and her family, thankfully. Hannah had moved off to the side, still glowering.

I trotted up to Megan and stopped. "The men who saw you," I said without preamble. "How far away, and what *exactly* did you see?"

"Um," she said. "About six hours' drive away. I saw . . . men. Human men, looking through my window."

"They weren't just standing in the parking lot and happened to catch a glimpse of you? They were actually *looking*?"

"Um," said Megan again. Then she paused, eyes

widening. "Yes. Yes! They were looking right at my window. Why would they do that?"

"Because you're right: they were following you, or at least they were waiting for someone like you. Hannah?" I turned. "I know what happened."

The gorgon matriarch had a long enough stride that she appeared beside me almost instantly, snakes hissing and tangling around her shoulders in threatening array. "What has the child done?" she demanded.

"Nothing," I said, forcing myself to meet her eyes. I had never been so grateful for my goggles. "Those men were probably part of a network, staking out all the major approaches to Columbus. There aren't that many. If you restrict yourself to the highways and the motels that still aren't part of a major chain, you could do it with twenty." My family could do it with fourteen. There was no need to go making things worse if I didn't have to.

"Why?" asked Hannah.

"Because they've been casing the community, potentially for months, while they lined up buyers for your kids. We've seen this kind of thing before. One of the sylph creches got raided a couple of years ago, and the only way we found the perpetrators was food poisoning at a motel diner." I half-suspected my dead Aunt Rose of having had a hand in that. Diners are part of her domain, and she doesn't like people who mess with cryptid kids.

None of us do. Children suffer the sins of their parents, and they shouldn't have to. They should be allowed at least a little time to be innocent, before they realize they've been born into an endless, slow-motion war.

Dee put a hand over her mouth, looking suddenly sick to her stomach. "Buyers?" she asked. "What do you mean, buyers?"

"I mean they weren't hunters, or there would be a lot more broken glass, and this wasn't some spur-of-the-moment smash and grab. They knew where the children were, they knew which ones they wanted, and they knew how to spot a gorgon. They probably made Megan as soon as she stepped into the lobby." I looked from face to face. "Megan may have accelerated their timeline slightly by coming home, but you can't blame her for that. You were being hunted."

"Poachers," said Frank grimly.

I nodded. "Yeah. Poachers." I turned to fully face Hannah. "I need your permission to do something you aren't going to like, and I need it right now, because we don't have a lot of time to waste."

She frowned. "What do you want to do?"

"My cousin Sarah is a Johrlac. I assume you know what those are?"

Hannah's frown deepened until it became a scowl. "If you believe yourself family to one of *those* monsters, I should kill you where you stand."

"Sarah's different. She's not like the rest of her kind. What she is, however, is a telepath." A fragile one, who was afraid to leave the house. What I was proposing would put her in danger. She could hurt herself again.

And it didn't matter. With as many moving parts as this plan must have had, we could be looking at dozens of buyers, scattered all over the continent. If we didn't find these children before they were separated, they were going to disappear forever. There are lots of things an unethical "owner" can do with a gorgon. They could be hunted for sport, or simply shot point-blank to make an "exotic" meal for some unethical fucker. They could have their fangs pulled to turn them into manageable domestics or be beaten into becoming killers and enforcers.

We had to save them. Sarah would understand.

I hoped.

"So?" said Hannah.

"So she's better than a bloodhound, and these people won't have bothered to invest in anti-telepathy charms. That sort of work is expensive, and there's no need for it when you're only planning to attack the local gorgons. If they're in these woods with your kids, Sarah will be able to find them. I need your permission to bring her here, and your word that you won't attack her."

"It's my job to keep these people safe," said Hannah.

"Keep them safe by letting my cousin in," I replied.

Hannah stared at me. I looked patiently back. She broke eye contact first.

"Fine," she said sullenly.

"Great, thanks. Megan?" I looked toward the younger gorgon. "You're with me. I'm going to need someone to navigate me through the confusion charms, and Sarah's going to want a look at those men you saw."

Megan blanched, but she stepped up to join me. I started to move toward the car. Dee grabbed my arm.

"Take care of my little girl," she said.

"I will," I said. "Take care of Shelby until I get back." Dee nodded and let go.

Together, Megan and I walked away.

Megan sat rigid and silent in the passenger seat until we were almost to the house. Then, in a small voice, she said, "I thought you'd be taller."

"I get that a lot."

"It's just that your sister's as tall as you are."

"Yeah, well, she got the good genes in the fam—" I stopped mid-sentence, slamming my foot automatically down on the brakes. The car came skidding to a stop. Fortunately, no one was behind us: that could have ended very badly for everyone involved.

I twisted in my seat to stare at Megan. She stared back, face framed by the long brown sweep of her wig. She could have passed for a terrified human girl in that moment.

Terrified. Right. She didn't know me, and it's not polite to scare your allies. I forced myself to take a deep breath, and said, "I have two sisters. Which one do you mean?" She couldn't mean Verity, Verity's short. Verity barely comes up to my chin. But she couldn't mean Antimony, either, because no one knew where Antimony *was*.

"Um," said Megan. "I mean Annie."

I stared at her for a few seconds before returning my attention to the road and starting the car moving forward again. Having something to distract me might keep me from shaking her until she either told me where my sister was, or the snakes atop her head decided to bite me.

"I see," I said. My voice was impressively neutral to my own ears. "Because she's been missing for a while now, and we're all really worried about her. Is there any chance you could tell me where she is?"

"No. I mean, I'm sorry. But I can't tell you because I don't know."

Of course she didn't. Annie did better in her basic survival training than any of us. I was never intending to go into fieldwork, and Verity has never really mastered the idea of "subtle." Wherever Megan had seen my sister, there was no chance that she was still there.

"Where *was* she?" I asked.

"Lowryland."

I somehow managed not to hit the brakes again. Of course. Of *course*. It made terrible, awful, perfect sense. Annie was on the run from the Covenant. The Covenant may hate magic in all its forms, but that doesn't mean they aren't willing to bend it to their own ends when the need arises. She had trained with them. Blood, sweat, and tears, those are all things that can be used to make a tracking charm, if you have the proper training.

Running to Lowryland would have confused any spells the Covenant tried to use to find her, because the sheer density of people meant a hundred false positives and unclear results, until it was impossible to narrow anything down, or even be sure that they were looking in the right place. It was a sideways sort of genius, and I was proud of my baby sister, even as I wished she had the sense to come in from the cold.

We've faced the Covenant before. We've always won. We always will.

"Do you have any idea where she was going?"

"I wish I did," said Megan. "She took our roommate and some other people, and she left. I don't think *they* knew where they were going."

So Annie wasn't alone anymore. That made me feel a little better. No matter how much we train, we're always better with backup. "Thank you for telling me. It's going to make our parents feel a lot better to know that she's all right."

"I think she's the sort of person who always winds up all right," said Megan, a little wryly. "If the world tries to tell her she's not, she'll just punch it until it starts playing nice."

"That sounds like Annie," I said.

"Can you . . . I mean, I assume eventually she'll go home," said Megan. "When she does, can you call my parents and let them know? I worry about her sometimes. I worry about all of them."

She wasn't naming names. That was probably a good thing: it's always best to play your cards close to the chest when you're not sure of people's safety. At the moment, however, it was endlessly frustrating. We've always known that Annie was alive—Aunt Mary would have told us if she wasn't—but that's *all* we've known.

At least this might help my parents sleep a little better.

"I will," I said. "In the meantime, how much do you know about Johrlac?"

Megan looked at me blankly. "I know we're going to pick one up, but I don't think I've ever heard of them before."

"You would probably have heard them referred to as 'cuckoos.' "

Her blank expression melted into horrified comprehension. "They're killers. Dangerous killers. They've wiped out entire communities, and they did it for *fun*." A note of bewilderment crept into her voice. "Humans kill because they're afraid of losing their place at the top of the food chain, but cuckoos kill because they can."

"Okay, you're not wrong," I said. "My cousin Sarah— the woman we're on our way to get—is a cuckoo, although she prefers the term Johrlac. She says cuckoo is pejorative." What she would *really* have preferred was a complete change of species. Since that's not in the cards—not even with the intervention of the crossroads, who can do a lot of things, but who can't transform a pseudo-mammalian wasp into a human girl—she makes do with a certain amount of caution with her language. We all have our own ways of coping.

Megan stared at me. "You *live* with one of them?"

"I do. Shelby and I both do. So does Annie, when she's at home. It's not a bad idea to be afraid of cuckoos: most of them are extremely dangerous. Sarah is different. I grew up with her. I trust her with my life."

"There was a human boy who used to hang out on my favorite NeoPets forum," said Megan. "His family ran one of those little roadside zoos. He used to post pictures of himself with their bear. He always said she loved him. That she was different. When he stopped posting, I went looking for news articles about the zoo. The bear killed him. Maybe she was different, but she wasn't different *enough*."

I didn't say anything. Megan wasn't saying anything new: she was expressing a fear shared by several members of my own family, my Grandma Alice among them. Cuckoos kill. It's what evolution designed them to do. Grandma Angela may be a CPA, and Sarah may be a math nerd, but they're both built to be killers, and there's always the chance that one day, nature will win out over nurture.

Of course, there are people who say the same about

my family. We belonged to the Covenant for centuries, after all: we are the descendants of killers who waded through rivers of blood to put humans at the top of the pecking order. An upsettingly large percentage of the cryptid population is waiting for the day when we decide to go back to the old way of doing things.

If I could believe in my family's ability to walk away from the Covenant, I could believe in Sarah's ability to walk away from the need to twist the world to her own desires. I had to believe in it, because she was family, too. There are more important things in this world than blood.

"So you're aware, Sarah knows what most people think of her, and her kind," I said. "She doesn't get mad about it, since she knows it's true, and she'd rather people have some warning. But once she's in the car, if you look at her and think 'monster' too loudly, she'll probably hear you, and we want her to be willing to help find your colony's missing kids."

Megan's cheeks flushed red as she turned her face toward the window. Maybe I was being a little heavy-handed. Whatever. I was about to ask Sarah to do something I knew she absolutely would *not* want to do, and it was going to be a lot easier if she didn't have someone sitting by, waiting to be murdered.

The driveway was still empty when we pulled up in front of the house. My grandparents hadn't come home yet. That would make this easier, since it meant Grandma couldn't argue with me about whether or not Sarah was ready to leave the house. It would also make this harder, since Sarah would probably try to say that she couldn't go out without permission.

"Come on." I stopped the engine, unbuckled my seatbelt, and opened the door. "No matter what you see, I need you to stay calm and keep your wig on, all right?"

Megan gave me a horrified look. She followed me anyway. I guess the fear of losing the children was stronger than her fear of an ordinary suburban home.

The living room was empty when I unlocked the front door. The distant sound of drumming echoed through the walls, faint enough to be easily mistaken for the thump of a faulty air conditioner. I closed the door before leaning over and rapping shave and a haircut on the nearest retaining wall.

"The sound will carry," I explained.

"Carry *where*?" she asked.

In answer, a tiny, cunningly camouflaged door popped open in the wall. The edges had been sanded until they were completely flush with the drywall around them, making it functionally invisible to anyone who didn't already know it was there.

"HAIL!" cried the mouse who had opened the door. It was dressed in the regalia of the Thoughtful Priestess, also known as my mother, which made sense: apart from the mice who were traveling with me, most members of the resident colony were adherents of her particular subsect of their faith. "HAIL TO THE RETURN OF THE GOD OF SCALES AND SILENCE!"

"Um," said Megan.

"Hey," I said, to the mouse. "I need to take Sarah out of the house for a little while. Can I leave a message for Grandma, in case she gets home before we do? She's going to want to know where we are." I didn't insult the mouse by asking if it would remember. Aeslin mice have perfect recall of everything they see or hear. They don't believe in written records, considering them fragile and fallible: for them, the oral tradition is all.

The mouse puffed out its chest with pride. "I Listen and Repeat!" it squeaked.

"Awesome. Okay. Tell her this: that the God of Scales and Silence has taken the younger Heartless One to the children of Stheno, for their offspring are in danger, and Sarah is needed to bring the young ones safely home. Tell her that the Unpredictable Priestess is also with the children of Stheno. If we do not return by sunrise, we have failed, and more aid is required."

"It shall be Spoken," said the mouse, bobbed its head politely to Megan, and withdrew into the hole, pulling the door shut with a soft but definite click.

"Um," said Megan again.

"Aeslin mice," I explained. "They're almost extinct, but my family has managed to preserve a colony. A pretty healthy one, too. Their population is still increasing."

"I've . . . heard of them," said Megan, looking suddenly awkward.

I had to swallow a laugh. "Let me guess, in the context of 'these were a delicacy, but no one can find them anymore.'"

She nodded, cheeks flaring red.

"Don't worry. Everyone shares the same food chain. Will you be okay here by yourself for a few minutes? I want to go get Sarah."

"I won't touch anything," said Megan.

"Cool. Be right back." I started up the stairs before she could change her mind and demand to come with me. Sarah already knew she was in the house, of course: I was wearing an anti-telepathy charm, but Megan wasn't, and she couldn't sneak up on a cuckoo if she tried. That was probably a good thing. Sarah has a harder time reading minds she hasn't encountered before, so Megan's presence was going to be less "invasive" and more "warning." It's always good to give the twitchy telepath as much advance notice as possible.

Her door was still closed. I knocked lightly. "Sarah? I know you're in there."

Silence.

"You don't have a car, you haven't gone outside voluntarily in months, and the mice would have said something if you'd wandered away. Open the door."

Again, silence, stretching long enough that I was afraid I was going to have to enter her room uninvited. Then the doorknob turned, and the door creaked open, just a few inches, just enough to let me see one large, accusatory blue eye peering back at me.

"You brought a *stranger* into the house," said Sarah.

"I did," I agreed. "Her name is Megan; she's Dee's daughter. She knows Antimony."

The door creaked open a little wider. "Annie? She knows Annie? Is she okay?"

"She was," I said. "You can ask Megan yourself, if you want; you'll just have to do it in the car. I need you to come with me to look for the missing children."

Sarah jerked the door all the way open, eyes going even wider in surprise and, yes, fear. "*With* you? You mean to where the gorgons live?"

"Yes." I looked at her steadily. "Please."

"No!" She took a step backward, moving deeper into her room, which was so scrupulously clean that it could have been a showroom display at IKEA. It hurt a little, seeing it that way. She's never been the most cluttered member of our family, but she used to at least keep a few personal touches in reach. "Gorgons, they aren't just *one* mind, not like humans are; they're all these little minds touching on one big central mind, and it's like standing in the middle of a snowstorm and trying to guess which flake is in control of all the others. It's confusing."

"But it's not painful," I guessed.

She bit her lip and didn't correct me.

"Sarah, their children are missing. Someone took them, and from the way it looks, that someone was a human, part of a group of humans. They're going to sell those children to the highest bidders. Do you know what happens to cryptid kids who get bought by humans?"

"Yes," she whispered. We didn't talk about it much, for a lot of reasons, but her older brother, my Uncle Drew, was one of those kids. He'd been stolen from the bogeyman community where he was born when he was too young to remember anything about it. My grandparents had saved him from his "owner," and his adoption had been an act of essential mercy. He had been afraid of his own species, as well as almost everything else, for years after his rescue.

"So you understand why we need to find them as soon as possible. There should only be two humans in the woods: me and Shelby. If you follow the sound of human thoughts, we'll find where they have the children."

"They could already be gone," she said.

I shook my head. "They were smart enough to set lookouts on the major roads in and out of the area. They're smart enough to go to ground for a few days, to let the heat die down and give the children time to accept their new reality." And to start pulling fangs. If they maimed a few of the older children, the others would fall into line.

It wasn't going to get that far. I wasn't going to let it.

Sarah closed her eyes.

"Please," I repeated.

"I could . . . I could lose control," she said. "I could *hurt* someone. I could get scared and decide I needed to be protected and *hurt* someone."

"You won't," I said.

She opened her eyes, looking at me gravely. "How do you know?"

"Because you're my cousin, and I love you, and I trust you, and you've never hurt anyone like that," I said. "Not even when you were a little kid. You were scared and you were running and you were looking for someone to keep you safe, and even then you didn't take over anyone's mind on purpose. Besides, who's going to take better care of you than I could? If you get scared, you'll just get behind me."

She smiled wanly. I still took it as a good sign.

"You think pretty highly of yourself, don't you?" she asked.

"Well, you know, I have it on pretty good authority that I'm not completely bad at my job," I said. "I mostly come home in one piece."

"So far," she said. Then, awkwardly, she added, "Do the gorgons, um . . . do they know you're coming here to get me? Not everyone likes having a cuckoo around."

"They know," I said. "I have permission." That, more than anything, would tell her how serious this was.

Sarah nodded. "All right," she said. "I'll come."

The ride back to the community was awkward, made even more so by the way Sarah sat in the center of the backseat, head bowed and hair covering her face, like she was preparing for the starring role in yet another remake of *The Ring*. Megan kept stealing anxious glances at her in the rearview mirror, and her wig was emitting a steady hissing sound that was almost comical while we were alone in the car but would become a serious problem if we got pulled over for some reason.

"Sarah, we're coming up on the barrier between the community and the main road," I said. "For me, it manifests as a bunch of illusions, and the strong desire to turn around and go back the way I came. If you start feeling like we shouldn't be here, try to remember that it's external."

"All right, Alex," she said, without lifting her head. Then: "Please ask Megan to be less afraid of me. It's like she's screaming and screaming in my ear, and I don't like it. It makes it hard to concentrate."

"Okay," I said. "Megan, hey, could you try to be less terrified of my cousin? Please, as a favor to me?"

"She can hear you," said Megan.

"I know, but she asked me to try, so I'm trying," I said. "Look, she's a nerd, all right? She does math for fun, she puts spaghetti sauce on her ice cream, and she reads too many comic books. She's not going to hurt you. She's here because she wants to help."

" 'Want' is a generous word," said Sarah. "I'm *willing*. Children shouldn't have to be afraid of the people who are supposed to take care of them. But I don't *want* to be out of my house, and I don't want to be around people who're afraid of me. It's not my fault I can read your mind."

"So don't," snapped Megan.

Sarah finally peeked out from behind the curtain of her hair. "Tell the snakes on your head to stop breathing," she said.

Megan's eyes widened. "What?"

"They're breathing. Tell them to stop." Sarah sat up straighter, pushing her hair out of her face and looking defiantly at Megan's reflection in the rearview mirror. "Well? I'm waiting."

"I can't do that!"

"And I can't stop having a certain low-level awareness of your consciousness. I'm not digging through your memories, all right? That would be rude, and it would be *hard*, and being out of the house is hard enough for me right now. I'm not changing your mind for you. If I were, don't you think we'd be best friends? You'd be sitting back here and braiding my hair and telling me about the cute girl in your immunology lecture series. Instead, you're sitting up there trying not to think about how scared of me you are and wondering whether your venom would petrify me before I could wipe your sense of self. I didn't choose my biology any more than you did, and it's not fair of you to sit up there hating me for it when I'm on my way to help save kids you care about. You need to stop."

Megan blinked and looked away, visibly ashamed. That was a nice start. "I'm sorry. I've never met a cu—a Johrlac before."

"Yes, you have." Sarah sounded genuinely apologetic. "I can see the scars. It probably happened at Lowryland. The dangerous ones, the *real* cuckoos, they like places with a whole lot of people. It makes it easier for them to pass unnoticed. I don't think you've ever been targeted, but they've brushed past you on the street."

"Is that supposed to make me feel better?" asked Megan.

"You can still remember my name, so yes," said Sarah. "I don't know what I can do to prove to you that I'm not a monster, other than continuing to sit here without killing you or warping your mind. I'm doing my best. Can't you please try to do the same?"

" . . . sure," said Megan.

I breathed slowly out, blinking as I realized that we were already through the barriers that should have slowed our approach. "Huh," I said.

"I noticed them," said Sarah. "I just suggested that maybe they didn't want to bother us, and they agreed. Compulsion charms are like tiny magical AIs. They're pretty easy to talk into doing what I want them to do."

"That's horrifying," said Megan.

"Welcome to my life," said Sarah.

The crowd of gorgons was still gathered outside the trailers. It had changed composition slightly, new faces replacing the old, the parents of the missing children standing out from the rest thanks to the looks of shattered horror that seemed permanently etched into their faces. Even if—even *when*—we got their children back, I wasn't sure those looks would ever fully go away.

Hannah was waiting when we got out of the car. She looked Sarah up and down, mouth twisting dismissively, and looked like she was about to say something cruel when she abruptly stopped dead and said, in a soft voice, "You're looking at my eyes."

"Yes," said Sarah. "People seem to prefer it when I look them in the eyes, and I try to be polite when I can. It balances the part where I'm always a little bit impolite, by human standards."

"You're not turning to stone."

My eyes widened, and I swore softly. Sarah didn't have goggles on. I should have realized before, but I'd been in a hurry, and she had managed never to look directly at Megan. Somehow, I had missed it.

"No," said Sarah. "I'm not quite a mammal, the way you think a mammal is, and I'm not a bird or a reptile or anything else that comes from around here. Your gaze doesn't work on me."

"I have more than just eyes," said Hannah, and bared her teeth, which were too sharp and too serrated to have any place in a human-seeming mouth.

"Your venom might work," said Sarah. "I don't know. I don't have blood, in the sense of platelets and hemoglobin and all those other sticky substances; it's possible the biological chain reaction that causes petrifaction would do nothing. I'd rather not find out, if you don't mind. I can't look for your missing children if I'm a lawn statue."

"And I'd really rather you didn't turn my cousin to stone," I said hastily. "She hasn't done anything to threaten you."

"Her existence is threat enough," said Hannah, slumping slightly, so that she was no longer looming over the pair of us with quite so much intensity. "Your woman is with Dee, speaking to the fringe. They should return soon."

The fringe was the other side of the community, built with deep roots and sturdy walls and an absolute policy of isolation from the outside world. Walter, who led the place, was Dee's brother. They didn't have the warmest family relationship. I wasn't entirely comfortable with Shelby going there without me, and I was absolutely aware that telling her so would be a good way to wind up getting yelled at for being a macho pig. She could take care of herself, sometimes better than I could.

"All right," I said. "I think Sarah and I are going to go meet them, if you don't mind. I want Sarah to have both the approved human presences behind her before we start scanning the woods for humans who *shouldn't* be present."

"And I am coming with you," said Hannah.

"No," said Sarah.

There was a long, dangerous pause. Finally, in a low voice, Hannah echoed, "No?"

"No," said Sarah. "You're scared of me. You don't want to be because you don't want to be scared of anything, but you are, and all the snakes on your head are picking up on that. They see me as a threat. They don't have a lot of room for thoughts, so they think the ones they have very, very loudly. You'll distract me."

"Please stay here," I said, before Hannah could start to argue in earnest. "If we find anything at all, I'll have Dee call Megan. I know Dee has a phone. I assume Megan does, too."

"Don't leave home without it," said Megan.

"You can come right over and fuck up whoever dared to touch your kids," I said. "But if there's even a chance that your presence means they don't get found, you can't come."

Hannah visibly deflated. "Everything about this day tells me I've failed my duties as protector of this community," she said. "For a daughter of Medusa, that burns."

The three known species of gorgon each claim descent from a different Gorgon of mythology. For the greater gorgons, like Hannah—half of Hannah, anyway, and as those genes seemed to have the dominant expression, it only made sense for her to think of herself as a greater gorgon—that progenitor is Medusa. They take their role as children of the most famous of the mythological Gorgons very seriously.

"You haven't failed," I said. "You're just standing back and letting people who are better equipped to deal with this specific problem do their jobs. Now, will you let us do our jobs?"

She nodded silently. I turned to Sarah.

"Follow me," I said. "I know the way."

The gathered gorgons parted to let us through, and we made our way out of the circle of mobile homes, into the woods that separated the main community from the fringe. Sarah sighed heavily and allowed her shoulders to slump as soon as the gorgons were out of sight behind us.

"There are so *many* of them," she said, voice caught somewhere between agony and awe. "How did I ever stand the density of people in Manhattan? My head should have exploded."

"I think you were less fragile then," I said.

Sarah scowled at me. "I want to be less fragile now," she said. "I want to be able to walk in the world and not worry that I'll pass someone who's thinking about doing a crossword puzzle and wind up stuck for hours wondering what three down was supposed to be. It isn't fair."

"I know," I said.

"And you know who hasn't called? Hasn't texted, hasn't even sent an email? Verity." Sarah's scowl deepened. "You, you moved into the house where I was recuperating, even knowing that I could be dangerous, that I wasn't always going to understand how to be gentle with people. Artie kept IMing me and texting me and sending me cute pictures of wasps and kittens. Even Annie sent me a bunch of cards, even if she couldn't come to Ohio. But Verity never did any of those things. She had time to go on television and start a war. She didn't have time to tell me she was sorry I got hurt."

"I think . . . I think she tried, right after it happened. I don't think you could hear her yet." It sounded like the excuse it was. Verity has always been great at running away from her problems. She's ashamed of failure in a way the rest of us aren't. It doesn't make her a bad person. It makes her a little inept when it comes to apologies.

"I'd do it again—choosing to be good means choosing to do what needs to be done even when no one appreciates it or thanks you. But I wish she'd sent a card."

I silently resolved to have a word with my sister the next time we spoke. "Yeah," I said aloud. "I get that."

We walked through the tangled trees, Sarah drifting almost aimlessly, yet always managing to wind up beside me when I paused to check on her. She might lack the intensive training that the rest of us got, but she still grew up in Ohio, and she knows her way around the forest. In a way, she's even better in the woods than I am, since ticks and mosquitoes don't bother her. She doesn't read as a food source.

Johrlac biology is weird. The more we learn about it, the more convinced we are that they aren't originally from around here. Whether that means "another dimension" or "another planet in this dimension" doesn't matter nearly as much as the fact that they're not going anywhere, and one day they might kill us all.

Some people worry about the robot uprising. I'm much more concerned about the cuckoos.

The trees began to thin, and we stepped out into the manicured, well-farmed land allotted to the fringe. Their small brick houses marched in tidy rows off into the distance, looking incredibly out of place in their agrarian setting. Farmhouses exist, yes, but they usually come with roads, and cars. These houses looked like they'd been swept straight out of some earlier time, predating even the Amish in their old-fashioned solidity.

Dee was standing outside one of the nearby houses, deep in discussion with her brother. He lifted his head and pointed at us, snakes writhing wildly. Dee turned. I waved. It was a perfectly ordinary exchange, rendered strange only by the situation, and it seemed to put Walter marginally more at ease. We were never going to be friends—I was the wrong species, for a start—but I had helped to save the community he belonged to, and it had earned me a certain grudging respect.

I lowered my hand as I realized what was missing from the scene. As I started to step forward, Sarah put a hand on my arm.

"It's all right," she said. "Shelby is inside the house. She needed to use the restroom. I guess the aversion to modern technology doesn't apply to plumbing."

"Where's her anti-telepathy charm?"

"She gave it to Dee. She's thinking about that now,

along with what I think is an Australian variation on that song about monkeys jumping on the bed. It's a pretty good way to keep me from digging deeper into her thoughts." Sarah sounded grudgingly impressed. "Dee was afraid I'd start looking in her mind and judging her, so Shelby gave her the charm to help. And so that if you got separated, like you are right now, you wouldn't be worried that something had happened to her."

"I love that woman," I said.

"Maybe you should finish planning the wedding," said Sarah. "I bet I could attend now, as long as I was careful and had a private room that I could go back to when the people got to be too much."

"We still need to find a venue that works for both our families and doesn't attract the attention of the Covenant," I said. "We're not in a hurry."

"I guess not," said Sarah.

I gave her a sidelong look. "Why? Do *you* think we should be in a hurry?"

"I like cake," said Sarah. "She's coming out now."

Shelby appeared on the porch, waving vigorously when she spotted us. We started toward her, and she met us halfway across the open space, a smile on her face and worry in her eyes.

"Only two kids missing here, both from the house nearest the wood," she said, voice pitched low. "I think our kidnappers looked at the walls, looked at the security, and decided they had a big enough haul. But there's no reason to have taken *any* kids from here unless it was on their way."

I nodded. The fringe was farther from the main road, which we already knew the kidnappers hadn't used: it was virtually impossible to get a single car in or out of the basin without being seen, and they would have needed multiple cars to manage their victims. "Did Walter have any thoughts about the paths they might have taken?"

"He swears the woods nearest the house where the kids were taken are impassable, and that if they weren't,

his people would have been able to track the intruders."
Shelby smiled mirthlessly, showing all her teeth. "That
means we start there."

I nodded. Impassable woods almost never are; there's
always a way to fight through the brush. Walter's people
were farmers, not hunters, and when they did hunt, they
did it by walking into the clearer woods on the far side
of the fringe and stunning deer with a glance. They had
no reason to understand the finer points of woodcraft.

"Got it," I said. "Dee coming with us?"

"It's her or an entire patrol of Walter's men; he's willing to send them to search in the opposite direction if
his sister goes along with us. They've been beating the
bushes all day, not finding anything, but that doesn't
mean he's giving up." Her feral smile dimmed. "Can't
say as I blame him. Kids deserve better than this."

"Yes," I said. "They do."

"How're you holding up, Sarah?" asked Shelby, focus
shifting to my cousin. "We really appreciate you coming
out and giving this a go. You just say the word if you
can't handle it, and we'll make sure you're taken straight
home."

"I'm already here," said Sarah. "Let's find these kids."

"I'll get Dee," I said.

"Good," said Shelby, smile finally dying entirely.
"Poachers don't like to be the hunted ones. I don't know
how much time we have."

Neither did I. I kept that thought to myself as I hurried
over to where Dee was waiting. It was time for us to move;
it was past time for us to bring those children home.

The woods Walter had identified as impassable and
Shelby had identified as our best starting point for finding the kidnappers were the sort of dense, tangled
woodland that Ohio excels at. It was easy to look at
them and understand why Walter wouldn't think they

were an option, although I was willing to bet he'd thought differently when he was a kid himself. Kids never look at a thorn briar or a hedge and think "I can't go there." They're a lot more likely to think "adults can't follow me," and charge full speed ahead.

Shelby and I exchanged a look. "Sixty seconds," she said.

"I can do it in thirty," I said.

"You're on," she replied, and we took off in opposite directions, both of us scanning the brush for signs of disturbance, or something we could use to make our entrance.

I was starting to think Shelby was going to win when I saw a single half-concealed footprint poking out from under a veil of scrub. I bent, tugging gently on the bush. It came away in my hand, revealing the beginning of a tunnel. "Over here!" I called and began pulling more brush away.

Someone had spent several days carefully cutting a tunnel through the wall of tangles that separated the fringe from the forest, making it as inconspicuous as possible. Walter and his people had probably walked past it repeatedly, never realizing how close the danger had come. Not for the first time, I wished Lloyd's cockatrice hadn't killed the lindworms that used to hunt around here. Gorgons don't do well with dogs, and the lindworms had been the closest thing they had to an early warning system.

Shelby crowded up behind me, Dee and Sarah following behind her at a slightly safer distance. "What've you got?" she asked.

"A way in," I said. "Sarah, you're behind me; I want you scanning for human minds as soon as we go through the break. Dee, you walk after Sarah, and be ready to stun anyone who charges us."

"And I've got the rear," said Shelby cheerfully. "Anyone who tries to sneak up on us is going to get a taste of old-fashioned Australian hospitality."

"What does that mean?" asked Dee.

"Means I'm going to smash their teeth in," said Shelby.

Dee blinked. "You're not this terrifying at work," she said.

"Eh, I try to follow the rules about not creating a hostile workplace," said Shelby.

"Come on," I said, before the two could go any farther down the path of their digression. "Stay close, stay quiet, and do whatever Sarah says."

"That should be the rule for always," said Sarah, sounding amused.

I stepped into the woods, pausing only to hang my anti-telepathy charm on a nearby branch. The odds of encountering another cuckoo out here were minimal, and I needed any advantage I could get.

The nice thing about tracking people through places where people don't usually go: every little motion cuts a trail. Better still, when our kidnappers had gone back to their hideout, they'd been weighted down with panicked, probably squirming children. There were broken branches. There were smashed plants. Best of all, there were footprints in the muddy earth, all of them scuffed and layered over each other, but still clearly made by human feet. There were two directions these people could have been going. We already knew they'd been to the gorgon settlement, and that they weren't there anymore. That only left one reasonable direction.

We were going the right way.

It was a good thing, too, because Walter had been right about these woods being wild and difficult. The brush grabbed at our feet and legs, and I would have been worried about ticks if not for the fact that Shelby and I basically bathed in insect repellent, while Dee and Sarah weren't tasty targets. The branches overhead shut out most of the ambient light, leaving us to move through a dim, dangerous world filled with inexplicable sounds and half-seen motions.

We had pressed almost half a mile into the trees

when Sarah stopped walking, putting a hand on my shoulder to signal me to do the same. I turned. Her head was cocked to the side. That was fine. Her eyes, always a blue so bright that it looked a little fake, were glowing white, bleaching the color almost entirely away. That was less fine.

"Which way?" I mouthed, thinking the words as loudly as I could.

Sarah pointed, not straight ahead, but off to the left. They'd been smart enough not to draw a direct line to their hideout. I didn't know whether to be impressed by their forethought or disappointed that this was going to be harder than it had to be. Then she held up both hands, fingers spread wide. Ten kidnappers. It wasn't an unreasonable number, considering how many children they'd snatched. I still winced.

Okay. If we were doing this, we needed to do it. I motioned for Sarah to step in front of me, then waved the others closer. Shelby produced a handgun from somewhere inside her shirt, holding it low to her hip, so that she could quickly raise and shoot if necessary. The snakes on Dee's head silently writhed into a strike position. They weren't hissing. Rudimentary as their minds might be, they understood that now was a time for stealth.

Sarah began to drift through the brush, stepping lightly, somehow skirting the worst of the snags and tangles. I followed close behind, drawing my own gun and holding it in front of me. If we could do this without shooting anyone, that would be great. I wasn't counting on things being remotely that easy.

We're almost there, whispered Sarah's voice. I opened my mouth to reply before I realized her words were in my head. She was talking in my head.

She hadn't spoken in my head since her accident.

The situation was dire, and there were endangered kids somewhere up ahead, along with ten kidnappers we'd have to evade or defeat, and for a moment, none of that mattered, because I was smiling too hard to care. Sarah was talking in my head again. Sarah was getting *better*.

She stopped in the shadow of a large bush. Voices drifted from the other side, low but audible in the overall quiet of the forest.

"—telling you, we can't go back." The first voice was male, and agitated, like he'd finally realized the scope of what they'd done and didn't like it. "Make no mistake; we kicked the wasp's nest with this one. We need to be miles away from here."

"Eggs, Carl. There are more eggs." The second voice was female, quietly calculating and unruffled. The mastermind of the pair, clearly. "We couldn't get them all last night, not with the brats to manage, but we can get them tonight. Do you have any idea what a gorgon's egg goes for on the open market? Fuck, we have six offers in already, and that's just on the nonviable ones."

Dee put her hands over her mouth, eyes wide and horrified.

"We go back," said the woman. "We go back, we get the rest of the eggs while the parents are looking for their kids, and then we never have to come back to Ohio. This funds us for *years*, Carl. We can't turn our backs on that."

The bush we were hiding behind extended in both directions, but there had to be a way around it. I pointed and nodded to Shelby, who nodded back and started moving. I beckoned for Dee to come closer, then held my hand out to Sarah in the classic "stop" position. Both of them nodded. Sarah stayed exactly where she was as Dee and I worked our way around the edge of the bush.

Sometimes people get the clever idea to carve picnic grounds into the local woods, encouraging "back to nature" tourism by serving up visitors as a buffet to the mosquitoes, ticks, and bears. This had clearly been one of those installations: the rotting remains of a creosote-soaked picnic table greeted us at the bush's edge, half-consumed by the undergrowth. On the other side was a large, manmade clearing, into which our kidnappers had jammed three RVs, their windows covered in tin foil and their doors sealed with padlocks that would probably raise a few eyebrows if they got spotted by the highway patrol.

There were no gorgon children in evidence. There were, instead, five humans, all heavily armed and dressed in military surplus camo. Three were standing in a loose semicircle, including a woman with a long brown ponytail who I assumed was our aspiring egg thief. The other two were closer to the RVs, each with a large assault rifle slung over their backs. They hadn't seen us yet. For one second, we had the element of surprise.

I motioned Dee toward the men with the big guns. She stepped out into the open.

"Hey!" she shouted.

All five kidnappers turned. The two closest to the RVs got an immediate eyeful of Dee's gaze and froze, falling limply to the ground.

The gaze of a Pliny's gorgon stuns but doesn't petrify. Their venom does the petrification. If she didn't bite them, they'd be fine. Honestly, though, I expected fangs to be in their future—and I wasn't going to intervene. Protecting the cryptid world from humanity sometimes means looking the other way when protection involves killing in self-defense.

The other three kidnappers weren't stunned, and they knew we were there now. I aimed my gun at them and shouted, "Freeze! Hands in the air, right fucking now!"

The two men complied. The woman laughed.

"Oh, please," she said. "We have you outnumbered. I don't know what you think you're going to accomplish, monster boy, but this isn't going to go your way. We're in charge—"

She stopped mid-sentence, eyes going wide, as Shelby stepped up behind her and pressed the barrel of her gun to the back of the kidnapper's neck.

"Howdy," said Shelby. "I don't think we're *that* outnumbered."

With five kidnappers unaccounted for, she was technically wrong, but from the look on the woman's face, that didn't much matter.

"Keys," I said. "Now."

"I don't think you want to do that, friend," said the woman. "Those little monsters are pretty riled up. They're likely to strike first and consider their targets later."

"Alex." Dee's voice was rich with horror. I risked a glance in her direction. She held up a small, curved object, her snakes writhing and hissing wildly, sometimes striking out at the air. I blinked, trying to make sense of what I was seeing.

Then I recognized it, and the fact that I didn't immediately whip around and shoot the woman who'd been speaking was a testimony to the strength of my self-control.

"You pulled their fangs," I said, voice soft and low.

"Only two of them," she said. "Most of our buyers want the merchandise intact. Still, you have to show who's in control."

"True enough," said Shelby flatly, and pulled back, striking the woman across the base of the skull with the butt of her gun. The woman yelped and staggered forward but didn't fall. Shelby pouted. "Aw. That always works in the movies."

"You crazy bi—" the woman began. Her words dissolved into a groan of pain when Shelby dug the muzzle of her gun into the back of her head again, right in the bruised spot.

"Language," said Shelby primly. "I believe you were about to give him the key."

"You're making a mistake," said one of the men. "Whatever these monsters are paying you, we can double it. Triple it, even."

"Sorry, but I'm not in the mood to profit from the

exploitation of children," I said. "My mother would never forgive me."

"Please," said the other man—Carl. "We haven't done anything yet."

"You scared them, and you pulled their fangs, and you call us monsters?" Dee sounded like she was on the verge of tears. "Get the keys, Alex. I want to go home."

"Wait," said the woman. "Alex? Alex *Price.* What the fuck, man? I thought your people were on humanity's side."

"We're conservationists," I said. "The human race is currently of least concern. Now give me the keys, before I make you extinct."

Glaring, she dug the keys out of her pocket and threw them on the ground. Before I could move toward them, Sarah stepped daintily around the bush, retrieved them, and walked toward Dee. All three kidnappers watched her go, looking confused.

"Do you see a woman or is it just me?" asked Carl.

"Sorry," said Sarah. "I'm leaking a little."

"It's all right," I said.

Sarah walked past Dee and stopped, tilting her head.

"Oh," she said. "I found your other kidnappers."

The woman laughed. Shelby hit her again, harder this time, and she fell. I trained my gun on one of the two remaining men, while Shelby switched her focus to the other. There was a click from behind me, as someone prepared to fire.

"I don't know why you people thought this was a good idea, but I think you're about to sing a different song," said a man.

"Sure," I said. "Dee?"

"I'm okay."

"An adult female will fetch a pretty good price," said the man. "For that, we'll go ahead and kill you quick."

"Uh-huh," I said. "How many of us are there? Right now, how many do you count?"

"Three," said the man, and paused. "Three?"

"About what I thought." Cuckoos are ambush predators. *Psychic* ambush predators. When they don't want to be seen—when they feel like they're in danger—they aren't seen, period. Even Sarah, with her bruised edges and her uncertainty, could manage the traditional cuckoo trick of disappearing in plain sight.

There was a sharp snapping sound from one of the RVs, like a padlock being opened. It was followed by the sound of a padlock dropping to the ground. A swarm of underage gorgons erupted from the RV, falling on the kidnappers like the wrath of Medusa herself. A few shots were fired, but they all happened as the men were falling, their guns pointed at the air.

I didn't have much time to waste. I advanced on the two remaining kidnappers, both of whom looked like they were about to wet themselves, and demanded, "How did you know about this place? *How*?"

"Angie!" gasped Carl. "She grew up around here, she'd heard rumors, and then that cockatrice got caught down by Cleveland, and we started looking! Mister, I don't know who you are, and I wouldn't tell anyone if I did, please, you have to save us, please, we didn't do anything, we didn't—"

"You pulled their fangs," I said softly and stepped to the side as the wave of immature gorgons descended.

It didn't take long for things to be over. Not after that.

Ten strange statues and three empty RVs were left to rot in the clearing. Maybe someone would find them and scavenge them for parts before they'd been totally destroyed by the weather. Maybe not. Either way, the gorgons wanted nothing to do with them. Their use had tainted them, and only time would purify that taint.

I did stop long enough to retrieve my anti-telepathy charm from the bush where it was hanging. Those things are *expensive*. Then I rejoined the others, as we led the children and carried the unhatched eggs back where they belonged. Home.

The two children whose fangs had been pulled were among the older abductees. Both of them had lost their baby fangs the year before. The damage, now that it was done, was forever.

"We don't *need* our fangs the way we used to," said Dee, watching as Frank tried to console the weeping parents. As the community's doctor, he was the only one who fully understood the medical consequences. "We don't hunt for our food. We cook it in kitchens like civilized people. Live prey is a treat, and mostly reserved for our snakes."

"I hear a 'but' there," I said.

"But they'll need to have their venom sacs expressed manually for the rest of their lives if they don't want them to become engorged and infected. This could make it harder for them to marry outside the colony. Not many people want spouses who can't defend themselves." Dee shook her head. "I know, I know, it's primitive and unfair and unreasonable, but we're dying out. We can't afford to take risks with our children."

"I know." Putting human values on cryptids is never fair. They have to live by the rules we set for them, however unintentionally, when we hunted them to the cusp of extinction. "The kidnappers are dead. Any buyers they might have had won't know where the colony is, because that's not how you keep your prices up. You can breathe, and shore up your defenses, and take care of your kids."

"And for this, we thank you," said Hannah.

I stiffened. "Okay, I don't know *how* you snuck up on me, but I'm impressed."

I turned. The community matriarch was standing behind me, an amused smile on her lips. It softened her. Made her look less terrifying.

"My apologies," she said. "I wanted to express my appreciation for your efforts. They won't be forgotten."

"I know." Shelby and Sarah were a short distance away, Shelby kneeling as she listened to a small child speak at length, Sarah watching. She didn't seem to have been traumatized by the day's events, thankfully. I suppose the proof would be in her nightmares, or the lack thereof. "I'm going to take my people and head home, if you don't mind. It's been a long day, and it's going to get dark soon."

"Of course," said Hannah. "And if ever you need anything . . ."

"We didn't come here looking for favors," I said. "We came here because Dee asked, and because we were needed. Just, please, try to remember that we're not your enemies. All right?"

Hannah nodded.

I waved to Dee and started for the car, motioning for Shelby and Sarah to follow. Shelby straightened, chucked the child on the chin, and trotted after me. Sarah came more slowly, but she came; that was really all that mattered.

"Well," said Shelby, once she was seated in the front passenger seat, her belt fastened, and her weapons all safely concealed. "That went better than I'd been expecting. No one we cared about died."

"Ten humans died," said Sarah.

"Ten *poachers* died," said Shelby. "Sometimes what you do matters more than who you are. Those people gave up their right to live as soon as they laid hands on a child."

"This calls for a celebration," I said, starting the car. "I'll drop you off at home and go pick up the makings for a batch of mudslides. I can make yours with ketchup instead of chocolate sauce, Sarah."

"Thank you, but Shelby can't have any," said Sarah.

I blinked. "What? Shelby can have whatever she wants."

"Oh, damn." Shelby closed her eyes and leaned her head back until it was resting against the seat. "I didn't get my telepathy blocker back from Dee, did I?"

"No, you didn't," said Sarah. "I'm sorry."

"Try to stay out of my head, will you, sweetheart? I need to talk to Alex when we get home, and I'd rather you didn't muddy the waters on me."

"Sorry," said Sarah again, meekly.

"There's nothing to be sorry about."

I squinted at her. "Shelby . . . ?"

"When we get home, Alex, all right? I just want to wait until we get home."

"All right," I said, and tried to focus on the road. It wasn't easy. I understand secrets—they're a necessary part of staying alive—but I don't like them between members of my family, and Shelby was absolutely a member of my family. We weren't married yet, but all that was going to do was make it legal. We were family in every way that counts.

Family. I paused, giving her a sidelong look as certain events of the last few days began taking on a whole new focus. Then I hit the gas a little harder. I wasn't going to risk a speeding ticket, but I was going to get us home as fast as I could. We needed to talk.

The driveway was, once again, empty. I said a silent prayer of thanks to whatever was keeping my grandparents out of the house as I pulled in and killed the engine.

Sarah waited until we were inside before announcing, "I have a headache, and I need to cry. I'll be in my room. Please don't knock unless the house is on fire." Then she climbed the stairs, not looking back.

Shelby glanced at me, twisting her hands anxiously in front of herself. "So," she said.

"So," I echoed. "Bedroom?"

"Please."

We climbed the stairs together, shrouded in awkward silence. Shelby went in first. I followed, closed the door, and said, in a loud, clear voice, "I will allow one representative of the faith to remain, in silence, to hear what is said. I invoke the Holy Ritual of Mouse, Alice Loves

You, But I Will Gladly Ward You From My Sleeping Quarters If You Try Me. Am I heard?"

"Heard and Obeyed!" squeaked several voices, from several corners of the room. The proclamation was followed by a skittering sound.

I counted silently to ten before turning my attention to Shelby, who was waiting patiently, if not happily. "Okay," I said. "How long have you known you were pregnant?"

Shelby blinked. "I—" she began, and caught herself, shaking her head. "No. I won't do that. How did you figure it out?"

"No coffee, no alcohol, you were sick earlier in the week, but I didn't catch it, which means it was probably hormonal, and the way you shut Sarah down once you realized she'd been reading your mind. How long?"

"Took the test yesterday; suspected for about a week," she said. "I was planning to tell you today, since we're both home, but then, well . . ."

"Kidnapping took priority," I said. "I'm kind of glad I didn't know. I'm not sure I would have been quite so happy to have you around that many gorgons if I'd known that you were, well . . ."

I trailed off as Shelby glared at me.

"Alexander Healy, if you think for one second that my being pregnant means I'm going to let you bench me—" she began.

"Are you kidding?" I asked. "I was nearly born in the middle of a manticore breeding pit. I know better than to try to make you stay home. But I also know myself, and I'm going to have to swallow a lot of 'please, don't die' reactions. Honestly, though, you wouldn't be you if you weren't demanding to come with me into the field, and since I fell in love with you, I'd rather you didn't change. That doesn't mean I won't twitch."

Shelby nodded, glare fading into open, earnest anxiousness. "I know we didn't plan for this," she said. "We've barely talked about it. I'm not even sure you want children."

"Sweetheart." I took a step toward her, offering my hands. After a moment's hesitation, she took them. I smiled. "I want children. I want children with you. I want *this* child, with you, more than I can possibly say, especially since I think I'm about to run out of words. Also, I want to tell my parents the *second* you're comfortable with it, because otherwise, they're going to find out from the mice."

"From the mice?" Shelby laughed. "How?"

"The mice have email," I said darkly.

She stopped laughing. She kissed me instead, and that was about as perfect a conclusion to the day's events as I could think of, so I kissed her back as the mice drummed in the distance, and everything was right with the world.

Price Family Field Guide
to the Cryptids of North America
Updated and Expanded Edition

Aeslin mice (Apodemus sapiens). Sapient, rodentlike cryptids which present as near-identical to non-cryptid field mice. Aeslin mice crave religion, and will attach themselves to "divine figures" selected virtually at random when a new colony is created. They possess perfect recall; each colony maintains a detailed oral history going back to its inception. Origins unknown.

Basilisk (Procompsognathus basilisk). Venomous, feathered saurians approximately the size of a large chicken. This would be bad enough, but thanks to a quirk of evolution, the gaze of a basilisk causes petrification, turning living flesh to stone. Basilisks are not native to North America, but were imported as game animals. By idiots.

Bogeyman (Vestiarium sapiens). The thing in your closet is probably a very pleasant individual who simply has issues with direct sunlight. Probably. Bogeymen are close relatives of the human race; they just happen to be almost purely nocturnal, with excellent night vision, and a fondness for enclosed spaces. They rarely grab the ankles of small children, unless it's funny.

Chupacabra (Chupacabra sapiens). True to folklore, chupacabra are blood-suckers, with stomachs that do not handle solids well. They are also therianthrope shapeshifters, capable of transforming themselves into human form, which explains why they have never been captured. When cornered, most chupacabra will assume their bipedal shape in self-defense. A surprising number of chupacabra are involved in ballroom dance.

Dragon (Draconem sapiens). Dragons are essentially winged, fire-breathing dinosaurs the size of Greyhound buses. At least, the males are. The females are attractive humanoids who can blend seamlessly in a crowd of supermodels, and outnumber the males twenty to one. Females are capable of parthenogenic reproduction and can sustain their population for centuries without outside help. All dragons, male and female, require gold to live, and collect it constantly.

Fūri (Homo therianthrope). Often proposed as the bridge between humans and therianthropes, the fūri is a monkey—specifically, a human—that takes on the attributes of another monkey—specifically, some form of spider monkey. Fūri transform instinctively, choosing their human forms for camouflage and their more simian forms for virtually everything else. A transformed fūri is faster, stronger, and sturdier than a human being. Offering bananas is not recommended.

Ghoul (Herophilus sapiens). The ghoul is an obligate carnivore, incapable of digesting any but the simplest vegetable solids, and prefers humans because of their wide selection of dietary nutrients. Most ghouls are carrion eaters. Ghouls can be easily identified by their teeth, which will be shed and replaced repeatedly over the course of a lifetime.

Gorgon, Pliny's (Gorgos stheno). The Pliny's gorgon is capable of gaze-based petrifaction only when both their human and serpent eyes are directed toward the same target. They are the most sexually dimorphic of the known gorgons, with the males being as much as four feet taller than the females. They are venomous, as are the snakes atop their heads, and their bites contain a strong petrifying agent. Do not vex.

Hidebehind (Aphanes apokryphos). We don't really know much about the hidebehinds: no one's ever seen them. They're excellent illusionists, and we think they're bipeds, which means they're probably mammals. Probably.

Jackalope (Parcervus antelope). Essentially large jack-rabbits with antelope antlers, the jackalope is a staple of the American West, and stuffed examples can be found in junk shops and kitschy restaurants all across the country. Most of the taxidermy is fake. Some, however, is not. The jackalope was once extremely common, and has been shot, stuffed, and harried to near-extinction. They're relatively harmless, and they taste great.

Jink (Tyche iynx). Luck manipulators and masters of disguise, these close relatives of the mara have been known to conceal themselves right under the nose of the Covenant. No small trick. Most jinks are extremely careful about the way they move and manipulate luck, and individuals have been known to sacrifice themselves for the good of the community.

Johrlac (Johrlac psychidolos). Colloquially known as "cuckoos," the Johrlac are telepathic ambush predators. They appear human, but are internally very different, being cold-blooded and possessing a decentralized circulatory system. This quirk of biology means they can be shot repeatedly in the chest without being killed. Extremely dangerous. All Johrlac are interested in mathematics, sometimes to the point of obsession. Origins unknown; possibly insect in nature.

Jorōgumo (Nephilia sapiens). Originally native to Japan, these therianthropes belong to the larger family of cryptids classified as "yōkai." Jorōgumo appear to be attractive women of Japanese descent until they transform, at which point they become massive spider-centaurs whose neurotoxic venom can kill in seconds. No males of the species have ever been seen. It is possible that the species possesses a degree of sexual dimorphism so great that male Jorōgumo are simply not recognized for what they are.

Laidly worm (Draconem laidly). Very little is known about these close relatives of the dragons. They present similar but presumably not identical sexual dimorphism; no currently living males have been located.

Lamia (Python lamia). Semi-hominid cryptids with the upper bodies of humans and the lower bodies of snakes. Lamia are members of order synapsedia, the mammal-like reptiles, and are considered responsible for many of the "great snake" sightings of legend. The sightings not attributed to actual great snakes, that is.

Lesser gorgon (Gorgos euryale). One of three known subspecies of gorgon, the lesser gorgon's gaze causes short-term paralysis followed by death in anything under five pounds. The bite of the snakes atop their heads will cause paralysis followed by death in anything smaller than an elephant if not treated with the appropriate antivenin. Lesser gorgons tend to be very polite, especially to people who like snakes.

Lilu (Lilu sapiens). Due to the striking dissimilarity of their abilities, male and female Lilu are often treated as two individual species: incubi and succubi. Incubi are empathic; succubi are persuasive telepaths. Both exude strong pheromones inspiring feelings of attraction and lust in the opposite sex. This can be a problem for incubi like our cousin Artie, who mostly wants to be left alone, or succubi like our cousin Elsie, who gets very tired of men hitting on her while she's trying to flirt with their girlfriends.

Madhura (Homo madhurata). Humanoid cryptids with an affinity for sugar in all forms. Vegetarian. Their presence slows the decay of organic matter, and is usually viewed as lucky by everyone except the local dentist. Madhura are very family-oriented, and are rarely found living on their own. Originally from the Indian subcontinent.

Manananggal (Tanggal geminus). If the manananggal is proof of anything, it is that Nature abhors a logical classification system. We're reasonably sure the manananggal are mammals; everything else is anyone's guess. They're hermaphroditic and capable of splitting their upper and lower bodies, although they are a single entity, and killing the lower half kills the upper half as well. They prefer fetal tissue, or the flesh of newborn infants. They are also venomous, as we have recently discovered. Do not engage if you can help it.

Oread (Nymphae silica). Humanoid cryptids with the approximate skin density of granite. Their actual biological composition is unknown, as no one has ever been able to successfully dissect one. Oreads are extremely strong, and can be dangerous when angered. They seem to have evolved independently across the globe; their common name is from the Greek.

Sasquatch (Gigantopithecus sesquac). These massive native denizens of North America have learned to embrace depilatories and mail-order shoe catalogs. A surprising number make their living as Bigfoot hunters (Bigfeet and Sasquatches are close relatives, and enjoy tormenting each other). They are predominantly vegetarian, and enjoy Canadian television.

Tanuki (Nyctereutes sapiens). Therianthrope shapeshifters from Japan, the Tanuki are critically endangered due to the efforts of the Covenant. Despite this, they remain friendly, helpful people, with a naturally gregarious nature which makes it virtually impossible for them to avoid human settlements. Tanuki possess three primary forms—human, raccoon dog, and big-ass scary monster. Pray you never see the third form of the Tanuki.

Ukupani (Ukupani sapiens). Aquatic therianthropes native to the warm waters of the Pacific Islands, the Ukupani were believed for centuries to be an all-male species, until Thomas Price sat down with several local fishermen and determined that the abnormally large Great White sharks that were often found near Ukupani males were, in actuality, Ukupani females. Female Ukupani can't shapeshift, but can eat people. Happily. They are as intelligent as their shapeshifting mates, because smart sharks are exactly what the ocean needed.

Wadjet (Naja wadjet). Once worshipped as gods, the male wadjet resembles an enormous cobra, capable of reaching seventeen feet in length when fully mature, while the female wadjet resembles an attractive human female. Wadjet pair-bond young, and must spend extended amounts of time together before puberty in order to become immune to one another's venom and be able to successfully mate as adults.

Waheela (Waheela sapiens). Therianthrope shapeshifters from the upper portion of North America, the waheela are a solitary race, usually claiming large swaths of territory and defending it to the death from others of their species. Waheela mating season is best described with the term "bloodbath." Waheela transform into something that looks like a dire bear on steroids. They're usually not hostile, but it's best not to push it.

PLAYLIST:

The right music is essential when fighting cosmic forces. Here are some songs to rock you through Antimony's big adventure.

"Happy Phantom"......................Tori Amos
"A Summer in Ohio"...............*The Last 5 Years*
"Midnight Radio"................... Dar Williams
"Go to the Woods" .... Dar Williams
"The Ballad of Mona Lisa" ...... Panic! At the Disco
"Cold Cold Water" ....Mirah
"Haunted" ....Taylor Swift
"You Were the Lie"......................Girlyman
"Coffee and Roses".................. Thea Gilmore
"Death of a Bachelor" .... Panic! At the Disco
"Tik Tik Boom".................... Britney Spears
"Paths of Desire".................. October Project
"Blood Red River" .... Beth Orton
"Attic Window" .... Idgy Vaughn
"Underwater".....................Tegan and Sara
"Evil I" .... Ookla the Mok
"Liar Liar" ....A Fine Frenzy
"Keep Your Heart".................. Belle Histoire
"Tall Towers" .... Tori Sparks
"Home"....................... Barenaked Ladies
"The Babysitter's Here" .... Dar Williams
"Shadows of Evangeline" .... Tracy Grammer

ACKNOWLEDGMENTS

And with that, Antimony Price takes a bow and leaves the stage, at least for now: she's done her part for the family, and she deserves a bit of a break. But the beat goes on, as it always must, and we'll be back next year for *Imaginary Numbers*, when Sarah Zellaby finally gets a chance to tell her side of the story. I'm so thrilled that you've all come with me this far. When I started telling this sprawling tale of cryptozoologists and secret societies and crossroads and chaos, I didn't expect to make it eight books in. Thank you all for reading.

As a life-long horror movie girl, there's something intensely satisfying about writing a story where a bunch of twenty-somethings face off against supernatural forces in a rickety old house in the forests of Maine. Big thanks to my New England experts, Shawn and Cat, and to Heath and Sebastian, who may not know as much as the long-timers, but are charming all the same. Thanks to everyone who's been dragged into a haunted house or evil corn maze over the past few years: this book, in many ways, is for you.

The team at DAW Books remains one of the absolute best groups of people I could hope to work with, especially Sheila Gilbert (my editor), Joshua Starr (the managing editor, who puts up with way too much of my nonsense), Katie Hoffman (I like her cats a lot), and Lindsay Ribar (she doesn't have cats, but she is extremely tolerant when I call her during the work day to wail). Everyone at DAW is amazing, and my life wouldn't be the same without them.

I know I sing the praises of the machete squad a lot, but that's because they're the absolute best and I adore them. Kory Bing continues to illustrate the amazing Field Guide to the Cryptids of North America, located at my website. Tara O'Shea provides dingbat and short story cover designs, as well as designing the overall look of my website. Chris Mangum, Kate Secor, and Michelle Dockrey complete the "home team," and I would be absolutely lost if they weren't here to keep shoving the map into my hands.

Aly Fell is back for this book's gorgeous cover art, and I couldn't be happier about that: I missed him immensely on our last adventure (although thanks again to Lee Moyer for stepping in and making sure we had a cover that matched the rest of the series).

Things are still good here in the Pacific Northwest, even if I saw less of my home than I wanted to during the past year. My beloved Alice, the first of my Maine Coons and the true owner of my heart, left us shortly before the publication of *Tricks for Free*. I traveled way too much in the aftermath, as a way to cope with my grief. The house is still too empty. I want my girl back. But everyone here stepped up and kept me flying straight until I was once again able to fly on my own, and I appreciate that more than words. I couldn't have made it without them.

Big thanks to all the conventions and bookstores that have played host to me over the past year, especially Borderlands Books and Flying Colors Comics, both in the

San Francisco Bay Area, both owned by very caring, very tolerant friends of mine. I am so grateful for the people I have in my life, and so fortunate that they like me as much as I like them. Thanks to Jay and Tea, for fancy cocktails; to Leah, for Emma Frost feels; to my agent, Diana Fox, for laughing at me when necessary; to Merav, for not laughing when it wasn't necessary. I adore you all.

Any errors in this book are my own. The errors that aren't here are the ones that all these people helped me fix. I appreciate it so much.

Seanan McGuire
The October Daye Novels

"...will surely appeal to readers who enjoy my books, or
those of Patrica Briggs." —*Charlaine Harris*

"I am so invested in the world building and the characters
now.... Of all the 'Faerie' urban fantasy series out there, I
enjoy this one the most."—*Felicia Day*

To Order Call: 1-800-788-6262
www.dawbooks.com

Seanan McGuire

The InCryptid Novels

"McGuire's imagination is utterly boundless. The world of her *InCryptid* series is full of unexpected creatures, constant surprises and appealing characters, all crafted with the measured ease of a skilled professional, making the fantastic seem like a wonderful reality."
                                                    —*RT Reviews*

"The only thing more fun than an October Daye book is an InCryptid book. Swift narrative, charm, great world-building . . . all the McGuire trademarks."
                                                    —Charlaine Harris

To Order Call: 1-800-788-6262
www.dawbooks.com

DAW 143

Seanan McGuire
The Ghost Roads

"Hitchhiking ghosts, the unquiet dead, the gods of the old American roads—McGuire enters the company of Lindskold and Gaiman with this book, creating a wistful, funny, fascinating new mythology of diners, corn fields, and proms in this all-in-one-sitting read."　　　　　　　　　　　　—Tamora Pierce

SPARROW HILL ROAD

978-0-7564-1440-5

THE GIRL IN THE
GREEN SILK GOWN

978-0-7564-1380-4

"In McGuire's beautifully written second story featuring hitchhiking ghost Rose Marshall, set in the same world as the InCryptid series, Rose must confront her most dangerous foe: Bobby Cross, the immortal who ran her down when she was only 16. . . . This stunning, richly imagined story of love and destiny features an irresistible heroine and is one of the accomplished McGuire's best yet."　　　—*Publishers Weekly*

To Order Call: 1-800-788-6262
www.dawbooks.com

DAW 144